WESTERN

Rugged men looking for love...

Fortune's Convenient Cinderella

Makenna Lee

The Cowgirl Nanny

Jen Gilroy

MILLS & BOON

Makenna Lee is acknowledged as the author of this work
FORTUNE'S CONVENIENT CINDERELLA
© 2024 by Harlequin Enterprises ULC
Philippine Copyright 2024
Australian Copyright 2024
New Zealand Copyright 2024

First Published 2024
First Australian Paperback Edition 2024
ISBN 978 1 038 91078 3

THE COWGIRL NANNY
© 2024 by Jen Gilroy
Philippine Copyright 2024
Australian Copyright 2024
New Zealand Copyright 2024

First Published 2024
First Australian Paperback Edition 2024
ISBN 978 1 038 91078 3

MIX
Paper | Supporting
responsible forestry
FSC® C001695

Published by
Harlequin Mills & Boon
An imprint of Harlequin Enterprises (Australia) Pty Limited
(ABN 47 001 180 918), a subsidiary of HarperCollins
Publishers Australia Pty Limited
(ABN 36 009 913 517)
Level 19, 201 Elizabeth Street
SYDNEY NSW 2000 AUSTRALIA

Cover art used by arrangement with Harlequin Books S.A.. All rights reserved.

Printed and bound in Australia by McPherson's Printing Group

Fortune's Convenient Cinderella

Makenna Lee

MILLS & BOON

Makenna Lee is an award-winning romance author living in the Texas Hill Country with her real-life hero and their two children, one of whom has Down syndrome and inspired her first Harlequin book, *A Sheriff's Star*. She writes heartwarming contemporary romance that celebrates real-life challenges and the power of love and acceptance. She has been known to make people laugh and cry in the same book. Makenna is often drinking coffee with a cat on her lap while writing, reading or plotting a new story. Her wish is to write stories that touch your heart, making you feel, think and dream.

Visit the Author Profile page
at millsandboon.com.au for more titles.

Dear Reader,

Welcome back to the exciting world of The Fortunes of Texas! I have always wanted to write a *Cinderella*-inspired book, and this story about Barrington "Bear" Fortune and Morgana Mills was so much fun to write. There aren't any talking animals, but I am curious to hear how many nods to the original fairy tale you discover while reading.

Bear is a wealthy oilman who stays away from his family for months at a time, but when he hears that his brother is alive after years in hiding, he travels to Chatelaine, Texas, to see him. He didn't expect to be so drawn to the beautiful maid who sings and dances while cleaning his room at the old motor lodge on the edge of town. Morgana is reluctant to share any personal details, but she sure has been asking a lot of questions about the Fortune family. He is determined to find out what she's hiding, and learns some interesting facts. Bear is a pro when it comes to closing million-dollar business deals, so why is he having such a hard time convincing Morgana to go along with a proposal that will benefit them both?

I hope you enjoy *Fortune's Convenient Cinderella*. As always, thank you for reading!

Best wishes,

Makenna Lee

DEDICATION

To Mackenzie.
We are so glad you've become part of our lives.
Thanks for making our son so happy!

CHAPTER ONE

A TALENTED FEMALE voice singing ABBA's "Dancing Queen" made Barrington "Bear" Fortune smile before he'd even unlocked his motel room door—with an actual metal key. The pretty maid he'd seen around the old motor lodge was standing on the foot of his bed, barefoot and on top of a pile of stripped-off sheets. She stretched to swipe her duster across the ceiling, and her knee-length white skirt swished around her slim legs as her hips swayed to the upbeat song.

Something warmed inside Bear's chest. He squeezed the key in one hand and his laptop case with the other, all in an effort to resist pulling her into his arms just to see what kind of dance partner this alluring and mysterious woman would be.

The door swung closed with a thud, and as she spun to face him, her feet slipped out from under her. She landed on her butt, bounced off the mattress and right into a standing position at the foot of the bed.

He chuckled, surprising himself with the sound of his own laugh because he hadn't heard it in months. "Wow. Impressive move."

"Mr. Fortune, I am so sorry! I don't usually stand on the bed, but there was a cobweb. Way up high." She stepped into a pair of black ballerina flats and smoothed the front of her uniform, a white cotton dress that buttoned up the front. A turquoise apron with big pockets was tied around her slim waist.

"It's fine. I was just jumping on the bed this morning," he said with a straight face. A skill he'd perfected while making business deals around the world.

Her eyes widened even further at his joke, and she worked her mouth, but nothing came out.

"Kidding," he said, then added, "Maybe."

That made her smile, and it lit up her face. Long, dark eyelashes feathered around eyes the color of vibrant rainforest moss, and a lush mouth that had caught his attention the very first time he saw her coming out of a motel room was quivering with a smile she was holding back.

"Once again, I'm sorry, Mr. Fortune."

"You don't have to call me Mr. Fortune. Please, call me Bear." He gave her one of his trademark grins that often made women giggle, or on occasion, give a kittenish purr of invitation. But this young woman only ducked her head.

"Bear. Got it. I'm Morgana. I'll be done in here in a few minutes." She scooped up the pile of sheets from the foot of the bed. "Or do you want me to come back later?"

"Now is fine. Take your time." He was alone so often and usually liked it that way, but having her in his room was... He couldn't put a finger on the feeling stirring inside him, but he wanted her around. The entertainment possibilities of having her in his room were intriguing. He put his laptop case on the bistro-sized table by the window. "And feel free to keep singing."

A rosy blush spread across her high cheekbones. "I can't believe you heard that."

"And I enjoyed it."

She tried to hide a smile as she stuffed the sheets into a canvas bag attached to her rolling cart. "This job can get a bit monotonous. Sometimes I have to entertain myself."

"I can understand that." He was enough of a lone wolf to be well acquainted with the art of entertaining oneself. He had years of practice and had taught himself to be okay with having no one else around.

Whether from desertion, death or deceit, each person who'd disappeared from his life had made him withdraw from emotional attachments a little more each time.

Tension gathered deep in his chest, just like it always did when he thought about his ex-wife, but he pushed it away in a well-practiced move. She and his former best friend had served him a large helping of harsh reality, proving being alone and keeping love out of the equation was the safest path.

Bear sat in one of two chairs that were molded out of yellow plastic with flecks of silver. Very retro and surprisingly comfortable. He pulled out his computer and opened a new oil lease contract he needed to read before tomorrow, but his mind kept wandering back to the pretty maid moving gracefully around his small motel room.

What was Morgana's story? Why was this beautiful young woman working in a motel? Was she a loner like him, or was there something more to her story? His family had warned him that Morgana had been asking a lot of questions about the Fortune family, the mysterious Freya Fortune—who was staying in this same motel—and the silver mine collapse sixty something years ago that killed fifty miners. Fifty-one if the two mysterious notes about there being a fifty-first miner were to be believed.

His siblings and cousins had moved to Chatelaine at Freya Fortune's request. Freya might be like a beloved step-granny to some of the Fortune family, but Bear felt like something was off about her. And he had no interest in her wish granting. His brother Camden's girlfriend, who was a journalist, also suspected Freya was hiding something. Maybe even playing a cat and mouse game with the Fortune grandchildren of Edgar and Elias Fortune.

But there was no denying that Freya *had* been making their wishes and dreams come true with the money from her late husband's will, and despite some ups and downs, all his siblings and cousins were happy and in love. It was all so confusing, especially with Morgana in the mix, but it was a riddle he planned to solve before leaving town.

With the alluring maid still in the room putting clean sheets on his bed, he couldn't concentrate. All he could think about was wrinkling those sheets...with her. He gave up on getting any work done and closed his laptop.

"Where are you from?" he asked Morgana.

Her hand paused momentarily as she smoothed the ivory bedspread. "Tennessee."

"Nashville?"

"No. A little farming community that no one has ever heard of."

"A country girl. So what brought you all the way to Chatelaine, Texas?"

"Oh, I forgot to give you fresh towels." She rushed into the bathroom with a stack of fluffy white towels from her cart.

Her evasive move made him even more curious. Morgana might be fond of asking questions, but her quick retreat into the bathroom suggested she didn't like to answer them. Intriguing and just the kind of challenge he enjoyed getting to the bottom of. And speaking of bottoms, hers had moved so enticingly as she danced. Could Morgana be the distraction he'd been looking for or was she a test of his willpower? They did say keep your enemies closer. But was she *really* an enemy?

That's exactly what he intended to find out.

He glanced around his room. At first, he'd been shocked

by the pink tub, sink and old square tiles, but he kind of liked the old motor lodge with its dated but not worn-out furnishings, and thanks to this entertaining maid, it was always clean. Since he'd made millions off his oil wells and by inventing drilling equipment, he'd become so used to luxury that one might think he'd snub these simple surroundings. But something about this place felt authentic in a way he'd forgotten, proving to himself that he wasn't completely jaded or spoiled by wealth.

Did he like a fine bottle of scotch, a suit tailored just for him and handmade Lucchese boots? Absolutely. But that didn't mean he couldn't appreciate the simpler things in life. And the Chatelaine Motel was the only lodging in town, so there was that. He'd had offers to stay with some of his family members, but he declined because he needed his orderly space and the quiet of being the only person in the room. However, he wasn't going to complain about the occasional singing maid being tossed into the mix.

Morgana breezed back into the room. "I ended up in town because my car broke down while I was on a road trip," she said as if there hadn't been a long pause in their conversation. "I stayed here at the motel while I waited for it to get fixed, and the owner, Hal Appleby, offered me this job. So, I decided to stay in town for a while." Her eyes darted to his for a moment. "What about you? What brought you to Chatelaine?"

"I came to see my brothers."

"Camden and West Fortune?" she asked.

"Those are the ones."

She fingered the small silver charm resting in the hollow of her throat. "West is the one who is back from the dead, right?"

"Yes."

Believing West was dead not long after his ugly divorce had put him into a downward spiral. Bear had started spending all of his time around strangers who didn't know anything about his past. He'd thrown himself into work and little else. Having his little brother back in his life was an unexpected gift that had begun to mend a small part of his damaged heart, but it would never be fully healed.

"I'm happy for your family," she said. "I can understand why you've come for an extended visit."

"I'm also working on a new business deal," he confided to distract himself from his own thoughts. "Then I'll be on my way to somewhere else far away."

Morgana cut another quick glance his way then refocused on meticulously organizing tiny bottles of bath products on her cart. "So, has Freya asked you about your biggest wish like she did with all the others?"

"You know about that?"

"Small town," she said by way of explanation. Rounding the bed, she fluffed a pillow, pulled something from one of her pockets and placed a foil-wrapped chocolate on top, but she still wouldn't fully meet his gaze. "What wish will she be granting for you?"

He ground his back teeth. Nobody went to this much trouble to give away money without gaining something in return. He barely knew Freya Fortune, the cagey woman who was claiming to be their step-grandma, but he had a strong hunch she was up to something. "I'm not interested in Freya's wish granting. Why are you asking me about it?"

"Just making conversation." She hurriedly opened the motel room door. "I'll get out of your way. Have a good afternoon."

"You, too."

She still wouldn't meet his eyes as she backed out of the open doorway, and when the wheels of her cart got caught, she gave an extra tug to get them to bump over the threshold. A roll of toilet paper tumbled off and unfurled as it rolled across the room.

She mumbled something under her breath that sounded suspiciously like damning all toilet paper to hell, and he fought a laugh he figured she wouldn't appreciate. Because the beautiful maid was trapped outside by her unwieldy cart, he snatched the roll up off the tan carpet.

"Think I'll just keep this."

"Excellent choice," she said, as if complimenting his selection of wine with dinner.

His lips twitched, and his mood that had started to sour when she'd asked about Freya's wish granting was once again lifting. This lovely young woman with her singing and dancing and unplanned humor might be up to something, but she was also good for his mood.

"See you around, dancing queen."

CHAPTER TWO

MORGANA WELLS—CURRENTLY USING the last name Mills—
rushed away from Barrington Fortune's motel room, the
metal wheels of her housekeeping cart squeaking and
clacking along the wooden planks of the second-floor
walkway that ran across the front of the Chatelaine Motel.
First, she'd been caught singing and dancing on his bed.
Then she'd finished off her ill-timed performance with a
roll of runaway toilet paper.

Way to completely and totally embarrass yourself.

Her face was flaming, and the blasting July 1 sun wasn't
helping. The rural farm community where she'd grown up
in Tennessee was in a valley near the mountains and had
milder summers. This Texas heat took some getting used
to. She glanced back at the door of his corner room. Kind
of like the challenge of resisting Barrington's magnetism.

"Bear," she whispered. The nickname suited him. When
he'd looked at her with smoldering eyes the color of the
most decadent chocolate, her insides had gotten all warm
and tingly. And that devilish smile…

She turned away and shook her head out of the clouds.
Those same eyes had flared with warning when she'd
asked what wish Freya would be granting for him. Something about the question had set him off, and she needed
to find out why. It could be an important clue.

Way to push things too far too fast.

She'd been looking for a chance to talk to him and see

what he knew about Freya Fortune and what information he might have to aid in her search for her grandmother, Gwenyth Wells. But she'd rushed things and he'd become defensive. Maybe she should ask her coworker, Rhonda, to clean his room from now on.

Her stomach did a little flip. She immediately dismissed that idea. The whole reason she was in Chatelaine was to gather information that would lead to putting her family back together. She just needed to go about things with a little more...*finesse*.

Morgana returned the cart to the storage room above the office that was centered below her on the ground floor. The old motor lodge sat at the tail end of Main Street, a bit removed from the action. It had fourteen rooms with decor that was stuck somewhere between the 1970s and 1980s. She had asked her boss about doing some updates, but guests seemed to like its back in time vibe, so he only made repairs rather than remodeling.

She opened the washing machine to start a load of laundry, and when she pulled out the sheets that she had stripped off Bear's bed, she caught the scent of his cologne and pulled his pillowcase to her nose. Notes of cedar mixed with cinnamon and fresh mountain air made her whole body sing in the best way possible, and she wanted more of the delicious feeling he roused. She had the inappropriate urge to take the pillowcase to her room but stuffed it into the washer instead.

There was another reason she wanted to be the one who cleaned his room. The intensely curious way he'd looked at her made her feel alive in a way she'd never known. He had the air of a man who knew the meaning of the word *passion*. And how to make a woman feel desirable. Morgana shivered.

Bear's charm gave her a pleasantly warm and tingly

kind of glow, with none of the usual signs that a guy was putting on a performance with less than chivalrous intentions. It was true that she hardly knew Bear, and she might be only twenty-five years old, but she'd always been able to sense when a guy was bad news. Her mom had set a good example over the years, never letting a man push her in a direction she didn't want to go.

Bear also had a wicked sense of humor. That was one big thing checked off her list of attractive qualities—along with the butterflies and tingles, of course. And she had little doubt he knew his way around a woman's body. But how did he treat a woman when they weren't in the throes of passion? There was a charisma about him that made her want to climb back onto his bed and test that theory, and this time rumple the sheets...with *him*.

"Absolutely the worst idea you have ever had," she mumbled to herself.

They were from such completely different worlds. Bear Fortune wore designer clothes, drove a luxury car that she didn't even recognize the emblem for, and she'd heard a rumor that he had a private plane. She, on the other hand, cleaned people's rooms, shopped at thrift stores, had an old red car that had faded to orange and barely ran, and she'd never even been on an airplane, private or otherwise. They might as well be Cinderella and the prince—without the chance of a happily-ever-after in a castle.

Morgana got all the laundry started and passed by Bear's room on her way to the stairs. She paused briefly as if he might sense her presence and fling open the door and invite her inside.

I'm being completely ridiculous.

She hurriedly took the stairs and collected what she needed from the downstairs storage room. Next on the list was Freya Fortune's room. She had asked the other maid if she could always be the one who cleaned Freya's room by using the excuse that she'd bonded with Freya's orange cat. It was true that she loved seeing the cat, Sunset, but there was way more to it.

She knocked on Freya's door and waited only a few seconds before the eighty-something-year-old woman answered, dressed in a pale pink linen dress, her ash-blond hair styled into a sleek bob that brushed her jawline, and carrying one of her designer purses that matched her shoes. She was classy from head to toe. If she had told people she'd been a Hollywood movie star back in the day, most of them would have believed her.

"Perfect timing. I have an appointment," the old woman said and rushed away before Morgana could get out a single word.

"Have a nice day, Mrs. Fortune," Morgana called after her.

The woman was forever dodging her at every single turn. She was being very secretive and it was so frustrating. More and more each day, she was convinced that Freya had information she needed in her search for the grandmother she'd never met.

What is Freya hiding?

She winced because she herself was being deceptive, but she meant no harm to anyone. Morgana was on a mission to reunite her family and solve the mystery surrounding the 1965 silver mine collapse. No one could know her true identity. Not yet.

And as far as locating her estranged grandmother, she'd been impossible to find. It's like she dropped off the face of the earth.

The cat rushed over to see her, and she picked him up, not caring that she'd have cat hair on her clothes. "How are you today, Sunset?"

The animal rubbed his fluffy head against Morgana's cheek and his purr motor revved to full speed. She cuddled him for a moment longer before getting to work. Once a week, she gave their extended-stay guest's room a deep cleaning, and the other days she just gave it a quick once-over and freshened the towels. Today was a full cleaning, which is probably why Freya had ducked out so quickly. She only stayed around when Morgana was doing something that wouldn't take more than a few minutes.

She started in the kitchenette area. It was a perk Freya had in her room that she and Bear did not. But if you were going to live in a motor lodge motel, she supposed it was a must. Freya had bought a fancy coffee maker and dishes much cuter than the plain white ones the motel provided. They were French blue with delicate white flowers around the edge. She had also replaced the old standard ivory curtains with raw silk ones in an icy blue and the bedspread was sapphire with throw pillows that matched the curtains. Morgana's eyes drifted across the room and landed on the bookshelf that was filled with an impressive number of classic novels and a small collection of thimbles. But there was no other sign that the old woman liked to sew. The thimbles made her think of her own mother who could use a sewing machine to create anything she set her mind to—including most of the clothes Morgana had worn while growing up on the farm.

Over the past few months, she thought Freya would finally reveal something that would help her discover what became of her grandmother. Freya had to have picked up some piece of useful information from her deceased husband, Elias Fortune. He must've disclosed something to her over the years, but so far, she claimed to know nothing.

At first, the widow seemed to be doing good deeds but slowly Morgana had begun to wonder if Freya had an alternative motive that wasn't so altruistic. From previous conversations with her new friend Haley, the reporter also had similar suspicions about Freya's reasons for being in Chatelaine. There was just something about the whole situation that didn't make sense, but she couldn't pin down exactly what it was.

Once she was done cleaning, Morgana came out of Freya's room just as the other maid, Rhonda, stepped from a room down the way. "Are you finished for the day?"

Rhonda swiped the back of her hand dramatically across her forehead. "Yes, thank goodness. This last room was a doozy. Beer cans and fast-food trash everywhere. I hate it when someone has a drinking party in their room."

"At least they weren't loud. Since my room is right above that one, I would know," Morgana said about her comped second-floor room. A benefit of working here for less pay than Rhonda was because the sweet, brassy divorcée lived in a small apartment in town.

The woman looked at her watch. "I have to get home and shower. I have an appointment to get my roots dyed before my date tonight." She touched her bottle blond hair that was currently twisted into a bun.

"Who's the lucky man?"

"Remember the guy I told you about who I met at Cowgirl Café? He saw me in GreatStore and asked me out."

"That's wonderful! Have fun on your hot date tonight."

"Oh, I plan to. We're having dinner at the Chatelaine Bar and Grill and then after that…" Her middle-aged co-worker waggled her eyebrows while fanning her face. "Who knows. I'll see you tomorrow, kid."

Morgana chuckled and waved before going into the small office where the motor lodge's owner, Hal Appleby, was click-clacking away on his ancient computer. She'd finally talked her mom into getting a laptop, and she was working on doing the same for Hal, but he was resistant and frequently muttered about newfangled technology. The sixtysomething widower was a great boss. Kind, generous and always willing to help out a friend.

"All the rooms are clean and ready for the next guests."

"That's great." He brushed his hand through his thinning gray hair. "We just got a reservation for two rooms for tomorrow. I'm going to put them in rooms three and four."

"Good choice. Did you have fun on your date last night?"

He shook his head and tried not to smile, but his cheeks were turning ruddy. "It wasn't a date. Just dinner with an old friend who has moved back to town."

"If you say so. I think she's a lovely lady and you shouldn't rule it out." Morgana sighed inwardly. It seemed like everyone was dating, except her.

The lobby door swung open, and a young couple came inside, so she excused herself and went back upstairs to her room. Only two doors down from Bear's. Hers was smaller than Freya's room with a real kitchenette, but using odds and ends, Morgana had turned one corner into her own version of a kitchen. Hal had kindly provided her with a mini fridge, hot plate, toaster oven and the plain white dishes Freya wasn't using. She was so thankful for all of it. The mini fridge sat on the floor under a garage sale table, and the other items were arranged on top.

Like her mom had taught her, she'd sanded and painted the table. The top was a soothing shade of blue with whimsical little fairies dancing up the tapered sage-green legs. When it was time to leave Chatelaine, she would try to sell the table for more than the few dollars she'd paid for it.

She made a mental note to keep an eye out for furniture that had been set out in front of houses on trash day. It was amazing to see the kind of things people tossed out. Refinishing and repurposing found items is how her mom had made extra money when times got tough—which had happened often. Following in her footsteps, she would fix up a few pieces and save the money. With a little extra cash, she could afford to get her car repaired properly and quit just throwing temporary fixes at it.

Morgana took a quick shower like she always did after she finished work for the day and then settled in to read *Cinderella Stories from Around the World*. The book had been left behind by a guest, and she was waiting to see if they wanted it mailed back to them. Hal had chuckled when she'd told him she was going to take the book to her room and read it, but fairy tales had been a love of hers for as long as she could remember. She knew the fantastical stories weren't true to life. The perfectly tied-up-with-a-bow happy endings weren't something you could very often expect to happen, but as she saw it, a girl had to dream.

By EARLY EVENING, Morgana finished the last Cinderella story. This one had been from the country of Germany. And now, she was hungry for something more than what was in her room, and she was too keyed up to lie around and watch TV. She needed to get out of these four walls, and she knew just the thing. A sweet woman who'd been a guest a few weeks ago had struck up a conversation with her about books, and when she'd checked out, she'd left Morgana a twenty-five-dollar Remi's Reads gift card as a tip. She'd been waiting to use it during the July Fourth sale they were having this week.

Morgana stepped out of her room at the same time Bear was coming out of his. Of course, her heart rate took off like the rapid pace of a hummingbird's wings. "Hey, neighbor," she said and locked her door.

He looked between her and the room she'd just come out of with her leather backpack purse over one shoulder. "Do you live here at the motel?"

A tickle of embarrassment swirled through her, and she tugged on the midthigh hem of her favorite periwinkle-and-white sundress but quickly reminded herself that she had nothing to be embarrassed about. There were several reasons Morgana had taken the job as a maid at the old motor lodge. One, because she was from out of town and needed a place to stay and the position came with a small single room. But more importantly, because Freya lived here. Morgana thought proximity would help develop a relationship. And now, having Bear Fortune staying at the motel, it was another good reason to remain here a little longer.

"Yes, I'm living here temporarily. It's a perk of working here."

"That's convenient. Where are you headed?"

She dropped her keys into her purse. "I need a new book because I finished the one I was reading. *Cinderella Stories from Around the World.* I'll be happy to let you borrow it," she said, testing to see if his sense of humor really was as good as she suspected.

He grinned. "Thanks, but I've already read that one."

She couldn't hide her smile. "I'm walking to Remi's Reads. It's a bookstore."

"I've been there. My cousin Linc Fortune and his wife Remi own it."

"Oh, that's right. There really are a lot of Fortunes around town." They started walking, and he followed her down the stairs.

"That's kind of far to be walking, isn't it?"

Morgana shrugged and rubbed the star charm on her necklace, like she tended to do when she was nervous.

She didn't want to admit that her car wasn't running—
again—and she didn't have the money to fix it yet. Maybe
she shouldn't be spending money on books, but they were
one of the few pleasures she afforded herself. "The walk
saves me from having to get a gym membership."

"I'm going over to my brother West's house, and I'm
happy to give you a ride to the bookstore if you want. It's
on my way."

She hesitated but only long enough to remember she'd
been looking for an excuse to get a closer look at his vehicle. The sleek silver car made her think of the magical
coach that took Cinderella to the royal ball, and her little faded orange car was more like the pumpkin, sad and
broken on the side of the road. Very fitting that she and
her mom had actually named her car Pumpkin. At least
once, she wanted to be the one who was riding in the ex-
travagant coach.

"A ride would be nice. Thank you for the offer."

"You're welcome."

Morgana walked beside him but neither of them spoke.
This would also be another chance to see if he knew anything to help with her search for her estranged grandmother, Gwenyth, widow of Clint Wells, the mine foreman
who was blamed for the disastrous silver mine collapse
sixtysomething years ago. *Unfairly* blamed. That much
she had discovered to be true.

Her progress had been slower than she would've liked,
but she couldn't afford to give up now. Reuniting her family was the whole reason she'd come to Texas. Her mother
wasn't even aware she was in Chatelaine. Morgana was
being secretive to protect her mom because talking about
the past was hard for her. At the age of eighteen her mom,
Renee, moved to Tennessee and started a new life in a rural
farming community where they made what little money

they had by running a farm stand selling everything from fresh produce, honey and handmade goods. Renee had worked hard to build a life for them far away from her own mother's need for vengeance. Getting her hopes up for nothing was unacceptable.

They stopped beside his sporty luxury car. She wasn't even sure of the make or model. The lights flashed as he unlocked it with the key fob, and then he opened the door for her to get in.

"Thank you," she said and settled into the tan leather bucket seat that hugged her body like a lover. A shiver rippled all the way to her toes.

She shouldn't be thinking about lovers while she was already working so hard to resist her attraction to Bear Fortune. The oil baron who was way out of her league. In the time it took for him to round the hood of the car, she'd inhaled the scent of leather and admired the curving lines of the dashboard. A strip down the center around the controls was made from real wood, inlaid in a chevron pattern highlighted with a glossy coating.

For a tall guy, he easily slid into his seat in one swift and graceful movement, making her think of the prowling wildcats she loved watching at the zoo. And when he started the car, it purred and rumbled like said large powerful animal.

"This is a beautiful car. Have you had it long?"

"No. I just leased it when I got back from Brazil. I've always wanted an Aston Martin."

So that's what this is.

He seemed to be making his dreams come true, and that gave her hope that she could accomplish a few of her own by his age—which she thought was early thirties. "How did you get the nickname Bear?"

"I think it was because West couldn't say Barrington."

"That makes sense." Morgana couldn't seem to stop her nervous chatter. "I would love to go to Brazil someday. I hear there are some amazing waterfalls there."

"It's true. Iguaçú Falls is the largest broken waterfall in the world."

"Broken? Does that mean a lot of them side by side?" she asked.

"Exactly." His long fingers drummed on the leather steering wheel and a smile played on his lips, but his eyes remained on the road ahead. "It's made up of a chain of waterfalls. There are two hundred and seventy-five of them all fed by the Iguaçú River."

"I also like learning facts about the places I go," she murmured. "That must have been a wonderful vacation."

"It was for work. I was there for about three months. But I did slip away for a week to visit the falls."

"Didn't I hear that you're in the oil business?" she asked.

"I don't know. *Did* you hear that?" He cocked his head and shot her a brief glance.

She sighed inwardly. He was a tough one, just like Freya. "I must have, or it wouldn't have come to mind."

"Where'd you hear it?"

Apparently two could play the question game. She pretended to think about it, even though she knew exactly where she'd heard it. "I believe it was at Cowgirl Café when some of your cousins were sitting in the booth behind me." She fidgeted with her star charm to calm herself. She needed to keep her head about her and not get all dreamy-eyed. "Do you like the oil business?"

"Do you always ask so many questions?" It was said with a grin that lifted one corner of his mouth.

"I'm delightfully inquisitive. I know all kinds of interesting facts about Chatelaine."

"Well, now I guess we know how that happened."

"I'm just curious by nature. Always have been." It was true. Lots of people had told her that—some of them while rolling their eyes as they said it.

"I was consulting on a new offshore drilling project for a company who doesn't want to cut down rainforest to drill on land."

"That's admirable. How does one get a job like that?"

"I invented a new type of drill bit."

"Oh wow. An inventor. Impressive."

He shrugged like it was no big thing.

The ride was over too soon as he pulled up in front of Remi's Reads, and she opened her door. "Thanks for the lift."

"You're welcome. See you around, neighbor."

"If you need anything at all, you know where I am." Heat washed over her face, and she winced at the suggestive way that had sounded. "Like fresh towels or…" Her voice trailed off before she could embarrass herself further.

"Or toilet paper?" he quipped, using the exact words she'd been trying to avoid.

"Have fun with your brother." She practically leaped from the car, closing the door and then waving as he pulled away. Watching him drive away in his fancy car, she understood why he didn't need Freya to be his fairy godmother. Bear could grant his own wishes.

CHAPTER THREE

SINCE THE SPEED limit on this stretch of road was only twenty-five miles per hour, in between looking out his windshield, Bear watched Morgana growing smaller in his rearview mirror. She hadn't gone inside, just stood in front of the bookstore, watching him right back.

"What am I going to do with you, Morgana the Curious? Full of questions and so spirited." He hadn't stopped thinking about her since she'd danced on his bed, and he wanted her back on it. With him.

Bad idea, dude. Really bad idea.

There was no denying the instant spark between him and Morgana. Something so tempting and evocative. Like the finest dark chocolate and ultrasoft cashmere against bare skin. But falling into bed with the maid that lived a few doors down was reckless. Not because he thought she was beneath him. Never that. He'd started at the very bottom in life, literally abandoned in a park. It was because she wanted something from his family, and he knew all too well how initial sparks could burn down a life.

With a button on the leather steering wheel of his Aston Martin, he changed the radio to a country station and made the turn toward his brother's house. He loved the way this car handled, powerful yet smooth. Maybe he'd have to do more than just lease it.

He pulled up and parked in front of West's new house where he lived with his fiancée, Tabitha, and their one-year-old twin boys. Since he'd come to town, watching his brother with his adorable twin baby boys was making something paternal stir inside of him. He made his way up the front walk, which was lined with well-manicured grass, and stepped up onto the front porch to knock. There were a couple of comfy outdoor chairs and toys scattered about. Signs of the family life his brother was living.

Bear had come here to see for himself that West was alive and well, but he intended to keep his distance from anything involving his past, including his grandfather's widow, which was a challenge since she was staying at the same motel. He'd made a conscious decision to be about the here and now and to focus on the future. Always trying to outrun his past could get exhausting, but getting too close to anyone came with a big risk of losing them. It's why he liked to move from place to place because no one knew him well enough to know his tragic backstory.

The door opened, and Tabitha smiled at him. "Hi, Bear. Come on inside. West is just finishing up with a phone call and will be out of his office in a few minutes."

He kissed her cheek. "Good to see you again." He followed her from the front door to the living room where his nephews, Zach and Zane, were curled up together asleep on a blanket on the floor. It was the cutest thing he'd seen in a long time. He sat on the couch, and she took the chair across the room.

"Everyone is so glad you've come to Chatelaine. We're also glad to find out what you've been up to."

"Did you think it was something scandalous?" he asked dryly.

She chuckled and flipped her long blond hair over her shoulder. "We'd all been making guesses. A few I can remember were a spy, private detective and I believe someone guessed exotic dancer."

He laughed loud enough at that last one to wake up one of the babies. "Oops. Sorry about that."

"It's alright," she said and watched to see if the child would settle back down. "It's time for them to wake up from their nap."

The toddler sat up, rubbed his eyes and then smiled at him. Bear got down on the floor beside them. "Hey, there…" He tried to remember which twin this was.

"That's Zach," Tabitha filled in helpfully.

His nephew crawled his way, which happened to be across the top of his sleeping brother. The second twin was understandably a little crankier, and his mom went over to soothe him.

The little boy continued making his way over to Bear and crawled into his lap. "What's up, Zach man?"

The toddler babbled unintelligibly, and in no time, both boys were bringing him toys and climbing on his body like a jungle gym. He'd only been around his nephews a few times, but they were sneaking into his very closed heart. At first it had surprised him, but after giving it a bit of thought, it also made him realize he was ready to be a dad.

The twins were giggling so hard at his silly faces that they were out of breath.

West came into the living room, and when Tabitha smiled at him, he crossed the room to give her a kiss. The love between them was obvious, and Bear really hoped they could make it last, even though he couldn't.

He no longer believed in forever love—catching his ex-wife with his best friend last year had knocked the fairy tale right out of him. Who can he trust if not a best friend and a wife? The answer? Himself. Only himself. He'd have to find a way to experience fatherhood without it including a wife. He could only count on his own actions and keeping his heart out of things was a must.

West sat down beside him and the boys. "Sorry about being on the phone when you got here."

"No worries. These two have kept me entertained."

The twins were excited to have two big guys to climb on now. However, when Zach and Zane began to get irritable and started squabbling with each other, their mother came into the room and scooped them up. "Time for you two rug rats to have dinner and a bath. Tell your Uncle Bear goodbye."

One babbled and one cried.

"Bye, boys. I'll see you again soon." He waved as their mom carried them away, one on each hip.

"Let's go out onto the porch and have a beer." West suggested.

"Sounds good."

Bear took a seat on the back porch while his brother grabbed the beers and thought about what he had observed over the last hour. West had come back from hiding after the criminal who threatened to hurt Tabitha had been killed and had the shock of a lifetime when he learned he was the father of twins. But he'd jumped in with both feet and become part of a real family. A *happy* family. His little brother was in love, and he prayed it was only the beginning of West's happily ever after. But most of all, he was grateful that his bro was alive.

West came out through the back door and handed Bear a long-necked amber bottle.

"Thanks." He studied his brother's face, noticing some of the lines of worry and stress had diminished.

"What? Why are you looking at me like I'm a science experiment?"

Bear shook his head and took a long pull on his drink, the ice-cold beer cooling his throat that had suddenly grown tight and burning from too much emotion coming at him all at once. "It's just really great to have you back from the dead, little brother."

"I can't tell you how good it is to be out of hiding. But if only I'd known…"

He knew what West was thinking without him saying it. If he'd only known Tabitha was pregnant.

West shook his head and rolled his shoulder in a new repetitive movement Bear had noticed since coming to town. He couldn't imagine what it would be like to have a bullet wound and was sorry his brother would have a permanent reminder of falling into the river after being shot and assumed dead.

"I missed so much." His voice was hoarse with tightly held pain.

Bear squeezed his uninjured shoulder. "But you haven't missed *everything*. And the boys are young enough that they won't remember a time when you weren't around."

"Good point." West took a long swallow of his beer.

"Tell me about the ranch where you were hiding out. How was it being a real cowboy?"

"The hard work at least kept me in shape, busy and exhausted enough not to go crazy. I can ride, rope, fix fence, brand cattle and a whole host of new skills."

"We sure are glad you're back with us," Bear said.

"Thanks, and we're all happy to see you, too. You know that it worries us when you're out of touch, but am I right to think you're living some of the adventure stories you told us when we were kids?"

Bear shot his brother a surprised look. "You remember those stories?"

"Of course. Your make-believe stories got us through a lot of tough nights."

They were quiet, remembering the nights their parents fought, saying more than three little boys needed to hear.

When they would argue about who had an affair or who'd spent too much money, Bear would gather them all in one bed and tell them stories about the most exciting adventures he could think of. Exploring and discovering and fighting for good.

His adoptive parents, Peter and Dolly Fortune, hadn't been the best parents in the world, and even though there had been nights he and his two younger brothers had to fall asleep to the sounds of fighting and slamming doors, he had loved them and they him. He missed them since their fatal plane crash five years ago. He often wished he had a thicker skin because loss was hard for him.

"I think I'll start telling Zach and Zane those kinds of stories at bedtime," West told him. "Without adults yelling in the background."

"Good plan. It's never too early to start." Bear's thoughts once again went to his desire for a child of his own. A child that he could love and tell bedtime stories to each night. This time with stories that were based on his real-life adventures. A wish Freya could not grant. He'd have to figure this one out for himself. But how to do it without involving the big three: romance, his heart and hurting another person. That was the question.

Bear stretched out his legs and propped one snakeskin boot over the other. "Part of the reason I've stayed out of touch with everyone is because I thought I'd lost you forever. I know it seems opposite to pull away from family at a time when it's been proven you can lose them in an instant, but that's what I did."

"You always have been a lone wolf. But you know, you don't have to be alone forever."

Alone. Like he'd been as a toddler when his birth family abandoned him in a sandbox at the park. Alone now because his wife had tossed away their marriage. Maybe he was meant to be alone, but he didn't feel like having that discussion with West right now. "I know. I'm working on it. I've just been really busy."

"Are you dating anyone?"

An image flashed in his mind. Silky dark hair, mischievous green eyes and a lush smile. *Morgana.* Why was the pretty motel maid coming to mind? Anything happening with her was a bad idea, just like it was the last time he'd thought about it.

"No one lately. Guess I'm not eager to jump back into the fire and get burned again."

"I can understand that," his brother acknowledged. "Will you tell me what happened with your marriage?"

Bear's chest constricted as if wrapped with a metal band like it always did when he thought of his ex-wife and his ex-best friend. "The short version is, I came home early from a business trip to surprise her. Instead, I was the one who got the surprise. Not a good one."

West winced and took a sip of his beer. "Let me guess. She wasn't alone?"

"No, sir, she was definitely not alone." Acid burned in his stomach, and he rubbed his eyes, trying to ease the picture that had been burned into his brain. "She was naked and so was the man I thought was my best friend."

"Damn. That's rough. Sorry you had to go through that."

He ripped off a piece of the beer's paper label. "You're lucky to have the twins. I thought I'd have a kid by now, but it hasn't been in the cards for me." If he wanted to make something happen, he was going to have to do it himself.

"It's worth trying love again. You need to give it another chance, Bear. It's worth it."

"No thank you. It's a been-there-done-that-and-don't-plan-to-repeat-it kind of thing. I've been abandoned, lost parents, lost a brother—only for a while, thank God—and been cheated on by a wife and a friend. I think I'll stick to only temporary hookups." He didn't want to bring up the fact that he wanted an heir, because the problem was how to make that happen without entangling his heart with a woman.

"Are you going to the Fourth of July picnic at the park? We're taking the boys."

He was glad for the change of topic. "I didn't know about it, but sure. I'll meet you there."

BEAR PARKED HIS car in the lot of the motel and saw Morgana struggling to get a piece of furniture up the stairs. She was lifting it up one stair at a time, then pausing to catch her breath before struggling to get it to the next one. He hurried over to her.

"Let me help you with that."

She looked startled to see him but then smiled. "That would be great."

It was a small dresser with the drawers removed. It was worn with a child's scribbles on one side and scars along the top. Something that should be going out of the motel and not being moved *into* it. "Does the owner often make you move furniture?"

She chuckled. "No. Someone set this out in front of their house for the heavy trash pickup, and I'm planning to refinish it and hopefully sell it."

He looked around them. "How did you get it from the house where you found it here to the motel?"

"I rolled it carefully down the road on my skateboard. But sadly, that doesn't work for the stairs."

"Wait, back up to the skateboard part."

"Someone gave it to me, but I can't do more than roll along on a flat surface. Do you skateboard?"

"Yes, but I haven't done it in years. Let me get this furniture for you." He stepped around her, picked up the dresser and went up the rest of the stairs. It weighed nothing compared to the equipment he regularly moved around on oil rigs. "Are we going to your room?"

"No. See where the drawers are stacked up beside that door? That's the storage room where I'll be working on it."

Once they got all of the pieces inside, she locked the door and then flapped her shirt to cool her body. "Thanks for your help. Want a cold drink? I have some in my mini fridge."

He should say no. The two of them being alone in her room wasn't his smartest move, but he couldn't make himself decline. Consequences be damned. "That would be great."

When she flipped on the light in her motel room, he took in her space. There were splashes of color and touches that seemed fitting for the woman he was starting to know. A jewel-toned patchwork quilt on the bed, a purple scarf draped over her desk chair, a few belts on a doorknob and a painted table served as a kitchenette. Little terra-cotta pots of herbs were lined up along her windowsill and her book of Cinderella stories on her bedside table.

"Nice place you have here."

She looked at him with a slight tilt of her head as if trying to assess whether or not he was being serious.

"You did a good job of making it feel like a home with the plants and colors and stuff," he clarified.

What do I think I am? An interior decorator? I sound like a dumbass.

"Thanks." She got two Coca-Colas out of her tiny refrigerator and handed one to him.

He worked the flip-top on the ice-cold can of soda and

it hissed as carbonated effervescence escaped, making his mouth water for the sweet, fizzy drink.

She rolled her cold can over her cheeks before opening it. "Mind if I ask you something?"

"Go for it."

"Why are you so against Freya's wish granting? Have all your dreams already come true?"

"The ones Freya could possibly grant have. I don't need her money. But I do have a wish I intend to grant on my own. I want an heir." Goosebumps popped up on Bear's skin. Why was he telling her this? He hadn't shared this with anyone. Barely even to himself.

She sat on the foot of her bed and ran the tip of one finger around the rim of her can. "You want to fall in love and marry and have a child?"

Just hearing the word *marriage* made his gut clench. "Love? No. Tried that. I don't believe in love."

Morgana's brow furrowed as if she felt bad for him. "I see."

"I only want an heir, but I'm stumped on how to do that without hurting another person."

"At least you aren't the kind of guy who goes around breaking hearts. But you do intend to love your child, don't you?"

He stiffened as his insides twisted. "Of course I'll love him or her. That's completely different."

He would never understand a parent not loving their own child and would never ever do what his birth family had done to him. He loved his adoptive family, but after his parents' death and then his whole marriage fiasco, losing people had become a sore point for him. That's why it had been so hard on him when they thought West was dead.

"Why don't you hire a surrogate?"

Morgana's voice pulled him from his spiraling thoughts. "That sounds complicated," he answered gruffly.

Bear leaned his back against the wall beside her desk with a heavy sigh. In the years since he'd become rich, he wasn't used to being hindered from getting what he wanted, but this situation was tricky. If a child was involved, everything had to be considered very carefully.

Morgana kicked off her flip-flops, tucked her feet beneath her and flashed him a nervous smile. "If you tell me everything you know about Freya Fortune, maybe I can help you find a nice woman to have your baby. Or an agency that handles that kind of thing."

Something jolted inside him at the thought of *this* gorgeous, vibrant woman being the one to have his baby, but rather than let it show, he casually crossed one boot over the other. She was young and beautiful, and he got the feeling she was looking for the kind of happy endings found in one of her books. And he did not fit into that mold. "Why in the world do you want to know about Freya so badly?"

"I'm just curious. I've been cleaning her room for months, and she is kind of fascinating. Why is someone like her living in a place like this? She is so stylish and clearly has the money to rent a house or at least an apartment."

He'd recently thought the same thing. "I have money and I'm staying here."

"Are you planning to stay here for months on end?"

"Well, no." He followed her gaze to a stack of notebooks on her desk beside a couple of books about Chatelaine.

"Remember when I told you I was on a road trip when I came here?"

"Yes. You said you were stranded here when your car broke down."

"I've been traveling around the country collecting stories and doing research for a book I want to write about how a town's history makes it unique."

"A book? Like a novel or a nonfiction book?"

"You think I can't write? I did have some schooling back on the farm," she said with an exaggerated Southern accent.

He chuckled. "No. I didn't mean that at all. I'm just surprised. But intrigued. So, if you're traveling to collect stories, why have you stayed in Chatelaine for so long?"

"Because I ran out of money, and I've had to pause my trip to make some," she admitted. "And while I've been here the last few months, some stories have caught my attention."

"Meaning the mine disaster and the Fortune family. *My* family."

"Yes." She picked at a loose thread on her quilt. "Among other things."

"Well, you've come to the wrong person to ask about Freya. I don't know a thing about her." He studied Morgana for a moment, waiting for her to look at him. His phone rang in his pocket, and he pulled it out to see if it was important. It wasn't but it felt like the right time to make an exit. "I should get going so I can call them back. Thanks for the drink."

She stood and opened the door. "And thank you again for helping me with the dresser."

"Anytime. See you around, dancing queen." Morgana's door had barely closed, and Bear already wanted to see her again.

CHAPTER FOUR

BECAUSE THERE HADN'T been many motel guests last night, work had been light today and Morgana was antsy and bored. She watered her little terra-cotta pots of herbs that were lined up on her windowsill and got herself a cold bottle of kombucha from her mini fridge. She so badly wanted to finally just come out with the truth of her identity—that she came to Chatelaine months ago to research her family history so that she could repair it. Until she got further along in her research, she had to keep the secret a while longer.

From under her bed, she pulled out the cardboard box of photos, letters and other information she'd collected while in Chatelaine. She'd started with limited information. She knew her grandmother Gwenyth's birthday was July 25 and had an old photo, but she hadn't been able to gather too much information because her mom, Renee, didn't like to talk about the grandparent Morgana had never met. She said it was to get away from Gwenyth's all-consuming desire for vengeance against the Fortune brothers for unfairly blaming her husband Clint Wells for the 1965 silver mine collapse and ruining the Wells name. What a wild family history she had.

Sighing, she sat on her bed and spread out the collection of clues. She didn't have the original notes left by a mystery person about there being a fifty-first miner, but she knew what they said. The first anonymous note had been found last fall behind Fortune Castle where the number fifty—memorializing the perished miners—was etched into the castle wall. A castle that was built by Wendell Fortune. The note said "There were fifty-one." A couple of months ago, another unsigned note had been tacked up on the community bulletin board in the park and said "Fifty-one died in the mine. Where are the records? What became of Gwenyth Wells?"

This note containing her grandmother's name was the one that was giving her the hope she needed to continue. There was someone else out there with the same questions she had. A couple of people had said their great-grandparents knew someone who died in the mine collapse, but no one had any real useful information.

Who was leaving these notes?

In her quest for answers, she'd been to the town archives at city hall and the ones at the *Chatelaine Daily News*, as well as the town's small history museum to read through old articles and study photos. From looking at old grainy photos of her grandmother that she'd found around town, the age range, and little things Freya had said and done, Morgana had started to wonder if Freya Fortune and her grandmother were one and the same, but that seemed so unlikely.

Freya is *Elias Fortune's widow*. Why would her grandmother ever marry the enemy who she blamed for killing her husband and ruining their family? It made no sense.

She spread out the faded photographs on the patchwork quilt that she'd helped her mom make years ago. She compared one she'd recently taken of Freya—without her knowledge—to a photo of her grandmother from the 1960s. But she just couldn't tell. Next, Morgana reread the stack of old letters Wendell's daughter, Ariella, had written to him, but once again nothing new or noteworthy jumped out at her.

Maybe it was time to make another trip to the museum. She slipped on her tennis shoes and started her walk. Bear's car wasn't in the parking lot. Too bad the prince of bachelors wasn't around to give her a ride in style.

The Chatelaine Museum was a modest old historical museum in a white adobe house with a red tile roof. It had aged wooden floors and photos hung gallery style on every wall, and the hallway had an enormous hand-drawn map of the town with street names written in a neat but faded cursive.

She hoped that after her recent research, something she saw would spark an idea, or she might notice something she hadn't before. The old flooring creaked as she stepped inside and closed the heavy wooden door. After saying hello to the young woman sitting at the front desk, she walked slowly along each wall, studying every photo and reading every description, but no matter how hard she looked, she had no more information than she'd started the day with.

Another waste of time.

Feeling a bit discouraged about all the dead ends and unanswered questions, Morgana came out of the Chatelaine Museum and shielded her eyes from the afternoon sun. Digging into her purse, she put on her pair of cheap sunglasses for the trek back to the motel. And all the while she kept an eye out for Bear or his Aston Martin, but there was no sign of her crush.

THE NEXT AFTERNOON, Morgana was walking to the town's Fourth of July celebration at the park and once again wishing she had the money to get her car repaired so she wouldn't have to depend on her own two feet all of the time.

"I'm the one who needs a fairy godmother," she mumbled.

A car pulled to a stop at the curb beside her. The automatic window rolled down and Wendell smiled at her. "Can I give you a ride somewhere, young lady?"

A fairy godfather worked, too. "I'm headed to the park for the Fourth of July celebration."

"I'm going that way. Hop in."

"Thanks." She climbed in and clicked her seat belt in place. She really wanted to ask Wendell about the missing letter he was supposed to be looking for, but she wasn't sure if she should jump right to it. "Are you joining the celebration today?"

He turned down the country music playing on the radio. "For a little while. I'm meeting some of the grandkids."

"Oh, good. How have you been feeling lately? I know your hip gives you trouble."

"I guess I'm about as okay as an old man my age can feel. Make sure to have fun while you're young."

"I'm working on it. Have you found the missing letter from your daughter, Ariella?"

"No, but I'll keep looking for it."

Morgana kept her sigh of frustration on the inside. She really needed to catch a break.

BEAR HAD NEVER been to the city park but found it easily. If he could navigate around the world, he could manage a small Texas town. The Chatelaine Fourth of July celebration was being held here, and he'd promised to meet his brothers. The park had beautiful trees, a walking path, a play structure and a covered pavilion with a concrete floor. There was a community bulletin board near the pavilion.

Bear had been told this is where one of the mysterious notes about a fifty-first miner had been posted.

The park was decorated with red, white and blue streamers, balloons and flags. Food trucks were lined up in one area with a tempting variety of food, sweets and icy cold beverages. The event was noisy and crowded but he spotted West and Camden in line for drinks. West had a cowboy hat on over his dark blond hair and his youngest brother had on a baseball cap.

Bear slipped up behind them and grabbed each of them by the shoulder like he'd done when they were kids and caught them doing something mischievous. "What kind of trouble are you two getting into?"

West slugged him in the arm. "Hey, brother Bear. Nothing yet. Other than getting caught giving the twins candy this morning."

"Glad you made it out to meet up with us today," Camden added.

"Me, too." He meant it. He was really glad to see his brothers. "I've had a lot of work that's kept me on my computer. Closing one deal and working on a couple of others."

Camden moved forward in the line. "Good to hear your business is doing well. You should be proud of your accomplishments."

"Really proud," West said. "Tabitha and my boys will be here any minute and might want a place to sit. Y'all go grab one of those tables before they're taken, and I'll wait here for the drinks."

"Where is your girlfriend?" Bear asked Camden as they wove through people to get to an empty table.

"Haley was here earlier but had a few things to do. She's meeting us later for dinner at Cowgirl Café. You're still going, right?"

"I'll be there," he assured his brother.

"How is it living in the motel?"

"It's fine. Clean and comfortable, but I sure do miss room service."

"The pretty, inquisitive maid can't help you out with your needs?"

Even though he knew the comment was said in good fun and only teasing, Bear's hackles rose, and he gave Camden a hard stare.

His youngest brother raised his hands. "Whoa. I know that look on your face. You're protective of her."

"No, I'm not." The lie rolled right off his tongue to land like a lead ball on his big toe.

"You know I'm just kidding around. I didn't mean anything by that comment."

"I know."

West joined them at the table with three iced teas. "No sign of Tabitha and the twins?"

Camden took one of the drinks. "Not yet."

"I want a child." The words left Bear's mouth in a rush and earned him blank stares from both brothers.

"Like adopting one?" Camden asked.

"No. Adoption worked out great for me and lots of other people, but I'm talking about a child who is biologically mine. I don't have any blood relations. Well, I do somewhere, but I don't know any of them."

"You know the blood running through your veins doesn't matter to us, right?" Camden said gruffly.

"Yes, I do"

"But I understand what you're saying." West crunched a piece of ice between his back teeth. "Looking into the identical faces of my boys, it's an amazing feeling you can't describe."

Now they were just getting too emotional, and he

needed to rein it in. "I also need an heir," Bear blurted out and got raised eyebrows from both men.

"You need one for your massive fortune?" Camden asked with a chuckle.

They clearly didn't realize how much money he'd earned off the patents for drilling equipment and oil wells. "Let me rephrase that. I *want* an heir. But how to get a baby is the challenge. How can I have a baby without involving romance, love or hurting a woman?"

His brothers looked at one another and then burst out laughing. "Dude, good luck with that," West said. "There's no way to escape any of the three, let alone one."

That answer wasn't reassuring in the least. They paused the conversation when Tabitha headed their way with the boys in a double stroller.

He chatted with his family, held his nephews and ate a hotdog. A little while later, Bear caught sight of Morgana across the park. She was dressed in denim shorts, a flowy white top with red flowers embroidered around the neck and sleeves, and she had a white daisy stuck in her ponytail. "I'm going to go say hello to someone."

West followed his line of sight. "Bro, do you know what you're doing? She's the one asking all the questions."

"True, but she wants to know about Freya as much as I do. I want to find out what she knows. Questions can go both ways."

"Just be careful," his brother said.

"Will do." Bear slipped away from the group and made his way over to where Morgana was examining things at a craft booth. "You look like you could use a snow cone."

She turned to him with a smile. "I think you're right."

They began walking side by side as if it was a completely normal thing for them to do. His hand tingled with a desire to reach out and take hold of hers, so he hooked his thumbs in the pockets of his jeans. Maybe West was right to tell him to be careful, because he realized that he did feel a connection and a sort of protectiveness for her. But *why*?

"Are you staying for the fireworks?" she asked.

"I hadn't really planned on it."

"Hal said there's a good view of them from the motel."

"That's handy. We can just step outside of our doors later and watch the show." That had sounded like an invitation, and he knew he shouldn't have said it, but he wasn't sorry. "But you're probably planning to watch from here."

"No. I'll be back at the motel. I don't think I can take being in a big crowd from now until after dark."

"A woman after my own heart. I'm not a fan of crowds either." They stopped in front of the food truck that served snow cones. "What's your favorite flavor?"

"Blue coconut. But I always end up with a blue tongue. If I'd choose watermelon, which I also like, at least my tongue would be red." Her hands moved animatedly as she talked.

He couldn't resist smiling at her excited chatter. They reached their turn at the window, and he ordered both of the flavors she'd mentioned and then held them toward her. "Take your pick."

She tapped her chin with her index finger. "I think I should taste each before I make my decision. Unless you're afraid of my girl cooties."

He laughed loud enough that a few people looked in his direction. "Nope. No fear here."

"Good." She took the watermelon snow cone and pressed her mouth to the soft, snow-packed ice, and then made a soft moaning sound of pleasure. "Mmm. Cold and sweet. That really hits the spot."

His brain went straight to places that it shouldn't. Like

the "spot" on her neck where a star charm rested against her skin that was rosy from the warmth of the day. Instead, he tasted the blue snow cone.

They started walking again in no particular direction. "Is it a really long flight from here to Brazil?" she asked.

"Pretty long. About nine or ten hours. I usually travel at night and try to sleep." Having a private plane helped make any trip a lot more comfortable.

"Where are you off to next?"

"I'm not sure yet. It depends on a few deals I have working." He held out the blue snow cone and they traded without having to say anything. Something about taking a bite of the watermelon snow cone where her mouth had been made him feel like a teenager who had a crush.

"It sounds to me like you don't like to stay in one place for long."

"That's true." He was a jet-setter, never settling in any place for too long. "Aren't you a bit of a traveler yourself? You mentioned being on a road trip."

"I'm only just getting started with my adventures. I've barely been anywhere, yet."

He found himself getting excited that she craved adventures just like he did. He had ever since he could remember, and now he was living them, but factoring in a woman he'd just met as part of any adventure was exactly what he should *not* be doing. "You were right about something. Your tongue is blue." He chuckled when she stuck it out to check.

"Let me see yours," she said and then grinned. "Yours is, too. Well, actually it's turning purple from the mix of red and blue."

At Morgana's request, they stopped at a booth for the animal shelter. Some of the hopeful pets were in kennels and a round pen had been set up in the center so people could get a good look at the excited puppies.

She dropped to her knees in the grass beside the pen. "I miss having an animal around."

"I guess they don't allow pets at the motel?"

"Freya has a cat."

"She does?" He knelt to rub the soft belly of a chocolate-brown puppy who licked his hand and wagged his tail so hard that his whole back end wiggled from side to side.

"Have you seen the orange cat running around the motel?"

"Yes. I thought it was a stray."

"He was, but now his name is Sunset. He attached himself to Freya, and since she is a semipermanent guest, Hal had no problem with it."

If animals liked Freya and she liked them, she couldn't be all bad. At least that's what he'd found to be true over the years.

"Aww, this one is adorable." She held up a puppy with sleek black fur and let him lick the tip of her nose.

"You shouldn't say that so loud," he whispered. "The others will get jealous."

"Never fear. I have plenty of good words to describe all of them. There's precious and darling and cutie-pie."

She continued naming the pups, but he was too busy focusing on the way her lips moved as she talked.

They stayed there long enough to pet all the cute animals who were looking for a permanent home. As much as he wanted a pet, he didn't have a home to take one to. He rented places that were conveniently located for whatever he was doing at the time. His skin prickled.

If I don't have a home for a pet, how do I expect to make a home for a child?

Whatever it took, he would figure it out. He had the money to make it happen.

Morgana touched his arm. "Bear? Are you okay?"

"Absolutely." He looked at his watch, hiding his face long enough to get his expression under control. "I'm supposed to meet up with my family."

"I appreciate you hanging out with me for a while," she said softly.

"It was my pleasure." He meant it. The words weren't just an idle pleasantry like they would be with some people. He truly enjoyed this woman's company. But all too soon, his time with her was up.

As much as he wanted to ask her to come to dinner with him, he couldn't. His family was cautiously wary about Morgana, with different members having different opinions about her. He knew she was sweet and could sing and liked to dance. She was funny and enticingly beautiful in her eclectic style, but he didn't know enough about her to bring her to a meal with his family. Just happening to meet up as a group would be one thing, but him purposely bringing her would look too much like they were more than casual acquaintances.

"Thanks for indulging me with two flavors of snow cones. Have fun with your family. I guess I'll see you around the motel."

Was that a flash of disappointment he saw on her face? He was feeling a bit of that himself. "Yes, you will."

AT THE COWGIRL CAFÉ, owned by his cousin Bea Fortune, his family had a big table in a back corner. Of course, the news about him slipping away to talk to Morgana had made the rounds. Some of them were curious if she was after his money and warned him that he'd have to look out for that kind of thing now that he was wealthy. But they didn't all feel that way. Haley thought Morgana was nice and didn't mean any harm to anyone. Bear was starting to believe the same thing, but he hadn't gotten as far as he had in business by jumping to conclusions too quickly. Caution and plenty of consideration was always a must.

Bear ate too much, but everything at his cousin's restaurant was so good. He ended up with ketchup on his shirt courtesy of one of his nephews and chocolate sauce from the other twin. He laughed a lot, which felt really good, but he made sure to leave in time to get back to the motel before the fireworks. Resisting the draw of watching them with Morgana was too much and he gave up fighting it because he just couldn't think of a good enough reason at the moment.

BEAR LEFT COWGIRL CAFÉ just before dark, and the sun was setting as he pulled into the motel. He found himself automatically looking around for Morgana, but she wasn't outside. Hopefully, she'd come out soon to watch the fireworks, but if she didn't, should he knock on her door? He parked his car and picked up a book that had fallen onto the floorboard before heading toward his room.

"Barrington, do you have a minute to talk, please?"

Bear stopped and turned to face Freya Fortune. He'd been dodging her but had been too busy thinking about the lovely maid to pay enough attention to his surroundings. It was unusual for him to be so unaware. Another reason not to let himself get too deeply involved with Morgana or any other woman. But he might as well get this talk with dear old step-granny over with, because he had some questions of his own. He glanced at his watch to suggest he had somewhere to be.

"Sure. I have a few minutes."

Her tense expression turned into a tentative smile. "Let's go sit over here."

He followed her to an outdoor seating area not far from her door. They sat in retro metal chairs that looked like they were from the 1950s and had been repainted many times. Currently, they were a bright cherry red.

Freya sat with a straight spine and folded her hands in her lap. As Morgana had mentioned the other day, she wore designer clothes and expensive jewelry and could clearly afford to live somewhere grand, yet she was living in an old motor lodge. He was only here temporarily to see his family and finish a business deal, but Freya seemed to be staying for the long haul. He couldn't understand why she hadn't rented or even bought a house in town.

"As I'm sure you've been told, I'm here to honor your grandfather's last will and testament," she said.

"Yes. I've heard the stories. My family has given me the rundown."

"You're the last grandchild on my list, and I'd really like to help you. Will you please tell me your most fervent wish?"

"That's private, sorry," he answered brusquely. "And it's not anything you can help me with."

She sighed and fidgeted with a large diamond ring. "There must be *something...*"

"I already have more money than I know what to do with. I don't need any of Elias's."

"Maybe I can help you with something money can't buy then. Just think about it."

The old woman seemed so sad and tired. He suddenly felt for her and didn't want to add to her distress by being rude. Maybe she really had loved Elias Fortune that much and her mission was meant to honor her deceased husband.

But the whole thing was all so strange. "I promise I'll think about it. Have a nice night, Freya."

"You, too, Bear."

He walked briskly toward the stairs to the second-floor walkway before she changed her mind and wanted to talk about something else. Bear had come here to see West and other family members. Not to get mixed up in old family drama and the wishes of a deceased grandfather he'd never known. He was about the here and now and the future. A future he would be in charge of. Wishing couldn't help him get what he wanted most. He'd have to do that for himself. Luckily, he had more than enough money to take care of and protect a child.

Once he was in his room, he took off the food-stained shirt he'd worn all day, washed his hands and face, brushed his teeth and put on a clean T-shirt. He was ready for some fireworks…of one kind or another. And he could think of a couple of good options. Discovering the taste of Morgana Mills's lips was currently top of the list.

CHAPTER FIVE

AFTER A DAY at the town's Fourth of July celebration in the park, Morgana took a refreshingly cool shower and changed into a red dress that showed off more cleavage than usual, but she'd found it at the secondhand store and couldn't resist. The cotton fabric fell in soft folds from the empire waist to right above her knees. It made her feel feminine and desirable.

Would this dress make Bear think she was trying to seduce him? She gazed at her reflection in the mirror on the medicine cabinet above the pink bathroom sink. She wasn't completely inexperienced, but she had no doubt that he had plenty of practice with women and was probably used to them dressing way sexier than this.

"You don't even know if you'll see him again tonight," she said to herself. But having hope was never a bad thing.

She brushed her hair once more and put on mint lip gloss. In preparation for what, she didn't know. Bear was likely still with his family somewhere celebrating the nation's birthday. Not to mention, she shouldn't be doing anything to encourage Barrington Fortune. The wealthy oil baron who wanted someone to have a baby for him. Not with him, but for him. Emphasis on the *for*. He wasn't a good dating option. Not good at all.

"So, what is it that you think you're doing then?" her rebellious reflection asked with a big grin like a lovestruck teenager. She rolled her eyes at herself and went to find her shoes.

When she turned down the music playing on her phone, the screensaver appeared. It was her favorite picture of her and her mom when she'd been about ten. They didn't look much alike, but they were best friends. Even so, she envied Bear and all the Fortunes their large extended family. She remembered wonderful celebrations back on the farm. Everyone there was *like* family, but when it came right down to it, it was only her and her mom.

The fireworks would start soon, so she slipped on her flip-flops to go outside. If Bear wasn't back at the motel, maybe Freya would like to watch the fireworks with her. It would be another chance to get to know the mysterious older woman. But when she opened her door, the rush of sensations in her belly were like the flash of Fourth of July sparklers.

"Hello, neighbor." Bear had his folded arms propped on top of the railing.

"Hey, there." He was wearing a plain white T-shirt that was bright against his olive complexion and was just tight enough to show off sculpted muscles without looking like he was trying too hard. A tease, which she'd discovered was very onbrand for him. "I wasn't sure if you were still with your family or not."

"I got back a few minutes ago."

The night sky lit up followed closely by a boom and shower of sparkly crackles. It was followed closely by another, the boom's vibration traveling through her body and making her shiver. The breeze carried the faintest hint of black powder and the spicy scent of Bear's cologne.

"Looks like you got out here just in time," he said.

"Want to sit on the stairs? They're facing the perfect direction to see the show."

"Lead the way."

She sat first, and he lowered to sit beside her on the top step. The colorful display went on in front of them, but she was more aware of his body so close to hers. The heat of him. The sizzle of energy. If she wasn't careful, she'd catch fire and be about as subtle as one of those cone-shaped fireworks that jetted a fountain of shimmery sparkles.

"Did you say something?" he asked.

Oh, Lord, what did I say?

She had a troublesome habit of expressing some of her thoughts aloud, and since she was frequently alone, it usually didn't matter. But right now, it mattered. "I was just exclaiming over the fireworks. They're so beautiful."

"Very beautiful." He was smiling at her when he said it in a low, seductive voice.

A shower of tingles danced over her skin, leaving her momentarily weightless. "Who taught you to flirt?"

He laughed, a deep and very pleasant sound. "I guess it just comes naturally. Do you want me to stop?"

"Let's not get crazy now. I wouldn't want you to go against your nature."

With his arm brushing against hers, he met her gaze full on. "You are a most unique woman, Morgana Mills."

Her throat tightened at the sound of a last name that wasn't hers. Being deceptive did not come easily, and she prayed her face wasn't colored with guilt. "I'm trying to decide if unique is a good thing."

"I like unique things, so yes, it's good." Another firework exploded and sparks reflected in his brown eyes like a galaxy of stars. "You're refreshingly real."

"I try to be."

"You're also really young," he remarked.

"Not that young. I'm closer to thirty than twenty."

Bear quirked a brow. "By how much?"

"Well…a few months."

That made him chuckle. "I've got seven years on you."

"Women mature faster. So, twenty-five and thirty-two are practically the same age." She was enjoying their quick back and forth banter. At first, he'd made her nervous, but she'd discovered he was easy to talk to.

At the same moment, they turned to one another to comment on a particularly spectacular firework, and her breath caught. They were so close she could almost feel the heat of his mouth, burning for their first kiss.

A door slammed behind them, and they sprang apart. A teenage girl, who was obviously mad, stormed across the walkway, and they had to stand to let her get down the stairs.

The spell was broken. Disappointing but likely for the best. Morgana reminded herself that she had no experience with men like him. Cinderella's magical night only lasted a short time, and it would be the same with the world-traveling Bear Fortune. Living happily ever after with a prince in a castle was only in fairy tales and movies.

Although…there was a castle in town, and it just so happened that Fortune Castle belonged to someone in Bear's family.

THE NEXT DAY, Bear went out to his cousin Asa Fortune's dude ranch for a family barbecue. The weather was as perfect as you could get for a summer day. It was still hot, but the sky was filled with thick clouds that blocked out some of the sun's most oppressive heat, and a steady breeze kept the air moving. It carried the mouthwatering scent of food on the grill and the earthy scent of plants. They were celebrating a combination of a birthday, an anniversary and something else he'd forgotten. He had five new cousins who no one had known about until recently. They were

Wendell Fortune's grandchildren, and he was still working on getting all their names straight.

He moved off to the outer edge of the group and stood in the shade of an oak tree while his siblings, cousins, and their families and significant others broke into groups to talk and laugh. Kids and toddlers were running around, and babies were crawling and crying. And Bear was hanging back taking it all in. He was fine with his own company, but being around so much family was making him want to spend more time with them than he'd planned.

As long as he could retreat to his own space now and then to recharge. But watching them interact was also making him want something more for himself. One couple, whose names he thought were Cooper and Alana, kissed and smiled at one another, and his mind flashed to Morgana. He cursed under his breath and took a long pull on his bottle of beer.

He did not want a serious relationship and absolutely not another marriage. That deal was off the table. All he wanted was a child of his own. And the occasional no-strings-attached company of a woman. Maybe a friends-with-benefits arrangement.

He enjoyed Morgana's company, but last night it had taken all of his willpower not to kiss her as they sat side by side on the stairs watching fireworks. And he'd almost given in to his desire when he caught the scent of mint from her glossy mouth and swayed in her direction, only to be interrupted by a pouting teenager.

He had a strong feeling Morgana would be a firecracker in bed, but the level of emotional attraction to her fun-loving nature could make it harder to keep his heart out of it. He wasn't sure if he could safely have a friends-with-benefits thing with her. She was young and struck him as a passionate woman who would likely want more than he had to give. He'd married a passionate woman, and that hadn't gone well at all.

His cousin Bea's fiancé, Devin Street, walked his way. He was the owner of the *Chatelaine Daily News*, and they'd only talked briefly, but he liked the man.

"I think you have the right idea hanging out over here," Devin said.

"Best way to take it all in. I'm also trying to figure out who belongs to who."

Devin laughed. "That might take a while. But I'm happy to help you out where I can."

"Do you know Morgana Mills? She's a maid at the motel."

"Yes. I know her. Morgana has been to my newspaper's archives a few times."

Bear swatted at a bee buzzing around his drink. "I know she's been asking a lot of questions about the Fortune family."

"She's also been asking about the 1965 silver mine collapse."

"She told me she loves history and wants to write a book. Do you think that's true or is she after something else?"

"Well, she goes through old town photos and really does read old articles and takes a lot of notes, so it's not out of the question." Scrubbing a hand over his jaw, Devin mused, "And being a newspaper man, I'm used to reporters who ask plenty of questions. So I guess it doesn't seem that odd to me."

That eased Bear's mind about her...somewhat. Before they could talk more about it, two little redheaded boys wearing blue superhero capes ran right between them, the smaller one chasing the bigger one with a foam sword.

"That's Jacob and Benjy. Your cousin Damon's kids."

Bear chuckled when the older one performed a very dramatic death scene that involved rolling around on the grass with a variety of accompanying noises. They certainly had a lot of energy. Another reason to have a kid sooner rather than later was doing it before he was too old to play with and chase after them. Which was admittedly many years from now, but he also wanted to be able to keep up with grandchildren as well.

THE NEXT MORNING, Bear closed his laptop after a frustrating but successful business meeting with people from three countries. He needed to rework a proposal, but right now, he was too distracted and couldn't give it his full attention.

He couldn't get Morgana out of his mind. The wheels of her cleaning cart clunked across the walkway outside of his room, and like a teenager who had no control over himself, he opened his door. "Good morning."

"Hi, Bear."

Her sweet smile made something warm swirl about in his chest.

"Is now a good time to clean your room? If not, I can come back later."

"It's perfect timing. I just finished a virtual meeting."

She was biting her cheek in an obvious attempt not to laugh. "Is that why you're wearing a dress shirt and tie with jogging shorts and no shoes?"

He glanced down at himself and laughed. "Yes, ma'am. That would be the reason."

"I don't blame you a bit. I would do the same thing."

He stepped back into his room and helped her pull the cart over the threshold, making a mental note to buy new ones for the motel. She and the other maid deserved to work with good equipment that didn't frustrate them.

He loosened his tie and pulled it off then started unbuttoning his shirt. He didn't have on an undershirt like he normally would, and he couldn't deny enjoying the flicker of interest he caught as she tried not to look at him standing there in nothing but a pair of shorts.

"I should probably start with the bathtub." Her gaze once again landed on him before she disappeared into the bathroom.

As she worked out of sight, he put on a supersoft Dolce & Gabbana T-shirt, a luxury he could now afford. He sat at his computer, scrolled through a couple of websites and ordered several of the best carts he could find. He had them shipped anonymously to the Chatelaine Motel and wondered if they would figure out that he was the one who'd done it.

All too soon, Morgana had finished cleaning his room and moved on, and he was bored. He called Camden and then West, but both of his brothers were busy and couldn't hang out. The baby twins giggling in the background had tugged at his heart and caused a flash of jealousy, which made him once again think he was doing the right thing by deciding to become a father.

Although he usually liked being alone with his thoughts, right now they kept returning to the dangerous idea of Morgana being the one to have a baby for him. It would make things so simple if she would agree to be his surrogate.

If she was the woman that he thought she was, Morgana was just who he'd been looking for in a mother for his baby. Why? It was simple. Her cheery personality and being funny without even trying. Her go-get-'em attitude when she did things like haul old furniture upstairs because she wanted to make something old new again. And yes, her beauty certainly didn't hurt matters. There could be attraction and fun between them, but allowing romantic love to get mixed up in things was a terrible idea.

He didn't want his child to have parents who fought because there was hurt and jealousy. Keeping romantic expressions of love out of the equation was the only way to assure that.

Morgana might be young, at only twenty-five, but she was down-to-earth and knew how to take care of herself. She called it the way she saw it. If she agreed to do it, he wouldn't have to go through a long-drawn-out search for a surrogate. Having her agree would make things so easy.

And fun.

He couldn't believe he was seriously considering asking her to be the mother of his child, but it would be mutually beneficial. She was a maid living in one room of a small motor lodge, and he knew she could use the money. While talking to the motel owner, Hal, he'd discovered why she walked everywhere. Her car had broken down and needed a lot of repairs that she was saving up for.

Bear stopped pacing and snapped his fingers. "I'll get her car repaired or just buy her a new one."

He shook his head, dismissing the idea of a new car. That was too much like a bribe. He would just repair the one she already had. Much easier to write that off as just one friend helping out another, and it would be a start to showing her how her life could be made so much easier. He could pay her a fortune to have his child and she'd never have to scrub a toilet or a bathtub for a stranger again.

That's it. His mind was made up.

I'm going to ask Morgana to have my baby.

CHAPTER SIX

MORGANA WAS ABOUT to make a sandwich when someone knocked on her door.

Please, let it be Bear.

The thought came in a flash, startling her with its intensity. Like one of the ladies on the farm in Tennessee used to say, this needed to be nipped in the bud right quick. She absolutely could not fall in love with Bear.

She looked through the peephole and her spirits lifted along with a giddy nervousness that made her pulse trip over itself.

Wish granted.

She checked her reflection in the mirror above the small dresser and then opened the door. "Hello, neighbor. Do you need to borrow a cup of flour?"

He smiled big enough to show perfect white teeth. "I wouldn't mind some sugar."

Was he hinting at something...like a kiss? "I actually do have sugar."

"What I'd really like to do is talk to you about something."

"Sure. Come on in." She stepped aside and swept out her arm as if ushering him into an exclusive event. "What's on your mind?"

Bear crossed the room, lowered halfway as if he'd sit on the foot of her bed, but then he straightened and started pacing. "I have an offer to discuss."

"Like a business deal?" She hadn't seen him like this. He was jumpy and unsure, and it was starting to make her nervous.

"Kind of." He paused and faced her. "First let me say, I don't think you're a woman motivated by money. I happen to have more experience than I'd like with people who are."

Where was he going with this odd topic of conversation? "I appreciate your assessment of me, but I'm not sure why you're bringing that up. Do you need an assistant or extra maid services or something along those lines?"

"No. Nothing like that. Well, I guess it would fall in the something else category. What would you think about a million dollars to have a baby for me?"

She laughed and waited for him to do the same and then get to the real reason for his visit. But he didn't laugh. He didn't even smile. "Wait. Are you being serious?"

"Yes, I am. Completely serious." He stood tall with his feet braced slightly apart. His body language now screaming *confident businessman*.

Suddenly dizzy, she sidestepped to her bed and sat down hard. "You want me to have a baby for you?"

"That's the idea."

Could he actually be serious? "And how do you see me fitting into my own baby's life?"

"I haven't thought that far ahead." He pulled out the wooden chair from her tiny desk, straddled it in the wrong direction and propped his arms on the back.

"I see, so you envision what? That I have this baby for you, hand him or her over, take my million and walk away?"

He grimaced and pinched the bridge of his nose that had a slight crook from being broken. "It sounds bad when you put it like that. I can assure you that I am in fact a human with real feelings and emotions."

Morgana wasn't so sure about that at the moment. How could he possibly expect her to go along with such a wacky idea? "I think you need to take some time and come back when you have a well-thought-out plan." Not that she intended to have his child, she just wanted to make him *think* about what he was doing. The enormity of the favor he was asking of her.

"You make a good point."

"I bet you're more prepared than this when you make big oil deals."

"You're right." He rubbed a hand through his thick, dark hair, and his exhalation was long and slow as if to calm himself. "I got excited about the idea and jumped the gun. Can we talk more about it over dinner tonight?"

A quiver swept through her. She might be unwilling to have his child for money, but dinner seemed so mild in comparison. It was too good to pass up.

Why am I so drawn to this man?

It really wasn't hard to figure out. He was charismatic in a way that drew her in and made her want to see what he'd do next, and he was so handsome that looking at him was a treat for the eyes, but his guarded heart made her own ache. Maybe she could help redirect his misguided notions. "Dinner sounds nice. Where are we going and what's the dress code? I only have one nice dress with me."

His smile eased into the one she saw most often. Playful and a little bit devilish. "You should wear your dress. I like down-home restaurants like my cousin Bea's Cowgirl Café, but tonight, we'll be fine dining at the LC Club."

The words *fine dining* made her pulse pick up speed. "I've never been there."

"You'll like it." He looked at the digital clock on her bedside table. "Can I pick you up in an hour and a half?"

"That works for me," she said, trying not to let her eagerness show too much.

Once she closed her door behind Bear, she leaned her back against it and covered her face. "What just happened?" She did a little happy dance.

She'd already taken a shower, so she curled her hair into loose waves and did her makeup a bit more dramatically than her normal two coats of mascara and a touch of neutral eye shadow. For a date at a fancy restaurant, she added darker shadow, eyeliner, blush and lipstick. The blush was probably unnecessary because her cheeks would be rosy just from being with a man she found so attractive. A man who was so wrong for her. She wanted love and marriage and children she would raise as a partner with her husband. Apparently, Bear had no desire to fit into that lifestyle.

"Plus, he doesn't even live here, and he'll be jetting off to who knows where before I know it."

Which meant that anything that happened between them would only be a fling, not a relationship, and certainly not her being his baby mama. Did she want to have a fling with Bear?

The raucous butterfly dance going on in her stomach gave her the answer. Yes. Yes, she did.

But *did* and *should* were two entirely different things. She'd never done such a thing. All of her romances had been committed relationships, but maybe this was something everyone needed to do at least once in their life. Have a brief, passionate love affair you could look back on and know you didn't miss out on anything.

"I'll see how things go tonight at dinner, and then I'll make a decision."

She didn't have to decide at this very moment. She pulled her one nice dress from the postage stamp-sized closet, held it out in front of her and sighed. It was a black dress without much flair. The fabric was silky with a fitted bodice, a scalloped off-the-shoulder neckline and a full skirt. She put it on and added a thin silver chain belt that matched the adornment on her pair of nice black sandals and simple silver hoop earrings. Then she put her ID, lipstick, some cash and her phone into the emerald velvet clutch she'd made from a fabric remnant leftover from when they made curtains to glam up their small cottage living room.

Morgana was finally ready, but she still had some time to kill before Bear would be here to pick her up. For their *date*. She squealed and spun to make her skirt flair out around her, just like her excitement. She really needed to chill and act her age. She was twenty-five. Not fifteen.

She'd FaceTime with her mom. That would calm her down, even though Morgana felt guilty about deceiving her mother about where she was living. But if Renee Wells knew her daughter was in Chatelaine—the town she said she'd never return to—or that she was searching for her grandmother, she would be unhappy. Morgana didn't want to upset her mom about anything until she established a connection with her grandmother.

She had hoped to be able to tell her mom she'd found Gwenyth Wells or at least have something to report long before now, but she still hadn't found enough clues.

I need to be a better detective.

She had the sudden urge to watch an old episode of *Murder, She Wrote*. Jessica Fletcher would know what to do, and probably would've had this thing figured out by now. Since they'd only gotten a few TV channels on the farm while she was growing up, she'd rewatched the complete series on DVD many times over. You'd think she would've learned a few tips and tricks for solving a mystery. At least she wasn't dealing with murder. Or *was* she? The silver mine collapse did have some suspicious circumstances surrounding it.

Morgana grabbed her phone and made the call. After a few rings, her mom answered. Her curly hair was pulled back with a leather headband, and her cheeks were pink from a day spent outdoors, probably in the orchard.

"Hi, honey. I was just thinking of you."

"What were you doing that made you think of me?"

"Looking at your baby picture on the mantel." Renee turned the phone to show her, as if she hadn't known it was there her whole entire life.

"Do you need me to take a selfie and send you a new photo?"

"Yes, please. I miss you. But I'm glad you're having a grand adventure." Her mom got comfy on their couch that was draped with several quilts that covered the worn spots. "You look so pretty tonight. Do you have a party...or a date?" she said with a wide grin that showed her dimples.

"Actually, I do have a date."

"Oh goodie, tell me everything about him. And start at the beginning..."

Morgana smiled and felt her tension begin to ease. There was no way she was going to tell her everything, but she was excited to share some of the details about Bear. Her mom was going to love the story about sharing snow cones.

BEAR STARTED TO pull on a suit coat, but decided it was too hot for that level of dress. Gray slacks and a pale pink Prada dress shirt would have to do. After a quick check in the mirror to make sure he hadn't missed a bit of shaving cream, he brushed his hair. It was getting long on top, and it was time for a trim, but he had no idea where to go for one in Chatelaine. In the oil fields he wore a hat, and it didn't matter if his hair brushed the tops of his ears, but when he was in the regular world, he took time to make sure his thick, wavy hair was brushed back in a style somewhere between messy and too perfect.

Kind of the way he'd describe himself. A mess on the inside, but to the rest of the world, he tried to always present himself as confident and completely in control.

He wasn't giving up hope that Morgana would change her mind and agree to help him have an heir. A child of his bloodline who he would love in a way that his biological family had not. They hadn't loved him enough to keep him. It they had given him up at birth that would be one thing, but to abandon him as a toddler in a park...

He growled in disgust and pushed that old wound back where it belonged. Buried deep in a past that he hated looking back on. Tonight was all about the future, and enjoying the company of a beautiful woman. And convincing her they could make a good partnership. He shoved his wallet into his pocket, grabbed his keys and locked his motel room door. Part of his not-so-thought-out plan was to show Morgana what life could be like with a cool million or so in her account.

He grabbed the small gift he'd bought for Morgana because it had made him think of her, walked the few doors down to her room and knocked lightly. It swung open a few seconds later and his stomach flipped even though he'd just reminded himself about keeping any deep feelings out of the mix. Her hair that was usually pulled back in a ponytail flowed loose and full past her shoulders, and her vivid green eyes were enhanced with makeup.

"Wow. You're gorgeous, dancing queen."

"Thank you." She glanced down to adjust her silver chain belt and clutched tightly to a small green purse with her other hand.

He hated seeing her nervousness and wanted her to be relaxed. His goal was for her to be smiling and happy, not only because he wanted her to consider his proposal, but because she deserved to enjoy the evening. As well as maybe giving him a clue as to why she was in town and what she was really after. Because even though her desk held a laptop and a stack of notebooks, he didn't really think it was to write a book about old town history. She read fairytales, and there was a pile of romance novels on her dresser. It just didn't seem to fit her personality, but there was always a chance he could be wrong.

"Since you read all those Cinderella stories, I saw something that made me think of you and I bought them." He held up a pair of short socks that were made to look like a pair of baby blue glass slippers with a little pink bow on the toe.

"Oh, Bear. Those are so cute! Thank you. My very own glass slippers." She took them and held them to her chest like they were precious jewels.

"I'm glad you like them."

"I really do." She walked over to her bedside table and put them on top of her Cinderella book.

"Are you ready to go?"

"I'm ready." She smiled and some of her self-consciousness slipped away to reveal the gutsy woman he admired.

As they went down the stairs, he offered his arm, and she hesitated only a moment before curling her hand around his bicep.

"You look very handsome. I like that you are man enough to wear pink. It looks nice against your olive complexion."

"Thanks. That's what the lady at the store said. And I'm not ashamed to admit that I've always liked pink."

Morgana's arm jerked slightly against his, and he followed her gaze. Freya was standing near the bottom of the stairs, staring at them as she wrung her hands. She always seemed a little anxious, but tonight she was also agitated. Was it because they were together? Freya was likely worried that the motel maid was after his money and had no idea that he was the one who was after something in their relationship.

Relationship? No, no, no.

A slap of warning gripped him. Partnership or team or any number of things were a better way to describe what he wanted with Morgana.

"Hi, Mrs. Fortune," Morgana said.

"Where are you two going?" Freya asked.

He took the last step down. "To dinner at the LC Club."

"Together?" Freya's voice rose in pitch, giving away her concern. He wasn't completely sure why. Did she know something about Morgana that he didn't? Some reason that they shouldn't spend time together?

"Yes. Just the two of us. We have a lot to talk about." He said it to see how she would react, and when the lines of worry on her face deepened, it was telling. She was not happy about it.

"Oh. I see. Well, enjoy your evening out."

"Thanks," Morgana replied. "See you tomorrow."

"Have a good night." They walked away from his stepgranny, and he didn't look back to see if she was still frowning at them. Freya and Morgana each had answers he wanted, and he was starting to feel like he was in a book or movie.

Now, the only thing to do was to wait and see whether it would be a comedy or a tragedy.

CHAPTER SEVEN

ONCE THEY WERE driving away from the motel and Freya was out of sight, Morgana relaxed into the leather seat. The radio was tuned to a classic rock station. It was her favorite era of music. Had she told him that or did he really like it, too? "What's your go-to music?"

"I like to change it up. Rock, country, blues and once in a while, heavy metal."

"That's a good mix. Freya likes to play jazz and sometimes big band music that makes you want to dance." She slid him a glance. "Speaking of Freya...did you get the feeling she was nervous about the two of us spending time together?"

"Yes. I got the same impression. She's clearly up to something, or worried about something."

"As much as I've tried over the months, I've barely gotten to know her. She's very private and dodges me most of the time."

"She won't give you an interview for your book?" he asked.

The muscles along her shoulders tensed, and she clasped her hands in her lap. "Nope."

She hated keeping Bear in the dark about who she was and the truth of why she was in Chatelaine, because despite what she'd told him, it wasn't by chance. She'd tasked herself with finding out what became of her long-estranged grandmother, discovering the truth behind the silver mine collapse and clearing the Wells family name.

He slowed as they neared a stop sign. "But she sure likes to be in other people's business."

"I'm sure your family has told you about the troubles many of them encountered when it came to the wish Freya was granting them. And before you ask, I know because your soon-to-be sister-in-law Haley told me."

"Is that so?" he asked.

"Yes. We've gotten to know one another over the months. We were working together on the mystery of the anonymous notes about the fifty-first miner until she made a decision to drop the story because she decided that her love for Camden was more important than writing an exposé for a newspaper."

"I'm glad to hear that she loves my brother that much. And now you've taken up where the two of you left off?"

She nodded. "Something like that."

"I do know that my cousin Asa ran into trouble buying Chatelaine Dude Ranch. Some craziness about him needing to be married to buy it."

"And then Bea's opening night of Cowgirl Café was a disaster with too many things going wrong at once to be considered coincidences," she added. She liked having someone to talk things over with again. She hadn't had that since Haley had decided she wanted nothing more to do with the whole mystery. But Morgana wasn't ready to give up.

"And just recently, my brother Camden had a lot of unexpected red tape getting his children's riding camp up and running. What do we actually know about my late grandfather Elias Fortune's widow?"

Morgana idly played with the star charm on her necklace. "Not as much as you'd think after all these months.

I've wondered if she's been doing all this wish granting without having the noble intentions that she wants people to believe."

"Why in the world would she go to so much trouble to grant wishes for people she doesn't even know only to destroy them? It doesn't make sense," he said.

"Maybe that's what we should focus on. Why is she going to so much trouble for people she doesn't know? Did she love Elias that much? Could it be to make up for the harm Elias and Edgar Fortune caused years ago?"

"You mean the silver mine disaster?" Bear asked.

"Yes. Apparently, it's well known around town that they were responsible for the silver mine collapse and not the mine foreman, Clinton Wells. But no official statement has ever been made to clear the Wells name." All these years later, her grandfather was still officially taking the blame.

Bear's thumb tapped the steering wheel in time to the upbeat song on the radio. "And then there are the two mysterious notes about how many died in the collapse."

She considered restating what each note said but mentioning her grandmother's name in the last one gave her pause. "I also have a collection of letters you might find interesting. Wendell gave them to me and Haley, and then when Haley decided she no longer wanted to pursue the story, she gave them all to me."

"Who are the letters from?" he asked.

"They're from Elias's secret daughter, Ariella."

He slowed to go around a curve in the lakeside road. "For real or is this your imagination adding to the story you want to write?"

Every time he mentioned her writing a book, another splash of guilt layered on like a thick coating of oil. She'd come up with that excuse on a whim and hated that she'd told him another lie. "A hundred percent real. Wendell had forbidden her to see the poor miner boyfriend she'd fallen in love with. In the last letter your great uncle said he'd read from her, Ariella admitted that she'd had a baby and was hiding the child, but it was time for her father to know the truth."

"Wow. My family has a lot of scandals and secrets. I would like to read the letters Wendell gave you."

"That's great. It will be more fun to have someone to talk to about it. You can be Watson to my Sherlock."

He gave her a playful scowl. "Why do *you* get to be Sherlock?"

"I think it's because…" She tapped a finger against her mouth. "Oh, I remember. Because I arrived in town before you."

"Hmm. Not sure that's very official, but I suppose we'll go with it."

"Excellent decision, Mr. Fortune. There is also a letter from Wendell to me and Haley in which he admits to being scandalized by his daughter's behavior——which seems a bit hypocritical if you ask me. Especially since she was a *secret* daughter."

"No doubt."

"Wendell assumes Ariella ran away with her baby after her miner boyfriend died. But he's not sure."

"So, one of the big questions is, what became of Elias's secret daughter, Ariella, and her child?"

ON THEIR DRIVE from the motel to the lake, Bear had learned more about his family and some about Freya, but he had not gleaned anything new about Morgana. Although she seemed so real and authentic, he had a strong feeling there was something she was hiding—just like Freya seemed to be doing. After valet parking, he helped her out of the car and led her toward the entrance. He held open the door of the LC Club, and she went in ahead of him.

At his request when he'd called in the reservation, they were seated at a table for two in a secluded corner with a view of Chatelaine Lake. After pulling out her chair, he sat across from her. They could be somewhat alone while having the safety net of being in a public place. It wouldn't do anything to stave off his desire for her, but they were a whole lot safer in a public place than being in one of their motel rooms. Especially with the way she was nibbling one corner of her mouth, making her full lower lip even plumper. And driving him *crazy*.

"It's such a beautiful view," she murmured as she looked out the large wall of plate-glass windows. The water was calm and glistening as the sun crept toward the horizon.

He wanted to say she was more beautiful than the view but that sounded cliché, so he just agreed. "Do you drink wine?"

"Sometimes, but I know next to nothing about it, unless it has a screw top. Will you order for me?"

"Absolutely. I can do that." He liked that she was being herself and not pretending to be someone she wasn't. It was a refreshing change from a lot of the women he'd known and dated. His chest tightened as he caught his line of thinking.

We're not dating.

"Let's decide what we want to eat first, and then I'll know whether to order you red or white. I'm having steak. They make a great one here."

"Steak sounds wonderful. I haven't had one since… Gosh. A while now." She licked her lips as if anticipating the taste.

Once again drawing his eyes to her tempting mouth. If she kept up this level of unconscious seduction, he was going to have a hell of a time not finding out what she tasted like, even if they were in public. "Since we're both having beef, let's go with red wine. While I was in Brazil, I started drinking Malbec from the Mendoza region of Argentina. I think you'll like it."

She traced a finger along a line on the menu. "Will it go well with the charcuterie board?"

"For sure."

"Oh, good. It says the board is mostly locally sourced ingredients, and I'd love to sample what the area has to offer."

He grinned. "I'm glad to hear it. I was afraid you'd be shy about ordering or eating anything."

"I'm shy about some things, but food isn't one of them." She lowered her voice like it was a secret. "I like to watch cooking shows."

"I'm not much of a cook, but I'm right there with you on the eating part."

"I would cook something for you, but I'm pretty limited with my single hot plate and toaster oven," she confessed.

He was sad for her that she didn't have the kitchen to do something she enjoyed. Most of the places he'd rented recently had killer kitchens that he rarely used. This is why staying at the Chatelaine Motel was good for him. He sometimes took the luxuries his money afforded for granted.

The waiter returned, and he ordered the wine, appetizer and steak dinners. The bottle of wine came out quickly and he watched her closely as she took her first sip. He'd seen the contorted faces a person could make if they didn't like a wine, but Morgana's expression was delighted.

"Do you approve?"

"I do. It's smooth with such a nice aftertaste." She held up her glass to swirl the wine and see the color with the candlelight shining through. She knew more about wine than she realized.

He told her about wine tasting in different parts of the world and she asked questions about his travels. The artfully arranged charcuterie board arrived shortly after.

"Beautiful presentation." She studied the options.

"I'm about to mess it up because I'm starving."

"Go for it," she said with a laugh.

He popped a toasted pecan half into his mouth then grabbed a slice of salami and a cracker.

She spread soft, white cheese on a cracker, drizzled it with honey and took a bite. "Mmm. The goat cheese is delicious. Almost as good as mine."

"You know how to make goat cheese?"

"I do. On the farm where I grew up, my mom and I were the ones who made it."

This was the perfect opportunity to dig a little deeper into her life without his questions coming out of the blue. "Are you an only child?"

"Yes. It's always just been me and my mom."

"Tell me about what it was like to grow up on a farm in Tennessee. What were you like as a kid?

"A bit of a wild child. I ran around barefoot as much as I could in the summer, and when it was warm enough, I swam in the creek. The water comes from melting snow in the mountains and is pretty cold. My hair was really long, and I usually had a braid or two."

"Somehow, I can see all that about you," he said with a smile. "Did you have animals and a garden?"

"A huge garden and an orchard. I know I said it was just me and my mom, but we weren't the only ones living on the farm. It's more of a communal farm with several families all working together. But we do have our own little house where my mom still lives. We have a farm stand along the road where we sell the produce, honey, goat cheese and other handmade goods."

"You had goats?" He popped an olive into his mouth.

"Yes. We also had chickens and a few dairy cows. Everyone had their jobs. My mom and I made the cheese and helped in the orchard, among other jobs, while others made the preserves and tended the bees and all the other farm stuff."

"It sounds like a storybook setting."

"There were times growing up when I thought it was so boring and such hard work, but looking back, it was a pretty great childhood." A wistful expression crossed her face. "Being an only child, I was sometimes lonely for other kids. I bet it's nice having brothers."

"It is. We looked out for one another while we were growing up."

"You're the oldest brother, right?" she asked.

"Yes. At thirty-two, I'm a year older than West and three older than Camden."

"Were you too young to remember when they were born? I always wanted a baby sister or brother. I love babies."

He liked hearing her say that about babies. It could help with his idea for her to have one, or it could backfire and be the reason she wouldn't have one *for him*. "West was already born when I was adopted."

"I didn't realize you were adopted. I guess that answers the question about why you don't look much like your brothers."

Bear hadn't meant to reveal so much. He didn't like talking about the past, especially his origin story. Sometimes he wondered if there was something about him that was unlovable. Why else would his birth family abandon him and then his wife climb into bed with his best friend? He pushed those thoughts aside and refocused on Morgana and the present moment. He was supposed to be getting her to talk about herself and not bemoaning about his painful past.

"West and Camden aren't lucky enough to have my dark good looks."

She swirled her wine and grinned. "Or your wonderful sense of modesty, I'm sure."

"Oh, of course. That goes without saying." He refilled her wine glass, and they continued their easy conversation with lots of laughter.

Even though his family hadn't been perfect, he was grateful to have been adopted as a toddler by Peter and Dolly Fortune. However, he reminded himself that part of the reason he wanted a biological child of his own was because he had no blood relatives. He wanted to look into eyes that shared a piece of his DNA.

How to make that happen without involving his heart was the ever-present question. He'd been harshly fooled by love and had no plans to repeat it.

MORGANA SAVORED EVERY bite of delicious food, and the wine—which was starting to make her giggly—was the best she'd ever had. Their date that she'd worried would be awkward was going really well. Almost *too* well. She was so attracted to Bear. He was engaging and smart and funny and kind, even if he did have a nutty idea about her having his baby.

As they walked from the restaurant out into the starry night, keeping her identity a secret for a moment longer felt wrong. "Can we take a walk along the lake path before we go home? I have something I'd like to tell you."

"Sure. A walk sounds good."

They fell into step, and when she slipped on loose

gravel, he reached out and steadied her. But instead of letting go, he slid his fingers slowly down the inside of her arm, leaving a trail of tingly sensations. His hand was warm and strong and comforting, but it wasn't as soft as she would've guessed. This wealthy businessman had calluses from some type of manual labor, but his nails were well manicured. Barrington Fortune was a contradiction she hadn't figured out, but she planned to do just that, and if it continued like this, it would be a lot of fun.

His thumb stroked the back of her hand in a lover's caress, but just when she thought they would walk hand in hand, he let go. And she instantly missed his touch.

Oh, boy. This level of infatuation could be a real problem.

She forced a smile. "Thanks for the save."

"Anytime." They began to walk along the winding pathway beside the lake. A light breeze blew across the water and carried the scent of damp soil. "What is it you wanted to tell me?"

"Since I arrived here in Chatelaine, I've been keeping a secret, and I haven't had anyone to talk to about it." She hadn't missed the way he stiffened at her words, but she couldn't continue to keep her identity hidden. Not with the way she felt about him.

"You can talk to me," he said.

"I just have one request. Will you promise to keep my secret for the time being?"

He studied her for a long moment. "If it's not hurting anyone, then yes, I will."

She took a deep breath and looked up to meet his curious gaze. "My real last name isn't Mills. It's Wells. Morgana Wells."

"*Wells.* Why is that familiar?" Before she could answer, his eyes widened. "Like as in Clint Wells? The mine foreman?"

"Yes. The one who was unfairly blamed for the mine collapse. He was my grandfather."

Bear stopped walking and shook his head like he was searching for answers. "The man who my grandfather Elias and his brother Edgar Fortune blamed for the mine disaster that killed fifty or more people?"

She was suddenly cold and wrapped her arms around herself. "Yes, from my research, that is what I believe to be true."

"Are you here because you want something from the Fortune family? Money? Revenge?"

She gasped and took a step back. "No! I want nothing more than answers." Only a few hours ago, he'd been the one who said she wasn't a woman motivated by money. Especially since she'd declined the million-dollar offer to have his baby. But she wasn't about to become a rich man's baby mama. Not for any price. "Revenge is what tore my family apart, and I'm trying to put it back together."

He raked his fingers through his hair. "Will you tell me more about what's motivating you then?"

"I'm here in Chatelaine looking for clues about what became of my grandmother, Gwenyth Wells. That's why I've been asking so many questions. I only want to reunite my long-estranged family. And if possible, clear the Wells family name."

Even in the light of the crescent moon, she could see the hesitancy playing across his handsome face. Her throat tightened. Had she made a mistake in revealing her identity?

CHAPTER EIGHT

BEAR HAD LEARNED to read people, but from the moment he found her dancing on his bed, Morgana had enchanted and intrigued him. He searched her face, and his tight lungs began to unlock. Gorgeous green eyes met his without a hint of shame, and her body language wasn't shrinking in on oneself like people did when they were lying or holding back. Her arms were held out and her palms up in an open, honest posture as if to say, *See me. All of me. I'm laying it all out for you.*

"Bear, I have no need of vengeance."

"I believe you."

He couldn't resist stroking her cheek with the back of his fingers and was pleased when the tension left her face. Bear could usually spot someone trying to fool him during a business deal, and Morgana wasn't one of those people. She was tough and spunky and being honest with him. And there wasn't a doubt in his mind that she also knew how to stand up for herself. So maybe there was a chance she would be able to handle an agreement to have a mutually beneficial partnership?

"Fair warning, though," she said. "The grandmother who I'm looking for is a whole different story. It was Gwenyth's all-consuming desire for vengeance that drove my mom to leave at the age of eighteen and start over in Tennessee. She made a life for herself and then for me, far away from the stress of her mother's vendetta."

"Your mom must be a brave woman."

"She is."

"I'm glad you told me your secret," he said.

"Me, too. It feels good to tell someone, and I want you to know the real me." The pea gravel crunched softly under her feet as she turned back toward the restaurant. "And one other thing. Although I am doing a lot of research, I'm not actually writing a book."

Bear grinned at her. "I had a suspicion, but I bet you could write a book if you wanted to."

He held out his elbow, and she hooked her arm through his as they walked back toward his car. He was surprised by her reveal, but she was so sincere about her reasons. And he could relate to wanting information about relatives you've never met. After Peter and Dolly found him abandoned at the playground, the police hit a dead end in finding his parents or any other blood relatives. But there had to be someone out there in the world who knew where he'd come from.

Morgana now knew that the Fortunes adopted him, and she might have told him her secret, but he hated his origins and had never confided the whole story. Not to anyone.

Now who's the one holding back and being deceptive? I'm a hypocrite.

A cool night breeze blew across the water and tossed Morgana's long hair against his shoulder, and she tucked it behind her ear. "I've been worried that if anyone discovers my true identity that they'll try to block me from finding out any more information and ruin my chances of finding my grandmother. Or what might have become of her." She sighed. "I don't even know if she's alive. She may have died years ago, but there's no record. It's like she disappeared from the face of the earth. I might be chasing a ghost."

The look of sadness on her face tugged at his suddenly vulnerable heart, and he pulled her into a hug. They swayed together in the dark while crickets and frogs at the water's edge sang their night songs. Her determination to find her grandmother made him reconsider searching for his birth family, but he immediately pushed the idea away. He had no interest in the long-ago past. There was no changing it, so what did it matter.

Tonight had started with the goal of convincing Morgana to have a baby for him—which he wasn't completely giving up on—as well as learning more about her. The evening had yielded more information than he'd expected, but their time together had also done something else that was not on the approved list. It had brought them closer.

"Have you given any more thought to forming a mutually beneficial partnership and having a baby?"

She gave him a melancholy look. "I'm not having a baby unless it's with someone I love."

It shouldn't come as a surprise that a woman like her wanted love and not money, but he couldn't afford to fall for the woman who gave birth to his child. And truth be told, he was starting to care about Morgana.

Well hell. This is less than ideal.

He was being cynical, which was all the more reason to keep his heart out of things. And protect hers. She wasn't willing to be the mother of his child, and he was coming to quickly realize that was probably a good thing.

On the drive back to the motel, they talked about music and books and movies. All safe topics. They discovered a mutual enjoyment of classic movies that had been made around the time the Chatelaine Motel was built.

Bear extended a hand to help Morgana out of his car and considered keeping it clasped with his, but he forced himself to let his fingers slide from hers. "I'll walk you to your door."

"Oh, my. I couldn't ask you to go so far out of your way," she teased as they made their way toward the stairs.

"It's my pleasure." He internally groaned. Why had he used the word *pleasure*? Now that's exactly what he wanted to give both of them.

He briefly squeezed his eyes closed as they stopped in front of her room. While she unlocked her door, he shoved his hands in the front pockets of his slacks in an effort to resist pulling her into his arms again. Because this time he might not want to stop.

Make sure she's safely inside, say good night and walk away.

"Thank you so much for the wonderful dinner and for listening to me." She placed her hand flat on his chest. "You have a good heart. Use it to really think about how you want your future to look. As for me… A baby would be a part of me, and I know that I could never accept anything less than being a full-time parent."

A sinking feeling settled hard and heavy in his stomach, and he knew Morgana would not be the mother of his child. "I understand."

But spending some time with her wouldn't hurt anything. He covered her hand with his and then brought it to his mouth to kiss her palm. When she swayed in his direction and grasped the front of his shirt, all his reasons for holding back evaporated in a cloud of mingled pheromones.

Like a synchronized dance, they were in one another's arms, and all he knew was the sweet warmth of her mouth. Her hands in his hair and his on her back, tracing the soft bumps of her spine. The chemistry flaring between them was more intoxicating than any wine. More powerful than he'd expected.

But then a car door slammed, reminding him they were outside—where anyone could see them.

MORGANA GRASPED HIS shoulders to steady herself. She saw her own surprise reflected in his dazed expression. Neither of them had been prepared for the sensual power of their first kiss. Her skin buzzed and delicious pressure built low in her body.

"Bear." Her voice was almost a whisper.

"Yes, sweetheart?"

"How much longer will you be in Chatelaine?" she asked.

"Probably a few more weeks."

That seemed like the perfect amount of time to have a short love affair and not get so attached that it hurt too much when it was over. She summoned up her big girl courage and decided to go for it. "Want to hang out with me until you go?"

His grin started at one corner of his mouth and spread into a full-watt smile. "That's an excellent idea."

Ask him to come in. A caution alarm clanged in her head. *Not yet! Too soon.*

"I'm glad we're in agreement," she said. "I'll see you tomorrow."

"Yes, you will."

She went up on her toes and kissed him, nipping ever so lightly on his lower lip. He made a very satisfied masculine sound deep in his throat. A shiver of anticipation zipped through her, and she took several backward steps into her room to keep herself from pulling him inside. Because she had no doubt he'd come willingly. "I had a wonderful time. Good night, Bear."

"Sweet dreams, dancing queen."

She closed the door and then walked to the center of

her room, unsure what to do next. She wasn't the least bit sorry she'd decided to spend time with Bear. She might be tipsy from the wine, but she was drunk on his kiss. And excited and eager to see what came next for them. She spun to swirl her skirt like she'd always done when her mom made her a new dress and she felt pretty. Bear made her feel pretty and desirable in a way she'd never experienced.

She hit Play on the old CD player she kept on her dresser. The one people teased her for still using, but she had a collection of CDs that she still loved to listen to. The first song off of *ABBA Gold: Greatest Hits* played softly as she undressed and took off her makeup. Because of Bear's nickname for her, "Dancing Queen" was her new favorite song.

She considered calling her mom to tell her about her date, but it was too late. Renee Wells was an early-to-bed and early-to-rise kind of person. She missed their in-person talks and wished she wasn't so far away. Even though her mom had worried about her setting off from a farm in rural Tennessee in a rattly old car and not much money, she hadn't been able to resist the allure of adventure.

And she had a strong feeling that Barrington Fortune was going to be one hell of an adventure.

CHAPTER NINE

ALONE IN HIS motel room, Bear lay on the surprisingly comfortable mattress staring at the ceiling. The power of Morgana's kiss had done something unexpected to him. It had become an instant addiction. A craving he couldn't stop thinking about.

Thank goodness she wasn't clingy or instantly talking about *couple* stuff. She had been the one to ask him to hang out *until* he left, and that was a huge relief. There was an end date to their time together. And that was a really good thing, because after hearing the awful story of Wendell's secret illegitimate daughter, he was less inclined than ever to bring romance and love into the equation. Ariella hiding a secret, forbidden love and a baby, and then her boyfriend being killed in the mine was all so tragic and sad. Ariella's child would be in her late fifties now. Had mother and baby run off after the mine disaster just like Morgana's mom had done?

His logical brain knew he had to go the surrogacy route, but there was an ornery-as-hell part of him that wanted Morgana to be the mother of his child. Could it be done without hurting her?

Impossible.

Hurting her was as likely as the sun rising and setting. He needed to stop torturing himself with the idea of her pregnant with his child.

With a growl, he rolled onto his side for a different view.

A thin ribbon of moonlight sliced through the gap in the curtains. It made him think of their walk beside the lake. Her vulnerability was endearing, but also a sign he needed to be careful with her young heart.

There was only one thing to do. He would find a surrogate like Morgana had suggested. Using someone he didn't have a relationship with to have his heir was really the best route to take. Just a contractual agreement, legal, nothing personal about it. No muss, no fuss.

THE NEXT DAY, someone knocked on Morgana's door and her first thought was that it was Bear, and her pulse began to speed up. "I have such a major crush on him," she whispered to herself on the way to her door.

The man she saw through the peephole was not her sexy neighbor, but instead, a man in his eighties—but she was glad to see him as well. He had something she needed.

Information.

"Hi, Wendell."

"Hello, Morgana. I have something for you."

She held the door open wider. "Please, come inside."

He eased himself onto the desk chair that Morgana pulled out for him and rubbed a weathered hand against his denim-covered thigh. "I'll get straight to the point. I found the missing letter from Ariella."

"Oh, that's good news!"

"I set it aside decades ago because I couldn't bring myself to read it. Then a couple of days ago, I found it in the back of a desk drawer. When I pulled it out, I remembered it arriving the day after the mine collapsed. I assumed it was a letter blaming me for the death of the man she loved, and that she never wanted to see me again. I guess I also worried it was something I wouldn't want to know.

There was so much going on. I shoved it in a drawer and forgot about it."

"What does it say? Did she run off with the baby?"

When Wendell cleared his throat and gave the slightest shake of his head, she granted him a moment to collect himself. She sat on her bed beside her laundry basket of clean clothes and casually pulled out a pair of shorts and started folding them as if she had nothing but time.

"I don't know what it says. It's still sealed." From his shirt pocket, he pulled out an envelope, yellowed and crumpled with age. "You take it."

"Are you sure? We can read it together if you want."

He shook his head again and put it on her desk. With a hand braced on the corner, he pushed himself up with a wince. "I'm sure. I need to go. Take care of yourself, young lady."

"You, too, Wendell."

Her heart was racing as she closed the door behind him. This letter from Ariella could be an important clue. She sat on her bed to open it but first held it against her chest and said a silent prayer that it held some of the answers she'd been searching for, and for Wendell to have some peace.

She slid her finger under the envelope flap, the old glue dried out and easily giving way. The thick paper crinkled as she unfolded it. The first thing she looked at was the date in the top right corner, and an electric jolt sizzled through her.

"That's the day of the mine collapse!"

Dear Father,
By the time you get this letter, my fiancé and I will be long gone. I'm sorry you don't approve of my choices, but tonight, I'm leaving our baby girl with a sitter while I go into the mine to get the man I love,

and then we plan to elope. I'll contact you once we
are married and settled and see if you want to meet
your granddaughter. And if you've forgiven me.

"Oh, no." Morgana's hand flew to her mouth, and a spiderweb of chills raced across her skin. "She went into the mine the night of the collapse. Ariella Fortune must be the fifty-first miner."

The short letter hadn't revealed anything about Gwenyth, but big wow. She had discovered the identity of the fifty-first miner. Wendell was such a sweet elderly man who'd been through so much. "How can I tell him that his daughter most likely died that night?"

With a heavy heart and cheeks streaked with mascara, Morgana folded it neatly and put it back into its envelope where it had been for almost fifty years. She had to tell Wendell before Haley or any of the other Fortunes. Although, there was one member of the Fortune family she could go to. Bear had become her confidant. They'd come to an agreement to share and keep one another's secrets. He wouldn't spread the news around before Wendell knew. And she really needed to talk to someone about this.

She cleaned up her smudged makeup and then went to see if Bear was in his room. She knocked and heard movement before the door opened.

"Hi…" His wide smile dropped away. "What's wrong? Come inside."

She rushed past him, clutching the old handwritten letter in her hand. "I made a discovery."

"Sit, sweetheart, and tell me what's going on." He patted the foot of the bed, and she sat beside him.

"Wendell finally found the missing letter from his secret daughter, Ariella." She held it up like it was Exhibit

A. "His daughter was the fifty-first miner." A fresh tear slid down her cheek.

Bear wiped it away with his thumb. "How can that be?"

"Read it." She watched his facial expression rapidly change as he read. "Pretty shocking, isn't it? And so sad. Young love tragically lost. At least they were together at the end, hopefully in one another's arms. At least that's what I'm choosing to believe." She sniffed and wiped away a few more tears.

He put the letter aside, drew her into his arms and they lay back on the bed with her head on his shoulder. "I wonder what happened to the baby?"

She sighed, settling herself against his side and taking the comfort he offered. "This brings up so many new questions. Who raised the baby, and does she have any idea she's a Fortune?"

"I don't understand why the babysitter wouldn't come forward and say she had Ariella's baby."

"I guess it's possible Ariella didn't tell the sitter the identity of the father, or maybe whoever it was felt too intimidated to tell Wendell Fortune. So many unanswered questions. It's all so tragic." She stroked her fingers across his chest as they talked, absent-mindedly exploring the dips and planes of his muscles through the soft fabric of his pinstriped dress shirt.

"It makes you stop and think. After believing for so long that West was dead, I have a new appreciation for how quickly things can be taken from you. You never know when it might be the last time you see someone."

She propped herself up on her elbow so she could see him. He was so handsome. So irresistible. "I guess the lesson is not to waste time and miss out on living?"

"That sounds right to me." He sat up to face her and cradled the back of her head, massaging her scalp and drawing her slowly closer. "What should we do about this idea of not missing out? Any thoughts?"

Showing him seemed a much better option than telling, and she couldn't wait another nanosecond for his kiss. Closing the small distance between them, she meant for it to be a soft, teasing caress, but when he slid the tip of his tongue between her lips, she lost her very thin hold over her good girl self-control. Their kiss became deep and searching as they fell into perfect rhythm.

He kissed a path along the curve of her neck and across her collarbone. "You have the most gorgeous shoulders. Do you want to know one of the things I find so sexy about you?"

"Tell me," she said, her voice sounding breathy.

"Your eagerness for adventure," he rasped, then rolled them until she straddled his hips.

As she looked down into Bear's mesmerizing dark eyes, *eager* was an excellent way to describe her current feelings. So were *excited* and *enthusiastic*.

She began to slowly unbutton his shirt. "Do you feel like having an adventure right now?"

"That's a brilliant idea." His hands slid along her thighs, and she shivered under his touch. "Let the adventure begin."

MORGANA SLEPT IN his arms after proving his theory that their passion would be fireworks. Her soft hair was fanned across his chest, and he trailed his fingers through its silkiness. Bear waited for the usual urge to get up and dressed and put necessary space between himself and the woman in his bed. But the urge never came. In fact, the impulse that filled him was to wake her up, make love to her again and hold her all night long.

An uncomfortable current of caution surged across his

skin, and he flinched. She shifted and mumbled something in her sleep that he didn't understand. This was the perfect time to get out of bed, but they were in his room. He should wake her up, but kicking her out felt all wrong. Next time they could go to her room, and then he'd be able to slip out of bed and go back to his own.

For tonight, though, Bear stayed right where he was, kissed the top of her head and held her a little tighter, letting his fingers play among the silky strands of her hair and lulling her back into a deep sleep. She didn't need to know that he was having a moment of weakness with a touch of freak-out.

Damn it. This is exactly what was not supposed to happen.

MORGANA WAS STILL riding on the delicious high from waking up in Bear's arms that morning, and she couldn't wait for the next time they could hang out.

She was behind the motel's front desk while Hal ran some errands when a delivery arrived. The driver brought in several large boxes.

"I'm sorry one of the boxes got torn open a bit." He pulled back a flap of cardboard. "It doesn't look damaged, but do you want to open it and check?"

"Sure. I can do that." She grabbed a pair of scissors and cut more of the packing tape. "Oh, it's a new housekeeping cart. It looks like it's completely undamaged."

"Very good. Have a nice day, miss."

"You, too." Morgana went back to finishing unboxing the shiny new housekeeping cart, and then tested it out around the small lobby. The wheels rolled smoothly, nothing rattled and there was more room on it than the old ones.

The lobby door opened again, and her boss came in with a bag of groceries.

"Hal, thanks for buying new housekeeping carts."

"What carts?" He glanced between the boxes and the one she was pushing around. "I didn't order these. I wonder if they were delivered to the wrong place?"

"I don't think so. It's your name and this address on the labels."

"Curious." He rubbed a hand over his belly that was straining the buttons of his shirt.

Morgana smiled and gave the cart another roll around the lobby as if she was a kid with a brand-new toy. "I have a pretty good idea where these came from. I think one of our guests ordered these."

"You think Mrs. Fortune bought them?"

"No. I think *Mr.* Fortune did." Her temporary knight in designer armor.

THE NIGHT BEFORE, Bear had slept better with Morgana in his bed than he had in months. Maybe years. All morning he'd been telling himself his restful night was only because it had been so long since he'd been with a woman, and he'd exhausted himself.

Morgana was young and an ardent lover. She also had a deeply romantic heart that hadn't yet been touched by heartache like his. She thought she knew, but she had no idea how bad it could be. Just last night, she'd cried about the young lovers who'd died in the mine disaster decades ago. If she had his baby she would want—and rightly expect—more than he could give.

Making love with Morgana had been incredible. Also, an incredibly risky move, but it hadn't been a mistake. How could he ever regret experiencing the chemistry they had together?

As if there wasn't already a long list of reasons, this was even more confirmation that she could not have his baby. He couldn't afford to have strong romantic feelings for the mother of his child, and he wouldn't be able to separate his feelings if he had a child with Morgana. What if they started fighting like his parents had? If they were together and then at some point they weren't, the baby would be shuffled back and forth between parents. Then his child would grow up in a broken home. But wait—

It would be worse than that because she'd told him there was no way she would give up custody.

Bear sat back down at the small desk in the corner of his motel room, opened his laptop and started doing serious research about surrogacy. He read articles and scoured countless agency websites. Once he'd made a long bullet-point list of all the most important things, he decided which agency he would call first. The ball was rolling, and all that remained to be seen was if it would be a winning goal or if it would roll back downhill and crush him flat.

A tiny voice inside him continued to whisper that Morgana should be the mother of his child, but without the heart involved.

Still impossible just like it was a few hours ago, bonehead. Why do I keep tormenting myself by even thinking about it?

She was also too tenderhearted to be a friends-with-benefits kind of woman. She deserved so much more than that. More than he had to give.

Someone knocked, and he yelled out for them to come in because he needed a distraction from his own thoughts.

Morgana opened the door. "Oh, sorry. It looks like I caught you right in the middle of something. I'll come back later."

"Stay." It was then that he recognized the calming effect she brought into a room—like a Disney princess with a halo of birds and small woodland creatures gathered near. He looked around at his scattered handwritten notes and crumpled wads of paper. Now was the perfect time to make sure she knew he was serious about his plans to have an heir. It would put some necessary space between them, because he could not allow himself to get used to having her in his daily life. "I was doing some research, and I'd like to tell you about it."

She easily pulled her housekeeping cart over the threshold and into the room. "How do you like my shiny new cart?"

"Very nice. Where did you get it?"

"I believe I have a secret admirer who wants to make my life a little easier. I think I'll find a creative way to thank them."

He returned her smile. "Sounds like a hell of a guy."

"How do you know it's a guy?"

"Just a hunch."

She came around behind him to see what he was doing and rested her hands on his shoulders.

He knew the second she saw the surrogacy website pulled up on the screen. Her fingers suddenly flexed against the tense muscles on each side of his neck.

He was doing this to protect her as well as himself. "I'm going to find an egg donor and a surrogate to have my child."

CHAPTER TEN

THE LIGHT AND cheery feeling of happiness that had put extra pep in Morgana's steps all day suddenly drained out as if someone had pulled a plug.

She slipped her hands from Bear's shoulders and clasped them behind her back so she wouldn't be tempted to touch him. The surrogacy website Bear was looking at was a giant flashing billboard announcing he was going ahead with his wacky plan, and he didn't see her in his future. Which he'd told her repeatedly, but apparently she wasn't very good at listening.

"You're really going to do it? You're going to hire a surrogate to have a baby for you?"

"I don't see any other way."

She walked over to his bed and sat down. "I think you're missing the whole point of it all."

He shook his head and ran a hand roughly through his hair. "I assure you I'm not. My point is, romantic love leads to disaster and estrangement."

"Not always. Love and family and sharing the joys and struggles of life with a partner can be wonderful. Watching your child grow and sharing the good as well as the difficult parts of being a parent. Supporting one another." Her mom had been a single mother, and Morgana had seen her struggles, and she didn't want that for herself or for Bear.

"I have something that can help. Money. I can hire the best to help me."

She ducked her head, letting her hair screen her face because she knew her expression would give away her disappointment. Not to mention the disapproval of his plan. "Are you going to go the rest of your life without loving a woman?"

"That's the plan." He crossed his arms over his chest and leaned back in the chair.

She suddenly felt cold and tucked her feet beneath her. From the things he'd previously said, she got the impression there were painful things in Bear's past that he didn't like to talk about, and she wasn't sure if now was the right time to question him about it. "That sounds...lonely."

"I didn't say I wasn't going to date and have casual connections."

Casual connections? Tension banded her chest. *That must be what I am to him.*

Of course it was. She was a temporary fling to him, but she had herself to blame because she'd been the one who suggested *hanging out* until he left town. She would have to seriously sort through all these feelings. Soon. "Oh, Bear. Who hurt you?"

He scratched his head and looked like he was making up his mind about something important. "I have an ex-wife. We were married a few years and then she and my best friend thought it would be a good idea to hook up when I was out of town on business."

"Damn. That's harsh."

"Do you know what's even harsher? Walking in on them."

Morgana winced. "I'm so sorry that happened to you."

"I lost a wife *and* a friend that day," he bit out.

"And you've lost your parents, too?"

"Yes, five years ago in a plane crash with my aunt and uncle."

Morgana wanted to go to him, but with his arms crossed so protectively over his body, she wasn't sure if he wanted her affection or not. "There are people who will stick by you and not break your heart. I've seen you with your family. You told me you were adopted, so that means the Fortunes wanted you."

"It's a little more complicated than that." He rubbed a hand over his face, tapped his bare foot on the floor and then came over to sit beside her on his bed. "When I was a toddler, Peter and Dolly Fortune found me sitting alone in a sandbox at a park."

Her breath snagged, but she managed to control her reaction. At least she hoped she'd hidden her shock. Silently, she put a hand on top of his and scooted closer to him.

"They looked for my family, but the police concluded I had been abandoned. They couldn't find my parents or any relatives, so the Fortunes took me in. West and I bonded quickly, and they adopted me."

She laced their fingers and leaned her head against his shoulder. "I know you might think it's cheesy to say, but they weren't forced to take you. They *chose* you to be part of their family."

He tipped up her chin and kissed her softly. "I guess you're right."

"I'm right a lot of the time. It happens quite frequently," she said with a smile, lightening the mood.

"I can believe that, sweetheart."

"Have you tried to find your birth family since then?" He shook his head.

"Well, if you wanted to, you could get a 411 Me DNA kit and see if you have any matches. I bet you would have at least cousins who might know something."

"I've thought about it. That's how my cousin Esme found out her baby had been switched at birth." A shadow crossed his face and he muttered, "But I'm not sure I want to. I don't need to search them out and hear a sob story or an excuse about why they didn't want to keep me."

She decided not to push the issue. "I heard about the babies being switched. What a relief Esme and Ryder got that figured out, fell in love and are raising the baby boys as brothers."

"Was Freya around when that happened?" he asked. "The switching babies part."

She thought back over all the information she'd gathered. "Yes. She was already in town. It's another weird thing that has happened while Freya is here granting wishes on behalf of her late husband, Elias Fortune."

Bear rolled his neck as if his muscles had suddenly tensed. "But from what the others have told me, my step-granny is the one who gave Esme the DNA kit. If she had something to do with the babies being switched, why would she have done that?"

"Good question. Maybe because of guilt for doing something wrong?" she said.

"Could be, I guess."

She stood and walked to her cart. "I better get your room cleaned."

"I only need towels." He leaned back on his elbows. "And a roll of toilet paper."

"Very funny." She grabbed a roll and tossed it at him. She loved this playful side of him.

"How many more rooms do you have after mine?"

"Yours is the last one."

He lay all the way back on the bed with his hands under his head and flashed a big grin. "Saving the best for last?"

"Something like that. Then I'll figure out what to do with the rest of my day. There are just so many options, and I can't decide…"

"You know, now that I think about it, my shower needs cleaning, and I've heard that it's easier to clean if you do it while you are actually taking a shower," he said.

She flashed him a cheeky smile. "If that's what you heard, then it must be true. Want to help me test the theory?"

"Do you really have to ask?" He rose from the bed and pulled his T-shirt over his head.

She admired the defined muscles of his back as she followed him into the bathroom and closed the door.

For several days they hung out with one another as much as possible in between work and his family obligations. One Sunday morning, they were snuggled together in her bed watching TV when there was an advertisement for the day's 1980s movie marathon.

Morgana propped herself up so she could see Bear. "Since I have the day off, want to stay in bed all day, eat takeout and junk food while watching movies that became classics before we were born?"

He chuckled and kissed the pulse point on her wrist. "Sweetheart, you had me at stay in bed all day."

"Even though the first two movies they're showing are *Sixteen Candles* and *Say Anything*?"

"Is *Say Anything* the one where John Cusack holds up the big boom box like the one you have on your dresser?" He pointed to her CD player that wasn't nearly as big as the one in the movie.

"Hey, funny guy, mine isn't that big, but yes, that is the movie. My mom loves it, and I used to watch it with her."

"I'm going to call the café and get an order delivered. What would you like?" he asked.

"The ricotta pancakes with lemon curd and an order of bacon, please."

"Bacon always sounds good."

She was in the bathroom brushing her teeth when she heard him placing the order, and she almost choked on toothpaste when she started laughing about his last request. She rinsed her mouth and climbed back into bed. "Did you order a side of chocolate sauce from the Cowgirl Café?"

"I did." He propped himself up against the headboard, the sheet pooling in his lap. "You never know when it might come in handy."

The day went by in a happy blur of laughter, food, making love and a long leisurely shower after he'd had chocolate sauce for dessert—right off the most sensitive skin of her belly.

MORGANA GRABBED HER keys and headed out to the parking lot to get something out of her car's trunk, but when she stood in front of the spot where it had been parked, it was empty. Her heart plummeted to the ground.

"Oh my God. Someone stole my car." She turned in a circle, just in case she'd forgotten where she parked. But Pumpkin was nowhere to be seen. "Why would anyone steal a car as old and rundown as mine?"

She had almost saved enough to fix it, but she certainly didn't have enough for a new car. Even another old clunker. She stood frozen in place for another minute. What was she supposed to do now? Live forever in the Chatelaine Motel? Her heart began to race.

"Morgana, what's wrong, kid?" Rhonda asked as she walked up beside her, with her own keys in her hand— which belonged to a car that was thankfully still parked in its spot.

"My car. It's gone! Someone stole it."

Her sassy coworker propped a hand on her hip. "What

do you mean? I just saw your car this morning on the way to work."

That surprised her. "You did? Where?"

"At the mechanic shop. They had it on a lift and were underneath working on it."

"Oh. Really?" Morgana tried to make sense of it all. How had her car gotten across town? It wasn't even running.

"You didn't know it was there?"

"No. Maybe Hal got tired of it collecting dust in his parking lot and had it towed over to the mechanic and convinced them to give me credit."

Rhonda laughed. "Honey, I think you might have a knight in shining armor. And their name is definitely not Hal. Sorry, but I've gotta run. I'm late for an appointment."

"See you tomorrow," Morgana called after her and then turned back to the empty parking spot.

Bear Fortune. Did you do this like you did with the new carts?

A smile pulled up the corners of her mouth, but then she glanced toward Freya's room. Had she done it? That was highly unlikely. The woman would hardly even talk to her, and Morgana wasn't one of the Fortunes who were getting their greatest wishes granted. There would be no reason for Freya to help the stranger who was always asking too many questions.

Morgana went straight to the lobby, and when Hall knew nothing about her car, it reinforced her hunch as to the identity of her benefactor.

Bear had gone somewhere with one of his brothers, and she didn't want to interrupt their time together, so she dismissed the idea of calling him. Reading her new romance novel sounded like a good way to pass the time waiting for Bear to get home. She came to a stop and pressed the heel of one hand to the knot in her chest.

This isn't home for either of us.

Nothing about this situation was permanent or lasting. He would leave first, and at some point, so would she. If she had a car when the time came.

Some people might be mad at him for making a decision about their car without asking, but she wasn't. Although, she did have to wonder about his motive. Was it another attempt at convincing her to have a baby for him? She would be disappointed if that was the case. He knew how she felt, and he was very clear about what he did and didn't want.

More likely, it was the generosity she'd witnessed. Like the time he left a thousand-dollar tip for the young waiter at the LC Club with a note telling him good luck at college. She doubted he would let her repay him, but that didn't mean she couldn't do something nice for him. She'd have to think of a few ideas.

When he drove up a while later, she closed her book and waved to him from the outdoor seating area. "You'll never guess what happened," she said as he got close. "My car was stolen."

"Is that right?" He grinned, and that told her everything she needed to know.

"Might you be the one who stole it, Mr. Fortune?"

"Guilty as charged, but I do plan to bring it back to you in better shape than it was."

"That won't be hard to do." She took his hand and started leading him upstairs. "But seriously, I really do appreciate the help. Thank you."

"You're welcome."

"Can I ask you why you did it?"

He followed Morgana into her room and closed the door behind them. "It was something that needs doing, and I have the means to get it done. Everyone deserves to have someone help them out now and then."

"My mom would adore you." She held her next breath and turned to put her book on the nightstand. This anti-committed-relationship guy probably didn't go for meeting parents.

"Moms always love me," he bragged and wrapped her in an embrace that made her shiver.

Relieved he wasn't getting twitchy about her comment, she kissed the strong line of his jaw. "I can believe that."

"Would you like to go to the lake with me tomorrow afternoon?"

"That sounds fun. I'd love to go," Morgana said.

"Cool. I was hoping you'd say yes. I rented a boat, and it has a cabin with a bed."

Her smile grew as tingles spread through her core. "How convenient. It must be a big boat."

"Not really. But it's big enough for an adventure."

"You know I'm up for an adventure anytime. You're spoiling me."

He swayed them gently from side to side. "Right again, dancing queen. It makes me happy to do it."

"So glad I can give you pleasure."

That earned her a kiss that demonstrated the fact. At first, she'd thought Bear was a playboy, but that was only surface-level camouflage. This smart, thoughtful, funny man knew what he was doing in the bedroom, and since both of their rooms had a bed smack-dab in the middle, they often found themselves in it.

"How do you feel about staying overnight on the boat?" he asked.

Her eyes widened. "Can we really do that?"

"Yes, we can."

"Well, in that case, I'm in. I guess we'll need to take food."

"We can order food from the café and stop by Great-Store if we need to. Pack a swimsuit and…that's about it."

She rested her head against his chest and made up her mind to enjoy her time with him—while she could.

CHAPTER ELEVEN

MORGANA STEPPED DOWN into the boat's cabin. "Wow! This is so much nicer than I expected. How did you even know you could rent something like this?"

Bear had learned that for the right price, you could rent luxury almost anywhere. "It's easy when you have a great assistant who is good at finding things. He handles leasing and booking hotels, condos, flights, cars and all the logistics."

"Very handy."

He was pleased with the boat he'd rented. It was a small but beautiful overnight cabin cruiser with a tiny bathroom. The private boat dock was in the affluent area of Chatelaine Lake. Located in a secluded cove, it would allow them to have a peaceful night alone. He dropped their overnight bags onto the bed.

If she was interested, he could tell her about some of his adventures. Scuba diving in the Maldives or hiking to Machu Picchu in Peru. They could pretend they were somewhere far away from Chatelaine—and all the real-life worries and problems that meant their time together was limited.

He unzipped his duffel bag to drop his keys and wallet inside. "We've got sodas, water, beer and a couple bottles of wine. So, let me know when—"

Her tie-dyed T-shirt sailed over his shoulder to land on the bed, and he forgot what he'd been about to say. He spun to see her in a little red bikini top and pair of denim cutoffs that were low enough to show her belly button. He'd seen her completely bare and beautiful, but this bikini with its string ties was even better than finding her topless. He let go of his keys without taking his eyes off her and heard them hit the floor. Just like he was hoping her shorts might do.

Her lips puckered in a way that he'd learned meant she was trying not to laugh. The sassy little tease knew exactly what she was doing to him. And he was enjoying it very much.

"Can we drive around the lake for a while?" she asked. "Maybe stop and swim somewhere?"

"You got it."

He reminded himself that boating and swimming *was* the reason he'd planned this mini adventure. Not for the use of the bed. They had two of those back at the motel that they could use any time. This trip was about more than that. He'd planned it because he enjoyed spending time with her, and their talks and the laughter always left him smiling. He pulled his own shirt over his head and stole a few kisses before they went up on deck, where she continued her deliciously slow seduction.

"Will you put this sunscreen on my back, please?" She held out a tube of cream. "And then I'll put some on you."

"It's a good thing you didn't ask me to do this while we were down in the cabin, because I would've been hard pressed not to pull that little string and untie your bikini top."

"Hmm," she purred. "I'll have to remember that."

They spent some time cruising around and exploring all the areas of Lake Chatelaine. They saw people waterskiing and fishing and enjoying the sunny day. When they were almost back to the cove where they would dock later, he slowed the boat. "How does this spot look for swimming?"

She came up behind him at the wheel and wrapped her arms around his waist. "Looks perfect to me."

"Excellent. I could go for a cold drink, too." He turned in her arms. "And a kiss."

"I can help you with one of those things right away." She eagerly proved her point.

As another boat drove by, he heard catcalls and whistles. He broke their kiss to see a group of college-age guys craning their necks to look at Morgana. He couldn't exactly blame them. He waited to see if she'd say anything about it, but she was so focused on him, she didn't even seem to have noticed. His chest warmed with her attention. She made him feel...special.

He dropped the anchor but turned around in time to see Morgana shimmying down her denim shorts.

"Catch me if you can, Mr. Fortune!" She jumped into the water with a whoop of excitement. When she resurfaced, the look of joy on her face made him chuckle. She was smart and mature with a good head on her shoulders, and even though she had a serious side, she had retained a youthful playfulness that he found so appealing.

She's irresistible.

His heart was in the danger zone, and he knew it, but that was a problem for another day. Today was too good to taint with worries he couldn't do anything about right now.

He tossed in the lounge floats, grabbed two cans of ice-cold beer and jumped in after her. She climbed up on the yellow float and flipped her long hair over the back to trail in the water behind her. Her bright red bikini was slowly driving him wild.

He stuck a can in the cupholder of each float and climbed onto the blue one. Hand in hand so they wouldn't drift apart, they floated near the boat and talked, sharing childhood stories. After they were tired and hungry from swimming, they lounged on the deck and snacked on fruit and cheese.

Morgana rolled onto her stomach to sun her back and propped herself up on her elbows. "Have you ever been on one of those giant private yachts?"

"A couple of times. Is that something you want to do?"

"I've never really thought about it," she admitted. "I've mostly thought about the locations I want to visit but not the mode of transportation."

He could easily imagine showing her the world, but that was something you did when you were in a relationship.

Maybe it doesn't have to be.

He *had* made it clear that he never planned to marry again. Maybe they could meet somewhere in the middle? He'd previously jumped to the conclusion that she wouldn't want a friends-with-benefits agreement, but she could make up her own mind about whether or not she wanted to get together now and then with an understanding that it would not become a forever thing. Future get togethers would be a lot of fun. It wouldn't hurt to talk to her about the idea. On another day.

He tucked her hair behind her ear. "Speaking of traveling, I have to take a business trip to Houston. I'll be gone for three days."

"For the big new business deal that you're working on?"

"Yes. Hopefully this will tie up some of the loose ends."

When the sun started to slip close to the horizon, he drove them back to the private dock. They watched the sunset from the deck and ate a delicious picnic meal he'd talked his cousin Bea into preparing for them. The wine with dinner was good, but Morgana's company was so much better.

"Bear, thank you for planning this day for us. It's been wonderful."

"Thank you for being so fun and easy to be with." He idly played with her long, tapered fingers, and she hooked her leg over his as they lay side by side on the deck. The night sky was clear and perfect for stargazing. He knew almost nothing about astronomy, but Morgana did and pointed out some of the major constellations.

When they saw a shooting star, he made a wish. The kind that was rarely granted, because having it all was a huge ask.

FOR TWO DAYS, Bear had been out of town on business, and Morgana missed him way more than she ought to. She couldn't stop thinking about him. How it felt to be in his arms kissing him. Sharing secrets. And the way his deep laugh surrounded her like a warm blanket.

"Why did I fall for him, setting myself up for the torture of missing him once he's gone for good?" she whispered.

She put away her housekeeping cart and headed toward the lobby for a cup of midday coffee. She'd been craving the crème brûlée flavored creamer she added to the small coffee, tea and snack bar she'd set up and been put in charge of. Moving around the few pieces of furniture, she'd made space in a corner of the small lobby, and it had been a hit with the guests.

Hal was reading a fishing magazine when she went into the lobby and gave him a list of maintenance issues that needed to be addressed. "Good afternoon."

"Morgana, I know you've been looking for extra ways to earn money, and I might have something for you."

"Great. What is it?" Even though her car was being taken care of, she could always use extra money in her savings for whatever situation popped up next. Pumpkin would need to be replaced at some point.

"It's really late notice, but the LC Club is looking for extra staff for a big fancy party. It would be a good chunk of extra cash."

She propped her arms on the counter. "That sounds like a good opportunity. Do you know what I would be doing?"

"Tidying up, removing glasses and hors d'oeuvre plates, and general bussing duties."

An upside-down feeling twisted her stomach. Not long ago, she'd sat in the fancy establishment eating and drinking fine wine at a secluded table with a gorgeous millionaire bachelor—who fully intended to remain single. He would also be leaving all too soon. Being spoiled by him would end. So, she would take this temporary job and get back to being the one who cleaned up after other people while they enjoyed themselves and celebrated.

Their dinner date at the LC Club had been a Cinderella moment, and she needed to remember that she lived in the real world. And she needed the money. "When is the party?"

"Tomorrow night. It's for Freya Fortune's birthday party."

Morgana gasped. That was July 25—the same date as her grandmother Gwenyth's birthday!

"Something wrong?" Hal asked.

"No. Not at all. Just excited to make some extra money." At least Bear was out of town and wouldn't be there to see her bussing tables while his family celebrated. "Can I have the number of the person doing the hiring?"

"Sure thing." He wrote the manager's number on a sticky note and handed it over. "I told them what a great employee you are. You'll have no trouble getting the job."

"Thanks, Hal." She rushed back outside without getting

the cup of coffee she'd gone in for. Her brain was hyped up enough just thinking about what the date of Freya's party could mean. "July 25. What are the chances?"

It was possible that Freya's birthday was earlier in the week or several days from now and the party was only on the twenty-fifth because it was a Saturday and convenient, but the coincidence... This was another huge clue that gave credence to her growing suspicion.

Is Freya really Gwenyth Wells?

Could the woman who dodged her at every turn be her grandmother? A woman who was so secretive and honestly, kind of sad and lonely. She should just walk up to Freya the next time she saw her and ask if she was really Gwenyth Wells. *Because if you are, you're my grandmother.*

She just might do it because enough was enough!

BECAUSE HER CAR needed so much work and they needed to order parts, Morgana didn't have it back yet, so Hal gave her a ride to the LC Club. He offered to come back and get her if she couldn't find a ride home after the event. She couldn't ask for a better boss.

The fancy party for Freya Fortune's birthday would be starting soon. None of the guests had arrived, but the host, Wendell, was there to make sure everything was ready. Morgana was arranging appetizer plates and silverware when she noticed him standing alone in one corner just observing the setup.

She made her way over to him. "Hi, Wendell. You certainly throw a nice party."

He shrugged. "Thank you, but all I did was write a check."

"Well, it's a very nice thing to do for your brother's widow. Is today her actual birthday?"

He thought for a minute. "She said her birthday was in July, and when I asked her when a good time for a party would be, she picked this date. But I'm not actually sure if it's her real birthday today or not."

Why was it so damn difficult to find out the truth? "I read the unopened letter from Ariella," she blurted out and then wished she hadn't. She shouldn't have brought up this topic right before the party started. She didn't want to ruin his night of fun.

Wendell took a deep breath. "Tell me."

She hesitated. "Maybe now isn't the time to talk about it—"

"I knew it. It's not good news." He wiped a trembling hand across his brow. "I can't wait another second. Just tell me."

She pulled out two chairs at the nearby table and motioned for him to sit. "The date of the letter was the same day of the disaster."

"I received it a day after that."

"Ariella wrote that she left her baby with a sitter for the night because she was going into the mine to get her boyfriend so they could elope."

"But if they'd both run off to elope, he wouldn't have been in… Oh." His eyes filled with tears as realization hit. "My daughter was the fifty-first miner."

She covered his wrinkled hand that was resting on the table. "Yes, I believe so. I'm so sorry."

His next breath came out shaky. "I remember something of hers was found in the mine after the collapse. I just figured it was her beau who'd had it."

"She also wrote that she would contact you at a later date to see if you wanted to meet your granddaughter."

"The baby." Wendell wiped his eyes. "Did Ariella say who was looking after the baby?"

"I'm afraid not." Morgana saw the catering manager watching them. "I'm sorry, but I should get back to work before I get fired. Are you okay? I won't leave you if you aren't."

"I'll be fine. You go do what you need to and don't worry about me. Your concern for me means a lot."

She stood and smoothed her white blouse. "We can talk more tomorrow or anytime you want to."

"Thank you, Morgana. Your family must be proud that you're such a kind and caring young lady."

His compliment made her feel good, but it also made her a little sad that she didn't have anyone except her mom to be proud of her. What a colorful family history the Fortunes had. What a family history she had herself. Maybe Bear was right to be disillusioned about the past.

Morgana went back to work but now she was upset for Wendell as well as grumpy about the whole Freya situation, and in general just feeling down in the dumps because Bear would soon be leaving for good. She just wanted to confront Freya and find out the truth once and for all, but she couldn't do it tonight. Just because she'd gotten in her head about her short romance coming to an end and was generally having a bad day, she didn't want to spoil the elderly woman's big night.

CHAPTER TWELVE

BEAR HADN'T THOUGHT his business in Houston would be finished by today, but they'd come to an agreement, signed contracts, and he'd made it back to Chatelaine in enough time to put on a suit and leave for Freya's birthday party at the LC Club. He'd knocked on Morgana's door as soon as he'd returned to the motel, but she hadn't been there. When he'd called her to see if she wanted to go with him to the party, she didn't answer, and he'd only been able to leave a voice mail. It worried him that he couldn't get ahold of her, but he reminded himself that he wouldn't always be around to look after her, and she was a capable woman.

While he'd been away, he thought about Morgana's suggestion to get a 411 Me DNA kit like Esme had and decided he'd do it. He'd already bought a kit and sent it off. If he got no results from sending in his DNA, and still wanted to take it further, he could hire someone to investigate. But he'd take it one step at a time.

Arriving at the LC Club reminded him of that first dinner with Morgana, and looking out over Chatelaine Lake brought to mind their boating adventure. The memories of their days and nights, their long talks and making love were something he'd have forever. He still hadn't talked to her about the idea of getting together several times a year because he was still debating whether it was a good idea or possibly the worst he'd ever had.

I'm being as decisive as a hormonal teenager.

The club's ballroom was filled with Fortunes of all ages. He liked seeing his brothers so happy. West was such a good father, and currently had a baby in each arm. Camden was dancing with the woman he loved while big band music played, and people were talking and laughing, but his mind was so far away from it all, the chatter faded into the background. He'd only been here a few minutes and already wanted to leave. Finding Morgana and spending what little time he had left in town with her was all he wanted to do. Preferably back at the motel, where they could be alone to talk and start saying their goodbyes. Now, he just wanted to get this event over with and see if his dancing queen was home.

And that was the problem.

His consuming desire for her was a sign that he'd let himself get too close. Too vulnerable. But he'd be gone soon, and after a period of adjustment, he'd be fine. Until then, there was no harm in enjoying what little time they had left. They'd made lots of memories, and he could reminisce about his sweet, sassy Morgana whenever he wanted. He'd hold dear their days and nights together and suspected she would as well.

Two of his cousins, brothers Damon and Max Fortune Maloney approached, both of them laughing about something.

"Didn't I see you drinking scotch on the rocks at our last get together?" Max said and handed him a short glass with a large, perfectly round ice ball surrounded by amber liquid.

"Yes, you did. Thanks."

"You looked like you could use a drink." Damon held up his cocktail in the universal sign for cheers.

"Am I that obvious?" Bear chuckled and took a sip. It was top-shelf scotch with a smooth, smoky flavor.

"The last time we were all together here at the LC Club was the big New Year's party our oldest brother Linc threw," Damon said.

Max swirled the ice in his drink. "It was an over-the-top splashy way to reveal he'd become a millionaire."

Bear had been somewhere on the other side of the world that New Year's Eve. "I've heard some talk about that party. Isn't that when your family started getting your money one person at a time from Wendell?"

"Yes, and I had to wait until last," Damon said.

The two brothers turned to their mother as she approached and started having a whispered conversation. All he heard was something about their sister and stopped listening.

One of the little redheaded boys that had been wearing a superhero cape the other day skidded to a stop in front of him with a cupcake in each hand. "You're the bear, right?"

He chuckled. "My name is Bear. It's short for Barrington."

"I'm Benjy Keeling Fortune Maloney. Look what I got." He held up one chocolate and one vanilla cupcake. "But Mama said I can only eat one."

The kid was cute and renewed his desire to become a dad. "Which one are you going to eat?"

Benjy licked frosting from first the vanilla and then the chocolate. Some of the colorful sprinkles fell into the front pocket of his white dress shirt. "I like the chocolate one." He held out the vanilla cupcake that was missing a sizable dollop of frosting on one side. "Want this one?"

"No thanks. I already had mine." He was trying so hard not to laugh.

Benjy shrugged. "That's okay. My little brother Jacob will eat it. Bye," he called over his shoulder as he dashed away.

Damon turned from the conversation with his mom and

came closer to Bear. "That was our little sugar monster. He's the oldest."

"Cute kid. You must've been really young when you had him."

"My wife, Sari, already had the two boys when I met her. But I adopted them once we got married, and then we had our baby girl." He smiled at his wife a few tables away. She was a lovely woman with long red hair like her boys, and she was holding their baby.

"You have a beautiful family."

"Thanks. I have to agree with you. I'm a lucky man."

Bear supposed some people could be lucky in love and make it work. He just didn't happen to be one of them. Sipping his cocktail, he scanned the room and his stomach fluttered when he saw Morgana on the other side of the ballroom. He was so happy to see that she'd been invited. But why was she holding a stack of dirty dishes? That's when he paid more attention to what she was wearing. A slim black skirt and white blouse with a black tie. It was a caterer's uniform.

She looked in his direction, and he started to raise his hand to wave, but she swiftly left the room.

No wonder she hadn't been at the motel. She was working at the party, and if he wasn't mistaken, avoiding him. But why?

WITH A STACK of dirty dishes teetering in her grasp, Morgana dashed through a doorway at the back of the ballroom that led to the kitchen.

What is he doing here?

He was supposed to be out of town working on a business deal that would make him even richer. Had he told her he wouldn't be home tonight because he didn't want to bring her as a date to a family party? Suddenly light-headed, she paused to get her bearings. That was an unpleasant thought. She didn't want to believe that he was embarrassed of her.

She had spotted Bear right before he saw her, and she hoped her pretense of not seeing him was convincing enough that he didn't know she was avoiding him.

Why am *I avoiding him?*

That was a question she should seriously consider. Seeing him here at the party when she hadn't expected to had thrown her off kilter, and she wasn't exactly sure what was wrong with her. True, she'd been a little down and grumpy all evening, but she'd never been ashamed about making an honest living.

She stowed the dishes where they could be washed and started refilling trays with hors d'oeuvres. Morgana wished she could just leave, but she had a job to do.

After their night on the boat, she fallen even harder for a man who could never be hers. And since he'd left for Houston, she'd discovered what it was going to be like to miss him. It was a reality check she didn't care for.

Seeing Bear amongst all the other finely dressed partygoers had stirred up a swirl of conflicting feelings. She wanted to run across the room, leap onto him and kiss him silly, but she also wanted to hide. And hiding was the cowardly emotion that had won out in the end. It was ridiculous. She cleaned his room all the time, but something about him being in a designer suit at a big fancy party and her toting around dirty dishes really highlighted the differences in their lives.

It wasn't like anyone was treating her poorly. Haley and some of the other women had chatted with her, and everyone was kind, but she felt so removed from the Fortunes all dressed in their finest with their great wealth on display. Most of all Bear.

Their futures looked nothing alike. He was a filthy rich bachelor who planned to remain that way, and even though they both wanted to be parents, she would not start a family without being married to a committed partner with mutual love binding them. She could not let herself settle for less and didn't see how she could make that happen when their futures looked so different. And sadly, she predicted Barrington Fortune would end up miserable if he kept his heart on lockdown.

She tended to some of the duties in the back so she wouldn't have to see Bear, but she couldn't stay in the kitchen all night. At some point she'd have to face her fears and feelings. And a little thing called reality.

She gave herself a pep talk the way her mom would do. There was nothing wrong or embarrassing about what she was doing. She was working and making ends meet. When she went back out into the ballroom with fresh trays, Bear was waiting for her right inside the door to the ballroom.

"Hello, beautiful."

She couldn't help but return his big smile. He had sought her out, proving he wasn't completely avoiding her. He looked so handsome in a charcoal suit, the pink shirt she loved and a silver tie. "Hi, yourself. I didn't know you were back in town yet." She held out the tray, and he took a bacon-wrapped pepper on a toothpick.

"I just got back. I only had enough time to knock on your door and then get dressed before coming to the party." He popped the bite-size hors d'oeuvre into his mouth and followed her as she took the trays to a long table set up along one side of the ballroom.

"You knocked on my door?"

"I did. I wanted to see you."

She shoved down the giddy feeling his words caused. He might've wanted to see her, but he had not said he'd planned to invite her to be his date to this party. Experiencing this very public employee and guest dynamic between them was something she couldn't ignore.

A stark reminder that what they had was not some real and lasting love story.

The fact was Bear was leaving soon, and he didn't want any kind of committed relationship. He was planning to pay a surrogate to carry his heir, for goodness' sake. If the option existed to use nothing more than a test tube, he'd likely do it because it would completely remove the risk of getting attached to the mother of his child.

"I should get back to work. I need to go get more trays of food and clear some dishes."

"Of course. Sorry. I shouldn't be keeping you." He swayed forward like he'd kiss her but only squeezed her hand and then stepped away. "Come find me when you get a break."

"Okay. I'll try." She once again fled for the safety of the kitchen.

Why did I start sleeping with him?

She sighed. Oh, yeah. Because she'd thought it was a grand idea to experience everything life had to offer and have a no-strings-attached love affair. Talk about living and learning the hard way. There was no chance of them ever ending up together. She'd been deceiving herself in a big way to even hope, and a fool to think she could sleep with him and not fall in love.

But for him…

I'm nothing more than a fling for Barrington Fortune.

MORE FOOD WAS SERVED, and dishes cleared. Morgana's feet were aching and so was her back as she watched people dancing and drinking and Bear laughing with his brothers.

Freya was standing alone, and it was the perfect opportunity to ask if this was her real birthday. She was almost certain that she'd put enough clues together to suggest that the elderly but vibrant woman standing beside an ice sculpture was her grandmother. Besides the age range and birthdate, there were little things she'd said and done over the months. She'd known that the bookstore was once a hardware store, and it's true someone could've given her that information, but the way she'd said it was as if it were firsthand knowledge. And then there was the major clue about her revealing to West and Tabitha that she had a daughter with whom she'd been long estranged.

She only had to walk up to her and ask, but she also had to tread carefully because she didn't want to ruin her special night.

Freya looked so elegant in a long champagne-colored dress with a gauzy shawl collar. Her ash-blond hair was in a fancy twist on the back of her head. She was observing her party with an odd expression that wasn't exactly joyful or melancholy but something in between that was tender and touching. She held up her left hand and gazed at her diamond ring. Who was she thinking of? Her late husband?

Morgana approached her with a smile. "Happy birthday, Mrs. Fortune. You look beautiful."

"Thank you. This is such a lovely party. But it makes me miss... Elias." Her words had trailed off to a whisper.

That must be why she looked so wistful. She really had loved Elias Fortune.

Morgana's chest tightened, and she frowned as hope faded. Loving Elias would suggest that Freya was not Gwenyth. Her grandmother never would have married the enemy. But she had to be sure.

"Is today your actual birthday?"

Freya stiffened ever so slightly, but it was enough for Morgana to know she'd struck a nerve.

"Excuse me, please. I'm needed over there," the old woman said and hurried away.

Way to just throw it out there with no finesse.

Now Morgana was even more confused. Why dodge her question if she wasn't Gwenyth? She sighed. This was not helping her frustration level. She'd walk right out the front door if she didn't have to work.

When she entered the kitchen, the manager waved her over. Her heart plummeted. Was she about to get in trouble? She shouldn't have been chatting with the guests. As if she needed another reminder of her place.

"Morgana, it's your turn for a break. Thanks again for filling in tonight on such short notice. Hal was right about you. You're a hard worker who also takes the time to make people feel welcome."

"Oh, wow. That's so nice to hear. Thank you."

"Take thirty minutes off your feet. There will be lots of work to do once the guests leave." Something clattered in the kitchen and the manager rolled her eyes with a sigh and went to investigate.

Morgana headed back toward the ballroom. Bear had told her to come find him if she had a break. Had he truly meant it? "Guess I'll find out."

She made a quick stop in the bathroom to check her appearance. All she could do was smooth her ponytail and add a dash of mint lip gloss from the tube in her pocket, and then she went back out into the ballroom. It only took a few seconds to spot Bear standing with his brothers, and she started walking their way but hesitated. Was this wise?

He saw her and excused himself from his family to head her way. "Hey, there. How's it going?"

"I'm on my break."

He held out his hand. "Excellent. Come join us."

She looked down at herself, feeling self-conscious in

her server's uniform. "I'm not really dressed for the occasion. I was thinking I'd just go outside or something."

"My lovely dancing queen, don't you know you're the most beautiful woman in the room?"

"There you go again with your master-level flirting."

He chuckled. "You bring it out in me, sweetheart. Don't you want to dance with me?"

"I do, but…" She adjusted the collar of her white blouse.

He held up a finger. "Give me one minute. Will you meet me by that door to the balcony?"

"I'll be there." She smiled, her tension beginning to melt away. She made her way through the thinning crowd and waited where he'd indicated. He returned shortly after with a bottle of champagne, two glasses, and over his arm was a beautiful red silk shawl she'd seen Haley wearing. She opened the door, and they went out onto the balcony.

"Why do you have Haley's shawl?"

"She let me borrow it." He put the bottle and glasses on the ledge of a planter, and then like her fairy godfather, he wrapped the silk around her shoulders and loosely tied it. "Red is your color. It makes me think of your little red bikini."

Butterflies were skyrocketing around her insides. She suddenly felt like Cinderella at the ball. Just like in the fairy tale, the clock was ticking, but she was going to make the most of every second. "You think I should wear more red?"

"Definitely." He gently pulled the hair tie from her ponytail, and with his hand on the back of her head, he fluffed her hair.

She closed her eyes and moaned as delicious tingles spread over her scalp. "You have a magic touch."

His warm breath fanned across her cheek as he whispered in her ear. "I'm just getting started, sweetheart."

She slid her arms around his waist and met his gaze. "Why are you doing this?"

"Because you deserve it. And I like to see you smile." He moved them into a slow dance to the muted music from the party. "Most beautiful woman at the ball."

"With the most handsome man." She rested her head on his chest and inhaled his clean and spicy scent.

They danced until the band took a break and then stood at the railing sipping champagne and looking at the lovely view. The night was breezy, and the water softly lapped against the shoreline. She jumped when a firework exploded in a shower of silver sparkles that rained down over the lake. It was quickly followed by another, the colors reflecting on the water.

"Did you do this?"

He chuckled and kissed her softly. "I wish I'd thought of it, but no."

"I wonder what the occasion is?"

In her fairy tale retelling of this Cinderella moment, the fireworks would be just for them. If only she had a glass slipper to leave behind.

CHAPTER THIRTEEN

BEAR WAS LEANING against his car outside of the LC Club while he waited for Morgana to finish working. Their time together on the balcony had been wonderful but far too brief, and he hated watching her go back to work when he knew she was tired. She'd told him that Hal gave her a ride out to the LC Club and another waiter was giving her a ride back to the motel because he lived nearby. That had made him instantly jealous, which was ridiculous.

Very soon it would be time for him to leave Chatelaine. Back to his regular nomadic lifestyle, which suddenly felt tiresome and a little depressing. Moving from fancy hotels and rented condos was getting exhausting. After watching his family members setting down roots in homes that they owned, he knew he needed to start thinking about doing the same.

Along with finding an egg donor, buying a house was a necessary step that had to be completed by the time a surrogate was carrying his baby. The big question was, where in the world to settle?

The back door to the LC Club's kitchen opened and he straightened, hoping it was Morgana, but it was only two young women who laughed and talked as they walked to a little black car. Once again, he wondered who the guy was giving her a ride. Was it someone closer to her age who wasn't jaded like him? Another flash of jealousy hit him. "Dammit. What the hell is wrong with me?"

His tie suddenly seemed to be choking him. He yanked it loose and walked another lap around his car, the fine gravel crunching under his Gucci shoes. At the heart of it, they were from very different worlds.

He was glad he hadn't yet brought up the topic of being friends who get together for special benefits several times a year. The jealousy curling through him proved *he* was the one who couldn't handle an arrangement like that with Morgana.

For a little while longer they could enjoy the short amount of time they had left together. He'd talk to her about it tonight. They could take their time saying good-bye. Then that would be the end of it. They'd be left with great memories.

This time the feeling in the pit of his stomach wasn't the flashfire burn of jealousy. It was…panic. And it was totally unacceptable.

Being here was a mistake. He needed to leave, but right when he opened his car door, Morgana came out the back door with a tall blond who looked like he was the star quarterback type. The kind of guy who had no trouble with the girls.

"Bear." Her smile blossomed—for him. Not the other guy. "What are you still doing here?"

He went around and opened the passenger-side door and tried to get his heart rate under control. *Get it together, dude.* "We're going to the same place, and I thought I could give you a ride."

She turned to the young man beside her. "Thanks so much for the offer of a ride, but I've got it covered."

"Maybe another time," he said and looked bummed as he walked away.

Bear couldn't blame the guy.

"Thanks for waiting for me," she said and came close enough for a kiss.

He pressed his lips to hers and savored the moment of connection. His anxiety started to melt away and he felt control returning.

On the drive back to the motel, she told him about her conversations with Wendell before the party and how sad he'd been. Now, finding out what happened to Ariella's baby was on the list of mysteries to solve.

She adjusted her seat belt. "When I got to the LC Club tonight, I was almost certain all the clues plus the date of the party meant that Freya was really Gwenyth."

"Now you don't?"

"I spoke to her toward the end of the night. But right before, I watched her staring longingly at her wedding ring. And then she talked about missing Elias, and it was obviously she had loved him." Morgana's tone turned pensive "So, I don't see how she could be Gwenyth. My grandmother was so set on vengeance against the Fortune brothers that there is no way she would've fallen in love with and married one of them."

"What about the birth date?"

She sighed. "She dodged that question, as usual. Another loose end that I can't seem to tie up."

He swung his car into his usual spot at the motel. "Your room or mine?"

She smiled and nibbled on her full lower lip in the seductive way that she had learned drove him wild. "Mine. I want to take a quick shower after working all evening."

"You can take a shower in mine. *With me*," he said with a big grin and leaned across the console to kiss her.

"Do you have shampoo that smells like flowers?"

He chuckled. "Nope. I do not."

"Then I guess you'll just have to join me in my shower."

"I'd love to take you up on that offer, sweetheart."

They walked up to her room, hand in hand and started kissing the moment the door was closed behind them.

Tomorrow would be soon enough to talk to her about him leaving Chatelaine. Tonight was too special to tarnish with talk of their imminent goodbye.

MORGANA'S WHOLE BODY was taking flight. The evening that had started out so crummy had turned into the kind of beautiful night she'd remember forever. She loved it when Bear kissed the spot right below her ear and then went on a slow and gentle exploration that made her shiver from head to toe.

"Too many buttons," he muttered as he worked on the top one on her blouse.

She giggled. "You have just as many."

He grabbed the lapels of his shirt like he was going to rip it open and send buttons flying across the room.

"Barrington Fortune," she said with a gasp. "Don't you dare rip this beautiful pink shirt. It's my favorite."

He growled but then grinned and returned to working on her buttons. "Maybe you better tend to mine."

"Good idea." She took his suggestion and ran with it all the way down to his belt buckle. Their arms were tangled, and they were laughing so hard it took twice as long as it should have.

He finally shrugged off his shirt and tossed it on her desk. "You can keep my shirt."

They left a trail of clothes from the doorway to the small bathroom.

There was an extra level of tenderness in Bear's touch. More intensity in his kisses. Something about tonight felt different. A little more special.

BEFORE MORGANA HAD even opened her eyes the next morning, she was smiling. Bear's chest was warm against her back and his arm was stretched out along her leg with his fingers splayed on her thigh. It made her feel so...calm and cared for. Like everything would be okay.

They'd made love late into the night, but she was on such a high from their romantic evening that she was wide awake. It felt like they'd jumped a level in their relationship, and she'd almost told him she loved him, but caught herself just in time. It was way too soon for that. Especially knowing how skittish he was about relationships.

They might not be planning a future together, but would he still claim what they had wasn't a relationship? How could he deny it at this point?

His deep, even breaths told her he was still sleeping, but she had a few ideas about how to wake him up. First, savoring the present moment was most important. It was so nice to feel safe and protected and...in love.

Oh, God, I'm so in love with Bear Fortune.

But was Bear in love with her, or just really good at seduction? She'd swear that she felt something new in his touch. A stronger connection.

The time on the bedside clock caught her eye, and she remembered she had to start work early this morning.

Nooo. Why today?

All she wanted to do was lounge in bed like they'd done the day they watched the 1980s movie marathon, but she had a commitment. Sighing, she slipped out from under the covers without waking Bear, and hurried into the bathroom to get ready for work.

He woke when she leaned down to kiss him goodbye. "Where are you going?" he asked in a sleepy, gravelly voice.

"Unfortunately, I have to start work early this morning."

"What time is it?"

"Seven."

He grasped her hand and tugged her down to sit beside him and then rested his head on her thigh. "What do you have to do so early on a Sunday morning?"

"For one, the other maid, Rhonda, is out of town and it's just me today. You know that big group who is here for a family reunion? They paid extra for breakfast, and I have to get it set up in the lobby." The large group had taken up the eleven rooms that weren't occupied by her, Bear and Freya.

"You have to cook?"

"No. It's only pastries, fruit, yogurt and little quiches made in muffin tins. I just have to warm them." The tiny kitchen tucked away at the back of the lobby wasn't the easiest place to do anything, but it had been her idea to offer a breakfast option for an additional charge. At the moment, she was thoroughly annoyed with her entrepreneurial ideas.

"Hurry back so I can have you for breakfast." He hiked up the skirt of her uniform and kissed her knee.

Something about the action was so tender that it threatened to make her cry. She needed to get out of here before she told him that even though she'd said she wouldn't, she'd fallen head over heels in love with him.

"I plan to clean your room last so you can be my reward."

He sat up. "Good plan."

"I started my coffee pot for you and you're welcome to anything in the refrigerator." She kissed him once more and then went to find her shoes. "It will be a few hours before I get back. When the big group leaves, which will thankfully be earlier than usual, I have to clean their rooms for another group who is coming for some event at the lake and are due for an early check-in."

He sat up and the sheet pooled in his lap, and the muscles of his chest and arms flexed as he stretched. It was enough to make her want to quit her job and climb back into bed with him.

"I have work to do as well. I have to prepare for a ten o'clock meeting."

"Where do you have to go for it?"

"It's virtual," Bear told her. "I'll just be in my room on the computer."

"I'll make sure not to interrupt. See you in a while." She blew him a kiss from the doorway.

"See you soon, sweetheart."

A few steps away from her room, Morgana glanced around to see if there was anyone who could see her, but deciding she didn't care who witnessed her happiness, she danced all the way to the office. The feelings coursing through her were like nothing she'd ever experienced. She felt light and floaty like she might drift up into a castle in the sky, but at the same time, powerful and grounded in a way that made her feel connected to the universe.

The day was too good to ruin with any thoughts of the Freya drama. It could wait until tomorrow.

She hummed and sang quietly while prepping breakfast and then taking care of the guests. As soon as they finished eating and checked out, she got to work on their rooms. When she was on the last of their rooms, she looked at her watch. At Freya's request, she had a set schedule for cleaning her suite—mostly so the old woman could avoid her. If she went right now, she'd be early. She'd started the morning with the mindset of not wanting to think about the elderly woman, but now, she wanted it done and over with.

She would ask Freya outright if she was Gwenyth Wells

and if she still refused to answer, she would tell her she was Renee's daughter and see if that got a reaction. It had waited long enough. Whether she was or wasn't her long-lost grandmother, at least she'd know one way or the other. Then she could concentrate on a path to the future she hoped to have with Bear.

She knocked on Freya's door, waited and then knocked again, but there was no answer. She used her key, and like always, called out once more before stepping all the way into the suite.

It was quiet and dark, except for the glow of the screen saver on Freya's laptop.

Morgana flipped on the lights and kneeled to pet the orange cat who'd hopped off the bed to greet her. "Hello, Sunset. Have you been a good boy?"

The cat purred and arched into her hand for a back rub.

On today's cleaning schedule, Freya's room was not due for a deep cleaning, but it wouldn't hurt to take her time in hopes the woman would return. But not too long because she was eager to see Bear.

The first time she'd met him, he had told her he'd be leaving town when his business deal was done, and from what she'd heard him say on a few work-related phone calls, she had the impression he would only be here another week or so. She had to make the most of it.

It was wholly unwise, but she was holding out hope that in the time they had left, she could make Bear see that he didn't need a surrogate to have a baby. She wasn't like his ex-wife and would never tromp on his heart the way she had done with his best friend. That he could have love in his life again. *With her*. Because loving him and having his child had moved to the top of her list of hopes and dreams.

Morgana went into the bathroom to gather the towels, and when she came out, she once again noticed that Freya's laptop screen was up. She stepped forward and then back and then forward again, battling with herself about what to do. Curiosity won and she sat down at the desk. There was no way she could get lucky enough that it wasn't password protected, but it wouldn't hurt to check. With a deep breath—and a quick prayer to forgive her for this breach of privacy—she clicked a key. The screen came to life, with no need of a password.

She gasped because she hadn't expected it to work, and guilt hit her, but she couldn't take her eyes off the screen. It was open to an unsent draft email. It looked like Freya was writing a letter to someone. When Morgana saw the intended recipient, her heart skipped a beat and then took off racing.

CHAPTER FOURTEEN

MORGANA PRESSED A hand to her stomach and the other one over her mouth and stared at the letter on Freya's computer screen. It started with the words Darling E.

"Could E be Elias? What is going on?" Was Freya writing it as catharsis even though Elias was dead? She refocused on the letter.

Darling E,
When I fell in love with a man named George Jessup, things started to change in my life. It was your love that helped me set aside my vendetta against Edgar and Elias Fortune for what they did to my family.

A whoosh of goosebumps spread across every inch of her skin, and she squeezed her eyes closed and tried not to get her hopes up too high. Considering the number of people who died in the mine, it was highly possible someone else also wanted vengeance against the Fortune brothers. But what were the chances? She kept reading.

Then when you went to the hospital, imagine my shock when I discovered your true identity. I was furious and felt betrayed even though you knew me as Judy Jones, an alias I created when I started my search for the Fortune brothers. But at the time, I was too blinded by emotions. I'd fallen in love with and married one of the very men I'd been hunting for vengeance against my first husband, Clinton Wells.

"No freaking way! It's been true all along. Freya Fortune is my long-lost grandmother, Gwenyth Wells. I knew it." Morgana shot to her feet but immediately sat back down to keep reading, too curious about what else she might discover.

That's right, I'm the mine foreman's widow who unknowingly married Elias Fortune. Once I discovered your true identity, I came to Chatelaine to restart my efforts for revenge. I took your will that said you were leaving everything to your and Edgar's grandchildren, and I told them all that at your request, I'd grant each of them their most fervent wishes—only to destroy them.

"Haley was right. She's been behind all of it."

Now, I am so ashamed of myself and so sorry for what I did when I first arrived in town. I sabotaged their lives, but then everyone was surprised and so happy when they discovered West wasn't really dead. It was then that I knew for sure that I had to stop. I realized that I truly cared about all of the Fortune grandchildren.

It's terribly tragic that I didn't learn my lesson the first time. Because of my obsession with vengeance, I lost my own daughter, Renee, to estrangement when she was eighteen. I've looked for her over and over, but I've never been able to find her.

I'm so sorry that I lied to your grandchildren about your

death. I'm still holding out hope, my darling, that you will come out of the coma and be able to read this letter.

"Oh. My. God. Bear's grandfather, Elias Fortune, is still alive? This is huge news."

Freya's email was so emotional, and it was clear she truly loved Elias. When Morgana tasted salt on her lips, she realized she was crying.

The lock clicked, the door opened, and Freya froze in place. Morgana was still sitting at her computer, wiping tears from her eyes. It was pretty clear that she'd invaded this woman's privacy, read the email and knew everything.

"I… Oh my." Freya burst into tears and ran away.

Morgana jumped up, tripped over the cat but caught herself before completely going down. Once she'd righted herself, she ran out the door after her. She now had the proof that Freya was Gwenyth, and she needed to tell her that she was her granddaughter. Her car was still here, but no matter where she looked, there was no sign of the woman who had apparently gone by three different names at different times in her life. Gwenyth Wells, Judy Jones and Freya Fortune.

Morgana leaned forward with her hands on her knees. The spike of adrenaline was waning and making her nauseous. She abandoned her search and went upstairs to find Bear. She peeked through the crack in the curtains to see that he was not on his computer so she knocked and then opened the door.

He turned from the tiny closet, and the smile immediately fell from his face. "What happened? Why are you crying?"

She sat on his bed beside the suitcase he was unpacking from his recent trip. "Freya is really Gwenyth Wells. I have proof."

He kneeled in front of her and took her hands in his. "Did you talk to her? What did she say?

She shook her head. "She ran off before I could tell her that I'm her granddaughter."

He pushed the half-empty suitcase aside, sat beside her and pulled her onto his lap. "Start from the beginning and tell me everything."

"Freya... I mean Gwenyth, came in and saw me reading a letter she'd written." From the comfort of his arms, she told him her grandmother had sabotaged the very wishes she'd been granting, and also that she'd looked for her daughter, Renee.

"Wow. You hit the payload of information."

"I really did. I have to tell my mom about this, but I'd really like to talk to Gwenyth first, so I have some idea of what to tell her."

"I'm sure she'll be happy no matter how you say it, sweetheart."

"Bear, I haven't told you the part that is going to shock you the most. Your grandfather, Elias Fortune, is alive."

His eyes widened almost comically. "For real?"

"That's what the letter said. She hopes he will come out of his coma and be able to read her letter."

"We should go look for her." His jaw hardened and she felt his arms tense around her. "She has some explaining to do. We need to see if she'll come clean."

"Now that I've read what she wrote and she ran away in tears, I don't know how she can deny it."

They left his room and started their search. When they had no luck, he finally called Freya, and she answered.

"Hello, Bear." She sniffed as if she was crying.

"Freya, where are you?"

"I needed to take a walk."

He put the phone on speaker so she could hear. "I'm with Morgana, and we're looking for you."

"Oh. Oh my. I guess you know everything?"

"I doubt I know everything, but I do know we'd like to talk to you, please."

She sighed. "Okay. Can you please help me call all of the Fortunes together so I can tell everyone the truth all at once? I hate the thought of repeating it over and over, but I will if it's necessary."

"I don't think there's any reason for that," Bear said. "This is a lot to explain. I'll call everyone, set up a meeting for tonight and then get back to you with the place and time. You're not going to skip out on us, are you?"

"No. I'll be wherever you tell me to be. As of right now, I'm done with doing the wrong thing."

A FEW HOURS LATER, Bear's brothers, cousins, their families, and Wendell and Morgana were all gathered together at the Cowgirl Café. Since it was closed on Sunday nights, they had the place to themselves. Plus, the advantage of having drinks and snacks readily available.

He could tell Morgana was nervous, so he put an arm around her shoulders and gave her a light squeeze as the last couple of people took their seats.

"What's all this about?" West asked and grabbed a nacho from one of the plates in the center of the long stretch of tables they'd pushed together.

Freya stood from her chair at one end of the table. "I have some things I need to tell everyone. I need to confess."

"This should be good," someone mumbled, and then someone else shushed them.

"When I met your grandfather, Elias, he was using a different name. I knew him as George Jessup. And he knew me by my alias, Judy Jones. It was completely unexpected, but we fell in love and got married."

"Hold up," Haley said. "You got married without even knowing each other's real names?"

"I understand that it's hard to believe, but it's true. It wasn't until I saw his last will and testament that I realized I'd married Elias Fortune. The very man I'd been hunting."

"Hunting?" several voices asked in unison, and then everyone started talking at once.

Bear stood and held up his hands in the universal sign for everyone to quiet down. "Let her finish. You're all going to want to hear this. Trust me."

Freya wrung her hands and waited for everyone to settle and give her their attention. "I was so angry and hurt when I discovered the truth of who I'd married that I acted without giving it enough thought." She took a shuddering breath and scanned the group, meeting everyone's gazes as if she wanted each of them to know she was talking directly to them. "My shameful plan was to grant your dreams and then destroy them, but it all unraveled because I grew to care about all of you so much."

Bear glanced up and down the table at the stunned faces. Everything from the wide eyes and slack jaws you would expect to see, plus a few others like the salsa dripping off a chip that was halfway to Asa's mouth.

"I was the volunteer who saw a nurse switch the babies and that's why I gave Esme the DNA kit, so she'd find out fast."

Esme sucked in a quick breath, then hugged the baby boy in her arms and reached over to take the tiny hand of the baby on her husband's lap. The two babies born on the same stormy night who were not related but were now being raised as brothers. The one Esme had brought home from the hospital and fallen in love with and the one who was her biological son who was being raised by a widowed father. The man who was now her husband.

"Esme, I am more sorry than you'll ever know," Freya choked out. "I don't expect you to ever forgive me, but I am truly sorry for the pain I put you through. I wish with all of my heart that I could go back in time and make better choices."

Esme leaned against her husband, Ryder, and kissed the top of the baby's head who was sitting in his lap. "Complete forgiveness might take some time, but…if you hadn't done it, I wouldn't be married to a man I love dearly, and I wouldn't have two adorable sons to love."

Freya then went on to spill the rest of her transgressions. She admitted to Asa that she had exaggerated his sowing his wild oats so the owner of the ranch wouldn't sell to him unless he was married. Then she confessed to Bea that she'd caused the mishaps on opening night of Cowgirl Café. The very place they were sitting in that had thankfully become so popular. Freya also divulged she had originally created red tape for Camden's horse camp, but quickly undid that because she couldn't bear to keep children from doing something so special.

"When West returned from the dead, I found myself so happy for him and all of you that I stopped my shameful vendetta." Freya steepled her pointer fingers and pressed them momentarily to her lips. "And because I have grown to truly care about all of you so much over the months. I completely understand if none of you ever wants to see me again." She sat down as if every bit of her strength had left her in a rush.

Morgana pushed a glass of ice water her way. "Have a drink."

"Thank you, dear."

Everyone was oddly quiet as they processed the wealth of information they'd just been given.

"I forgive you," Wendell said. "I can identify with making poor decisions and wishing you could change things you've said and done."

Bear's cousin Asa put an arm around his wife, Lily. "You know, you actually granted more wishes than you think. If you hadn't done what you did, I wouldn't be married to this amazing woman. You led us to love, and I'm willing to forgive you."

"Thank you." Freya wiped a tear that slid down the soft skin of her papery cheek. "But you might want to hold that thought until I finish telling you everything."

"There's more?" Camden gritted out.

Bear and Morgana shared a knowing look, and she laced her fingers with his under the table.

Freya took one more sip of water, and then cleared her throat. "Elias is alive."

Now, no one was quiet. Everyone was talking at once and getting louder.

She held up her hands and tried to shush them.

"Let her talk. I want to hear this," Wendell said loudly enough that everyone immediately quieted.

"Elias is in a coma at a private hospice care facility on the Texas Gulf Coast. In Galveston."

There was another moment of stunned silence before Bear steered the conversation to the information Morgana most wanted to hear. "You've only gone by the name Freya since you came here?" he asked.

"Yes. That's right. I became Freya Fortune when I arrived in Chatelaine."

"No wonder you didn't always answer the first time someone called your name," Wendell said.

"What do we call you?" Bear's brother Camden asked. "Freya Fortune, Judy Jones or… What was the other one?"

"Gwenyth Wells," Morgana said.

The elderly woman pressed her fingertips to her lips as if to hold in emotions. "I haven't gone by the name Gwenyth in so many years. But I would like to be that person again. I liked her so much better than the bitter woman I've become."

Morgana squeezed Bear's hand and then stood. "Can I say something?"

"Why not," West said. "What else could there possibly be that would surprise any of us?"

Bear snorted. "With this family? Hold on to your cowboy hats, boys and girls." He winked at Morgana and mouthed, "You've got this, dancing queen."

CHAPTER FIFTEEN

BEAR'S SUPPORT MEANT so much to her and gave her that little extra bump of courage and calmness she needed to continue. "You all know me as Morgana Mills, but that's not my real name."

"*Another* secret identity?" Bea asked.

"My name is Morgana Wells." From the corner of her eye, she caught several confused expressions, but she focused on the woman she'd been seeking for months. "I'm the daughter of Renee Wells."

"Oh, my goodness. You're my granddaughter." Freya clasped her hands to her mouth, and once again, everyone was stunned by the news and talking at once.

Morgana put a hand on Freya's shoulder when she swayed in her chair. "It's okay. Take a breath."

Tears welled and began streaming down Freya's cheeks. With trembling hands on the table, she pushed herself to stand and pulled Morgana in close. "I'm so sorry, sweetie. I should have known. I've been so blinded by my need for revenge, and I've been so horrible."

Morgana hugged her back, and her own cheeks were wet and her heart full. "I found you. It'll be okay."

Bear stayed close to them while still giving them a moment of privacy, and everyone else was up and talking in whispers with animated movements.

Her grandmother put both hands on Morgana's cheeks. "How could I not know? My beautiful granddaughter."

"I guess I should've said something sooner. I just wanted to be sure."

"I'm so glad you came looking for me, and so sorry that I made it so hard for you. Looking back, now I understand why you were asking so many questions. I'm glad you didn't give up on this stubborn old woman." Freya pressed a hand to her chest. "Does your mother know you've been looking for me?"

"No. I didn't want to get her hopes up until I knew for sure." Morgana looked at her watch. "I'll call her tomorrow."

"Tell me everything. Where have you been all these years that I couldn't find you?"

"I grew up on a big communal farm in rural Tennessee. That's probably why you couldn't find us." Morgana caught Bear watching her from across the room and returned his smile.

Her grandmother followed her gaze. "You really like him, don't you?"

"I really do." Her stomach filled with butterflies.

Heaven help me, but I'm so in love with that man.

"Tell me more about growing up on a farm."

"It was a good life, but I did have to work hard." She smiled softly. "Now I know that's a good thing because I know the value of a hard day's work."

"Were you born in Tennessee?" Freya asked.

"I was. We have a doctor who lives on the farm, and I was born at home."

"Renee always was drawn to a simple life. I hope she's been happy."

"She has. She loves working in the orchard and with the animals." Morgana sat with her grandmother for a while longer and gave her a brief overview of the last twenty-five years in Tennessee.

Some of the Fortunes approached the two of them and told Freya that they would be happy to welcome her into the family—even though they'll be keeping a watchful eye. Freya said she couldn't blame them, and their welcome was more than she deserved. Esme and Bea asked to talk to Freya privately and offered to give her a ride back to the motel.

Before Freya left with them, she hugged her granddaughter one more time. "Can we spend time together soon?"

"I'd love that." Her cheeks were starting to ache from smiling. "I'll see you tomorrow."

"I'm looking forward to it, dear."

As she watched her walk away with Esme and Bea, Morgana began to think about the best way to reveal such big news to her mom. Should it be over the phone or video chat, or should she go home and tell her in person? No, it would take too long to travel back to Tennessee, and Freya… *Gwenyth* was too excited for it to take that long.

It was getting late, so they all moved outside and began to say their goodbyes. While Bear was talking to his brothers in the parking lot of Cowgirl Café, Morgana caught up to Wendell before he could get into his car.

"Wendell, do you have a second to talk?"

He stopped and turned to her. "Certainly. Do you have another juicy secret?"

"No, but I do have a thought I'd like to run by you." Over Wendell's shoulder, she caught sight of Bear hugging each of his brothers. "What if the two notes about the fifty-first miner have been left by Ariella's child? Maybe she discovered her identity and is searching like I've been doing."

He shook his head and rubbed the back of his neck. "That's a good thought but it's impossible."

"How can you be so sure?" Bear's arm slid around her waist, and she leaned into him.

"Because I know who it is. It was me," Wendell said.

Shocked to the core, Morgana put a hand on the elderly man's arm. "*You* left the notes? Why?"

"I did it hoping someone would investigate and find out what became of Ariella. I've been too afraid to delve into it, afraid to discover that my daughter perished in the mine instead of running off with the baby." His eyes welled with tears. "And now that I know that is exactly what happened, I want to find my granddaughter."

"I think that's a wonderful idea," she said.

"I should've said something inside while we were all gathered together, but there was so much else being revealed that I thought I should wait. Once things settle down a bit, I'll look for my granddaughter, just like you looked for your grandmother and found her."

"Why wait?" Bear said. "Now that we have more information, I think it's time to hire a private investigator."

"You know what? You're a smart young man." Wendell slapped Bear on the back good naturedly. "I'm going to go hire one right now."

The old man hugged Morgana and whispered, "Don't let time slip away like I did. Share what's in your heart."

As Wendell walked away, she reached for Bear's hand, and he laced their fingers. His touch sent comfort spiraling through her.

"It's been a big day," Bear said.

"It certainly has, and now I'm exhausted."

"Let's head back to the motel." He kissed the top of her head and they moved toward his car.

Bear had been clear from the start. He did not want a serious relationship. Never planned to marry again. And he wasn't interested in love. At least those were the words he'd said, but she had begun to suspect he was only trying to convince himself, because the way he was with her told a different story. One where there were feelings deeper than two people just hanging out like she'd originally suggested.

She gazed at him. Bear was the most romantic man she'd ever known. A delicious combination of masculine, thoughtful and tender. Was Wendell right? Should she tell Bear that she'd fallen in love with him? "How are you feeling about everything that happened today?" she asked him cautiously.

"Me? I'm fine. I never knew my grandfather but hearing that he's still alive is a good thing. It's you I'm concerned about."

"I'm good. Happy but emotionally exhausted."

"I bet. You've been busy. We know who Freya really is and all the other secrets because you kept after it and found the answers you were looking for. Do you need to call your mom in Tennessee and give her the news?"

"I do, but I'm so wound up right now that I need to calm down first and get my thoughts in order." She sighed. "You'd think by now I would've planned out exactly how to tell her I found her mother, but I'm not sure. I just want it to be perfect."

"Want to come back to my room and I'll give you a back rub to help you relax?"

She leaned into him. "That's an offer I can't resist."

But in truth, it was *him* she couldn't resist. Maybe Wendell was right. She should just go for it and tell Bear what was in her heart.

IN HIS ROOM, Bear sat on the end of the bed and pulled off his boots while she remained standing.

Morgana's decision to tell him what was in her heart

had given her a burst of energy. "I have one more thing to tell you."

"It couldn't be more surprising than some of the things we've learned today. Lay it on me, sweetheart." He stood and came over to her.

She put her arms around his neck and liked the way he cradled her hips and pulled her closer. "I know that relationships or any talk of love scares you."

"I don't think *scared* is the right word. It's more like caution."

"Cautious can be good, but… I guess it's all the coming clean and secrets being revealed that have given me the courage, so I'm going to go with it." She let her fingers trail up into his hair. "I'm in love with you."

He stiffened and dropped his arms. "Morgana—"

"Bear. Let me finish while I still have the courage. I want to have your baby, but not just to give our child to you and only be a part of their life. I want to be the mother of your child…and your wife. We can be a real family where everyone loves everyone." The expression on his face made her warm cozy feelings flash freeze into blocks of ice around her heart.

"Sweetheart." He shook his head and crossed the small room. "You don't understand. You're young and haven't been through what I have." He grabbed a stack of jeans from a drawer and then dropped them into the open suitcase.

The sudden chill increased to encompass the air in her lungs. Why was he putting things *into* his suitcase? Maybe he just wasn't thinking about what he was doing. "Are you packing or unpacking?"

"I'm packing."

"Another business trip so soon?"

He came back over to her and took both of her hands in his. "It's time for me to leave Chatelaine."

"And me." Her voice quivered and her whole body went painfully numb and empty. "For good? You're leaving because I love you?"

He closed his eyes and rested his forehead against hers. "You've always known my time here was temporary. You know I don't do serious relationships."

She pulled her hands free from his hold and turned to the window. That was so much crap! The man was lying to himself.

"I'm sorry, Morgana. This is exactly what I didn't want to happen. I never wanted you to get hurt."

"I understand." She didn't understand it at all, but she suddenly felt so defeated and empty. She knew there was nothing she could say to make him love her.

"I wish it could be different."

With her throat and eyes burning, she swallowed back the pain and tears and spun to face him. "Thank you for fixing my car and for…everything." She opened the door and stepped out. "Goodbye, Bear."

Fleeing from his room was difficult, but running from the heartbreak was going to be infinitely harder.

CHAPTER SIXTEEN

BEAR HAD BROKEN his own rule. He'd hurt Morgana, and it was torture.

He glanced in his rearview mirror long enough to see the Chatelaine Motel growing smaller and smaller until it was gone from view. His stomach was twisted in knots, his head throbbed, and his heart felt like it was being squeezed by a vise grip. He was leaving behind a part of himself, but there was no other choice.

If he turned around and went back to her and then truly lost Morgana at some point, it would crush him even more than it had when his marriage ended.

Where had he gone wrong? Had he not been clear enough when he told her about his rules and plans, or was Morgana just more naive than he'd thought?

The drive to Houston went by in a blur, and now Bear sat in the dark living room of his furnished rental condo with a glass of scotch in his hand and heaviness on his heart. The city skyline at night was impressive and made him think of watching fireworks with Morgana on the balcony at the lake. He wished he could share this view with her, because without her… It was unimpressive and only reminded him that there were people out there who were living their lives. Loving spouses and children and building homes to share with their families.

He tipped back his crystal glass and drained every last drop.

Bear knew he couldn't be what she needed. He was older and jaded and too broken for someone as sweet and as innocent as Morgana. She was young and full of big dreams and sparkling butterflies. At some point, one of them would end up broken. There was no reason to set yourself up for that kind of pain.

MORGANA HAD BEEN curled up in bed ever since Bear left the night before. She'd called and told Hal she was sick and couldn't work. It might not be true in the normal sense, but she was heartsick. Her stomach hurt, her head hurt, and she was humiliated and berating herself for being so foolish. He'd been clear about what he did and didn't want, and she should've listened. But still...

She had filled with a love like she'd never known only to be crushed under the weight of the walls around Bear's heart. He was apparently right about her being naive. She was embarrassed that she'd been so gullible.

Their ending hadn't been as tragic as him catching his wife with his best friend, but heartbreak was still so much more painful than she'd known it could be. Finally knowing what real romantic love was and losing it so rapidly was enough to give a girl whiplash.

Bear had taught her what it was to be in love with someone, and just as quickly, he'd taught her about heartache.

She'd been so wound up and excited after the family meeting that she'd put off calling her mom, and now she was too emotionally crushed for the big reveal. Her mom would instantly know there was something wrong, and it would ruin the big surprise she'd been working on for months. Morgana wanted the conversation to be nothing but joyful when she told her she'd found Gwenyth. And right now, she was anything but that.

A knock on her door startled Morgana, and she clutched the pillow closer to her chest.

Could it be Bear? Did he come back?

For a few more seconds she let herself hope that he'd returned to sweep her off her feet, but she knew her fairy tale was over, and she couldn't bring herself to move. Because if she crawled out from under the covers, she'd have to face the real world. She just couldn't. Not yet. She wanted to lose herself in sleep and not have to feel the searing ache of not having her love returned. Morgana didn't intend to let her pity party go on for long— she just needed a few more hours to lick her wounds.

The knock sounded again.

What if it really is him?

She threw back the covers and went to the door to make sure, but one glance through the peephole killed her hopes.

"Morgana, are you in there? It's Haley."

With her foolish hopes dashed, she opened her door and did her best to keep her lips from trembling.

Her friend studied her face. "Oh no. This won't do."

"What won't?"

"I was afraid of this," Haley said. "You've been crying. Can I come in?"

"Sure." She turned away but left the door wide open for the other woman to come inside.

Haley flipped on the light and then sat in the desk chair. "It's true? Bear left Chatelaine?"

"He's gone."

"It's not just another business trip?"

Her throat burned as she held back tears. "No. He's gone for good. He's moved on with his life, and I'm not in it." Morgana sat on her bed and then flopped onto her back to stare at the ceiling. "I fell in love, and he didn't."

Haley sighed. "I'm so sorry."

Morgana told the other woman everything that had happened between her and Bear. Well, *almost* everything. Some of the memories were precious and only for her.

"I've seen you two together and the way Bear looks at you…" Haley came over to sit beside her and reached down to give her shoulder a comforting squeeze. "The man loves you. I think he just can't admit it. Give it some time. His family lives here, and he'll be back to visit them."

Morgana shook her head. She knew that before this trip Bear had been out of touch with his family for months, and he'd likely do it again. "I'm not so sure about that. He's pretty set on not having any kind of serious relationship with a woman, and clear about what he wants out of life. A wife is not on his list, but having a husband *is* on mine."

"I'm glad you are smart enough to know yourself and what you want long term."

Emotionally exhausted from the conversation, Morgana abruptly changed the subject. "Have you found out anything more about the possibility of you having a fourth sibling?"

"Not yet, but though none of us can wrap our brain around the possibility, my sisters and I are still going to look into the rumor that we're actually quadruplets and have a brother," Haley said.

"Please let me know if I can help in any way."

There was another knock on her door, and she caught her breath again before she could stop herself. She had to stop torturing herself with false hope. Barrington Fortune wasn't coming back to her this time. She answered the door to see her grandmother.

Freya's bright smile turned into a frown. "Are you alright, honey?"

The way she said it reminded her so much of her mom, Renee, that she lost the small amount of control she had over the tremble in her lips and tears spilled from her eyes as Morgana motioned for her to come inside.

"I didn't realize you had company. Hi, Haley," Freya said.

Haley stood. "I'm going to get going and let you two talk. Morgana, call me. Anytime."

"I will. Thank you for coming to check on me."

When the door closed behind her friend, her grand-mother sat on the bed and patted the spot beside her. "Come tell me what's going on. Is your mom upset to hear that you found me?"

"No. I haven't called her yet. I'm so sorry. I know you're anxious but…" Her voice choked up as she took a seat.

"It's Bear, isn't it?"

She nodded with her lips pressed tightly. "It didn't work out."

She repeated some of the things she'd just told Haley, and they talked for a couple of hours.

Freya told her own stories of heartache and shared the hard-earned wisdom of where she went wrong and how she would do things differently if she could.

Getting advice was a bit of a comfort, and Morgana now had some perspective. "I think I'll take a shower, so I look presentable before I have a video chat with Mom."

"That's a good idea. I'll be in my room if you need me. And just like Haley said, you can call or come to me any-time. Day or night."

"Thanks, Grams."

The old woman's eyes lit up. "Oh, I like that name. I can't tell you how wonderful it is to hear it."

It was also nice to be able to say it. Morgana was feel-ing a little bit stronger and was once again excited to call her mom.

Morgana got in the shower and had one more cry about

Bear before washing her hair. Once she was dressed in her favorite sundress, she put on some makeup to conceal her dark circles and red-rimmed eyes. Then she got comfy on her bed and dialed her mom's number for a video call.

"Hello, honey. How is your adventure going?" Renee's big sun hat shaded her face as she walked through the pasture where the dairy cows grazed.

"It's going good." Small lie, but as far as their family went, it was nothing. "I have several things to tell you. First, I'm in Chatelaine, Texas."

Renee stopped walking. "Why? Are you just that curious about where I used to live?"

"I was definitely curious, but there's more. I found your mother," she said in a rush.

It took a lot to shock her supercalm and down-to-earth mom, but Morgana had done it. Renee Wells stood motionless with her mouth attempting to say words, but nothing was coming out. She took a few steps back then sucked in a startled breath.

Morgana caught a glimpse of her mom falling butt-first into the water trough before the phone sailed through the air to land with a view of the sky through the branches of her favorite climbing tree.

"Mom! Are you okay?" Morgana started to laugh and sprang up off the bed as if she could do anything from halfway across the country. But then her stomach plummeted when she heard what sounded like crying. "Mom," she yelled, not even knowing if she could hear her. Then the sound became very familiar laughter, and her tension eased.

Renee picked up the phone, her hat gone and her curly hair wet and clinging to her cheeks as they both continued laughing. "Well, that certainly cooled me off. I can't believe I fell in the water trough, but I thought you said you found my mother."

"Maybe you should sit back down, but this time not in the water."

Her mom leaned her back against the tree instead. "Are you trying to tell me that really is what you said? You found Gwenyth?"

"Yes. I found her. I met my grandmother, and she's been looking for you for years."

Renee wiped her cheeks, and this time it wasn't because of water from her unexpected dip in the cattle trough. "Really? I can't believe you found her. Is that what you've been doing this whole time?"

"Yes. Don't be mad."

"I'm not mad, honey."

"Thank goodness. It took me a while, and you won't believe all the twists and turns I ran into along the way."

She told her mom all the details of her search. The ups and the downs and all the unexpected secrets that were revealed along the way.

"I'm so glad you're willing to get together with your mother. Do you want to come here or for us to come home to Tennessee?"

"Maybe we should start with a phone call and see where it goes from there," Renee said softly.

"Sounds like a good plan, Mom." She smiled. "I'm going to give you her number so you can call her."

Once Morgana hung up the phone, she realized how hungry she was. In a little while she would go down to her grandmother's room, check up on how their conversation went and see if she wanted to go out for something to eat. Because if she continued to mope and crawl under the covers in her room, she'd cry herself to sleep all over again.

AFTER A LONG workout in the condo's fancy gym and then a shower, Bear pulled a T-shirt over his head and caught the lavender scent of the laundry soap Morgana used at the motel. He held the collar to his nose, inhaling as memories came at him hard and fast. Missing her wasn't going to be as simple to get over as he'd told himself it would. He tugged on a pair of jeans and felt a lump of fabric near his knee.

"What is that?" He shook his leg until whatever it was fell out the bottom and landed beside his foot. He bent to pick it up, and his throat tightened. It was one of Morgana's glass slipper socks.

It must have gotten mixed up with his stuff the last time she'd done his laundry, even though he'd always told her she didn't have to. He held it to his chest for a moment, then feeling silly about being so emotional, he folded it before putting it in a drawer with his own socks.

"This feeling really sucks," he mumbled as he went to the bar area of the condo. He'd told himself he wouldn't try to drown his sorrows with a drink, but that was a goal for tomorrow.

Ice clinked in the Swarovski crystal glass as Bear took a sip of scotch, the burn of it sliding down his throat, mimicking the way his heart felt. It was ridiculously expensive and his favorite, but it tasted like dirt in his mouth. He drained it in one quick gulp and then shuddered.

After forcing himself to do some work on his newest project, he realized it was the middle of the night, but he still couldn't sleep. He leaned back on the uncomfortable black leather sofa that was positioned to look out over the Houston skyline. The furnished condo his assistant had rented was a penthouse. It was modern, sleek, minimalist and quiet as a tomb. Bear had once craved this kind of order and solitude. But now?

There was no one singing or laughing or gently brushing his cheek. No kid's toys scattered about like they were at West's house. No love. He felt…empty. Completely empty. It was a physical pain in his chest. He missed his brothers and the twins and his whole extended family. But most of all, he missed Morgana. He missed her more than he'd ever missed anyone.

He grabbed the remote control and turned on the huge television that was mounted on one wall. An old episode of *The Golden Girls* was something he would normally never watch, but at the moment he didn't care. He just needed the droning noise of it to fill up some of the emptiness.

He would only be in Houston for a month while he tied up loose ends with his new business deal, so he really didn't need this large two-bedroom place. It seemed so over the top and unnecessary. He'd grown used to his cheap motel room, and he ached with every fiber of his being for the woman two doors down. A hollowness in the pit of his stomach left him feeling unsteady.

"Morgana, my dancing queen, what did you do to me?"

THE NEXT MORNING, Bear sat at the kitchen breakfast bar with a cup of strong coffee and scrolled through his email, scanning for anything that needed his immediate attention. He paused on one from 411 Me DNA.

"It's my DNA results. That sure was quick."

He opened the email and stared at the information. Along with 50 percent of his heritage coming from Mexico, there was also Italy, Wales, Scotland and Sweden. He also had DNA matches. None were parents or siblings, but he had lots of distant cousins, a couple of first cousins and one aunt.

As he stared at the information he'd been looking forward to, and at the same time dreading, he wasn't sure how to feel. There was an option to send a message to DNA matches, but he brushed it off. He had enough information.

And frankly, since he'd left Morgana, there wasn't much he cared about, including the new work project he'd normally be pumped to start. He'd lost his desire to take off for a foreign country, and he had no appetite.

He tossed his cold untouched toast into the garbage. This level of emotional response wasn't normal for him. "This has got to stop."

Bear poured a fresh cup of coffee and took a seat on one of the stools at the breakfast bar. With work pulled up on his laptop, he tried to fall into the rhythm that usually came so easily, but thoughts of Morgana and his family in Chatelaine kept flashing in his mind. He'd left town so abruptly that he hadn't even been able to say goodbye to everyone in person.

Two cups of coffee later, he changed his mind about contacting his birth family. For the first time ever, he knew for certain that he had blood relatives, and the curiosity was nagging at him. There was possibly someone with all the answers to a lifetime of questions. Mainly, why was he abandoned?

He closed the work document that he couldn't focus on and typed a message to his aunt. He told her he was adopted as a toddler and was curious about his birth family and asked her to contact him. Once he sent off the email, he went for a long run, hoping the physical exertion would exhaust him enough to be hungry and to get some sleep, so he wouldn't stress over whether his aunt would get back to him or not.

Fortunately, he didn't have to wait long. That evening, he received a phone call from an unknown number, but he answered right away.

"Hello. This is Barrington Fortune."

"Hi, Barrington. This is your aunt Rita."

His pulse picked up speed. "Thank you for getting back to me, and please, call me Bear."

"Bear. That is so fitting. I love it. I'm sure you have a ton of questions for me."

"I do." He walked to the huge windows overlooking the city. "First, what was my birth name?"

"Seth Sanchez."

Hearing his birth name for the first time was a surreal mixture of unknown and déjà vu. "Are my parents living?"

Her sigh was soft, but he heard it, and he knew the answer before she said it. "They both died many years ago. Your father, Carlos, in a construction accident shortly after you were born, and your mother, Silvia, died of cancer a few months after you went to live with the Fortunes."

His throat burned as he pressed the heel of one hand against his chest. "She knew she had cancer when she… left me in the park?"

"Yes. That's exactly why she did it. Her cancer was terminal, and she didn't know what else to do. We were very poor and lived with my grandmother who was seventy-five and not in the best health herself. I was only fourteen years old, and your mother was nineteen."

"Why didn't she contact the state or put me up for adoption?"

"Your mama and I were in the foster system for a little while before my grandmother took us in. We didn't have a good experience, and she didn't want that for you." There was a long pause. "I wanted to keep you *so badly*, but I was too young, and my grandmother was too old, and we had no other family. I was already grieving the sister I knew I would lose way too soon and letting you go was the hardest thing any of us ever did."

He heard her sniff in a way that suggested she was crying. "I imagine it felt like an impossible situation."

"It really was. We all loved you so very much. Giving you up broke our hearts more than you can imagine. When your mom discovered she had cancer, she couldn't see any other way. She was sick and desperate to find a better life for the son she adored."

He had imagined all kinds of scenarios for why he was abandoned, but this act of desperation hadn't been one of them. "Why did you say the name Bear was fitting for me?"

"Two of your favorite things were bears and digging in the dirt. On the day Mrs. Fortune found you, you were wearing a blue shirt with a cartoon bear on it and holding your favorite stuffed bear. It was also one of the words you knew how to say. Is that why they gave you your name?"

He shook his head. "I have no idea. I always thought it was because my little brothers had trouble saying Barrington, but I do remember having a black bear with a blue bow tie."

"That's the one. Your dad bought it for you."

He was pretty sure he still had it in a box somewhere in storage, but he didn't admit that to her. "How did my mother decide where to leave me?"

"We scouted around and found a park that was always filled with nice families. It was in a really nice area of town where rich people came with their kids. She put you in the sandbox, which was your favorite place to play. Because as I said, you loved to dig in the dirt as if you were searching for something."

"I still do. I'm in the oil business."

She laughed. It was a musical tone that made him smile. "That is also so fitting."

"I invented some drilling equipment."

"Oh, Bear. Your parents would be so proud of you. I know I am."

"Tell me more about the day she took me to the park," he rasped and sat on the edge of the sofa.

"We hid in a wooded area that bordered the park and watched to make sure nothing bad happened to you. Only a few minutes later, a mom with a toddler about your age came over to play in the sandbox. When she realized you were alone, she picked you up and held you, comforting you while she waited for the authorities. I was young, so I don't know all the details, but somehow, my sister found out where the other mom lived. Silvia was tiny and before she got too sick, she would dress as a young boy and walk our dog past the Fortune's house so she could make sure you were okay. Until she just didn't have the physical strength any longer."

Bear swallowed a lump in his throat. "I can see how that would be impossibly hard on her. Hard on all of you."

"It really was. Silvia made us swear to keep quiet and let you be adopted by a family who could give you so much more than we could. It broke all of our hearts," Rita confessed. "A few years after that, I almost ended up in foster care myself when my grandmother died, but I turned eighteen a month later. I went into the navy and then became a lawyer when I got out. I work with the foster care system, trying to make sure children don't fall through the cracks."

"That's wonderful. I'm sure…" It still felt so weird to call Silvia his mom. "Your sister would be proud of you for dedicating your life to such a worthy cause."

"Are you married or have any kids yourself?" she asked.

"No. It's just me." A flash of pain made him grimace, but he shoved it down in a way he'd become a pro at doing. "And you…?"

"I'm married with two daughters, and we live in Vermont."

It was all so achingly sad yet sweet, and he realized his cheeks were damp. He didn't even know when he'd started crying. "I really appreciate you telling me everything."

"Bear, never again think you weren't wanted. We all three cried an ocean of tears missing you."

"Will you tell me more about my parents?"

"Of course."

They talked for nearly an hour, and he found out all kinds of details about his parents, Carlos and Silvia Sanchez. They made plans to get together in person just as soon as he could get to Vermont. The second he hung up, he wanted to tell Morgana everything he'd learned about his origin. He might've been abandoned, but he was loved and wanted in a way he'd never imagined.

He ached to talk to his sweet dancing queen. To see her. To hold her. And it was 100 percent his fault that he couldn't.

CHAPTER SEVENTEEN

AT HIS FAMILY'S REQUEST, Bear drove an hour and a half from Houston to Galveston to meet Freya, Wendell, his brothers, and his three cousins, Asa, Esme and Bea. He was the first to arrive at the private hospice facility where Elias had been for months. It was a huge two-story home that had probably been built in the early 1900s and had been immaculately restored.

Even though he was in a coma, Freya wanted everyone to be there all together at least once. Bear wasn't fit company for anyone but hadn't been able to deny her. His brothers and Wendell were the next to arrive. He raised a hand in greeting and walked toward them as they got out of the car. He so badly wanted to ask about Morgana, but he bit down hard on the inside of his cheek instead.

"Are you doing alright?" West asked as he studied Bear's face.

He tried to harden his features to hide the vulnerability that had crept in. "I'm fine."

Camden snorted and shook his head. "Someone's a liar, and his britches are going to catch on fire."

"I have to agree with your brothers." Wendell squeezed Bear's shoulder in a grip that felt weaker than only days ago. "You look a bit worse for wear compared to how you did back home, young man."

The word *home* made Bear wince, and he knew they

saw it. "It's a small adjustment period. No big deal." But he was starting to seriously doubt his own words.

"Weren't you the one who gave me the advice not to let fear of getting burned again keep me from the woman I love?" Camden said.

Bear shrugged. "That's what I thought you needed to hear, not what I expected for myself."

Before they could once again call him a liar, a maroon SUV pulled up and the rest of the group piled out. This time, Bear worked even harder, forcing a mask of cheerfulness to fit his face. Thankfully, his cousins didn't know him as well as his brothers because his state of happiness didn't seem to be in question with them.

"Thanks for meeting us here today," Freya said, but her expression told him she wasn't happy with him, and it wasn't hard to figure out that it was because of the way he'd left. The way he'd broken her granddaughter's heart.

The eight of them went inside the house and crowded into Elias's private room. Other than the medical equipment around his bed, it looked nothing like a hospital. It had plush carpet, expensive furnishings and fine art on the walls.

Freya—who he'd have to start thinking of as Gwenyth—sat on the edge of her husband's bed, took his hand and kissed his forehead. "I'm here, my love. I brought your brother Wendell and yours and Edgar's six grandchildren."

Wendell sat in the plush armchair closest to the bed but didn't say anything. He looked as if he needed to get his emotions under control first.

Freya told them the sweet story of how they first met and then a funny one about when Elias tried to catch a raccoon that had gotten into the house. It put everyone more at ease with the situation and the atmosphere became more relaxed.

Wendell cleared his throat. "I've been waiting to have all of you together again so I can share the newest development. I'm sure you've all been told by now that I'm the one who wrote the notes about the fifty-first miner."

"So we would look for your daughter," Esme said with a nod.

"Yes." He told them some of what Bear already knew. "I always wondered what happened to my daughter Ariella, and now I know she died in the mine with her baby's father. For way too many years, I was too ashamed of my actions and how I treated her to reveal anything about her. But with all the secrets coming out lately and with the help from some of you, I've located her daughter. I—I have another granddaughter."

"Oh, that's wonderful." Bea said. Everyone else joined in with well wishes and questions.

Bear smiled. One he didn't have to fake. He was happy for his great-uncle because he finally had answers to questions he'd been holding on to for way too long.

Freya gasped, interrupting Wendell's story. "He squeezed my hand!"

They all moved closer as she kept talking to Elias and stroking his cheek. "Please wake up, darling. Everyone is here to see you, and I want so badly to talk to you."

Elias blinked his eyes and groaned. He tried to speak but coughed.

"I'll get a nurse," someone said from behind Bear.

Freya soothed her husband with tender touches. "Don't try to talk yet, my darling."

"Water," he croaked in a voice hoarse with long disuse.

Wendell was closest to the pitcher of water and poured a glass, and then Freya helped Elias take a small sip.

"Sweetheart," Elias whispered and lifted a trembling hand in an attempt to touch her face.

She took his hand in both of hers and lifted it to press his palm to her cheek. "I've missed you so much. I love you."

"Love you. Nice to see…" He struggled for a breath. "Your pretty face."

The door to the room opened. "Mr. Fortune, I'm so glad to see you're awake," a nurse said. "The doctor is on his way. Let me just get a blood pressure reading." She came around on the opposite side from Freya and started her assessment.

Elias looked around the room full of people and his eyes widened as if he'd only just realized they weren't alone.

"Some of your family has come to see you." Freya started introducing them one at a time. "And your brother Wendell is here, too."

Wendell stood from the chair and took Elias's hand. "Hello, little brother."

"I'm sorry." Elias's voice was still hoarse and gravelly. "So sorry, Wendell."

"Instead of dwelling on the past, let's focus on the future." Wendell swept out his arm to encompass the Fortune six. "Look at all these young people who are here to see you."

"Tell me," Elias coughed and struggled for a breath.

A doctor had come in midway through the introductions and was listening to his heart and lungs, but Elias tried to shoo the man away.

"Just let me do a quick check, Mr. Fortune," the doctor said. "Then you can visit with your family."

"Your lives. Tell me," Elias insisted weakly.

Not knowing what to say about his life, Bear hung back. Everyone talked about the person they loved, their kids, their ranches and homes. He was the only one without a significant other waiting at home. He squeezed his eyes closed and rubbed his forehead.

I'm also the only one without a permanent home.

His rented condo was empty, impersonal and too cold. But that's the way he'd said he wanted it to be. He'd made his bed, so to speak. When his turn finally came, he stuck to only telling his grandfather about his work in the oil industry.

"Black gold," Elias said with a weak grin.

"Let's give them some time alone," Esme suggested once they'd each told him about their lives.

Everyone other than Freya stepped out of the room to give her and Elias a chance to visit. All seven of them settled in a sitting area richly decorated with pricey antiques and artwork. Someone offered them coffee and a variety of homemade cookies. They were the first thing that had tasted good to him since leaving Chatelaine. Since leaving Morgana.

The group talked about West's twins and random other topics, and the whole time he was waiting for someone to mention Morgana, but no one did. The same nurse who'd taken Elias's blood pressure stepped into the room and relayed Freya's request for them to come back.

"I'm afraid it won't be long now," the nurse said softly.

They filed into his room, and Bear's stomach hardened into a knot.

Freya lay stretched out on the bed beside Elias with her hand on his chest. She was crying softly.

They all remained silent, and Wendell sat on the other side of the bed and covered his brother's hand with his own. The only sound was the beeping of medical equipment and a bird singing a mournful tune in a tree outside of the window.

Elias's eyes fluttered open, and he gave his wife a faint

smile and whispered something. A moment later, he closed his eyes. For the last time.

The soft beeps from a monitor marked that Elias's heartbeat had begun to slow. When it became a flat line, Bear inhaled a sharp breath that caught painfully in his throat. Just like that, in only a few heartbeats, Freya had lost her partner. There was nothing she could do to stop it from happening. The person she loved was lost to her.

This was one of the reasons he couldn't be with Morgana. He had no choice but to leave Chatelaine. He'd had to make her understand…he couldn't be what she needed.

But why had Freya willingly put herself in this position?

Because she got to be in love, said a voice in his head before he could stop it.

Several people were crying along with Freya, and while he knew they were all glad they'd been here at the end, Bear really needed to get out of here. Seeing Elias and Freya's love for one another and then so quickly watching death come between them was stirring up his own turbulent emotions.

After an appropriate amount of condolences and goodbyes, Bear was getting ready to head back to Houston when Freya followed him toward the front door and stopped him with a hand on his arm.

"Barrington, do you have a minute to talk before you go?"

His skin felt too tight, and he really wanted to get out of here and be alone to sort through his jumble of emotions, but he'd broken her granddaughter's heart, and she deserved to get her licks in.

"Sure. Let's sit over here." He led her to a tiny sitting area near the front door and they sat on the couch. "I'm glad you asked me to come here today, and I'm so sorry about your loss."

She squeezed his hand. "I think Elias woke up because all of you were here. He could hear us talking and laughing about memories. All of you being here gave him the strength of will to wake up for a little while. I'll always be grateful for this last bit of time with him."

"As you should. I'm glad you had a chance for a proper goodbye."

"Whether or not you want to hear it, I'm going to share some of my hard-earned wisdom."

There wasn't much doubt what this was about. Now that Freya knew Morgana was her granddaughter, she'd gone into maternal protection mode and was probably going to give him a scathing lecture about loving and leaving an innocent young woman. He mentally groaned. But he knew deep down he deserved whatever she had to dish out.

"I'm listening."

She took one shuddering inhale. "I've wasted so many years being miserable and seeking revenge when I should've been enjoying my life and my family. Way too many wasted years that I can never get back."

"I hear you, but I have too much baggage for someone as sweet as Morgana. I need to keep moving."

"You can't outrun your past, Barrington. Trust me on this one. I have years of experience. The heart is always going to be involved." She looked at him with a heartfelt, broken smile. "Don't do what I did. I've seen you and Morgana together. I know she loves you, and if you'll look in-side—" she put a hand on his chest, patting lightly over his heart "—I think you'll find that you love her, too."

He was suddenly too choked up to speak.

"Think about what I've said, please. Love is worth everything." Freya pulled a tissue from a box on the side table and then stood. "Be safe on your drive. I'll see you soon. I hope."

BEAR TURNED UP the music on the car stereo, but it couldn't drown out the thoughts buzzing like a swarm of bees in his head. What Freya said was true. He was always trying to outrun his past and not get too close to anyone and risk losing them.

But I lost Morgana anyway.

He groaned. "I've gone and fallen completely in love with her."

His feelings for Morgana were not the same as the love he'd felt for his wife, or rather, what he'd *thought* was love. With his dancing queen, it was somehow deeper. Stronger. More complex.

But what about her well-being? I've already hurt her.

Another thought struck him with a harsh slap. If he didn't think he was enough for Morgana, how was he supposed to be what a child needed? If he had a baby using a surrogate, he could hire a whole team of nannies and it wouldn't be enough. Why was he even considering bringing a child into the world who would never have a mother? Why would he want to subject his child to that?

Oh my God. I'm being such an ass. A pigheaded, selfish fool. He realized he was speeding and eased his foot off the accelerator.

"What the hell am I doing?" Bear said to the empty car. "Me leaving Chatelaine hasn't made anyone happier. I walked away from her because I'm scared. She was right. I'm afraid to open my heart."

By the time he got to Houston and stood in the middle of the condo, he knew he had to do something to fix his mistakes. No one was happy with the way things were. Least of all him.

"I love Morgana. I have to get to her and tell her."

Bear's whole body was practically vibrating with a combination of excitement and nerves as he threw clothes haphazardly into a suitcase, not caring what was getting wrinkled or if any of it even matched. Now that he'd made the decision to go after the woman he loved, he couldn't get there fast enough.

The last thing he did before leaving the condo, however, was grab one special item and stuff it into his front pocket.

BEAR PARKED IN his usual spot at the Chatelaine Motel and immediately saw Morgana standing beside one of the new housekeeping carts in front of the downstairs room on the far corner. He wanted to call out to her and have her wave enthusiastically or blow him a kiss. The rush of love for this woman made his heart beat so fast he was short of breath. She was so lost in thought that she hadn't seen him yet, and he watched her for a minute longer.

And he did not like what he saw.

She wasn't singing or dancing or even smiling. Her hands moved sluggishly as if it took all her effort to organize the mini bars of soap and bottles of shampoo.

I did that to her.

Disgust filled him. Hot shame and regret. He'd been the one who crushed her beautiful spirit. The one who made her pretty eyes glaze over with a faraway sadness that tore at him.

He quietly moved closer. "Hi, sweetheart."

She stiffened on a small intake of breath and briefly closed her eyes as if saying a prayer before looking up at him. "You're here."

"I am. Sorry it took me so long."

"What are you doing here?" She wrapped her arms around herself as if she was cold.

"I forgot something."

She clutched the star charm on her necklace. "I cleaned your room, and I didn't find anything of yours."

"Did you look in *your* room?"

Her eyes filled with hurt as she frowned. "You want your pink shirt back?"

"No." He held out a hand, but she didn't take it. "I'm not here for my shirt. I came back for *you*, sweetheart. I came back for the woman I've fallen head over heels in love with."

She took a step back, and his heart sank. What if it was too late? What if he'd blown his one and only chance? He had bared his truth, and the next move was out of his control. She might very well tell him to take a long hike across a short cliff. Bear had never been so scared.

But then an idea came to him, and he went with it before he overthought it.

MORGANA PRESSED A hand to her chest as if that could slow her hurtling heart rate. Bear Fortune was standing in front of her saying all the right words, and she wanted to fall into his arms, but now she was the one who had her guard up. He'd always said she didn't know heartache, but he'd been the one to teach her that lesson. The hard way.

She'd never seen him this unsure, and when he started backing away from her, she thought he was leaving, but he pulled out his phone. His fingers moved across the screen, and he held his phone above his head like a miniature boom box.

As the song "Dancing Queen" played from Bear's phone, she smiled for the first time and moved a few steps closer. Close enough to touch but she clasped her hands against her tumbling stomach. He was reenacting a movie scene with a modern twist, and it was so sweet and on-brand for the kindest guy she'd ever known.

"But, Bear, what about the risk to your heart?"

He put his phone in his shirt pocket and caressed her

cheek in the most tender move she'd ever seen from him. "My heart is yours, Morgana Wells. I love you, sweetheart. I started falling in love with you the moment I found you standing on my bed singing and dancing, but I was being too…"

"Cautious?"

"Scared. I'm not afraid to admit it anymore. Now, the only thing that frightens me is living the rest of my life without you. I want to sleep beside you every night. I want to make babies with you and build a life together wherever you want to settle down." This time when he held out his hand, she slid her fingers across his palm. "Will you give me another chance to show you how much you mean to me?"

The pressure that had felt like a physical weight on her heart began to lift. With a smile she led him into the empty motel room she'd just cleaned and closed the door behind them. "You want to build a real family together?"

"Yes. More than anything. Completely real in every way possible. A mom and a dad loving one another and sharing the duties of raising children. And I'm not trying to say that you need to have a baby right away. There's no timetable. I just want to start a life with you. Kissing you every morning and every night. Loving you."

She smiled and released the breath she'd been holding since the day he drove away. Morgana stepped into the comfort of his arms and wrapped hers around his neck. "I'd like that very much. I love you, Bear."

He drew her into a deep, achingly sweet kiss and then she buried her face in his neck, breathing in his scent. She wanted to stay this way forever and not risk this being a dream.

"I know it's only been a few days, but I've missed you so much, sweetheart."

"So have I." She tipped up her face to look at him. "But how are you going to kiss me every morning and night when you travel so much for work?"

"I'm glad you asked. I'm hoping you'll want to travel with me, and then when you're ready for children, we'll both stop traveling."

She jumped onto him and wrapped her legs around his waist, loving his strength and how he could hold her this way with no trouble. "That's something else I'd like very much."

"Then, in that case, you should give your notice to Hal. Your cleaning days are over, sweetheart. It's time you had some pampering and a real adventure." He gazed adoringly down at her. "I want to take you to see waterfalls in Brazil and pyramids in Egypt and beaches where you can wear your little red bikini. I'll take you wherever you want to go."

She slid a hand up the back of his neck and into his thick hair, her grin blooming into a smile so big that it made her cheeks ache. "So, you're offering me the world?"

"As much of it as I can give you." His kiss was soft, his tongue barely teasing her lips before easing back to smile at her.

"I can't wait for our first adventure."

He slid a hand low on her back and urged her closer. "Do you know where I want to go first?"

"To bed—I mean the beach?" She giggled and liked the sound of his answering deep laughter.

"I like the way you think. Both excellent options, and that first suggestion is one we should check off the list very soon."

"Agreed. But I'm curious, where is it that you want to go?"

"To a farm in Tennessee where you grew into the woman I love."

Her heart filled with so much love that she felt like she was floating. "You came here to sweep me off my feet, didn't you, Mr. Fortune?"

"Yes, ma'am. I sure did. And speaking of your feet…" He put her on the bed, dropped down to a knee and took one of her shoes off.

"What are you doing?" she asked with a giggle when he tickled the sole of her foot.

He pulled something from his pocket and slipped it onto her bare foot. When she realized it was her missing Cinderella sock, a lovely shimmer of tingles settled over her whole body. "Look at that. It's a perfect fit."

"Let the adventures begin, my love."

EPILOGUE

On a cloudy day when the sky itself seemed to know they were sad, the Fortune clan and family friends were gathered at Fortune Castle. Although Morgana's heart was filled to bursting with love, it was a sad day because one member of the family was no longer with them. She straightened the flower arrangements clustered around the eight-by-ten-inch photograph of Wendell.

They'd chosen one that wasn't a stuffy portrait in a suit but rather a candid shot of Wendell smiling at a family barbecue. It suited the loving man he'd become by the end of his life.

Bear slipped his arm around her waist and kissed her cheek. "How are you doing, sweetheart?"

She nestled against his side and breathed in his familiar scent. "I'm alright."

Morgana was so glad that she had talked to Wendell on the phone the day before he passed away peacefully with his granddaughter by his side.

Wendell had left a letter with his lawyer, asking his relatives to hold a celebration of life at his home, Fortune Castle, rather than a somber funeral in a church. He wanted it to be a celebration of Fortunes and of all that the word *Fortune* means.

Once all the guests had gone and it was only the family, they sat in one of the large rooms of Fortune Castle, sharing memories of the unique man who had been in their lives for way too short of a time.

"There's one more thing I want to tell everyone," Bear said. "I've set up a foundation that will make restitution to the families of the miners who were killed in the collapse."

"That's so generous. What a great idea," West's wife Tabitha said.

"We're also dedicating a plaque to my grandfather, mine foreman Clinton Wells," Morgana informed the family.

"That's such a wonderful gesture. I love it," her grand-mother said and held a hand to her heart. "Your grandfa-ther would be so proud of you."

"Tell us more about your last conversation on the phone with Wendell and what you've learned about his grand-daughter," Haley said. "Not everyone has heard the story yet…"

Morgana snuggled closer to Bear. "Wendell was finally reunited with his long-lost granddaughter, Wendy Wind-ham Fortune, and he died peacefully with her at his side. Wendell also decided to leave her Fortune Castle."

Everyone was full of rapid-fire questions. Where is Wendy from? Is she married? Does she have children? How did she feel about her grandfather?

Morgana briefly explained what little she knew. "I don't really know very much. Wendy has six adult children, three women and three men. Apparently, they have a com-plicated past and have decided to claim their family name of Fortune and move to Chatelaine."

"Wow. That's a lot of new family members," Camden remarked. "I'm so curious and can't wait to meet them."

"You'll get that chance sooner than you think," said Eliza, the real estate agent in the family who had mar-ried Max Fortune Maloney. "I heard that they bought a huge working cattle ranch in Chatelaine Hills on the far side of the lake."

Asa sat forward to put his drink on a coffee table. "That's a really wealthy area."

"And they'll be moving to town in only a few days," Morgana said.

Bear chuckled. "It's always a wild, unexpected ride with the Fortune family. I can't wait to see what happens next."

* * * * *

The Cowgirl Nanny
Jen Gilroy

MILLS & BOON

Jen Gilroy writes sweet romance and uplifting women's fiction—warm feel-good stories to bring readers' hearts home. A Romance Writers of America Golden Heart® Award finalist and short-listed for the Romantic Novelists' Association Joan Hessayon Award, she lives in small-town Ontario, Canada, with her husband, teenage daughter and floppy-eared rescue hound. She loves reading, ice cream, ballet and paddling her purple kayak. Visit her at jengilroy.com.

Visit the Author Profile page
at millsandboon.com.au

Dear Reader,

One of the reasons I enjoy writing a series is developing a setting and cast of characters through multiple books. *The Cowgirl Nanny* is the third book in my Montana Carters miniseries for Harlequin Heartwarming, following *Montana Reunion* and *A Family for the Rodeo Cowboy*.

Although each book also stands alone, many characters, human and animal, recur, as does the High Valley, Montana, setting and the Carter family's Tall Grass Ranch. I hope you feel at home among this welcoming community of family and friends.

In *The Cowgirl Nanny*, champion barrel racer Carrie Rizzo is taking a break from rodeo and gets a summer job as a nanny for widowed rancher Bryce Carter's two children. As much as Bryce and Carrie like each other, they can't risk their hearts on anything more. She's returning to rodeo and his late wife was the love of Bryce's life. However, friendship can turn to love and an unexpected new beginning might be just around the corner.

I enjoy hearing from readers, so please visit my website, jengilroy.com, and contact me there, where you'll also find my social media links and newsletter and blog sign-ups.

Happy reading!

Jen Gilroy

DEDICATION

For Joan, with love from "Jen up the hill."

Thank you for your friendship, wise counsel
and staunch support.

CHAPTER ONE

"WHOA THERE, BUDDY." Bryce Carter grabbed the black-and-white goat by its collar. "Where do you think you're going?"

The goat stared at him with a yellow petunia plant half out of its mouth. It bleated and looked back over its shoulder at a miniature red barn by the entrance to Squirrel Tail Ranch's activity center.

"There's always something more interesting on the other side of the fence, isn't there?" Bryce scratched the goat's neck as children's laughter echoed from behind the barn. He shook his head at the trampled flower bed and picked up the rope trailing from the goat's purple collar. "Folks will be looking for both of us." In Bryce's case, those "folks" were his two children—the most important people in his world—and he'd promised them he'd be here half an hour ago.

Leading the goat, Bryce stopped by the red barn and scanned the busy scene. A young woman, likely a college student, drove a tractor pulling a wagon piled with hay and excited children. The principal, who'd been Bryce's fifth-grade teacher at the same school his kids now attended, waved.

"Daddy." Eight-year-old Paisley ran toward him, two blond pigtails bobbing. "When you weren't here when you said you'd be, Cam was scared something bad happened. I said I bet you were rounding up that mean old bull."

She wrapped her arms around his waist while her six-year-old brother, Cam, who'd trailed behind, hung on to Bryce's arm.

"It wasn't the bull, and Big Red's not so bad." Not since Bryce's brother, Cole, had taken the animal in hand. "I was checking crops in the far fields, and the truck had a flat tire. I had to stop and change it." He gestured to his mud-spattered jeans. "Sorry I'm late. I couldn't call because I didn't have cell service. I hope I didn't miss too much." He'd wanted to get here early so he could share the last part of this field trip with the kids, but, once again, life had conspired against him.

"It's okay. Everyone's still here," Paisley said. "Where'd you get that goat?"

"He was in the flower bed near the guest welcome area. He must have gotten out of the petting zoo."

Except for the surrounding fields, rented out to grow grain and other cereal crops, Squirrel Tail was more a re-sort and tourist attraction than a working ranch. Owned by Shane Gallagher, a friend of Bryce's mom who'd moved to Montana from Wyoming a few years ago, Squirrel Tail now hosted events. Besides school field trips like this one, they also held birthday parties and company team building events and offered luxury bed-and-breakfast accommodations and meditation and wellness retreats.

"We went on a nature walk and learned how to build a rabbit hutch. Wanna come see?" Paisley asked.

"Sure." His daughter still hugged him, and Bryce inhaled her sweet little-girl scent. With her blonde hair and pale blue eyes, she didn't look like her mom, but with her outgoing personality, kindness and love of animals, Paisley was like Alison, Bryce's late wife, in other ways. Cam, though, had inherited Ally's bright blue eyes and chocolate-brown hair. He looked so much like the girl Bryce had fallen in love with when her family had moved to town because of her dad's job, and she'd joined his sixth-grade class.

Bryce grabbed his cowboy hat as it caught in a gust of wind and bent to his son's level. "You okay?"

"Yeah." Cam stared at the ground and dug his sneakers into the dirt. "Mr. Gallagher said I'm good with horses."

"You're a natural like your uncle Cole." Bryce ruffled Cam's hair. His son needed a haircut. Something else for Bryce to add to this weekend's to-do list.

As a group of boys around Cam's age raced past, Cam moved nearer to him.

"Has anyone seen a…?" A thirtysomething woman with light brown hair in a high ponytail stopped by Bryce and the kids. "Here you are, Sammy. You're an escape artist, aren't you?" She grinned and glanced at them.

Paisley giggled again. "My daddy caught the goat."

"Thanks." The woman brushed her hands against her faded blue jeans. "It wouldn't be good to lose one of the owner's animals my first time here. You must be Paisley and Cam's dad."

"Yeah, I'm Bryce Carter." He took off his hat and held out his hand. She wasn't one of the regular teachers or classroom assistants. He knew all of them well because he'd either gone to school with them, or they'd been working here when he was a student. He hadn't seen her around Squirrel Tail Ranch before either.

"Carrie Rizzo." When she shook Bryce's hand, his palm tingled as it met the warmth of her strong grip. "Shane Gallagher needed extra help with today's school visit. My aunt and her friend volunteered and brought me along. I've only been in High Valley a few days. I'm here on vacation."

"Welcome." Bryce stuck out his hand to Carrie again before realizing they'd already exchanged handshakes.

He was flustered because of the flat tire and being late. It had nothing to do with that unexpected spark of awareness when he'd held her hand in his.

"Can we help you put Sammy back in the pen?" Paisley hopped between Bryce and Carrie. "The rabbit hutch is near there."

"If it's okay with your dad, sure." Carrie glanced at Bryce.

"Please, Daddy?" Cam still clutched Bryce's arm, but there was more enthusiasm in his voice than Bryce had heard for weeks. "I can show you my favorite bunny. He's called Buster. Mr. Gallagher let me feed him."

"That'd be great." Bryce swallowed the lump in his throat. Between work and trying to keep day-to-day life on track, he didn't have much time for fun with the kids. He fell into step with Carrie as Paisley and Cam went ahead. "Who's your aunt?"

"Angela Moretti. She's my mom's oldest sister." As Carrie took Sammy's rope from Bryce, her fingers brushed his, and there was that tingle again.

"Mrs. Moretti's a family friend, but I don't remember you ever visiting High Valley."

"I didn't. Mom and Aunt Angela had a big argument when they were younger and didn't speak for years. They finally reconciled last Christmas." Carrie shook her head. "I'm sorry I didn't get to know Angela sooner. I'm also sorry I won't be here longer. High Valley's a great town and everyone's so kind and welcoming."

Bryce nodded. He'd had a lot of kindness from folks in High Valley since Ally died, but he needed to get better organized instead of depending on everyone's good nature.

"Paisley and Cam are wonderful kids. They were both in my small group today. Paisley's really caring toward her brother. You must be proud." Carrie's smile blossomed.

She had a great smile, like Ally, but it was different than his wife's. And while Ally had been tall and slender, with eyes as blue as the mountain cornflowers that grew wild here from late spring through early summer, Carrie was shorter with a more athletic build. She also had green eyes that sparkled and a dusting of freckles across the bridge of her nose.

Bryce stopped himself. He couldn't keep comparing every woman he met to Alison. Ally was gone, and she wasn't coming back, no matter how much he wished she could. "I sure am proud of Paisley and Cam. They're friends as well as brother and sister and look out for each other. I also try to do my best for them."

"It shows," Carrie said. "In our art session, they used poster paint to make handprints. Paisley said they do them around this time every year and stick them in an album. That's a fantastic idea. A special memory too."

"My wife started that album when the kids were babies." In the past few years, Bryce's mom had added items, but whenever she'd ask him to take a look, he'd find something else to do. The album, along with everything else Ally had made for him and the kids, hurt too much, so he'd packed those reminders away. Now they lurked in boxes stacked in a closet, like ghosts of the life he'd lost. And the album was on a shelf in the guest bedroom where he wasn't likely to see it.

"Look, Daddy." Paisley called. "Sammy must have gotten out here." She pointed to part of the fence where wire had come loose. One of Shane's ranch hands was fixing it, with help from a girl who handed him tools from a red metal box.

A small group of parents and kids patted the other goats, and Angela Moretti and several members of the Sunflower Sisterhood, a local women's group Bryce's mom belonged to, chatted nearby. The penned goats bleated at Sammy, who bleated back, and two horses in a nearby pasture joined the animal chorus.

"The bunny hutch is over here." Cam tugged on Bryce's arm as Paisley held a paper cone with special animal food pellets in front of Sammy to help lure him into the pen.

"Ms. Rizzo has to go home next week, but I want her to stay here longer." Paisley's expression was hopeful. "I also know a way she could. She could look after Cam and me for the summer. Since Grandma can only babysit us on Saturdays, you still hafta find someone else, don't you? I heard you tell Uncle Cole when he came over last night."

"Yes, but…" Bryce hesitated.

"Please?" Cam joined in with unexpected enthusiasm. "Ms. Rizzo said she'd love to see me play soccer."

"I'm sure your dad already has someone in mind." As she closed the pen's gate behind Sammy, Carrie's cheeks pinkened.

"Ms. Rizzo's on vacation. She wouldn't want a job as a summer nanny." Bryce spoke at the same time as Carrie.

"Why not?" Paisley tugged Bryce's right hand while Cam did the same on his left. "Ms. Rizzo said she's looking for a summer job to keep her horse in feed. You don't want Teddy to starve, do you?" Paisley and Cam gave Bryce matching disapproving expressions.

"Job or no job, Teddy will be fine," Carrie reassured the children.

"Paisley's right," Bryce said. "I *am* looking for a summer nanny, but so far, I haven't had any luck. I'd prefer an adult rather than a high-school student."

"Carrie's wonderful with children," Angela said as she and her friend, Nina Shevchenko, joined them near the fence.

Nina nodded. "She's a natural, all right. Kind but firm."

"Your mom says you need help." Angela chimed in again, and everyone nearby murmured agreement.

"If I can find a stable to board my horse, I'd be interested in the job, sure. Teddy's here at Squirrel Tail, now but that's temporary." Carrie knelt to tighten the fastening on one of Cam's sneakers.

"She could board Teddy at our ranch, couldn't she?" Paisley continued tugging Bryce's hand. "Ms. Rizzo's a professional barrel racer. If she looks after me and Cam, she could give me barrel racing lessons too. What do you say?"

"Hang on." Bryce took a deep breath. He'd come to pick up his kids, not look for summer childcare, but as his mom often said, "The Lord moves in mysterious ways." With only a few days of school left, hiring Carrie might be the perfect solution to one of the problems keeping him awake at night.

"Between kids, women and goats, you're outnumbered." Shane Gallagher came out of a shed behind the petting zoo. "Oh no you don't." He grabbed Sammy's collar as the goat tried to escape again.

"If you're free tomorrow, why don't you come out to our ranch?" In the midst of the chaos, Bryce spoke to Carrie in an undertone. "I can tell you more about what the kids and I need. Although Paisley got ahead of herself, we've had a cancellation, and there's a horse boarding space free in our barn. I can hold it if you want."

"That'd be great. Anytime tomorrow would work for me." Carrie's face was still flushed.

"How about eight thirty in the morning? Cam has soccer practice later, and Paisley has gymnastics."

"That's fine." Carrie's green gaze met his. "You've got a lot on your plate."

Somebody told her about Alison. Bryce's breath stuttered. He wouldn't have to explain what was still inexplicable. And when Carrie smiled again—a smile filled with understanding and compassion—it was like the sun slipping out from behind dark clouds.

"See you tomorrow. I'll get directions to your place from Aunt Angela." Carrie gestured to Cam, who, the rabbit hutch and Buster forgotten, leaned against her with his eyes half-closed. "Cam's almost asleep on his feet. You probably want to head home."

"Yeah." Bryce took a step back. For a few seconds, it was like he'd had a connection with Carrie that went beyond the kids. A connection like he'd only ever experienced with one other woman, his wife.

Except, he'd loved once and well. His focus was on his children and the family ranch. The romantic part of his life was over.

THE NEXT MORNING, Carrie took in the view through one of the floor-to-ceiling windows in Bryce's house. Set back from the main road via a tree-lined driveway, the one-story ranch style had an open-concept floor plan with the eating area and kitchen connected to this spacious family room. The window overlooked a pasture, encircled by a split-rail fence, where several horses grazed. Near a water trough, a cute foal nuzzled its mother.

"Take a seat." Bryce came through from the kitchen holding a tray with two mugs and a plate of cookies. He nodded toward a duck-egg blue L-shaped sectional sofa along one wall. "I tidied up last night after the kids went to bed. The place isn't usually this neat." He set the tray on the table facing the sofa and offered Carrie a mug of coffee.

"You didn't have to clean up for me. Homes are meant to be lived in." Apart from a basket of children's books and Paisley's and Cam's backpacks beside a big fireplace, the room was almost too tidy, with none of the scattered toys and games she'd expected. From what she'd seen of Bryce's house so far, from porch planters empty of flowers to this room with the furniture at precise angles, it had an air of sadness as if part of its soul was missing.

"There's lived-in, and there's chaos. We're more the latter." Bryce gave her a wry smile and sat on the other end of the sofa beneath a big TV. In jeans and a white T-shirt, he looked younger than his midthirties. Although Carrie hadn't fished for information, Aunt Angela had told her about Bryce as well as the rest of the Carter family.

Carrie tried to look more confident than she felt. "Where are Paisley and Cam?" The house was silent, and country sounds—cattle lowing, a whir of insects and birdsong—filtered through the half-open windows.

"At my mom's. We've got a big spread here at the Tall Grass. Mom lives at the main ranch house farther along the driveway. She's on her own there except when my sister, Molly, visits from Atlanta. My oldest brother, Zach, and his family live a few miles away in a house our great-grandparents had before they built the main place. Mom needed the kids to come by for a fitting of the outfits she's making them for my brother Cole's wedding."

"Paisley's excited about being a flower girl. She told me about it yesterday." Carrie sipped her coffee. Aunt Angela had mentioned Cole Carter's wedding. Between contributing food, organizing flowers and making decorations for the church and reception hall, the women of the Sunflower Sisterhood were all involved in wedding preparations.

"That wedding is Paisley's favorite topic of conversation. Cole's fiancée and her daughter live in town. With wedding planning in full swing, their house is Paisley's favorite place to be. Cole's moving there after the wedding, but for now he's bunking in one of the ranch's outlying cabins. I joke there are days I'm tempted to join him for some peace." Bryce laughed and set his mug back on the table. "So, about the nannying job." His manner became all business. "I should tell you—"

"It's fine." Carrie set her coffee aside too. "Paisley put you on the spot. I have a lead on a summer job at the Bluebunch Café, and there's bound to be casual work in haying season. I left my contact details at the Squirrel Tail Ranch too. They hire extra staff for special events. I also have a freelance web design and marketing business."

As she moved to stand, Bryce shook his head. "Wait. If you want the nanny job, it's yours. My kids like you, and from what I saw yesterday, you're great with them, but Cam especially..." He rested his beard-stubbled chin in his hands. His short brown hair was damp, as if he'd just had a shower, and an errant curly lock flopped over one of his eyes making him look both rakish and vulnerable.

"What about Cam?" Carrie settled on the sofa again and made herself focus on the children instead of her urge to brush that piece of hair away from Bryce's forehead.

"He's always been a quiet kid, but he used to be a happy one too. The past few months, he hasn't been himself. He's either lashing out in anger or withdrawn. He hardly plays with his favorite toys, and apart from soccer, he isn't interested in the sports or activities he once enjoyed. I talked to the pediatrician and took Cam to see a few counsellors, but none of them have been able to reach him. I don't know what else to do." Bryce looked at his bare feet. "Cam's having trouble at school as well."

"When Cam was assigned to my group yesterday, his teacher asked me to keep an extra close eye on him." Between school staff and a parent volunteer, Carrie had heard lots about Cameron Carter. While he'd been fine with her for the field-trip activities, the word was he spent more time in the principal's office than with his class.

Bryce rubbed one hand across his eyes then looked up at her again. "Yesterday, when Cam was with you, I saw the boy he used to be." He drew in a breath. "My son needs help, and maybe you can help him."

"I'll try." Carrie was one of life's helpers and a giver too, but there was a fine line between giving and people pleasing. Often, she tried to make others happy at the expense of herself. "I heard about your wife. I'm sorry."

"Ally passed three years ago. She had cancer. It should get easier but…" His shoulders slumped. "Cam hardly remembers his mom, and even Paisley has forgotten a lot about her."

"Do you talk about Ally with them?" Having been close to her grandmother who'd died ten years before, when Carrie was in her early twenties, she knew how important it was to keep a loved one's memory alive.

"Not really. It's hard for me too." He shoved that lock of hair away as if daring it to fall forward again. Bryce had a square, serious face with deep-set blue-gray eyes, and Carrie got the impression he didn't smile or laugh often.

She took another mouthful of rich, full-bodied coffee and let it linger on her tongue. She'd half accepted the job without knowing anything about it. That was unlike her, but she was desperate and didn't want to have to dip into her savings. She didn't have new freelance projects lined up, and casual part-time jobs wouldn't pay enough for her to board Teddy. She also didn't want to return to Kalispell and rely on her parents or cross paths with the ex who'd dumped her for a woman she'd thought was a friend.

Although hurt pinched her heart, she straightened, determined to leave the past where it belonged. "What kind of nanny are you looking for? Live-in or daily?"

"Daily to start, but live-in if needed. Monday to Friday mostly but likely some weekends too. Meal preparation, grocery shopping and laundry if you have time."

"That sounds fine." The pressure in Carrie's chest eased. "I'm flexible. Aunt Angela's happy for me to stay with her, or I can live here when you need me to."

Bryce exhaled as if in relief. "Ranching isn't a nine-to-five or Monday-to-Friday job, and things come up unexpectedly. I'm also a volunteer firefighter and do agricultural consultancy. I might need you to work extra hours at short notice." His expression was almost pleading.

"I understand. Although I grew up in Kalispell, my mom's parents had a ranch, where I spent vacations. I can work whatever hours you need. Except for training with my horse, I don't have anything else planned this summer."

And she'd love to stay in High Valley. It would be a chance to prove to herself and everyone else, her parents especially, that her barrel racing career was only on pause. She needed to stop trying to please her folks and follow her own path instead of the one they wanted for her. For far too long, she'd let her parents assume barrel racing and freelance work were temporary. Unless she stood up to them, she'd be in that office in the family construction company before she knew it, wearing a suit and working a desk job. She suppressed a shudder.

"Paisley said you're a professional barrel racer." Bryce's voice broke into Carrie's thoughts.

"Yes." Her stomach quivered at the warmth and interest in his expression. "I had a few minor injuries and need to take time out, but I'm returning to the circuit this fall." Everybody had setbacks. How you handled them was what mattered. This summer was her time to reset, regain her mojo and come back even stronger. "I also went to college and studied business and marketing. That's where my freelance web design and marketing work comes in." It gave her another source of income and added to the money she was saving to buy a small farm or ranch of her own. Once she had it, she wanted to practice sustainable agriculture like she'd learned from her grandparents.

"Paisley's only eight, but she's already set on pro-level barrel racing." Bryce shrugged. "Before he retired with an injury, Cole was a professional rodeo cowboy. My dad rode on the circuit too, so rodeo's in Paisley's blood. I don't want to discourage her from setting a goal and going after it, but I want her to be realistic too. Cole had to sacrifice a lot to make that life work."

"It's tricky, and you have to want it, but I love it. Paisley might change her mind, though."

"Perhaps, but she's a determined girl." Bryce's expression was tight. "Having you around for the next few months will be great for her as well as Cam."

"I'm happy to help all of you." This job would help Carrie too.

"I forgot to mention we have two dogs, and there's always barn cats running around. Are you okay with pets?"

"Love them." Her ex didn't like cats or dogs. In retrospect, it was one of many signs they weren't right for each other.

"Great. Have a cookie?" He passed her the plate. "They're chocolate chip. My mom made them. Some say she's the best baker in High Valley."

As Carrie took the plate, Bryce's hand brushed against hers, and she drew in a sharp breath. There it was, that same spark of attraction she'd felt yesterday. "I'll have a cookie to go." A door slammed, a dog barked and Paisley's voice echoed from the rear of the house. "With soccer and gymnastics, you have a busy day."

"I do, but..." Bryce hesitated as the kids raced into the

family room with their arms open for hugs. "We haven't talked about a start date, but is there any way it could be today? We haven't talked about money either, but I'll pay you more than the going rate. As I mentioned, I'll include horse boarding too. For free, if I didn't make that clear."

"Please say yes, Ms. Rizzo." After hugging his dad, Cam moved to sit beside Carrie.

"Today's fine. I'll let Aunt Angela know." Joy mixed with excitement shot through Carrie at the thought of the money she'd be able to save this summer, but she didn't want to take advantage of Bryce's generosity either. "I appreciate the horse boarding, but you should charge me. Giving it to me for free is too much."

"No, it's not. You're a lifesaver. Horse boarding's the least I can do."

As Bryce's gentle smile wrapped around Carrie like a warm hug, it also reminded her of what she couldn't let herself forget.

Despite that spark of attraction to Bryce, as his kids' nanny, he was her boss. He was also a grieving widower devoted to his late wife. Even if Carrie were ready to date again—which she wasn't—he was off-limits.

The setbacks that had knocked her life off course had made her think about what she truly wanted. From now on, she wouldn't let anything or anyone—especially a man—distract her from her goals. She'd learned that lesson well, and the betrayal still stung.

CHAPTER TWO

"GOOD JOB." In the fenced pasture behind his house, Bryce balanced the bucket as Cam tipped the last bit of water into a horse trough. He raised his hand for a high five, and his son's small palm connected with his. "Get your backpack, and I'll walk you to the end of the lane. You don't want to miss the bus on your last day of school."

"Why can't I stay home with you and Carrie? It's not like we'll do anything important today anyway." Cam's smile disappeared as he took his backpack from where he'd left it outside the fence.

Bryce patted Cam's hunched shoulders. "School's like a job. You have to show up even if you don't feel like it. Besides, you get off early today, and Carrie's picking you and Paisley up to go swimming. Aren't you excited about that?"

"Nope. I don't wanna go to school *or* swimming." Cam dragged his feet in the gravel driveway as Carrie and Paisley came out the front door with Penny and Otis, their beagle-mix dogs. "I feel sick." He sniffed and gave a hollow cough. "I guess I hafta stay home."

"Oh no, you don't." Bryce ruffled Cam's thick hair. He'd forgotten about that haircut. He'd have to ask Carrie if she could take Cam later this week. After only a few days, Carrie had made a big and positive difference in all their lives. Bryce didn't feel like he was always rushing, and today he'd even eaten breakfast at the table with the kids instead of grabbing something to take to the fields.

"What's with the sad face, kiddo?" Carrie joined Bryce and Cam, and the boy wrapped an arm around her waist. "Don't you like school?"

Cam shook his head.

"You only have one more bus ride and a half day." Carrie's voice was encouraging. "I've got a surprise for you and Paisley this afternoon too."

"What?" Cam finally raised his head.

"It wouldn't be a surprise if I told you, would it?" Carrie laughed and tugged Paisley's ponytail. "Race you to the end of the lane? First one to touch the mailbox wins. Ready, set, go!" She took off, and the kids and dogs followed. "You too, Bryce." She gestured over her shoulder. In the morning sun, Carrie's hair gleamed with golden tints, and her ponytail had a pink ribbon like Paisley's.

Bryce froze and then broke into a jog. Although Paisley and Cam might not remember, he and Ally used to run to the end of the lane with them when Paisley caught the school bus too.

"Go, Cam. We can't keep up with you." Carrie bent and said something to Paisley, and his daughter nodded and slowed her pace.

"I won." Cam touched the mailbox and squealed with excitement.

"You sure did." Carrie hugged him and then Paisley. "And here's your dad bringing up the rear. Early chores tire you out?" She gave Bryce a teasing grin.

"No, it's…" Bryce blinked away the sudden moisture behind his eyes. He had to focus on the present and not mar this moment with sadness or regrets. "Your mom was a fast runner too. Way faster than me."

"I never knew that." Paisley looked him up and down. "What else was Mommy better at than you?"

"Lots of things." An engine rumbled, and the yellow

school bus appeared in the distance as Carrie corralled the dogs.

"What things?" Paisley still studied him. "You never talk about Mommy, and I want to know."

"Maybe your dad doesn't—" Carrie glanced at him over the kids' heads.

"It's okay." Bryce forced a smile. "If you want, we could make a list of things your mom was great at after supper tonight."

"Really?" Paisley's expression said she expected Bryce to forget or change his mind.

"I promise. See?" He held up his phone. "I'll make myself a note."

As the bus stopped with a hiss of brakes, Paisley's mouth trembled, and then she flung her arms around him in a tight hug.

Most of all, Ally had been great at loving the kids they'd made together. Bryce's chest compressed. "Off you go. Have a good day. Love you." Paisley let go of him and boarded the bus to join her friends.

"You too, Cam." Carrie gave him a gentle push toward the bus steps. "It's only a few hours until I pick you up. You can manage that."

"I guess I have to." Cam hunched over as if to make himself smaller, trudged up the steps and took the seat closest to the driver.

The driver waved before closing the door, and the bus started up again.

As they turned to walk back along the lane to the house, Carrie broke the silence. "Do you know what that's about?"

"Cam not wanting to go to school, you mean?" Bryce called Otis and Penny back from sniffing a field of new baby bean plants.

Carrie nodded. "He didn't want to get on the bus either."

"He's been that way for a few months now. I've tried and so have his teachers and the bus driver, but he won't talk about it."

"I'll try too." Carrie patted Bryce's arm and gave him an encouraging smile. "I have the whole summer with him and Paisley."

Bryce's arm tingled like his hand had the day they met, and his gaze caught Carrie's and held. Her green eyes, filled with concern for Cam, were the same color as the bean plants. The color of life, rebirth and hope.

"It's—"

"You—"

Bryce gestured to Carrie to go first.

"That surprise I mentioned to the kids?" Carrie patted the dogs. "I'm taking them for ice cream at the Bluebunch Café after we swim. My mom always did that with me on the last day of school. It was a special treat I looked forward to. If you have time, you're welcome to join us. I'm sure the kids would love it."

Bryce would love it too, and although he didn't have time, Paisley and Cam were more important than ranch work. "That sounds good. Text me before you leave the pool. I'll meet you at the café."

"Will do." As Carrie smiled at him, there was that connection again, even stronger this time.

Although Bryce had never thought about dating or remarrying, he didn't have to shut himself off from fun and happiness—or family and friends either.

Going for ice cream wasn't a big deal. It was the kind of thing Ally would have planned too. Besides, it was for the kids. As long as he focused on the kids and ignored whatever that tingle was with Carrie, he'd be fine.

"I HAVE TO go in here and get something for my aunt Angela before I go home, but I'll be back to make breakfast for you tomorrow morning." Outside the Medicine Wheel Craft Center on High Valley's main street, Carrie knelt beside Cam and used a paper napkin to wipe chocolate ice cream from around his mouth. "I hope you like the lasagna I made. All you and your dad have to do is cover it with foil and heat it in the oven. Easy." She grinned at Bryce. "I used stuff in your cupboards and freezer. The kids and I will pick up groceries tomorrow. Make a list of what meals you'd like, and Paisley and Cam can help me make them."

"That would be great." Bryce straightened his cowboy hat. "Come on, kids. I parked the truck around the corner."

"I don't wanna go home without Carrie." Cam's voice rose in a whine. "Why can't she have supper with us? It's not fair." He stamped one foot in his small cowboy boot.

"Maybe someday soon I can have supper with you. Like if your dad has to work late." Carrie cupped Cam's chin in her hands. "Remember what I said?"

"We don't whine, and when we want something, we ask nicely." Paisley's voice was smug.

"Okay." Cam's grin was sheepish. "Would you read to me tomorrow please? I can pick out books tonight."

"I'd love to read to you tomorrow, and I can't wait to see what stories you choose." Carrie hugged the little boy, and he wrapped his arms around her neck. "Now go with your dad like he asked." She got to her feet. "You're going to make that list about your mom tonight too. It'll be tomorrow morning before you know it."

As the kids put their used napkins in a nearby trash can, Bryce spoke in an undertone to Carrie. "How did you do that?"

"Do what?" She moved toward the craft center's door, which was propped open to let in the balmy June air.

"I thought Cam was going to have a meltdown, but instead he..." Bryce gestured to where Cam and Paisley patted a golden retriever stopped with its owner on the sidewalk.

"I talked to the kids about what they can expect from me, and what I expect from them. I want us to have fun together this summer and for the kids to trust me, but..." Carrie stopped at the expression on Bryce's face. Had she overstepped? She'd never worked as a nanny, but she'd done lots of babysitting and taught pony club. She also remembered what it was like to be a kid.

"It's fine, and you're right. I guess I can learn from you." Bryce's half smile was as sheepish as his son's had been.

"We can learn from each other." Carrie's heartbeat sped up as Bryce rubbed a muscular hand over one of his beard-stubbled cheeks. If she'd met him under any other circumstances, she'd have thought he was gorgeous, but she couldn't let herself think such things about her boss. "You know Paisley and Cam best, but for me kids are a lot like horses. You adapt your training to what the animal, or child, needs but they both need rules. It helps them feel safe and secure."

"You're a wise woman." Bryce's voice had a husky note that was almost intimate. "See you tomorrow?"

"You bet." Carrie put a hand to her throat as her eyes caught his. Her ex, Jimmy, had blue eyes, but not like Bryce's. She'd never met anyone with eyes like his—so soft and gentle but with a teasing glint too.

Her mouth went dry, and warmth suffused her chest as she turned and went into the craft center, brushing a set of wind chimes that tinkled.

"Welcome." A woman's voice came from behind a weaving loom set up by the front window.

"Hi." Carrie swallowed. Despite those beguiling eyes, Bryce was off-limits. "I'm Carrie Rizzo. I'm here to pick up the tapestry wool my aunt, Angela Moretti, ordered. She texted me it was in and asked me to drop by."

"Here you go." The woman stepped away from the loom and blanket she was working on and handed Carrie a paper shopping bag. "I'm Rosa Cardinal. Well done out there with young Cam." A broad smile creased her face as she smoothed her thick shoulder-length gray hair.

"You saw?" Carrie took the bag and slipped the straw handles over her wrist.

"Heard too with the door and windows open. I'm part of the Sunflower Sisterhood and a good friend of Bryce's mom, Joy. You're exactly who Paisley and Cam need. Bryce loves his kids, but he lets them get away with too much." Rosa shook her head. "It's understandable since they lost their mom, but Cam especially needs consistency and routine."

"I hope I can offer him something positive." Carrie glanced around the spacious store filled with beaded dream catchers, framed abstract paintings in bold colors, glass display cases of colorful pottery and silver jewelry, as well as tapestries, rugs and other woven items.

"You already have, and you'll keep on the way you're going. I have three grown children of my own and fostered countless more. I know someone who's good with kids when I see them." Rosa took Carrie's hand and shook it, her grip firm. "I'm glad to meet you. Angela's so happy you're staying for the summer. She hasn't been the same since her husband passed, and it's good for her to have family close."

"I'm glad to be with her." Carrie looked around the craft center again. "You have a beautiful space."

"It is, isn't it? I moved in a few years ago. It used to be the old train station. My business outgrew my kitchen table. Now it's outgrowing this place too." She laughed. "It's a good problem to have. I've hired three women to work with me this summer in the store, and I'll need some high-school kids part-time when it gets really busy in July and August." She stopped and studied Carrie. "Ordinarily, I'd want to interview you, but Angela's opinion and what I heard and saw out there tell me that won't be necessary."

"Interview me for what? I already have a job with Bryce." Although Carrie enjoyed craftwork, it was a hobby, and she wasn't as skilled as Aunt Angela, let alone a professional like Rosa.

"Angela said you do web design and marketing."

"Yes, freelance. Is there something I can do for you?"

"A new website for a start and likely more. Consider yourself hired." Rosa stuck out her hand again. "Flexible hours. Whenever you can fit the work in around those precious children."

"I'd be happy to help you, but you haven't seen my work or asked for a project proposal or quote."

"Oh, I've seen your work. Angela showed me the website you created for that jewelry designer in Idaho and other projects too. She might not show it, but she's proud of you."

"I don't know what to say."

"*Yes* would be a good start." Rosa's warm laugh made Carrie laugh too.

"Then yes, of course." Carrie took Rosa's hand in hers as they shook on the deal. What was that expression about good things coming in threes? The nanny job, free boarding for Teddy at the Tall Grass Ranch and now a freelance job. It was almost too good to be true.

"We'll work out the details later. You'd better get home. Angela will have supper waiting." With a squeeze, Rosa dropped Carrie's hand. "Better days ahead, that's what my mom said." Rosa's dark eyes were as warm as her laugh. "Angela says you've had some bumps in your life, but you've got gumption. I like gumption."

Carrie straightened her shoulders and returned Rosa's smile. In only a few days, her life had changed for the better, and that was because of High Valley and its people.

But maybe it was also because she'd let herself be open to opportunities. And for the first time in what felt like forever, she was excited about what might happen next.

CHAPTER THREE

JOY CARTER OPENED the barn door and waved at Carrie, who unlatched the back of the horse trailer hitched to a red pickup truck. "Hi. I'm Bryce's mom, Joy." She joined Carrie by the trailer as a rich, red chestnut with a crooked white star between its eyes stuck its head out. "I'm here to lend a hand to get you two settled."

"Thanks. Meet Teddy." Carrie rubbed the horse's neck. "He's my best friend, aren't you, boy?"

Teddy bobbed his head and nickered at Joy in welcome.

"He's gorgeous." Joy studied the quarter horse with an experienced eye. "Looks like just over fifteen hands in height. Good weight too."

"He's also fast and strong. We've won a lot of races together." Carrie's head was close to Teddy's, and he nuzzled her, the affectionate gesture showing Joy their close bond.

"I expect you'll win lots more." Joy took Teddy's lead rope so Carrie could shut the horse trailer. "Hi, Teddy. Welcome to the Tall Grass Ranch." Standing at a slight angle, she approached him from the left, made eye contact and gave him her hand to sniff. "We've given Teddy a stall on the end near the barn door so he can be part of what's going on." Joy glanced at Carrie. "Bryce cleaned it out last night. He said Teddy's a sociable guy. One of my other sons, Cole, manages the horse barn, but Bryce wanted to take care of Teddy's stall personally."

Bryce rarely had anything to do with the horse barn,

so his insistence on getting this stall ready told Joy there was something going on. Offering to be here to help Carrie get Teddy settled was a way for Joy to find out what that "something" might be.

"That's really nice of Bryce." In jeans, cowboy boots and a white T-shirt under a checked flannel shirt, Carrie looked like she belonged on a ranch. Her brown hair was pulled back in a thick ponytail, and her battered brown cowboy hat was working headgear, not a fashion accessory. She smiled as she retrieved the lead rope from Joy and led Teddy toward the open barn door. "I've only worked for him a few days, but Bryce and the kids have been great at making me comfortable."

"You'll be a big help to all of them this summer. You too, Teddy. The kids are excited to meet you." The sweetness of Carrie's smile and the kindness in her expression made Joy warm to her. "Paisley and Cam need the one-on-one attention they can't get at a day camp."

"In you go, boy." Carrie soothed Teddy as he stopped by the stall door. "They're fun kids. Bryce took them to the fields with him this morning so I could move Teddy from Squirrel Tail to here."

"They're lively kids too." Joy hesitated. Carrie seemed sensible and practical. Joy owed it to her, as well as her son and grandchildren, to speak her mind, and if she didn't do it now, when would she? "But the whole family's struggling, and I don't know how to fix it." She leaned on the half door of the neighboring stall and patted Daisy-May, an Appaloosa and the gentlest horse on the ranch.

"Maybe you can't fix it or them." Carrie filled a feed bucket from the container Joy indicated. "You can help, sure, but people have to fix themselves."

"That sounds like the voice of experience." All Joy knew of Carrie was the little Angela had said about her niece at the last Sunflower Sisterhood meeting, supplemented by Paisley and Cam's excited chatter about their new nanny. Bryce hadn't said anything at all and, even though her youngest son was quiet, that told Joy something too.

"I guess so." As Teddy stuck his nose into the feed bucket, Carrie checked the automatic waterer and closed the stall door. "I shouldn't talk. This summer is about fixing myself." She turned to face Joy. "Aunt Angela respects my privacy, but it's not a secret. I had a few injuries, minor ones, but enough to keep me off the rodeo circuit. And then, somehow, I lost my mojo. Along with stuff in my personal life, everything added up. I need time to rest and reset before I return to competitive barrel racing."

"You're smart to recognize what you need." In her early sixties, Joy was only now figuring out what she needed in life—but maybe, and even if she'd started earlier, it would always be a work in progress. "I'm guessing there was a man somewhere in there too?" She wasn't prying; she was only interested because Carrie was looking after her grandbabies.

"You guessed right." Carrie greeted Daisy-May and introduced her to Teddy. "I'm over that relationship, but from now on, I won't let myself think about settling down."

Where had Joy heard that one before? She suppressed a smile. Carrie sounded like Cole, but in a few weeks her restless middle child would marry sweet Melissa and be a stepdad to Mel's daughter, Skylar. He'd only needed to meet the right person. Maybe Carrie did too.

Joy considered the younger woman as she spoke to Teddy and Daisy-May, her voice reassuring and calm. Horses and children both tested boundaries and acted out when they were bored or tired, but they also loved to play. Most importantly, horses and kids lived in the moment.

Somebody needed to drag Bryce out of the past and help him live the life he still had. Could Carrie be that person?

"Hey, is that Teddy?" Paisley skidded to a stop by Joy and pointed to the horse.

"It sure is." Carrie overturned two empty buckets so Paisley and Cam, who followed his sister, could stand on them to greet the horse at eye level.

"Can I let him sniff my hand?" Cam asked.

"After you say hello and if your dad says it's okay." Carrie glanced at Bryce, who'd joined them. "Outside the competition arena, Teddy's pretty easygoing." She rubbed the horse's ears. "He's kind too. See the kindness in his eyes?"

The same kindness as in his owner's eyes. As Joy looked between Carrie and Bryce, something flashed between them. Awareness…maybe even a brief soul-to-soul bond. Joy had had that bond with her late husband. From the moment she'd met Dennis as a young girl, she'd known he was the one for her, and that hadn't changed over all their years together.

"Go ahead." Bryce spoke to Cam, who held out his hand to Teddy, and then Paisley did the same. "Whatever you or Teddy need, ask one of the ranch hands or Cole." Bryce waved Cole over to be introduced. "Or me, of course." His cheeks reddened, and he pulled his hat farther down over his face.

"It's all great." As Carrie greeted Cole, her cheeks were pink too.

"You'll see my oldest son around as well, but not until next week," Joy added. "Zach, his wife, Beth, and their daughter, Ellie, are visiting friends in Chicago. That's where Beth and Ellie are from. We all run the ranch together. It's been a family operation for several generations."

"It always will be." Cole grinned at Carrie. "I hear

you're a barrel racer. I'm retired now, but I rode rodeo for a lot of years. We might have crossed paths."

"We probably did. I certainly recognize your name. Everybody's heard of Cole Carter."

"Hopefully for the right reasons," Cole joked.

As Carrie and Cole talked about rodeo acquaintances, and Paisley and Cam played with the barn cats, Joy moved closer to Bryce. He stood apart from the group, and his blue-gray eyes were somber.

"Are you okay?" She touched his arm.

"Why wouldn't I be?" His laugh and smile were too bright. "The crops are doing well, so if we get rain at the right time we'll be set."

"I'm talking about *you*, not the crops." Mr. Wiggins, Joy's favorite barn cat, nudged Joy's ankles, and she picked him up for a cuddle, scratching the black patch on top of his head.

"I'm fine, Mom. You worry too much." Bryce avoided Joy's gaze. "The kids are doing great. Carrie's fantastic for them."

"I'm glad." She gave him a one-armed hug. If Bryce didn't want to talk about his feelings, Joy couldn't make him. "Life goes on, and I want you to be happy."

"I'm happy with my kids and work. That's enough." Bryce shrugged.

"After your dad passed, I thought the same, but life can give you an unexpected second chance. You don't want to miss out."

"I'm happy you and Shane are dating. I like him. We all do. Dad would have too." Bryce kept his eyes fixed on his kids.

"Shane's a good man, but we're taking things slowly." Joy still couldn't believe the kind and handsome owner of the Squirrel Tail Ranch had come into her life and seemed to have every intention of staying there. "I'll grieve your dad for the rest of my life, but that doesn't mean I can't let myself be open to happiness again. It's a different kind of happiness, that's all."

Bryce shook his head. "Zach and Cole are settled, and I am too. If you have to worry about someone, worry about Molly."

"I *do* worry about your sister." As much, if not more, than Joy worried about her sons. Despite having the big-city life and nursing career she'd always wanted, Molly didn't seem happy in Atlanta. "I worry about all of you and always will. It comes with being a parent." And after losing her oldest son, Paul, who'd died from complications of cystic fibrosis in his early twenties, she worried about her other children even more.

Bryce nodded and then stared at the barn floor. "Leave it, okay? I'm not Cole or Zach. I already met the love of my life and married her. I'm not looking for anyone else, so you don't need to interfere."

"I didn't exactly interfere with your brothers. I only—"

"Grandma." Cam tugged Joy's arm. "Teddy likes me. Come see."

"He likes me too, even more 'cause I'm older and know more about horses." Paisley joined in.

"But I'm a better rider than you were at my age and—"

"Teddy likes both of you," Carrie interjected. "Remember what I said about bragging and competing with each other?" She crouched to their level to speak to both kids.

Over the kids' and Carrie's heads, Cole gave Joy a meaningful look and then, as he gestured to his brother, a teasing grin.

Joy shook her head. Carrie *was* fantastic for Paisley and Cam, but she could be fantastic for Bryce too. She wanted all her kids to be happy, and there was nothing wrong in wanting to look out for them, no matter how old they were.

She glanced at Bryce, who stared at Carrie with a new softness and yearning in his expression.

Or in giving people a gentle push when they needed it.

"DON'T FORGET TO wash your hands, Daddy. You should change your shirt too. There's yucky stuff all over it." Paisley screwed up her face in distaste as she greeted Bryce at the back door of their house.

"That 'yucky stuff' is good, clean Montana dirt." He pulled off his boots and grinned at his daughter, who wore a pink ruffled bib apron his mom had made for her. "But yeah, I should change." He ducked into the mudroom, closed the door and took a clean shirt and pair of jeans from a hook. They hadn't been there this morning, so Carrie must have left them for him when she'd done laundry. It was the little things she did without him asking her to that made his life easier.

"Where's your brother?" Bryce slid out of his dirty garments and washed up in the utility sink before getting dressed in the fresh clothing.

"Reading with Carrie." Paisley talked to him from the other side of the door. "We baked chocolate brownies. I helped Carrie cook dinner too, and Cam set the table."

"Something sure smells good." In the six days Carrie had worked for him, Bryce's life hadn't only gotten easier, but his house now felt like a home. A jug of wildflowers sat in the middle of the kitchen table. Delicious meals were ready for him after a long day of ranch work. There was clean laundry when he and the kids needed it. And most of all, he had happy children and more time to spend with them.

"It's spaghetti and meatballs." As Bryce opened the

mudroom door, Paisley took his hand, and Penny and Otis tumbled around his feet. "Carrie used her family's recipe from Italy."

"Sounds fancy." Bryce followed his daughter to the kitchen, where the scent of rich spices and meat was stronger.

"No, it's not." Paisley shook her head. "Carrie said it's good, plain Italian home cooking. I wish we were Italian."

"No such luck, kiddo. The Carter family's English, Scottish and Irish. On your mom's side, you're Ukrainian and German with a bit of Dutch thrown in."

"You're a wonderful mix of countries and cultures like lots of Americans," Carrie said as she and Cam came into the kitchen. Cam carried a stack of books and put them on the shelf between the kitchen and the family room. Then he fed the dogs without being asked. "Dinner's ready, and there's a salad in the fridge. I should get going and—"

"Can't Carrie stay? Please?" Cam's expression was hopeful, but his voice didn't have even a hint of what used to be a too familiar whine.

"If you're free, it would be great if you could stay later tonight." Bryce turned to Carrie. "One of my crop-consulting clients called when I was on the way back to the house. I have to work tonight. The guy needs a report by tomorrow morning." After he got the kids to bed, Bryce might have to pull an all-nighter. "I'd pay you extra, of course."

"I don't have any plans, so I can stick around until the kids' bedtime." Like Paisley, Carrie also wore an apron—a green gingham one that had belonged to Ally.

"Yay!" Paisley and Cam shouted.

Bryce opened the fridge to get the salad. There was no reason Carrie shouldn't wear Ally's apron. Bryce had told her to make herself at home, and the apron, like Paisley's, had been in one of the kitchen drawers. It unsettled him, that was all, seeing another woman in Ally's place.

"Wash your hands, kids, and then we can eat," he said, putting the salad bowl and servers one of Ally's cousins had given them for a wedding present on the table.

"Tough day at work?" Carrie untied the apron and hung it from a hook near the kitchen bulletin board. The same hook Ally had once hung it from and the board where he and the kids had pinned the list they'd made of things that Ally was good at. Whenever Bryce looked at that list, his chest tightened and his vision blurred. But having it there made it seem like his wife was still part of the heart of their home.

"It was okay." Bryce rubbed the back of his neck. "I spent most of it on horseback. Since I don't spend as much time in the saddle as Zach and Cole, I'll sure feel it tomorrow." He winced as he pulled out his chair at the head of the table.

Carrie sat in the chair next to Cam's, leaving the seat at the other end of the table empty. "It must be weird for you having me, still almost a stranger, here in your house with your kids. If there's anything I can do to make it easier, tell me, please." Her hair curled in tendrils around her face, and her expression showed concern.

"It's fine, it's…" He hesitated but the kids were still in the bathroom with the faucet running. "I miss my wife, and you cooking dinner and all the rest reminds me of how things used to be. I should be okay with it by now but—"

"There's no timeline for grief." Carrie took paper napkins out of the holder and set them at each place. "The kids showed me the list you made with them where they wrote that their mom was a great cook. Did that apron I was wearing belong to your wife?"

Bryce nodded, suddenly too choked up to speak.

"After I wash it, I'll give it to you to put away. If there are other things you'd rather not see around or have me use, let me know." Carrie got up to drain the pasta.

"It's not that." Bryce stared at his empty plate. "The memories hit me when I least expect."

"I understand." Carrie ladled pasta into a serving bowl.

"Ally was my whole life. I'll never stop missing her."

"The kids showed me pictures of their mom. She was beautiful."

"Beautiful inside and out." Bryce took the bowl of spaghetti, now topped with fragrant meatballs in a tomato sauce, from Carrie as Paisley and Cam sat in their usual places at the table.

"Are you talking about Carrie?" Paisley glanced between them as Carrie poured milk into the kids' glasses. "When we were at the feedstore, Mrs. Taylor said Carrie was beautiful."

"Mrs. Taylor was talking about my barrel racing because she's a fan of the sport." Carrie's face went red. "You shouldn't repeat things you overhear."

"But you *are* beautiful. Almost as beautiful as Mommy." Cam looked between Bryce and Carrie too.

"Let's eat. I'll serve. This salad looks great. Is it another Italian recipe?" Carrie was attractive, and although Bryce was a widower, he was also a man. The sooner he diverted this conversation, the better.

"Yes, it's one of Aunt Angela's favorites. She gave me her recipe." Carrie tucked Cam's napkin into the top of his shirt.

"Wait, Daddy." Paisley bumped his arm as Bryce picked up a serving spoon. "We hafta say thanks for the food first."

"Of course." Bryce bowed his head and said grace, the

familiar words comforting and soothing him. Paisley and Cam needed this kind of life and routine.

He did too. As he opened his eyes and looked around the table, he realized how much he'd missed times like this. It was only an ordinary family dinner, but it was the most special meal he'd had since before Ally had gotten sick.

"Promise me?" Ally had looked at him with those blue eyes that had always seen what he was thinking and feeling. "I know you'll miss me, but I want you to find happiness without me."

"I promise." Bryce had clasped her thin hand and lied to her for the first and last time. He'd have said and done anything to ease her passing, but how could he be happy without the other half of himself?

"Daddy?" Paisley nudged his arm again. "I'm hungry."

"Sure. Right." He served salad and then the pasta, busying himself with passing plates and asking Paisley and Cam about their day.

"Please sit up straight and don't gobble your food, Cam. Remember?" Carrie softened the gentle admonishment with a smile.

"'Cause it's good manners and means my tummy won't hurt after eating." Cam's face was smeared with tomato sauce.

"That's right." Bryce straightened too. He'd eaten too many meals on the run or in front of the TV, but a family mealtime, like his mom and then Ally had insisted on, was important.

He glanced at Carrie, who now helped Cam twirl spaghetti around his fork, while the two of them laughed at a joke Paisley had told.

Bryce had never imagined thinking about another woman, let alone being drawn to one like he was to Carrie. However, she was his employee. He had no business looking at her in any way apart from as the kids' nanny.

Carrie laughed again, Otis barked and Penny lay beneath the table at Bryce's feet.

His heart squeezed. Home, family and love were all right here. Not as they'd once been. He'd never get back what he'd had with Ally, but maybe he could find something new.

His gaze drifted to Carrie once more. Something that would be good for all of them.

CHAPTER FOUR

"Is THAT WHEELBARROW too heavy for you?" Carrie called to Cam as she spread clean bedding in Teddy's stall.

From behind the tack room door, with the wheelbarrow still in the middle of the barn's main aisle, the boy shook his head and put a finger to his lips.

"Eli Minden's here for a riding lesson." Paisley grabbed more straw from a bale. "He's mean."

"Mean how?" Carrie used a pitchfork to fluff the straw.

The tack room door slammed shut as Cam disappeared.

"He takes kids' lunches and stuff." Paisley found a broom and swept up straw and shavings into a pile.

"What kind of stuff?" Carrie kept her tone neutral. Cam had seemed happier since school ended, but it was still a struggle to get him to go to his swimming lesson or do other things away from the ranch.

"I don't know." Paisley shrugged. "I've only heard other kids talking."

Carrie put the pitchfork away and went to the open barn door. The Carter family offered riding lessons to locals as well as children and teenagers staying at Crocus Hill, a summer camp for young people with disabilities. One of the camp's riding instructors sat astride a gray horse with a group of children on ponies clustered around her.

None of the kids looked threatening, but appearances could be deceiving. Besides, Carrie was an adult, not six.

She turned back into the barn as Cam came out of the tack room carrying several broken halters.

"Uncle Cole asked me to get these out for him. I forgot before," Cam said as he put them on a shelf. "I can move the wheelbarrow now." He stood behind the big barn door, out of sight of the group in the corral.

"It's okay. I can handle it." Carrie poked her head around the door. "After we finish here, want to take a walk to the creek? We could look for dinosaur fossils." Cam loved dinosaurs, and the flat path to the creek was his favorite spot to hunt for traces of the great creatures that had once roamed the Montana plains.

"Fossils are boring. I'd rather have a barrel racing lesson." Paisley looked behind the door too. "What are you doing?"

"Nothing." Cam stepped farther into the shadows, and his lower lip wobbled.

"No barrel racing lesson until I talk to your dad," Carrie said, stopping whatever objections Paisley looked set to raise. "Besides, you have your swimming lesson."

"I don't want to look for fossils or go swimming," Cam said. "Can't we go back to the house and watch a movie?" He poked his head around the door as the riding instructor and students left the corral to ride toward the creek path.

"Swimming first and a movie later. Your dad's already paid for those swimming lessons. You seem to like them once you're in the water. Is it your teacher?" Carrie studied Cam's bent head as they moved the wheelbarrow to the back of the barn.

"Forget it." Cam darted back into the tack room before Carrie could question him further.

After they'd washed up in the tack room sink, Carrie linked hands with both kids. "There's not enough time to go fossil hunting anyway." Cam's tense stance relaxed as they came out into the empty corral. "Why don't we visit Teddy instead?" Each day, Cam and Paisley opened up to her more, but it took time to grow trust.

And only an instant to break it. Carrie's stomach clenched at the memory of what her ex had done. Cheating was bad enough, but doing so with a friend was worse. It doubled the hurt and betrayal. Although she'd convinced herself she was over it, Carrie was warier now and less open with her feelings. She wouldn't risk her heart again anytime soon, if ever.

"Hey, boy." Carrie called to her horse and opened the pasture gate to let Paisley and Cam go through it ahead of her.

Teddy trotted across the field and nickered in welcome.

"How are you doing, Teddy Bear?" He nudged her face with his head, and she rubbed his favorite place behind his ears. Unlike people, horses didn't let you down. And when horses gave you their trust, as long as you continued to respect and treat them well, that relationship was for life. She dug in the pocket of her jeans for treats and let the kids take turns feeding Teddy.

"You're tickling me, Teddy." Cam giggled as the horse nuzzled his flat palm. "He's got a bigger mouth than Paisley's pony."

"A bigger everything." Paisley stood on tiptoe to pat Teddy's neck. "He's a giant compared to Luna." She giggled too.

"Uncle Cole's horse is the real giant." Cam pointed to where Cole led a gorgeous blood bay gelding around a corner of the barn. "We're not allowed near Bandit unless Uncle Cole's there."

"That's a good rule for any horse except your own." As Carrie ran her hand along Teddy's back, he whinnied and tossed his head in Bandit's direction.

Bandit responded with a whinny of his own, and Cole waved. At his side, his fiancée, Melissa, an animal physical therapist who worked at a clinic in town, checked something on the big horse's right front leg.

"Daddy." Paisley ran to the pasture fence as Bryce's truck pulled up, and he parked and got out of it.

Carrie's heartbeat sped up as Bryce came toward them carrying a paper bag. He was bareheaded and without his usual cowboy hat; the sun made his light brown hair look almost blond. Beneath his checked, snap Western shirt, his shoulders were broad, and he walked with confidence in a pair of worn jeans and boots, his head up and shoulders back.

As she and Cam followed Paisley to the fence, Carrie mentally shook herself. There was no reason for her to act like a high-school girl checking out a cute guy. Bryce worked on this ranch, and she was looking after his kids. They were both doing their jobs. Except, she was more pleased to see him than she should be.

"Hey." Bryce helped Paisley and Cam sit atop the white-painted fence. "Carrie?"

"Hi."

"I was… Teddy…the water trough likely needs filling." Her tongue tripped over itself.

"No problem." Bryce waved to a teenage ranch hand and asked him to take care of it.

"When I was in town, I got you a present. It's for all of you, but Carrie gets to look first. Hold on, kids." He passed the bag to Carrie. "I hope you like it."

She fumbled with the pale-green ribbon that tied the bag's handles together. "What's in here?" She grinned, building anticipation for the kids as she pulled out a swathe of green tissue paper. "Something fabric." She fingered it and drew out a multicolored swirl on a cream background.

"It's an apron. With animals on it and your name." Paisley leaned closer to take a look.

"Three aprons." Carrie took two smaller garments from the bag. "With all our names."

"Except for the names, they're the same," said Cam, nodding his approval as Carrie handed him the apron with his name embroidered in blue on the bib.

"How many different animals can you find, kids? Count them." Carrie swallowed a lump in her throat as the colorful pattern blurred.

"There's a horse and cow."

"A fox and squirrel."

Paisley's and Cam's voices rose and fell with the new game.

"Thank you." Carrie turned to Bryce, who stood by the fence with the children.

"With all that cooking and baking you're doing for us, I thought you could use it. Cam said we only had what he called 'girls' aprons,' so Rosa made these. She thought the fabric would be fun for the kids. And I...well... I thought you'd like it too. The red matches your T-shirt."

"It's perfect." Carrie's breath caught. This gift was sweet, thoughtful and, because it was personal, one of the nicest things anybody had ever done for her. If you had the money, it was easy to buy expensive presents but Carrie had simple tastes. This apron meant more to her than the impractical mini designer bag her ex had given her last Christmas. And way more than the headache-inducing perfume he'd handed to her, still in its airport duty free bag, the day after her birthday. "Red's my favorite color."

"Mine too." He cleared his throat. "I should get back to work."

"Likewise. The kids have swimming." They spoke at nearly the same time.

But Bryce lingered as if he wasn't in any hurry to leave. "Paisley said tacos are on the menu for supper tonight. I won't be late." He stuck his hands in the front pockets of his jeans.

"Great. Tacos. The kids are excited about making them." *His* children. The children of a grieving widower.

Even if Carrie liked Bryce, she liked him as a friend and the kids' dad, she told herself. Nothing more.

BRYCE GUIDED HIS HORSE, Maverick, across the hilly terrain and drew in a lungful of crisp morning air. He stopped Maverick at the top of a small rise and scanned the landscape spread out in front of them. The wheat was a rippling field of green, and in the adjoining pasture, red and white cattle grazed in the shadow of the distant Rocky Mountains.

Carrie liked the apron he'd given her yesterday, but what he'd intended as a friendly gift had suddenly seemed like more. And why had he mentioned her red T-shirt? He shook his head as embarrassment rolled over him again. Ordinarily, he had no problem talking to women, but Carrie was different. Around her, he was either tongue-tied or said the wrong thing. It wasn't like he wanted to date her. He didn't want to date anybody, and he'd crossed paths with plenty of nice single women since Ally had died. Yet, he hadn't reacted to any of them like he did to Carrie.

Maverick's ears twitched, and a long-billed curlew stuck its head over a tuft of rough grass before popping back down again.

"It's okay, little one. We don't mean you any harm." Bryce chuckled as Maverick turned his head as if to ask who else was around for him to speak to. His dad had taught Bryce about birds, plants and animals and to respect the natural world. He still tried to live and work by those lessons.

Hooves thudded, and then Zach reined in his horse, Scout, while Cole did the same with Bandit. Bryce greeted his brothers, who, like him, were dressed for ranch work in jeans, Western shirts, boots and cowboy hats.

"That new variety of wheat you tried looks good." Zach gestured to the green field.

"I just checked the moisture, and if Mother Nature cooperates, we should have a bumper crop. The barley's thriving too." Bryce settled his hat more firmly on his head. He and his brothers trusted each other to do their own jobs. While they sometimes worked together, like today when Zach had asked Bryce and Cole for help herding cattle, they never competed with each other.

"Does a good crop mean we can invest more in my rodeo stock contracting venture?" Cole asked. "I've got a lead on a prize bull in Colorado."

"As the saying goes, don't count your chickens, or bulls, before they hatch." Bryce turned Maverick around to follow his brothers to the cattle pasture. "We need a new baler."

"And the roof on the main barn could do with replacing," Zach added.

Cole and Bandit circled the first cow, their movements slow and calm. "It's lucky we have Beth on our team. She's a magician with money."

"She is, but even if she wasn't, I'm a lucky man," Zach said as he and Scout circled several other cows bunched together.

Bryce's chest constricted. His brothers were happy, and soon Cole, like Zach, would be married. Apart from Molly, who was much younger, he was the only one of the siblings on his own. He stared down one cow who gave him the bovine equivalent of teenage attitude. Paisley and Cam were challenging enough now. How would he cope when they reached adolescence?

"Good girl," he told the cow as she reluctantly joined the others. Without Bryce having to do much, Maverick rounded up the remaining stragglers, and now Zach and Scout led the cattle in a slow line as Cole and Bandit brought another group onto the meandering trail. "That's the way." Bryce guided Maverick in a slow, zigzag pattern behind the herd. His job was to keep the cattle calm, moving forward at their own pace and focused on where they were going rather than where they'd been.

That was good advice for life too. Cole, Zach and Bryce were close in age, but Bryce had always been the little brother. Nevertheless, he'd been the first to marry and start a family. But now, while they'd moved ahead, Bryce was stuck in the past.

"You guys need a hand?"

Bryce turned at Carrie's voice. "If you want to join us, sure. Where did you come from? It's your day off." And the kids were with Bryce's mom.

"I hadn't taken Teddy out for a good ride in a few weeks. We both need the exercise." Carrie sat easily in her saddle, at one with her horse like the experienced rider she was.

As Carrie and Teddy matched Bryce and Maverick's zigzag pattern, Bryce waved at Cole to let him know he didn't need more help and for his brother to join Zach at the front of the herd.

"Not that I came looking for you. I wanted to stay within cell service and close to home since I'm on my own." Carrie was intent on the slow-moving line of cattle.

Bryce held back a smile. On a big ranch like the Tall Grass, you could ride for miles without bumping into anyone. While her explanation made sense, something about it also told him she thought she needed to justify herself.

Home. Although it hadn't been long, Carrie already seemed at home on the ranch and in Bryce's house. It was comfortable having her ride beside him too.

"I'm interested in what you're doing with your grain crops." Carrie and Teddy eased a curious calf back into line with its mom. "How often do you leave fields fallow?"

Bryce stared at her and snapped his mouth shut when he realized he'd opened it in astonishment. "Not as often as I'd like to."

As Bryce talked about soil quality and estimated yields, Carrie asked more questions and even suggested a few things he'd considered but hadn't yet tried.

"I used to go out to the fields with my grandpa at his ranch. I learned from him. I've studied on my own too." When they reached the new pasture, Cole joined them at the rear of the herd, riding on Carrie's other side.

"Thanks. Great job." Cole gave Carrie a high five.

"My pleasure." Carrie returned the gesture with a friendly smile. "I like ranch work. Let me know if there's anything else I can do. When I'm not with Paisley and Cam, of course." She smiled at Bryce too. "They come first."

"I expect Zach could use extra help when Melissa and I are on our honeymoon." Cole's expression softened before becoming businesslike. "I'd also like to get your opinion on a mare. I want to breed barrel-racing horses as part of a stock contracting venture."

"Sure," Carrie said. "Let me know when and where."

As she chatted with his brother, Bryce rode ahead. Carrie had many years of rodeo left. Barrel racing was her life, like Paisley, Cam and this ranch were his. Bryce was fooling himself thinking she belonged here.

And despite a flicker of what might have been regret, Bryce couldn't let himself want anything different.

CHAPTER FIVE

"WHAT DO YOU THINK?" At a table in the craft center's workroom, Carrie showed Rosa mock-ups of new logos and color schemes that could be incorporated into her website design.

After a lot of late nights and early mornings hunched over her computer, Carrie was pitching a proposal to her first client in High Valley. If Rosa liked her work, she might recommend her to other business owners. As a freelancer, Carrie relied on word of mouth to build her business and grow her nest egg.

"I think you're a genius." Rosa's eyes twinkled. "I love all your suggestions. It'll be hard to choose only one."

"That's great." The knot in Carrie's chest loosened. She was good at her job but—just as anticipation and anxiety hit her when she and Teddy thundered along the alley to enter the rodeo ring—she got nervous presenting ideas to a new client. "Why don't you ask your employees, crafters and customers for their input? It's useful to get other perspectives."

Rosa nodded and pointed to an image on Carrie's laptop screen. "With this one, it's like you saw inside my head. It's similar to the original medicine wheel design I came up with when I started my business but a lot better. You're talented."

"Thanks." Carrie's face warmed with pleasure. "At each stage, I try to understand my client and their business. No matter which design you choose for your new website, you can then carry the same look and feel over to your business cards, customer packaging and your storefront and gallery signage, so everything is consistent."

"You've made my gallery and craft center look…" Rosa paused. "It feels like my kitchen-table business has reached the big time."

"From what I've seen, you left your kitchen table behind long ago." Carrie gestured to the workroom where craft supplies and products of every description filled the shelves that lined the walls. "You're a successful entrepreneur, so you need to make sure others see you and your business that way."

"I suppose I do." Rosa laughed. "I still get my best ideas at that old pine kitchen table, though. It's also where I feel closest to my family and roots. That table belonged to my mom and her mother before her. When I work there, it's like they're by my side guiding me."

Carrie had lost those connections and roots when her grandparents died and their ranch was sold. More than the house in Kalispell where she'd grown up and her mom had hired a professional to redecorate every few years, that ranch had truly been home. Working in the fields, milking parlor and horse barn had sparked Carrie's dream of having a ranch or farm of her own.

As Rosa looked through the presentation again, Carrie's thoughts drifted to Bryce and how they'd talked when she'd helped herd cattle four days before. She already knew he was smart. Those framed undergraduate and master's degree certificates in his home office said he was good at academics. But he was a working rancher too, and she'd been impressed by how he applied the latest scientific and agricultural research to real-life issues. He understood the ins and outs of sustainable farming too, and she'd almost told him about her own dream. Instead, she'd stopped her-self. That dream was too private and special to share with many people.

Her ex, Jimmy, had dismissed it and her, calling it a foolish idea. Like her parents, he wanted her to quit bar-rel racing and settle down in Kalispell. *Get a real job.* His words echoed in her head. She had a *real* job. Two, includ-ing her freelance work. With a farm, she'd have a third, and she was determined to succeed at all of them.

"If you email me these slides, I'll get some feedback and let you know any other questions and the design I want to go with," Rosa said.

"Sounds good." Carrie gathered up her notes and lap-top. Since Bryce had needed her to stay late a few days last week, she had this afternoon off, even though it was a Wednesday.

"Hello, there." A light tap sounded on the half-open workroom door, and Joy Carter came in. She was followed by Paisley and Cam; Zach's wife, Beth; Cole's fiancée, Me-lissa; and several teen girls, one of whom must be Ellie, Zach and Beth's adopted daughter.

"Carrie." Paisley gave her an exuberant hug. "Are you helping us make wedding decorations? I'm making paper flowers. Grandma taught me." Paisley sat beside Carrie.

"Grandma taught me too, but she asked me to work with her on candles for the centerpieces." Cam sat on Carrie's other side. "That's a very important job."

"Both jobs are important, but no, I'm just leaving to go back to Aunt Angela's." Carrie wanted to update her busi-ness plan and email some past clients to ask if she could provide them with anything new.

"Can't you stay, please?" Paisley's puppy-dog expres-sion mirrored the one Penny and Otis gave Carrie when they wanted a treat.

"We'd love to have you join us." Joy sat across from Carrie and set boxes holding scissors, glue, pastel-colored tissue paper and other supplies in the middle of the table. "By we, I mean the Sunflower Sisterhood." She gestured to the other women who'd joined them, including Aunt Angela and her friend, Nina Shevchenko.

"Please do." Rosa patted Carrie's shoulder as she and Nina set out more chairs. "Consider it your official welcome to town."

"Okay." Carrie wanted to meet more people here, and it had been ages since she'd done any crafts.

She exchanged greetings with the others, who introduced themselves if they hadn't met her before. Lauren, who was married to a Carter cousin, gave riding lessons at the ranch. Carrie nodded at Diana, a ranch owner whose daughter had been in Carrie's group when the school visited Squirrel Tail.

Kristi from the Bluebunch Café waved at Carrie from the opposite end of the table. "I want to talk to you about designing new signs for the café. Rosa says your work is great."

"I'd love to, thanks."

In the hubbub of ten or more women and girls talking at once, Carrie took a deep breath. She was comfortable in the rodeo world, but she knew people there. She wasn't shy, but she was more at ease one-on-one than in groups.

That was another reason she didn't want the job in the family construction company. While she enjoyed her freelance work, leading a team and having to be what her mom called "the face of the company" mingling at cocktail parties and golf days wasn't for her. Somehow, she had to make her parents understand that.

"How can I help?" As Paisley and Cam went to work

with Joy, Carrie turned to Beth, who held a roll of white satin ribbon.

"Want to make bows for the church pews with us?" Beth chuckled. "Ellie's at the age where she'd rather be with her friends." She indicated the group of girls who'd set up a workstation at a smaller table on the far side of the room.

"My Lily's the same." The woman beside Beth, Kate Cheng, sighed. "I miss the days when she didn't want to leave my side, but it's part of growing up and becoming independent. At least I still get to be around little ones at school."

"You're a special-education teacher, right?" Carrie remembered Kate from the field trip too.

"Yes. I also cover shifts at the school library when needed. That's where I got to know Cam." Kate gestured to where he was absorbed in sticking white candles in tall clear glass holders.

"He mentioned he spent time in the library at lunch and recess." Carrie took a length of precut satin ribbon from the pile in front of Beth and watched as Beth demonstrated how to make a bow and affix a loop to the back so it could be hung over a pew.

"He did, and that worried me. For kids who love reading, the library's their happy place, but it seemed more like Cam was hiding out." Kate started making another bow. "He sat in a reading nook, but he never had a book. Instead, he stared out the window into the playground. Both the librarian and I tried to talk to him, but he shut us out. After that, he'd take a book off the shelf and pretend to read."

Beth's expression was troubled. "We've all tried to help Cam at home. Even Ellie." She nodded to her daughter. "Ellie's biological mom died, so Ellie went through a rough time too, but Cam wouldn't talk to her either." Beth held one end of the slippery satin ribbon as Carrie tweaked her first, lopsided bow. "We're stuck as to what to do next so we're glad Cam has you in his life. Out of all of us, since you don't know him as well, you might just be the one who can help him."

"WATCH ME GO, DADDY." In the fenced pasture nearest to Bryce's house, Paisley trotted around a barrel pattern with Luna. As girl and horse approached each barrel, Paisley sat deeper into her saddle and pushed her weight into her stirrups.

"Looking good, kiddo." For a girl who loved speed, his daughter rode slowly and carefully, and she talked to Luna as they made the circuit around the small course.

"Carrie says it's better to go slow and steady first." Paisley drew the pony to a halt beside Bryce. "Mr. Gallagher loaned us those boots to protect Luna's legs and this special saddle. He has lots of barrel racing tack, and he said Luna and me could use it as long as we want."

Since Squirrel Tail Ranch was set up for visitors, Shane's stable was fully equipped. He was generous too, but extra generous when anyone in Joy's family needed something. While at first it had been strange for Bryce to see his mom with a man who wasn't his dad, he liked Shane. The older man made his mom happy, and in the past year, Bryce had gotten accustomed to her spending time with him. "That's great. I hope you thanked Shane."

"She did." Carrie joined him by the fence. She wore the apron he'd given her, and it fluttered in the light breeze. "She made him a special card."

"We also made him his favorite peanut butter cookies." Cam held Carrie's hand and wore his matching apron.

"Supper will be ready in twenty minutes. Untack Luna and wash up, please, Paisley."

"We have a yummy surprise for you." Cam grinned as Carrie untied his apron so he could follow his sister.

"I can't wait." Bryce leaned against the fence. "You need help, honey?" he called to his daughter, who led Luna toward the barn.

"Nope," she said over her shoulder. "Carrie says if you're old enough to ride a horse, you're old enough to take care of it. It's about responsibility." She stumbled over the word and then said it again correctly.

"That's right." Bryce tilted his face skyward. The sun hung above the western horizon, and white clouds topped the distant mountains like fluffy meringue on a pie. He loved this place and everything about it, and like his dad had taught him, he taught his children, carrying on a legacy from one generation to another.

At his side, Carrie studied the vista too. "I never wanted to live anywhere but Montana. Although Kalispell has its charms, ranch country feels like home for me."

"Me too." He noted the awe on her face. The same awe that must be on his. "It makes me feel small but big at the same time." He gestured to the vast landscape.

She nodded. "That's why how we take care of this land matters so much. I'm only one person, but I still have a duty to do my part."

"We're all part of a larger system. Animals too." Bryce didn't often speak about what was in his heart, but something about Carrie made it easy for him to open up to her. "We have to take care of them as well."

"And each other." Carrie paused. "Before the kids come back, I need to talk to you about something."

"Sure." Bryce stopped considering cloud patterns. "What's up?"

"It's Cam."

Bryce's good mood evaporated. "What's wrong now?" He'd thought his son was doing better.

"It's the same as whatever was going on at school. I keep trying to talk to him, but just when I think he's going to be honest with me, someone interrupts us." Carrie rubbed a hand across her face. "I need one-on-one time with him. Yesterday, when I made decorations with the Sunflower Sisterhood for Cole and Melissa's wedding, I talked to Kate Cheng. You know the special-education teacher at the school?"

Bryce nodded. "Kate's great. Even though it isn't her job, she's always been there whenever Paisley needs someone to talk to."

"Although Kate hasn't worked with Cam, she got to know him because he spent a lot of time in the library this spring."

As Carrie told him what Kate had said, a familiar knot formed in the pit of Bryce's stomach. "That's when I noticed things were off with Cam. I feel so guilty. What kind of dad can't help his child?"

"You're a good dad, the best, so there's no need for guilt."

At Carrie's words, a weight he hadn't realized he was carrying lifted from Bryce's shoulders. He'd felt guilty hiring Carrie to look after the kids, but she made all their lives better. Maybe he was too hard on himself. Since Ally passed, he'd tried to do everything for his children, and except for his mom, he'd never wanted to ask anyone for support. But maybe he needed to admit he was struggling and let himself depend on others.

"Kate thinks Cam has buried whatever the trouble is so deep, he can't talk to anyone about it. She also wonders if someone's threatened Cam so maybe he's afraid to talk."

Anger spurted inside Bryce. "Cam's six. Who'd threaten a little kid?"

"Another child most likely. Remember when you were Cam's age?" Carrie touched Bryce's arm before yanking her hand away and putting both hands in her apron pockets. "Children bully each other, and unless an adult spots what's going on and can intervene, the child being bullied might be so scared they can't see a way out."

Bryce's skin tingled where Carrie had touched him, and awareness of her surged through his body. Not as his employee but as a woman. "I…it's…what can I do?"

"If you plan a special afternoon away from the ranch with Paisley, I'll spend that time with Cam. We need to work together to make the kids understand it's a reward, not a punishment, so neither of them feels singled out or excluded. How does that sound?" Carrie's cheeks were flushed as if she'd felt that awareness between them too.

"Great. Sure. Of course. Anything for Cam." Bryce cleared his throat. "It'll be good for me to have one-on-one time with Paisley." He wanted a close relationship with his daughter, but the years were going by fast. He needed to nurture that father-daughter bond while she was still little. When she entered the preteen years, it would be too late. And he wanted her to feel comfortable coming to him when dealing with the challenges every teenager faced.

"What about tomorrow?" The sun caught Carrie's hair and highlighted gold tints in the brown. Her eyes had gold in them too, like spring green wheat mixed with rich harvest gold.

"Sure. I…" Bryce drew closer.

"Carrie." Paisley and Cam ran toward them, calling as one.

"Uncle Cole's untacking Luna, so can we work on our puzzle before supper?"

As Paisley looked between them, Bryce reared back, and Carrie stepped away too, bumping into the fence.

Carrie waved away Bryce's concern. "Sure, but let's go inside and wash our hands first."

She shepherded the kids to the house and left him by the fence surrounded by sky and fields.

Except now, he didn't feel big *or* small. He felt alone.

CHAPTER SIX

"YOU'RE GREAT AT ART." Carrie passed Cam a green crayon and chose a yellow one for herself. It was another gorgeous Montana summer afternoon, and they sat at the glass-topped patio table on the deck behind the ranch house, shaded by a turquoise umbrella.

"I like drawing pictures. I do art with Mrs. Rosa sometimes." Cam concentrated on coloring a green field, where he'd already drawn several bay horses. "She's nice. You're nice too." Cam drew another horse. "Not like some people."

"What people?" Carrie made her tone casual as she drew a golden sun.

Cam shrugged, gripped the crayon tight and dug it into the pad of paper.

"If you can't tell me, why don't you talk to Penny and Otis?" She called the two beagles from where they lay in the sunshine near the containers of flowers and herbs Carrie and the kids had planted. "Dogs are good listeners." She scratched Penny behind her ears as Otis leaned against Cam's bare legs.

Cam shook his head. "I'd get in trouble."

"Not with me, your dad or anyone in your family." How could Carrie get Cam to open up to her? He had the weight of the world on his slight shoulders, and although she'd expected him to want to go to town with Bryce and Paisley, he'd seemed relieved to stay at the ranch.

"Eli said I'd be in big trouble if I told." Cam made a chopping motion across his neck.

"That's exactly when you have to tell your dad or another adult you trust." *Eli Minden*. The boy Paisley had mentioned and one of the kids Cam had hidden from behind the barn door the day of that riding lesson. Eli was also in another swimming class at the same time as Cam's.

"But Eli's mean and he's bigger than me." Cam picked up Penny and buried his face in the dog's fur. "And him and his friends they..." His shoulders heaved.

"They what?" Carrie knelt by Cam's chair and stroked his hair. "I won't let anything bad happen to you. Your dad won't either."

"They take my lunch, push me into bushes." Cam's words were punctuated with choked sobs. "They say bad things about me, so none of the other kids want to play with me."

Carrie made herself stay calm. "Did anyone else see or hear Eli and his friends say and do those things?"

Cam nodded and cried harder. "Lots of kids, but they're scared of Eli."

"None of that's okay. It's also not your fault."

"Eli said it was *all* my fault. And then..." Cam gulped. "The first time it happened, I said I'd tell the teacher, but Eli said if I did, something bad would happen to Daddy and Paisley. Like with Mommy."

"Oh, sweetheart." Carrie hugged Cam tight. "Your mommy got sick. It just happened. It wasn't anything to do with Eli or anyone else. Your dad and sister are fine."

"Really?" Cam raised his tearstained face, and Penny and then Otis whimpered, perhaps sensing his distress.

"Really and truly." Carrie took a deep breath. "Were Eli and his friends mean to you every day?"

"Mostly. On the bus too and now at swimming, and he's joined my soccer team." Cam erupted in more sobs.

"No wonder you're so upset." Carrie was upset too, but she had to keep her emotions in check for Cam's sake. "It's good you told me what's been happening because now I can try to fix it. It sounds like Eli hasn't learned how to be kind to other kids. It doesn't make what he's doing right, but maybe there's bad stuff going on in his life, and he hurts others because he's hurting. As for his friends, some kids are followers."

"My dad says you hafta think for yourself." Cam's blue eyes were solemn.

"He's right, but it's okay to ask others to help when you need it." Something Carrie still hadn't fully learned.

"Eli's mom and dad are selling their ranch and moving to town. They're gonna have to live with Eli's uncle in an apartment. I heard Eli say he has to share a bedroom with his baby sisters." Cam rested his chin on Penny's head. "Maybe that's why he's mean."

"It could be." Carrie hesitated. "But for now, we have to think about how we can make things better for you. Can we tell your dad?"

"Yes, and Uncle Cole." Cam gave her a tentative smile. "He was a famous rodeo rider. I bet Eli would be scared of him."

"Your whole family will want to help, and your teachers too, but scaring Eli isn't the answer."

"You mean two wrongs don't make a right? Grandma learned me that." Cam let out a heavy sigh.

"Your grandma *taught* you that, and she's right." Carrie smoothed Cam's tousled hair. "Why don't we make a plan?" Starting with texting Bryce.

"Can it be going to the museum and having hot dogs for supper? Paisley and Daddy are doing something special, and you said we'd do something special too." His adorable grin popped out. "I didn't get to go to the museum on my class field trip 'cause I was throwing up, but I heard they have amazing dinosaur bones. Big ones."

"Sure, we can. The best plan is having fun." Carrie stood as Cam tossed a ball across the backyard for the dogs to chase.

"Play with us, Carrie." Cam ran after the barking dogs.

"Okay." She followed them across the lawn and retrieved the ball from Otis. "Now you catch." She sent the ball through the air to Cam.

Life was complicated no matter how old you were, but talking about problems helped.

Cam sent the ball back to her, but Otis caught it, mid-throw.

When Cam rolled on the grass with the dogs and laughed, Carrie joined them.

Maybe she hadn't lost her mojo, only temporarily misplaced it. And helping Cam was good for her too.

"WAY TO GO, CAM." At the edge of one of High Valley's soccer fields, Bryce jumped up and down and cheered as his son kept control of the ball before taking a shot on the net.

Carrie joined in the cheering, as excited as Bryce and the rest of his family, who'd all turned out to watch Cam's game.

"It's only been a week, but what a change in Cam." Under the noise of the crowd, Bryce spoke into Carrie's ear. "He's a happy kid again, and it's all thanks to you."

"Sometimes kids are able to talk more easily to a new person. I'm glad he finally opened up and I could be there for him." Carrie clapped as one of Cam's teammates made another good play. "And while I figured out what's been going on, you talked to the swimming teachers, soccer coach and school principal. Teamwork." She bumped Bryce's elbow.

"Who then all talked to Eli and his parents." Bryce bumped her elbow back. It was a teasing gesture, but for a second it felt like it could have been more. "That poor kid. Eli's been struggling as much as Cam. None of us knew the family was so close to the edge money-wise. Or that the parents have been going without food themselves to feed Eli and the girls and so Eli could still take part in sports."

"Bullying's never right, but it's not surprising Eli acted out." Carrie's voice was warm with sympathy. "I talked to Kate, and she said with all the stress at home, Eli was likely looking for attention."

"In the wrong way. And Cam was a victim, but Eli's one too." Bryce caught a whiff of Carrie's floral scent. It was fresh, light and had a crisp note, a combination that was a lot like her.

"Now both boys can get the support they need. That the town's pitching in for the Minden family in ways that won't embarrass them is wonderful." As Carrie grabbed a bottle of water from the cooler, her hand brushed Bryce's bare arm, and his skin prickled.

They were talking about his son. That was where his attention should be, not on how soft Carrie's skin felt against his. "For Cam, I'm sure talking to the counsellor the principal recommended will be good. But being able to be an ordinary kid again is best of all."

"It sure is." Carrie's smile lit up her face. "He already seems more confident, and when he goes back to school in the fall, it'll be a whole new start."

The Carter family cheered again as Cam scored a goal.

"Did you see that?" Carrie jumped up and down and pointed to the field.

"Yeah." Bryce's throat was thick as Cam ran around

and exchanged high fives with his teammates. Scoring a goal was great, but Cam had achieved something even more important—he'd conquered some of his self-doubt. All made a little easier with Eli taking a break from soccer and swimming.

"That's my brother!" Paisley shouted, and Bryce lifted her up so she could get a better view, while Carrie moved away to speak to Beth, Zach and Ellie.

Bryce's mom looped an arm through his. "It seems things are working out."

"Yeah, life's more settled, and Carrie's fit right in."

"She's good for you." His mom scanned the field, where the game was wrapping up. "You look happier and less stressed."

"Having support at home is great." Bryce kept his tone neutral. "It sure eases the pressure on me."

"In a lot of ways, I expect." His mom's tone was also neutral. "You must—"

"Beth? What's wrong? Mom? I need you." Zach's panicked voice interrupted them.

As Bryce and his mom rushed to join the rest of the family, Carrie knelt beside Beth who lay on the grass. "Did she hit her head when she fainted?"

"No, I caught her and sort of eased her down." Zach's face was pale, and he grabbed a sweatshirt from Bryce to make a pillow to put under his wife's head.

"It's okay," Bryce's mom reassured Beth as her eyes flickered open.

"I'm fine. I just…" She gave Zach a small smile as he crouched on her other side, now joined by Melissa and Cole.

"Low blood pressure again?" Melissa smiled at Beth too as she took out the first aid kit she'd brought to the game as the unofficial team physical therapist. "Paisley, honey? Can you please run to the cooler for a cookie and juice box for your auntie Beth?"

"Sure." Paisley darted away.

Beth looked at the worried faces that surrounded her and Zach. "Melissa already knows because I fainted a few days ago at her place when we were doing some last-minute wedding preparations. Zach and I had planned to tell the rest of you after Cole and Melissa's wedding, but...go ahead, Ellie." She squeezed Ellie's hand.

"Mama Beth and Dad are having a baby. I'm going to be a big sister."

"It's still early days, but that's why I fainted." Beth put her other hand in Zach's as he helped her sit up.

"Oh, my dears." Bryce's mom hugged Zach and Beth and then Ellie too, as congratulations broke out.

"I'm happy for you, bro." Bryce clapped Zach's shoulder. "When are you guys due?"

"Between Christmas and New Year's." Zach's voice was husky. "We were already a family with Ellie, but this baby is an extra special blessing. We're so lucky." He thanked Paisley for the juice and cookie and stayed close to Beth as she ate and drank.

"That baby's lucky too." Bryce spoke around the lump in his throat. "You and Beth are great parents."

"You'll have to give me baby care tips. When Ellie came into my life, she was half grown. This time around, I'm starting from the beginning." As he looked at his wife and stepdaughter, Zach's face was filled with love and pride.

"You've already got the most important thing covered and that's love. The rest of us will pitch in with practical stuff when you need it." Like Bryce's family had done for him and Ally after Paisley and Cam were born.

His gaze drifted to Carrie, who was in the middle of his family group like she belonged there. Paisley and Cam clung to her as she answered their questions about babies and shared their excitement about having a new cousin.

In identifying the bullying situation, Carrie had given Cam a fresh start. Could Bryce let himself think about a fresh start too? And maybe even being happy like Ally wanted?

CHAPTER SEVEN

"I DIDN'T EXPECT you and Luna to learn that new pattern so fast." Carrie clapped as Paisley stopped her pony at the end of the course.

"We've been practicing between lessons."

"I can tell. Your balance is lots better, and you're remembering to focus on where you're going rather than where you've been." So much in horsemanship was relevant to life, and teaching Paisley the basics of barrel racing was teaching Carrie too. As much as she could, nowadays she focused on her future, not her past.

"Where's Cam?" Paisley glanced around for her brother.

"He's with your dad." She'd given Cam a riding lesson earlier, but he'd gotten bored watching Paisley, so Bryce had offered to keep him busy in the barn. "We'll have another lesson after your uncle Cole's wedding." Carrie held Luna still as Paisley dismounted.

"Why not tomorrow?"

"It's the day before the wedding, remember? Between decorating the church and reception hall and going to the rehearsal and party afterward, we'll be too busy." Although Carrie was happy for Cole and Melissa, part of her would also be relieved when the wedding excitement was over. The place inside her that had once hurt like a raw wound was less tender now, but she wouldn't be human if seeing another couple's radiant happiness didn't make her remember what might have been.

"Sorry? What did you say?" She turned to Paisley and pushed the hurt—and the memories—back where they belonged.

"I asked if I'll be ready to compete in kids' events at horse shows soon." Paisley's expression held hope and the kind of self-confidence Carrie wanted to rediscover.

"Not barrel racing yet, but if your dad says it's okay, you could start showing Luna this fall." When Carrie would have left the Tall Grass Ranch, High Valley and Paisley behind. "I started competing when I was about your age." This job had always been temporary. She couldn't let herself get too attached to any part of it, including the kids. "Events should be fun, though, and not about a ribbon." Part of Carrie getting her mojo back was remembering why she'd started riding in the first place. Like Paisley, it was for a love of horses and rodeo sports. What happened in the competition arena was secondary.

"Why can't I have fun *and* win ribbons? I want blue ones, and I'm going to hang them from a line on my bedroom wall." Paisley gave her pony water. "I bet Luna wants blue ribbons too."

Carrie wasn't surprised Paisley wanted a first-place ribbon, and you needed a competitive spirit to accomplish many things in life—it was certainly needed to succeed in rodeo. However, maybe Carrie had focused so much on competition she'd lost sight of fun and, apart from her freelance work, almost everything else in her life? "Slow and steady, remember? You have lots of time to win ribbons of all colors."

"It would still be good to start with a blue one and… hey, there's Daddy and Cam." Paisley waved. "You want to go riding with us, Carrie?"

"Don't you want time on your own with your dad?" Like all the Carters, Bryce was a natural on horseback.

In jeans, a Western shirt, hat and boots, he resembled any other rancher. Yet, even if he hadn't been astride Maverick, Carrie could still have picked him out of a crowd at a hundred feet.

"You're welcome to join us. I finished work early, and it's a beautiful day." Bryce and Cam drew their horses to a stop by Carrie.

"I should get dinner started and—"

"Can we get pizza, Daddy?" Cam asked. Over the past few weeks, Cam had had a growth spurt, and riding Trixie, one of the summer camp ponies, he looked less like a kindergartener and more like a boy ready to start first grade.

"Good idea. Carrie must need a break from cooking for us." Bryce's slow smile made her heartbeat speed up.

"Making meals is part of my job, but I like cooking." She especially liked cooking for a family. When Bryce had to work late, which now happened several times a week, she stayed at the ranch for dinner. She enjoyed being part of family dinnertime too. "Riding would be fun. It'll only take me a few minutes to get Teddy tacked up."

"Already taken care of." Bryce smiled again, and a flock of butterflies took off in Carrie's stomach. "Cam wanted you to ride with us before Paisley asked. Since he was sure he could convince you to say yes, one of the hands looked after Teddy while I helped Cam with Trixie."

"That's great, thanks." Carrie looked beyond Bryce and Cam to see Heidi, a part-time ranch hand, leading Teddy out of the barn. "On the road, I'm used to doing everything myself."

"If we can do something to make your life easier, why not?" Bryce guided Maverick out of the way as Heidi and Teddy approached. "That's what friends and family do, and you return the favor. Giving Paisley and Cam riding lessons and rounding up cattle aren't in your job description."

"I like making people happy." Carrie greeted Teddy, thanked Heidi and swung into the saddle. "Besides, Paisley's doing really well. Cam too." And sharing her love and knowledge of horses with Bryce's kids fulfilled Carrie in ways she hadn't known she needed. "See how he's sitting?" She gestured to the children as they rode ahead of them along the creek path.

"Toes up and heels down. He's got his shoulders back too." Bryce rode at Carrie's side. "I've been trying to teach him that horseman's stance for weeks. How did you manage it?"

"No expectations maybe?" Carrie studied Cam. He had the makings of a good cowboy, but more importantly, there were lots of signs he'd grow up to be a good man. "Since Cam felt bad about himself because of the bullying, it makes sense he wouldn't sit tall on horseback. Hunching his shoulders might have been an unconscious way of making himself smaller so as not to attract attention. He's standing taller too."

"I hadn't made that connection."

"Why would you?" Carrie glanced at Bryce from under her hat brim. "You can't notice everything about your kids. I'm with Cam all day right now, and I'm still getting to know him. Maybe it's easier for me."

"I guess. It seems like yesterday he and Paisley were babies, and look at them now." Bryce's voice hitched. "Before I know it, they'll be wanting to go to horse shows, learning to drive and going on dates."

"Those last two can wait, but Paisley already asked me about entering kids' events at shows this fall." As they walked their horses along the creek path, white butterflies darted alongside, and a crow eyed them from a low branch of a juniper tree. "She's ready, but I told her it's your call."

"So I'll be the bad guy if I say no?" His expression was quizzical, almost teasing.

"That's being a parent, isn't it?" As the path narrowed, Bryce's denim-clad knee brushed Carrie's leg, the brief contact making her nerve endings hyperaware. "Paisley also wants turquoise cowboy boots with rhinestones. She saw a girl on TV with a pair and fell in love."

"Absolutely not." Bryce shook his head and gave a mock glare. "If I say no to the boots, I could say yes to a horse show. What do you think?"

"I think you've got a winner. Then when Paisley says if she can't have the boots, she wants turquoise eyeshadow, you can be outraged and say she can have the horse show or nothing." As they rounded a curve in the path, Carrie's knee bumped his, but Bryce didn't move away.

"Turquoise eyeshadow? At her age? Is there anything else I should know?" His eyes twinkled, but there was a warmth in them too, and the way he looked at her was less teasing and more admiring.

Carrie's breath sped up, and the hairs on her arms quivered as feelings she'd tried to suppress roared into life. "Paisley's a sensible kid, and lots of girls her age like trying makeup. If she—"

"Did you see me and Trixie trot?" Cam called. As if he'd thrown a bucket of cold water over her, Carrie jerked her attention, and her leg, away from Bryce. "Sorry, honey. I missed you. Why don't you go again? I'm watching now."

"I'm watching too." Bryce avoided Carrie's gaze. And, as if by unspoken agreement, when the path widened again, they were both careful to ride a distance apart.

Cam and the pony trotted to where the path ran alongside the creek, and Carrie and Bryce clapped.

"Great job," Bryce said as they joined the kids. "If you

keep going as you are, you'll soon be ready for a pony of your own."

Carrie made herself smile and praise Cam before she rested her cheek on Teddy's thick mane, seeking the comfort only her horse could give.

She liked Bryce. It would be easy to fall for him like she'd fallen for his children. However, attraction was easy and fleeting. A lasting relationship was harder and more complicated. That kind of relationship also required opening her heart and giving it fully to someone else. Something she wasn't sure she could risk again.

"You're my guy, aren't you, Teddy?" she whispered into the horse's ear, then rubbed his neck.

She had to fight that attraction to Bryce. It was the only way to protect herself—and keep her tender heart safe.

"STAND CLOSER TOGETHER and smile." In the church lobby, Bryce snapped a photo of Paisley and Cam in their wedding outfits. "I can't remember the last time you two looked so clean." Or the last time Cam looked so much like Ally. He pushed the emotion away. Today was about celebrating and sharing Cole and Melissa's happiness.

"Now a picture with Carrie." He gestured to her to join the kids.

Carrie wore high-heeled beige sandals and a pale green dress that nipped in at her waist then floated out to skim her knees. Bryce almost hadn't recognized her when she'd arrived at the church with his mom, Beth and the children. Along with the dress, which highlighted curves he shouldn't let himself notice, she'd done something new with her hair. It hung in loose curls around her face and cascaded down her back in a silky brown ripple. On an ordinary day, she was pretty, but today she was downright gorgeous.

"Carrie made me have a bath last night and then a shower this morning." With the impromptu photo session over, Cam made an offended face.

"Only because you, Cameron Carter, got into that mud puddle outside the barn after breakfast." Carrie straightened Cam's purple Western string tie, which was a smaller version of the one Bryce wore. "You have to be spic-and-span for your uncle's wedding, and now you're so clean you squeak."

"Squeak how?" Cam looked at Carrie with a puzzled expression.

"Like this." She tugged his arm, made a squeaking noise and Cam laughed. "At the reception, you can take off your suit jacket and have fun, but for now, you need to look and behave like a cowboy in his Sunday best. Like your dad and Uncle Cole."

"You sure do." Bryce took off his son's small white cowboy hat, while Carrie fixed the bow on Paisley's pale purple flower girl's dress. "Cowboys take off their hats in church, remember? Also, as your grandpa Carter would have said, because there are ladies present."

"Oops." Cam put a hand to his mouth. "But Paisley's not a lady."

"Not yet, but since she's your sister, that's even more of a reason for you to be considerate of her, don't you think?" Carrie asked, giving Cam his white satin ring bearer's pillow.

"To grow up to be a good man, a good cowboy and a good rancher, I hafta start now by being polite, honest and respectful to everyone, even my sister." Cam repeated words Carrie had evidently asked him to remember.

"And I hafta be the same, even to Cam when he bugs me," Paisley agreed. "Except I want to be a good woman, a good cowgirl and a good doctor so I can fix Cam and other cowboys up if they get hurt."

"That sounds like a fine plan, both of you." His kids were growing up, and Carrie was helping them become good citizens like Bryce wanted. She had a gentle way of teaching that made lessons stick. She also led by example, and along with Bryce's mom, Molly, Beth and now Melissa, Paisley and Cam had good female role models.

"The car with your aunt Melissa, her parents and the bridesmaids just pulled up." Carrie retrieved Paisley's basket of pink, white and purple flowers from a table near the door and handed it to her. "It's almost time. You remember from the rehearsal what to do?"

The kids nodded with matching solemn expressions.

Carrie turned to Bryce. "Shouldn't you be at the front of the church with Cole and Zach?"

"Yeah, I better see if Cole needs anything." That was the best man's job, and he and Zach shared that role today. He had come to the lobby to make sure the kids were okay when Carrie texted him they'd arrived. "See you guys soon. Mind your manners, remember?"

"Of course, Daddy." Paisley gave him the kind of eye roll he'd thought was reserved for a teenager who was borrowing the family car and being reminded to drive safe.

Over the kids' heads, he grinned at Carrie, and she grinned back. Then he walked up the center aisle and joined his brothers. "All set?" He focused on Cole. That was who he should be thinking of, not how fantastic Carrie looked and the warmth and connection between them when they'd shared that smile.

"I'm more nervous today than if I was waiting in the chute to ride the meanest bull in Texas." Cole's usually ruddy face was pale, and his brother looked as serious as Bryce had ever seen him. "I want to marry Melissa, but this part with all these people is a lot more stressful than I expected."

On Cole's other side, Zach's voice was reassuring. "It's important to celebrate finding the woman you want to spend the rest of your life with. All of us are here for you and to welcome Melissa into our family."

Then the musical trio—a violinist, a guitarist and a banjo player—began to play, and the soloist sang the first words of "Take My Hand," Emily Hackett's "Wedding Song."

"Here goes." Bryce nudged Cole's ribs, but his brother was oblivious. Instead, his gaze was fixed on the back of the church, waiting for his first glimpse of Melissa. Exactly like Bryce had once waited for Ally.

As the romantic lyrics echoed around the church, Melissa's bridesmaids—her two sisters and Molly—walked down the aisle to join the men. They were followed by Cam and then Paisley with Melissa's daughter, Skylar, in matching dresses and awed expressions.

Bryce gave his kids a discreet thumbs-up as they reached the front and turned to wait for the bride.

Beside him, Cole sucked in a breath and then Melissa appeared, escorted by her mom and stepdad. All brides were beautiful, but the love and trust on Melissa's face as she looked at his brother made Bryce's heart flip. He couldn't avoid thinking of Ally and their own wedding. He also couldn't not think about the unfairness of their life together being cut so short.

Cole greeted Melissa and took her hand as Reverend Ralph stood in front of them and started the service. He'd been their family's minister when Bryce was a child and had come out of retirement to officiate at this wedding.

As Cole and Melissa exchanged their vows to love, honor and cherish each other, Bryce's thoughts wandered.

Several generations of Carters had married in this church on the corner of a quiet street in High Valley's oldest neighborhood. And today, half the town had gathered to see Cole and Melissa happily join their lives together.

In a front pew, Bryce's mom patted her eyes with a tissue. She had her own memories of marrying Bryce's late dad here. Shane Gallagher sat behind her, along with Carter aunts, uncles and cousins. All the members of the Sunflower Sisterhood were here too, with Rosa at the end of a row, ready to give a reading. Ranching families Bryce had grown up with, Melissa's coworkers and members of both the bride's and groom's extended family and friends from Montana, California and Canada filled the pews to the back of the church and up into the loft. Weddings weren't only about the bridal couple. They were also about family, friends and community.

Cam held out his ring bearer's pillow for the exchange of rings and then stepped back to his spot between Paisley and Skylar. He beamed at Bryce, who nodded approval.

Bible readings, several more songs and the homily passed in a blur. Although Bryce avoided looking at Carrie, he was still hyperaware of her seated behind Paisley, Cam and Skylar, there for the kids if they needed her.

"I now pronounce you husband and wife. You may share your first married kiss." Reverend Ralph blessed Cole and Melissa. A smattering of applause broke out, the couple kissed and one of Cole's rodeo friends cheered.

"You did it, bro. Congratulations." Bryce patted Cole's shoulder, and Zach congratulated the newlyweds too. Then Bryce was in a line paired with Melissa's youngest sister as the musicians and the soloist launched into Tim McGraw and Faith Hill's moving duet "The Rest of Our Life."

As he waited to recess out of the church, Bryce's eyes smarted, and he dug in his jacket pocket for a tissue. The burning behind his eyes was for Ally and the past, but for Cole and Melissa too, and all they'd overcome to find *their* happily ever after.

When he passed Carrie, his gaze caught hers and lingered.

And instead of thinking of the past, Bryce thought about the rest of his own life and what it could be. A life he didn't spend alone, but with another good woman by his side.

Moving on from Ally didn't mean letting go of her because she'd always be in his heart. But maybe there was room for someone else there too.

Someone like Carrie.

CHAPTER EIGHT

AT THE SIDE of the dance floor in High Valley's community center, Carrie tapped one foot to "Cowboy Take Me Away" by The Chicks. Since it was a country wedding and a country crowd, she knew most of the songs on the DJ's playlist, including this one. And now that the wedding and formal part of the reception were over, she'd taken off her heels and replaced them with boots, like most of the female guests.

Cole and Melissa danced past her, Melissa's white cowboy boots peeking out from under the ruffled hem of her dress. The couple looked so happy they glowed.

"Want to dance?" Cam held out his hand like he'd seen Cole and the other men do.

"I'd love to." Carrie clasped his small palm and studied his flushed face and the dark shadows beneath his eyes. "It's been a long day, and it's not over yet. You can sleep in as long as you want tomorrow." She included Paisley and Skylar, who stood behind Cam. Skylar was having a sleepover with Paisley, and Carrie was staying overnight in the guestroom at Bryce's to help with all three kids.

"And then can we make blueberry pancakes?" Paisley asked.

"If you want to, sure." Was her pride in Paisley and Cam today how a mom felt? She was as proud of the kids as she was of Teddy when the two of them completed a clean race in a personal best time. Yet, her pride in these children was different, although she couldn't explain how or why.

As Skylar went to dance with her mom and Cole, Carrie took Paisley's hand too. "Why don't the three of us dance together? We don't want to leave your sister out, do we, Cam?"

"'Course not." Cam bowed and drew them onto a quieter part of the dance floor where they wouldn't collide with Bryce, Zach and a group of Carter cousins doing a "Boot Scootin' Boogie" line dance to the Brooks & Dunn song of the same name.

With Cam and Paisley on either side of her, Carrie counted steps. "On four, put your left heel up—that's the same side as the hand you write with, Cam. Clap your hands and then reverse." Their boots echoed on the floor in time to the music. "Nice. You two look like you've done this dance before."

"We have. Lot of times with Daddy. A bunch of other dances too." The tip of Paisley's tongue stuck out of her mouth as she concentrated on the footwork. "Grandma says he's the best dancer in our whole family."

"I can see why." Carrie's gaze slid to Bryce. While the Carter brothers all stood head and shoulders above most of the other men in terms of height and good looks, when it came to dancing, Bryce was also head and shoulders above Cole and Zach. With good rhythm, neat footwork and a smooth style, he seemed to glide across the floor like Fred Astaire in the old musicals Carrie loved.

Focus on the kids. They are the only reason you're here. "I lost my step count. Let's start over." She turned back to Paisley and Cam, and they tried the routine again, getting into the groove of the song alongside the other dancers.

"It's the cowboy cha-cha," Paisley said as the music changed. "That's for two people." Her smile dimmed.

"We can make it work as a line dance with three." Carrie listened to the beat. "I'll show you." She demonstrated, and the kids copied her.

"It's better in a couple, though." Before she realized what was happening, Bryce took Carrie's hands and led her into the dance. "Watch us, kids. Carrie and I'll show you how it's done. Can you take a picture of us, Paisley? Here's my phone."

Carrie's face heated. Bryce's hands were warm and callused like hers. "I was okay sticking with the kids." They posed for the photo while Paisley took a picture and then gave the phone back.

"But I bet you'd like a turn with someone who won't step on your toes." Bryce laughed and held Carrie close.

"Cam only stepped on my feet once, and he's not heavy." This closeness with Bryce was only because of the dance. It didn't mean anything important.

"The kid's learning." Bryce dipped Carrie, and she relaxed into the music, the dance and her partner.

"He has a good teacher in you." She was used to being independent, but in a partner dance, one person had to lead, and she was happy for Bryce to do it. He had the same confidence on the dance floor as everywhere else, but now he was attuned to her in a way that was new. "I thought men who could dance were almost an endangered species."

"Not in my family." Bryce drew her even closer. Unlike some men Carrie had danced with, who hauled her around like she was a steer they were trying to wrestle, each of Bryce's movements was smooth, as well as gentle and courteous. "My dad was a good dancer, and he and my mom danced together most Saturday nights at home. They taught all of us kids. When my grandparents could babysit, my folks went dancing at a place in town. Mom says date nights are important. Along with mutual respect and shared interests, dates keep the magic and love alive."

Carrie wanted that kind of relationship, one that was a true partnership, like her parents had. Although her mom had given up ranch life to move to the city, marry Carrie's dad and work with him in the family business, she'd always seemed happy with that choice.

The music changed again, and their steps slowed as Darius Rucker's voice wrapped around them singing "History in the Making."

Bryce turned Carrie in his arms, so they were face-to-face and almost cheek to cheek. A hint of his spicy aftershave mixed with her perfume. Under her hand, the muscles in his arm where he'd rolled up the sleeves of his white dress shirt were taut and lightly covered with short hair. Her hand trembled in his and her stomach fluttered.

When the song ended, they stilled, caught in the moment.

"We should...the kids..." Carrie made herself step away.

"Of course." Bryce dropped Carrie's hand and invited Paisley and Cam into their circle.

"You dance almost as well as Daddy." Paisley studied Carrie through narrowed eyes. "Mommy was an excellent dancer. The best ever."

"I'm sure she was." Paisley couldn't be jealous Carrie had danced with Bryce, could she? "If your mom were here, she'd be really proud of how you both handled yourselves today."

"Grandma says Mommy is always with us. In our hearts and watching over us." Paisley glanced between Carrie and Bryce. Her lower lip stuck out, and if her eyes could talk, they would've said, "Leave my daddy alone."

"What a lovely way of keeping your mom close." Carrie laced her fingers together.

"I talk to Mommy sometimes. Cam and I both do." Paisley spit the words out.

"That's great." Carrie was way out of her depth, and from Bryce's uncertain expression, he was as well. "I talk to my grandparents too. I miss them, and that's how I keep them close."

And her grandparents would have wanted her to be happy. When her grandma had left her some money, Carrie had invested the small inheritance in what she called her "farm fund." Thanks to this nannying job, her dream wasn't as far out of reach as it had been.

"Listen. It's my favorite song." Unaware of any undercurrents, Cam did his version of a disco-style dance, his arms and legs flailing to "Electric Boogie."

"Shall we? I remember this one from when I was a kid." Bryce flung his head back as he slid across the floor with Carrie and the kids following.

"An oldie but a goodie." Carrie moved in time to the music. It had been a long and tiring day. Paisley likely wanted to dance with her dad herself. She shouldn't read anything more into the girl's sullen expression. "The DJ at my eighth-grade graduation dance played this song. Whenever I hear it, I remember my science teacher calling out 'boogie woogie woogie,' and all of us joining in."

Bryce, Paisley and Carrie clapped as Cam showed off more moves, and then they joined a conga line with some of Melissa's Californian and Canadian family members.

"I can't remember the last time I had so much fun." As the dance ended, Carrie fanned her hot face and asked the bartender for a pitcher of water and glasses.

"Me neither." Bryce leaned against the bar as the kids joined Skylar and several other children at a table with crayons and coloring sheets. "I could hardly keep up with you guys."

"It's me who couldn't keep up with you." Carrie made her tone light. "It's been a great party."

"Here's the photo Paisley took of us, along with some I got of you dancing with Paisley and Cam." He tapped his phone. "There, I sent them to you."

"Thanks." She'd look at them later when she was alone. That way, she could linger over them and pretend…no. Carrie mentally shook herself. "Aunt Angela's having fun." Carrie gestured to where her aunt danced with a group of friends. "It's been awful for her since my uncle passed, but she says she's ready to get out and mix with people again."

"A small-town party has a way of bringing folks together." Bryce filled glasses with water for them, and Carrie took a long drink, the refreshing coldness slipping down her throat.

"It's like the rodeo community in some respects." Except, for Carrie, this wedding reception was more fun than any after-rodeo party. While rodeo was often called a family, today Carrie had been drawn into the Carter and High Valley families, and that was different. These people were connected not only by bonds of blood, but a history far beyond a shared sport, and she liked the sense of belonging it gave her.

"Lots of rodeo people are here for Cole. This wedding could be good for ranch business too." Bryce finished his water. "I talked to a stock contractor friend of Cole's from Colorado. Heath told me about a new forage barley they're trying. I'd like to give it a shot here."

"I talked to Heath too. He and his wife are a nice couple." Since they were committed to sustainable ranching, Carrie had enjoyed chatting with them and gotten lots of great tips. "I'll take the kids home soon. It's late, and they're high on chocolate cupcakes, excitement and adrenaline. If they color for a few minutes, they should settle down before getting into the car."

"Let's hope so." Bryce's smile was wry. "If you'd like me to—"

"I wanted to say what a wonderful family you two have." A blond woman in her early sixties stopped beside Carrie. "Paisley and Cam have been as good as gold all day, and the two of you are such loving and caring parents. I'm Melissa's third cousin, Marion Koehler, from Calgary." She stopped to take a breath.

"We're not... I'm not... I'm the nanny." Carrie introduced herself. "Paisley and Cam are Bryce's children. Bryce is Cole's younger brother."

Bryce's laugh sounded forced. "Carrie's great with the kids."

"I'm so sorry." Marion put a hand to her mouth as a gray-haired man joined her. "I'm always putting my foot in it, aren't I, Randall?" She looked at the man before introducing him as her husband. "I saw you dancing, and you looked...anyway...a nanny is almost part of the family, aren't you?" She patted Carrie's arm.

"No harm done." Bryce assured her.

"Bryce and the kids treat me like family." Hopefully, the muted light of the reception hall would hide Carrie's red face. She supposed it was an honest mistake. Zach and Cole were both married, and Molly, who'd arrived the day before from Atlanta, was with a group of her high-school friends. Only Bryce had attended the wedding on his own.

"It's all good then." Marion turned away to order sodas from the bartender.

"I'll check on Paisley and Cam and let them know we're leaving soon." Carrie avoided Bryce's gaze, but as she skirted the dance floor to reach the coloring table, she felt his eyes follow her.

The one time she'd thought about settling down, it had gone wrong. And now, except when it came to horses and work, she didn't trust herself to make good choices.

"Ten minutes until home time, you two." She knelt beside Cam and admired his field of red cattle.

Rodeo and family life also didn't mix, let alone making a go of her own ranch. No matter how good that sense of family and belonging felt right now, Carrie wouldn't give up her dreams. Even if she couldn't quite convince her heart she meant it.

"I CALL THIS meeting to order." At her seat at a table in the Bluebunch Café, Joy tapped a teaspoon against her water glass and tried to sound firm. Although Sunflower Sisterhood meetings weren't formal, there were a few things she wanted to tell the other women at their last get-together before the fall.

"That expression about herding cats comes to mind," Rosa said as the hubbub of female conversation continued. She chuckled and took out the lap blanket she was knitting. "It's been four days, but have you recovered from the wedding excitement?"

"Hardly." Joy laughed too. "It's wonderful having happy and exciting things going on, and I don't want them to end. Molly being able to stay a few days longer is fantastic. She's also lending a hand with ranch work while Cole and Melissa are on their honeymoon."

She glanced at her daughter, who sat at another table with Beth and several younger women. Molly's eyes were purple-shadowed, and she had a new brittleness about her. Whenever Joy tried to talk to her, Molly brushed off her gentle questions. Tomorrow, she'd fly back to Atlanta and a life Joy wasn't truly part of.

"Having Skylar stay with me is fun too." She couldn't

help Molly if her daughter wouldn't talk to her. And even if Molly did open up, except for video calls and sending care packages, Joy couldn't do much from two thousand miles away. "With Paisley and Cam in and out as well, it's like having my own children at home again but without so much responsibility."

"Being a grandma is the best." Rosa nodded. "I hope you don't mind, but I invited Carrie to join us. She'll be along as soon as she finishes a few things for my website."

"That's fine. I intended on inviting Carrie to this meeting myself, but I got caught up in wedding planning and then hosting Melissa's family." Cole and Melissa were perfect for each other, and her once restless son was happy and settled like Joy had always wanted for him. If Bryce and Molly could find that same happiness, she could rest easier.

A buzzer sounded, and Kristi, the café's owner, opened the front door and welcomed Carrie. The Bluebunch closed at six, but Kristi let them use the café for evening meetings.

"Sorry I'm late." Carrie hovered in the entryway before Joy patted the empty chair beside hers.

"We haven't started yet." Joy tapped her glass with the spoon again as Carrie greeted Rosa and the others, and the various conversations ceased. Joy stood and scanned the circle of faces. "Since we don't meet in August, tonight's our last gathering until September." Thanks to her college classes, she'd gotten better at public speaking, and she was among friends, but it still wasn't easy. She was pushing herself out of her comfort zone, though, and that was what mattered. "Before we start tonight's icebreaker activity, I have a few announcements. First of all, thank you for your hard work in making Cole and Melissa's wedding so special."

Joy waited until the clapping died down and then remembered to pitch her voice so everyone could hear. "From our support of the food bank, to volunteer placements for our middle-school students at local businesses and ongoing fundraising for our biggest project—making the arena more accessible—we've had a successful year. Thanks to Angela and Nina for leading the arena fundraising project. We all hope you'll stay on." The two widows were contributing to the community again, and getting involved had helped them as well. Joy was happy to see how, like sunflower plants, they'd blossomed.

"We will," Nina said, and Angela nodded.

More applause.

"I handed out the financial report earlier." She acknowledged Diana, who, along with running a ranch, worked part-time as a bookkeeper and kept the group's books. "You can read it at your leisure. Since we keep these meetings fun and informal, Rosa suggested something to round out the year that will help us get to know each other better, especially our new members. Rosa?"

"Some of you may have played 'what's in your purse' before, and if you have, you know it's a lot of laughs." As if on cue, muffled laughter broke out, and several women clutched their bags. "You earn points for particular items on this list. It doesn't include things like wallets or phones because we all carry those around. We're looking for more interesting stuff that says something about who you are. My daughter in North Dakota put the list together, so like the rest of you, Joy and I are seeing it for the first time tonight, although I've agreed to keep score." There was more laughter as Rosa waved a brown envelope and withdrew several sheets of paper. "If you don't have a purse, a backpack is fine."

"But I…" Carrie looked around with an embarrassed expression.

"In this crowd, you won't be the first to carry horse

tack around with you. Or paint brushes and pots." Joy sent Rosa a teasing glance.

"I might need them in an emergency." Rosa opened her bag, a patchwork tote of her own design.

"Like painting an SOS sign if your car breaks down on a back road with no cell service," Angela said above more laughter. "It's always good to be prepared for the unexpected."

"Angela's right," Beth said as she cradled her small pregnancy bump.

"Okay. Let's start, shall we?" Joy waved to get the group's attention. "Diana?"

"Nothing too interesting, although I do have a pair of underwear for my youngest just in case." She held up a pair of cartoon-patterned boys' briefs. "A stain removal pen, an envelope with business receipts, a granola bar and safety pins."

Rosa totted up Diana's points.

"You want to go next, Carrie?" Although they'd spoken to each other almost daily at the ranch, either with Paisley and Cam or when Carrie was seeing to Teddy, Joy couldn't say she'd gotten to know her yet. While Carrie was always friendly, it was as if she held part of herself back.

Carrie unzipped her backpack. "A red hair scrunchie." She pulled it out and stuck it on her wrist. "A broken rein, a pack of gum, a USB stick and a picture Paisley drew for me. It's of us riding together." She held it up to show everyone.

As the others admired the crayon drawing of two horses and riders in an emerald green field, Joy flicked a gaze to Carrie's half-open backpack. She wasn't being nosy. She was interested because the pack had a helmet holder similar to one she'd like. Carrie's pack had space for a water bottle too.

Joy drew in a soft breath. Although she'd suspected there was something more than friendship between Bryce and Carrie, she hadn't had proof. Until now. Under the guise of picking up a paper napkin, Joy leaned closer. A picture stuck out from an envelope with High Valley's photo-center logo. Joy had the same envelope in her own purse because she'd printed out wedding pictures to mail to family members who hadn't been able to attend and also didn't use email.

But while Joy's photos featured the bride and groom, Carrie's was of her and Bryce. She'd known they'd danced together because Paisley had mentioned it, but Joy hadn't thought anything of it. But this picture was important. Joy slid her reading glasses from atop her head to get a better look. The tenderness in Bryce's expression, how he held Carrie so close and how the two of them gazed into each other's eyes...

"Joy? We're going around the table clockwise, so it's your turn." Rosa's voice broke into her thoughts.

"Sure. I dropped this." She waved the napkin, but the others were still talking about Paisley's art and how many points Carrie had earned.

"Cam's also good at art. Here's a picture he drew for me." Joy rummaged in her purse for the drawing of her sunflower field Cam had given her earlier. "I have wedding photos, a mini manicure kit and a grocery-store gift card I won at the last bingo night."

As the game continued, Joy stole a glance at Carrie, who was now talking to Diana about irrigation systems.

Although Bryce might not have let himself admit it, he was well on his way to falling in love with Carrie. And all the signs were that Carrie reciprocated the feeling.

After Zach and Beth had gotten together, she'd promised Zach she wouldn't interfere in his life or anyone else's, and so far she hadn't.

Cole and Melissa had only needed a gentle nudge. Would that work for Bryce and Carrie too? Like Joy, Ally had wanted Bryce to be happy. Anything Joy did would be for her son as well as the woman she'd loved like a daughter.

And her precious grandbabies. Although Bryce likely hadn't admitted it, Paisley and Cam needed a nurturing motherly influence, and Carrie would be perfect.

Now Joy had to help her son see what was right in front of him. But first, she had to bide her time, watch and wait for the right opportunity.

CHAPTER NINE

"IT'S ONLY FOR a few hours. Besides, when did you last take a break?" Carrie spoke to Bryce over one shoulder as she hung a ball in Teddy's stall for him to play with.

"I take time off when I need to. Like for the wedding." Bryce finished putting away extra feed buckets and tried to avoid Carrie's intent green gaze.

"You were there for Cole and Melissa, which is what family does, but when was the last time you had fun with your kids?"

"At the wedding." He'd had fun with Carrie too, maybe too much because the more time he spent with her, the more off-balance he felt.

It was like when he was a kid and had taken swimming lessons at the pool in town. While Zach and Cole had run along the diving board and plunged into the water without thinking twice, Bryce had teetered at the edge of the board. Although he'd been scared to dive in, he hadn't wanted to go back to the pool deck either. Yet, when he finally launched himself off the board and sliced into the water exactly as the teacher had shown him, he'd wondered why he'd been so frightened.

Carrie huffed out a breath. "All I'm asking is that you come to Squirrel Tail with the kids and me this afternoon for the children's event. It's like the school field trip but unstructured family fun instead of learning focused." She glanced at the kids playing with the barn cats in the hayloft and lowered her voice. "Paisley and Cam need time with you. Paisley especially. Since the wedding, she hasn't been herself. Maybe she's still tired. It was a lot of excitement and build up for a girl her age, and she's bound to feel flat now it's over. But whatever's wrong, some special time with you might help."

Guilt churned in Bryce's stomach. In the past six days, Paisley had talked back to him twice and slammed her bedroom door after he'd spoken to her about her rudeness. Although that behavior might well be because she was overtired, Bryce couldn't shake the sense something else was also going on.

"I've wondered about Paisley lately. I appreciate you caring about her. About both kids. I'll come to the event with you." Work could wait. He'd devote this afternoon to the children.

"Great. As for caring about the kids? I do care, truly." For a second, something flickered in Carrie's eyes, as if maybe she cared about him too. Then her tone turned teasing. "Are you sure the ranch won't fall apart if you leave it for a while?"

"Who knows what might happen?" Bryce teased her back. "But yeah, Zach and the hands can manage." He wasn't irreplaceable, and the work would always be there.

"We're leaving right after lunch, so see you back at the house?" Carrie paused at the bottom of the hayloft ladder. "We can take my truck."

"Sure." He hesitated. "You're good for all of us. Me as well as the kids. Thank you." His voice wobbled, and he made a clatter of grabbing a dustpan and broom to cover it.

"It's my pleasure." Carrie beamed before she clambered up the ladder and joined the kids. The sound of their happy voices made him wish he could take the whole day off, not only the afternoon.

Several hours later, in front of a bunny hutch at Squirrel Tail Ranch, Bryce crouched beside Paisley as she explained how she and Cam had helped build it.

"I hammered in this nail right here." She pointed to one of the sides. "I used a drill too."

"You did great," Carrie said. "Shane and I were with the kids the whole time." She reassured Bryce.

"Michael Kim almost chopped his finger off. There was blood everywhere." Cuddling Buster, his favorite bunny, Cam shook his head. "Even on the grass."

"Don't exaggerate, honey," Carrie said. "Michael's finger bled, sure, but he didn't need stitches, and Mr. Gallagher and I took care of it." She turned back to Bryce. "Don't worry. Shane had child-size tools for them to work with, and they wore goggles. Michael cut his finger on the rough edge of a piece of lumber. He wasn't using a saw."

"I wasn't worried exactly. I trust you, and Shane too." Bryce began to protest.

"You weren't there, so I'd be surprised if you weren't worried. Kids have accidents. You must have when you were a kid." Carrie scratched a gray-and-white bunny between its ears.

Like all children, Bryce had had the usual mishaps, but back then he'd felt invincible. After losing Ally to the cancer that came out of nowhere, and his dad in a farm accident, he'd become more aware that life could be short and more protective of his children too.

"Buster's asleep, so can we go in the bouncy house?" Cam tugged on Bryce's arm.

"Sure." Bryce stood and brushed grass from his faded jeans as the kids and Carrie put the rabbits back in their hutch.

He'd changed out of his work clothes, but maybe he should have worn something fancier than his usual jeans and Western shirt. In crisp denim shorts, white sneakers and a white T-shirt with a barrel-racing pattern in glittery pink, Carrie looked casual but more dressed up than she was around the barn or when looking after the kids. No matter what she wore, though, Bryce could barely keep his eyes off her since the wedding. And he kept sneaking glances at his phone and the photo Paisley had taken of him and Carrie dancing. At town and family parties, he'd danced with other women since Ally had passed. Why did dancing with Carrie feel so different and momentous?

"You hafta bounce too, okay?" Paisley gestured to the red-and-yellow bouncy house on the other side of the grassy area from the rabbit hutch and petting zoo.

"Sure." They sat on a bench and took off their shoes as, opposite them, Carrie and Cam did the same.

"Only you and me, okay?" Paisley lowered her voice.

"But we're here as a..." Bryce stopped. He'd almost said "family," but even though they felt a lot like one, they weren't. "A group," he substituted.

"I want to be with you. Not Carrie and Cam." Paisley stuck out her bottom lip.

"Feeling left out, are you, Ladybug?" He tried to ruffle her hair, but she jerked away.

"Mommy called me Ladybug. I thought you'd forgotten."

"I'd never forget something so important." He jerked his chin to indicate to Carrie she and Cam should go ahead. "I've been really busy lately, but I'm never too busy for you and Cam."

"It's always Cam." Paisley picked at the pink nail polish she'd worn for the wedding. "Or Carrie."

"What do you mean? With Eli being mean to him, I thought you understood why Cam needed extra attention. I also thought you liked Carrie."

"I do like her. And Cam, well, he's Cam. It's…" Paisley let out a long sigh. "Forget it."

"I'm your dad. I can't forget it." Bryce hesitated. "If you're upset about something, I want to make it better."

"It's nothing." She gave him a bright smile. "Eli Minden was really mean to Cam. When school starts again, I'm gonna be mean to Eli too."

"No, you won't." Bryce took Paisley's hand as they walked to the bouncy house. "Eli *was* unkind to Cam, but he said sorry, and everyone deserves a second chance." *Even me.* Bryce caught his breath. Although he'd always believed in second chances, that was for others. Why hadn't he given himself the same grace and compassion?

"I guess, but I can still *imagine* being mean." Paisley watched a boy near her age do a series of somersaults.

"You could, but why waste your imagination on something that isn't nice and kind?" Bryce tugged one of her braids as he followed her onto the bouncing area.

"I'd rather imagine being a world champion barrel racer." Paisley held Bryce's hands as they bounced together.

"There you go."

"Hey, watch me, Paisley." The boy showed more acrobatic moves.

"That's Noah. He goes to my school, but he's going into fourth grade," Paisley said. "He's here with his aunt and older cousins."

Bryce watched the kid too, who he now recognized from a youth hockey team Zach coached. And when Noah returned to his family group, and Paisley started talking about barrel racing, Bryce hoped this meant order had been restored. The daughter he knew seemed to be back.

Carrie and Cam joined them, Cam chattering about how high he could jump and taking Bryce's hand to show him.

"Let's jump in a circle holding hands." Cam's mouth and blue T-shirt were stained pink from the frozen strawberry treat he'd eaten earlier, and his hand was sticky in Bryce's. His eyes shone as he twisted his wiry body into pretzel-like shapes. "You too, Carrie."

"Okay." She grinned, and her mouth had a strawberry-pink tinge too.

When her hand connected with Bryce's, he kept bouncing even though the biggest part of him stilled. Although Cam and Paisley continued to talk, the only person Bryce was truly aware of was Carrie. The warmth of her palm and how right it felt in his. How the sunshine on her pretty hair also illuminated her sweet face. The way she smiled at the kids and him too and gave them her full attention. Those freckles on her nose he'd like to trace with a fingertip before kissing. And how he'd like to hold her close like he had when they'd danced, finding safety and comfort in her embrace.

"Bryce? Are you all right?" Carrie's voice yanked him back to reality.

"Are you gonna throw up, Daddy? You look like Paisley did that time at the fair before she—"

"I'm not going to be sick, Cam. It's fine, Carrie." Bryce bounced to a stop and put a hand to his head. "It's hot out here, that's all. Why don't we get lemonade?"

"Good idea." Carrie still looked at him as if he'd grown another head. "We should find some shade too. The kids want to swim, and the children's pool has an awning."

As Bryce left the bouncy house in a daze, he barely heard Carrie or his children. All that jumping around must have really rattled him. That was the only explanation for why he'd let himself think about Carrie in such an intimate way.

As if she were special to him rather than the kids' nanny. As if he wanted her to be part of all their lives forever.

"HERE YOU GO." An hour later, Carrie wrapped a swim towel around Paisley "Is that better?"

Although she still shivered, Paisley nodded and sat on one of the lounge chairs beside the children's pool.

"You'll soon warm up, but I'm done swimming too. I'll stay here with you while your dad plays with Cam." Carrie gestured to Bryce and Cam, who, still in the pool, tossed a beach ball between them. She pulled up another chair under the shaded awning and wiggled her toes. "Our pedicures lasted well, didn't they?" She nudged Paisley's foot with hers.

"Yeah." Huddled in her pink unicorn-patterned towel and with wet hair plastered to her head, Paisley appeared younger than eight.

"You looked like you had fun this afternoon. Especially with Noah in the bouncy house." Carrie hadn't missed Bryce's classic protective dad expression when the boy had shown off for Paisley's benefit. "Are you and Noah friends?"

"Kind of. He's nice. He goes to after-school club with Cam and me. One time, he stopped a kid from pulling my hair." Paisley studied her pink toenails.

"Is he the kind of boy you might like?" Most kids had crushes. Bryce likely didn't have anything to worry about—the kids were so young—but Carrie owed it to him to make sure.

"Just as a friend." Paisley rolled her eyes. "Noah wants to compete in rodeo too, so that's mostly what we talk about."

"If you want to invite him to the ranch, your dad or I can call his parents and set something up. You can invite your other friends too." Now that Carrie thought of it, Paisley didn't mention any friends apart from Melissa's daughter, Skylar. At her age, Carrie had had playdates with friends all the time.

"It's not important." Paisley squeezed water out of her hair.

"Is something bothering you? If so, I hope you know you can talk to me. I might not be able to fix whatever it is, but I've been told I'm a good listener. I remember being your age, and I know sometimes it's hard." Carrie toweled her own hair.

"How could you know what it's like? You had your mom when you were my age. You *still* have her. Cam and me are the only kids in the entire school, probably the whole town, who don't have a mom. And then at the wedding, when you and Daddy were dancing, I heard…" Paisley gulped and buried her face in the towel.

"Your dad and I danced together because we're friends. We didn't mean to make you sad or upset." Carrie put a gentle hand on Paisley's heaving shoulders and sent Bryce a look, silently telling him to distract Cam a while longer. "Can you tell me what you heard?"

Paisley shook her head.

Carrie patted Paisley's back. She hadn't missed the covert glances she and Bryce had attracted at Melissa and Cole's wedding, and although people in small towns liked to talk about their neighbors, it usually wasn't hurtful.

But while she'd tried to pretend dancing with Bryce was as innocent as when she'd danced with Cole and Zach, it wasn't. She wouldn't have printed that picture of them together otherwise. A picture now tucked in a plain envelope in her bottom dresser drawer beneath a pile of hoodies, where nobody but her would see it.

"Whatever you heard was likely gossip and didn't mean anything important."

"It meant something *very* important. A lady talking to Mrs. Shevchenko called me a motherless child. I'm not motherless. I had Mommy." Paisley raised her tearstained face.

"You did, and you still have her, sweetheart." Carrie smoothed wet hair away from Paisley's face. "You're not motherless at all." From everything Carrie had heard around town, Alison Carter had been a devoted mother and wife whose husband and children were the center of her world.

"That's what Mrs. Shevchenko said. I like her."

Carrie liked her aunt Angela's friend, Nina Shevchenko, too. She'd give her a call tonight and ask what had been said. If there was anything else Carrie could do to reassure Paisley, she needed the whole story. "Did Cam hear what the lady said?"

"Nope. He was goofing around. But the lady also said if Daddy got married again, me and Cam would have the mother we needed. Like we didn't need Mommy." Carrie opened her arms, and Paisley flung herself into them as her words came out between choked sobs.

"You'll always need your mommy." Carrie hugged Paisley tight. "Even if your dad marries someone else, she wouldn't replace your mother, not ever. Your dad would make sure of it. He's that kind of man." As far as Carrie knew, Bryce wasn't even dating anyone, so the issue was hypothetical, but it broke her heart to think of how Paisley must have worried.

"Really?" Paisley sniffed and rubbed a hand across her face.

"Really and truly, but you need to talk to your dad." She exhaled as she tried to think of how best to help Paisley understand. "Look at Ellie. Her real mom passed too but she and Beth were best friends, so although Beth became Ellie's guardian, she'd never take Ellie's mom's place. Beth's there for Ellie like a mom, but she also keeps Ellie's real mom's memory alive." Carrie didn't know Beth well, but when they'd chatted at the Sunflower Sisterhood meeting, Beth had mentioned talking with Ellie about her mom and displaying photos.

Paisley gulped. "Ellie says she now has two moms."

"There you go." Maybe Beth and Ellie could talk to Paisley too. Carrie had been so focused on Cam and the bullying she hadn't realized Paisley was struggling. "From now on, when you're worried about something, will you promise to tell me, your dad, your grandma or someone else you trust?"

"I promise." Paisley took a tissue from Carrie and mopped her tears. "It's okay if you dance with Daddy. If he does ever get married again, I wish it would be to someone like you."

"I'm your nanny. I work for your dad." Carrie's stomach lurched. "Besides, I'll only be around this summer, but I know…" She rushed on to forestall more tears from Paisley. "You and Cam are the most important people in your dad's life. He'd never share his life with someone who wasn't right for *all* of you." Someone who'd be around all the time to pick up the kids from school, help with homework and tuck them into bed each night.

Carrie's refusal to leave the rodeo circuit had been a recurring argument between her and Jimmy long before he'd gone off with her friend. Neither of them had been willing to compromise.

"For your art project next week, what do you say about focusing on your mom? You could share your memories of her through stories and drawings. If you did it on poster

board, we could get it framed, and you could hang it in
your bedroom." With Rosa's guidance, Carrie did an art
project or craft with the kids each week, and it was fun
for her as well as them.

"I'd like that." Paisley sniffed. "But what about Cam?
He doesn't remember anything about Mommy, only stuff
other people have told him."

"You can tell him about her, and maybe he could talk to
your mom's parents and her sister." After Alison's death,
her parents had retired to a town in Idaho to be closer to
their other daughter and grandchildren, but they video
called Paisley and Cam several times a week. "I'll try to
think of something special for Cam's art project."

"What kind of something special?" Cam hugged Carrie
from behind, his wet arms encircling her neck.

"We were talking about your mom and our next art project. Here's your towel. Dry off, you're getting me all wet
again." Carrie caught Bryce's gaze. "I hope that's okay?"
She'd wanted to comfort Paisley, but she hoped she hadn't
gone too far by talking about Alison.

"Yeah, I can get the old photo albums out," he said, his
voice gruff. Then he grabbed his own towel and rubbed
his face and hair.

"Those albums in boxes in the basement?" Paisley
asked. "You said we couldn't look at them."

"I guess it's time. For all of us." Bryce draped the towel
around his shoulders and gathered up the kids' sunhats
and backpacks.

Carrie turned away to make sure the children had their
flip-flops, water bottles and Cam's ball.

She shouldn't admire the breadth of Bryce's shoulders,
or how good he looked in swim trunks, his body fit from
daily hard physical work. She also shouldn't think about

how a man who was such a good dad would also be a good husband.

Carrie was with this family for a short time and doing her best for them. That had to be enough. Yet, she couldn't help wanting more.

CHAPTER TEN

THAT EVENING, Bryce shut Paisley's bedroom door and rejoined Carrie in the family room. "I appreciate you staying over tonight on such short notice."

"No problem. You have an early start tomorrow. I understand what working with freelance clients is like. When they need to meet with you, you have to be available." Curled up cross-legged on the sofa, Carrie looked both comfortable and at home.

Thanks to her, Bryce's house continued to look more comfortable and homey too. A cozy, horse-patterned blanket was draped over the back of the sofa. Baby spider plants grew in pots on top of a bookcase, and the fridge was decorated with Paisley and Cam's artwork. Nowadays, Bryce liked coming home after work. He also liked talking to Carrie about his day. She knew more than he'd expected about agriculture, and she listened and asked intelligent questions.

"Paisley and Cam had fun this afternoon. They were so tired they were asleep almost as soon as they got into bed." He sat beside her on the sofa with Otis and Penny snuggled between them. "I had fun too."

"It was great. I'm on the road so much with rodeo, I'd forgotten what it was like to spend time with a family doing something fun." Her smile was pensive. "I love my folks, but when I was growing up, they were often busy with work. My dad's in construction, and my mom has an

office job. I spent vacations with my grandparents, so…"
She hesitated. "I had some big trips with my parents, sure.
New York City, Florida and even Italy once, but it's the
little things, you know? They make the best memories."

Bryce nodded. He'd gotten so caught up in work and
trying not to think about what he'd lost he'd forgotten those
little things and the importance of cherishing the every-
day. "Cam liked the bouncy house so much he wants a
trampoline."

"You have enough space, and lots of stores are having
summer sales, so you might be able to get a deal." Carrie
offered Bryce a snickerdoodle cookie. She'd made a batch
for the kids, but he must have eaten half of them. "It would
also be nice for Paisley and Cam to invite kids from school
over to play on it. It might help them make more friends."

"Yeah." His heart sank at the thought of handling a
group of kids on his own. He could ask Beth or Melissa,
but he'd gotten used to Carrie being here and, like today,
the two of them working together as a team.

"Paisley wants to invite Noah to the ranch. She says
he's a friend, nothing more."

"Watching Noah showing off for Paisley, I guess it
brought out my protective dad instincts." Bryce savored
the delicious, soft, cinnamon-flavored cookie. "Sometimes
I can't believe how fast the kids are growing up. How am
I going to cope when they start dating?"

"Try not to worry about the future. Enjoy the now." Carrie's laugh was light. "Like I should talk. I worry about the
future too, but Paisley and Cam are showing me how
to live more in the moment."

Bryce exhaled. "You're right." She was right about a
lot of things, not only the kids.

Carrie picked up her mug of cocoa and drank. "Today,
Paisley talked to me about her mom and how much she

misses Ally. I tried to help, but it was tough. There's nothing I can say to make that kind of loss better."

"I heard part of what you said, and you did fine." Bryce's throat clogged. "It's hard for me to talk about Ally with the kids, but, like when the three of us made that list of things Ally was good at, today you reminded me I need to make sure we keep their mom's memory alive."

And as he'd overheard Carrie comforting his daughter, saying and doing what he'd never been able to, he realized the magnitude of his mistake. Not only in not talking about Ally with the kids, but also in being so sure he'd never be able to open his heart and life to anyone else. But, like Carrie had said, she was the kids' nanny, and she'd only be around for the summer. He couldn't let himself think about anything long-term.

"Sorry, what did you say?" he asked.

"The client you're meeting tomorrow, what kind of farm do they have?" Carrie looked interested, her expression bright.

"It's small but growing. Spence started with ten acres five years ago, and now he's up to twenty." And as he talked about his work, and Carrie asked questions, Bryce found himself opening up to her.

"I want to have a farm, a small ranch really, but to start, my main focus would be agricultural crops." Having finished her cocoa, Carrie nibbled a cookie. "My grandparents were big on protecting the environment. I want to practice sustainable farming too." She hesitated. "I don't talk about it much. A lot of people, guys especially, think women having a farm or ranch is foolish. Some still have a problem with women in agriculture."

"They're the foolish ones." Bryce rubbed Penny's floppy ears. "If a ranch is your dream, you should go for it. Don't let anyone hold you back. Look at Diana. She's a better rancher than many men. Ranching's changing and for the better, I say. If Paisley wants to work here on the Tall Grass, I'd encourage her the same as Cam."

"That means a lot." Carrie's voice was low. "Thank you."

The heat of attraction rushed through Bryce. It hadn't mattered he'd never been able to talk with Ally about his work. Their relationship was built on their long history together, the children, friendship and steadfast love. But talking with Carrie, someone who understood what Bryce was trying to achieve, fulfilled him in a way he hadn't known he'd needed. "My oldest brother, Paul, was big on sustainability. He had a vision for this ranch based on environmental stewardship. He had cystic fibrosis and died when I was in my late teens."

"I'm so sorry." Carrie reached across the sleeping dogs and put her hand on top of his.

"If Paul had lived, we'd have worked together on the agricultural side of the ranch, so now I want to carry on what he believed in. He was an artist too. As long as he was able, he'd go out with his easel or sketchpad and draw the landscape and birds and animals."

"Do you have any of Paul's art? It would be nice for Paisley and Cam to see their uncle's work and hear about him. Cam especially has real artistic talent. I wondered where it came from." Carrie gave him a dimpled grin. "Now I know."

"I've got a framed oil of the creek in winter and some of Paul's watercolors of cattle and horses." They were in a box in Bryce's basement because, as with Ally's things, it hurt Bryce to see them. "I guess I could hang them up. That oil would look nice here in the family room."

"If it would be easier, we could do that together this

weekend." Carrie squeezed Bryce's hand before letting go. "Get the kids involved."

"That would be good for all of us." He picked up his now cold cup of cocoa and set it back down again. He enjoyed the feeling of Carrie's hand on his and felt an odd sense of loss when she took it away. "Ally would have liked you."

"I'm sure I'd have liked her as well. Everybody around here speaks highly of her."

There was a question in Carrie's green eyes. One that had been there earlier too when she'd talked about Paisley missing Ally. A question—and an issue—Bryce had avoided for too long.

He took a deep breath. "I'd also like to display some photos of Ally and other things, like ornaments. She collected pig figurines." He smiled at the memory. "She belonged to this online group with other collectors. They raised money to support endangered pig breeds. For her birthday and Christmas each year, I'd give her a pig-themed gift. It was a joke between us. One year, we all, the kids too, had matching pig Christmas sweatshirts." For the first time, that memory brought joy and healing instead of pain.

"Why not raise heritage pigs? In Ally's memory." Carrie's voice was light.

"That's a fantastic idea." One Bryce should have thought of himself. "I could try Herefords. They're a great American breed. Gentle and easy to handle. When the kids are a bit older, they could even show them at their 4-H club."

"There you go." Carrie reached for her phone on the coffee table. "It's late, and you have an early start tomorrow. I should get settled in the guest room." She grabbed the mugs and the empty cookie plate to take them to the kitchen. "Text me when you get to the client's farm. The kids like to know where you are."

"Of course." Bryce woke the dogs and went to let them out the back door as Carrie put the dirty dishes in the dishwasher. "I…thank you."

"For what?" Carrie's back was to him, her voice muffled by the clatter of dishes.

"Tonight. It was good to talk." And with that talk, something important had changed for him and between he and Carrie. Carrie wasn't Ally, and he didn't want her to be. Apart from reminiscing about his wife and their marriage, he'd been focused on Carrie. Ally would always have a special place in his heart, but now Carrie did too.

As a friend, he reminded himself while he let the dogs back in and headed to his own room at the other end of the house.

He set the alarm on his phone and crawled into his king-size bed, which felt bigger and lonelier than ever. Even though Carrie was fast becoming his favorite person apart from the kids, and even though she understood him better than anyone, he could handle this friendship thing. It would be a mistake to want more.

"It looks great, doesn't it?" Kristi gestured to one of the framed posters Carrie had designed that now hung beside a chalkboard listing the daily specials at the Bluebunch Café.

Carrie loved making clients happy, and the thrill of seeing her work in public never faded. For Kristi's new logo, menu and signage, she'd drawn inspiration from both the local area and the café building's history. The design incorporated the old tin ceiling, reclaimed barn board walls, bluebunch wheatgrass and High Valley's "big sky" vista. The result was timeless but also fresh and modern, and it captured the warmth and the whimsical feel of both the café and its bubbly owner. "I'm glad you like it."

"I don't just like it. I *love* it. I called the printer earlier to order postcards of the posters. Tourists have been asking for them." Kristi handed Carrie a bag with three cornbread muffins, the decorated gingerbread cookies Paisley and Cam had chosen and several bottles of apple juice. "After seeing what you did for Rosa, I'd like to hire you to update the café's website too."

"Sure, I'd be happy to take a look and give you a quote." When Carrie nodded, Kristi gave the kids a new variety of trail mix to try. "How does tomorrow evening around seven work for you?"

"Great, see you then. You caught me at a busy time." Kristi turned to a couple who'd approached the counter and asked for half a dozen morning glory muffins to go.

No matter what time Carrie stopped by, the café was always busy. Waving goodbye to Kristi, she held the takeout bag in one hand and guided the kids to the café door with the other. High Valley's charming main street was thronged with visitors, but even in tourist season, the small town had a laid-back, easygoing vibe Carrie liked. From the sidewalk, she waved at Joy, who'd just gotten out of one of the ranch pickup trucks parked in front of Rosa's craft center.

"Watch for cars, kids." When the traffic stopped, they crossed the wide main street at the temporary summer crosswalk and greeted Joy.

"Grandma." Paisley and Cam hugged her, and then Joy wrapped Carrie in a hug too.

"I'm glad to have three helpers." A smile lit Joy's face as she stepped away to take her grandchildren's hands.

"It's no problem." With Joy's friendliness, Carrie's heart felt full. "We're happy to pack orders with you and Rosa." She bent to speak to the children at their level. "It's something fun to do before swimming, isn't it?"

"Everything we do with Carrie is fun." Cam's expression was serious.

"It is." Paisley chimed in. "Daddy and us and Carrie redecorated yesterday."

As they went into the coolness of the craft center, where Rosa and two of her summer staff answered questions from a bus tour group, Joy glanced at Carrie and then back to the children. "Redecorated how?"

"We put up pictures of Mommy, and Uncle Paul's art. Daddy also showed us Mommy's pig collection and let me arrange it in a special cabinet," Paisley said with a tone of importance.

"I helped too," Cam added. "Me and Paisley also named some of the pigs. One's Carrie. She's pink and white with a curly tail."

"That's sweet." Joy's eyes widened with something that looked like speculation, along with approval and maybe hope.

"You named a pig for your mom too." Awkwardness curled in Carrie's tummy. "And your dad. Don't forget to tell your grandma about raising Hereford piglets." She needed to change the subject before Joy got the wrong idea and imagined Carrie could be part of her son and grand-children's lives longer-term.

Carrie put the food in the small staff kitchen and then regrouped with Joy and the kids in Rosa's workroom. Craft items, packing boxes, paper, customer orders and other supplies were on a big table in the middle of the room, and boxes almost ready for shipment were stacked by the door.

After giving Paisley and Cam rolls of Medicine Wheel address labels and showing them how to stick them to the packed boxes, Joy joined Carrie at the table. "You did a good thing. Bryce and the kids need to remember Ally and Paul. It's part of healing and going on with life." As she covered two dreamcatchers in bubble wrap, Joy's blue eyes were soft with emotion. "I've tried for more than a year to get Bryce to bring out photos of Ally and things that were important to her. Ally's folks and sister have too, but he wouldn't budge. You managed to get through to him, and I'm grateful."

Carrie tucked white tissue paper between the folds of a crib blanket patterned with bears, deer and buffalo. "Paisley talked to me about missing her mom, so I wanted to help. I don't know what I did, not really."

"Maybe Bryce was finally ready to listen, but whatever or however, it's a blessing." Joy patted Carrie's arm. "Bryce was close to Paul, but, like with Ally, it was as if he had to shut that part of himself away to cope with his grief. Then, he got stuck."

"Paul's paintings are beautiful. Did he ever show them in exhibitions?" Carrie found a box and tucked the baby blanket inside, along with one of the gallery's cards.

"No, he planned to, but then…he passed." Joy's mouth worked. "I try to keep Paul's memory alive in whatever way I can. I want to celebrate his life, not focus on how it was cut so short. I have lots of his pictures displayed at the house and around our summer camp."

Carrie closed and taped the box and found the shipping label, checking off the order against Rosa's list. "What would you think of having a retrospective exhibition? It could be a special event with music and refreshments. Not selling the paintings but raising money for a charity?"

Joy's hands stilled on the dreamcatcher box. "That's a wonderful idea. Maybe it could support a charity for children and teenagers with special needs, similar to Camp Crocus Hill. We set up Crocus Hill in Paul's memory."

"Then what about having the campers make art too?" Carrie had only seen them when they came to ride at the main ranch, but someone had mentioned Crocus Hill had an art studio. "We could make the event a showcase for Paul and the camp, along with other local artists. I saw something about an art club in the weekly newspaper."

"That would be perfect. It's too late to organize anything this summer, but perhaps we could hold an event in the fall or for the holidays." Joy's face was animated, and her eyes sparkled. "Everyone will pitch in. Paul was a member of that art club."

"I could design marketing materials. No charge." Ideas popped in Carrie's mind. Although this wasn't the main reason for her offer, it would be a way of promoting her business, and she might make contacts that would lead to new work. "I'll talk to Cole and some of my rodeo contacts. With a Western focus, we might be able to get corporate sponsors interested."

"That's so kind and generous, but you won't be here in the fall, will you? I'm getting ahead of myself." Joy wrapped another parcel of dreamcatchers while Carrie tackled a queen-size circle-of-life blanket. "I suppose you could work remotely and, with enough notice, come back to town for the actual event."

"I guess." Carrie had also gotten ahead of herself. She focused on the card included with the blanket that explained its design and how the colors symbolized different life stages.

"When are you going back to barrel racing?" Joy fixed a shipping label to the box with the dreamcatchers.

"Apart from a small charity event later this month, my first official competition is in Colorado after Labor Day. I practice with Teddy most days after work, so we should be ready." Carrie felt better than she had in years. Along with increased mental sharpness, she was getting back into peak competitive physical form. But, although she was excited about returning to competition, she'd miss being with the kids. And she'd miss Bryce even more.

"I'd love to come and watch. I grew up in Missoula, but I spent summers with family in High Valley. That's how I met my Dennis and learned about horses and ranching. Now I can't imagine horseback riding not being part of my life." Joy chuckled. "No more jumping, though, so I'm learning dressage. I never tried barrel racing, but I have a friend who's still doing it in her late fifties. Linda competes in senior rodeo. She loves it, although she says she doesn't bounce as easily as she used to."

"Good for her. I hope that's me someday." Carrie laughed too. "If you're interested, I can give you and your horse, Cindy, a barrel-racing lesson."

"That would be fun. Not that I'll ever reach the heights Paisley's aiming for, but I'd love to try a new sport." Joy gave her granddaughter a fond smile. "I always say there's a time for everything in life. Because you missed out on something once doesn't mean you can't have another chance at it. While it might not feel or be the same as when you were younger, as long as you're breathing, you can still try."

Except for motherhood. Carrie wanted a family and had expected to have one with Jimmy. But he'd said no man would want to be with someone who was away more than they were home. Even if she found the right person, would he accept her wanting rodeo *and* family life? Or had Jimmy and her parents been right all along that sooner rather than later Carrie would have to settle down?

"This blanket's the last." She folded one of Rosa's prize-winning Cree Star blankets into a tissue-lined box and added the information card. "Ready for snack time, kids?" she called. The children had finished with the address labels and were working in the activity books Carrie had put in their backpacks. "I also brought snacks for you and Rosa." Carrie turned back to Joy.

"Women like you, Beth and Melissa inspire me," Joy said. "You know what you want in life, and you go for it."

"Hardly." Carrie shook her head. "I'm a work in progress."

"You and me both, honey." Joy linked her arm through Carrie's as they moved to the kitchen.

"And me." Rosa's rich laugh rolled out as she joined them. "I say having it all means having what's right for you. If you aren't happy with *who* you are or *where* you are, change it. That's the beauty of life."

As Carrie helped Paisley and Cam set out the food and drinks on the table in the staff kitchen, she considered what Joy and Rosa had said. Who she'd been—yesterday, last month or last year—wasn't who she had to be forever. She *could* change.

High Valley was currently a small phase in Carrie's life. But what if she looked for a property nearby? If she found one in her budget, she could put down more permanent roots here. For things like an exhibition of Paul's art, she wouldn't be a visitor. She'd have a place to come home to, somewhere she belonged. Her new friends—Joy, Rosa, Kristi, Diana and the Sunflower Sisterhood—as well as High Valley could be part of her life for always.

And Bryce wasn't like Jimmy, so she shouldn't judge him by that standard. If she wasn't working for him, who knew what might happen?

CHAPTER ELEVEN

BRYCE DROVE WHAT had once been his dad's red tractor around the outer edge of the hayfield. With the mower hitched to the back of the tractor and a clear blue sky, everything was perfect for haying. These days, though, and even if the weather was overcast, he went about his work with a new lightness in his heart.

As he rounded a corner, he waved at Cole, who drove a green tractor in the next field over. His brother, still a starry-eyed newlywed, raked the hay Bryce had cut the day before. After Cole pulled the hay into rows, Zach would bale it. Haying season meant the whole family worked even more closely together than usual.

Bryce stopped the tractor near a small stand of trees and wiped his face with a red bandanna.

"Here you go, Daddy." Paisley handed him a bottle of water from a cooler.

"Thanks, Ladybug. You guys started raking here. That's great."

Carrie and the kids were involved in haying too. Although they each had their own jobs, having Carrie alongside him was comfortable. And whenever he spotted her in the distance or, like now, up close, he got warm inside.

"It's hot work." Carrie leaned on a pitchfork.

Bryce nodded as he drank the cold water. In jeans, a light long-sleeved shirt, work gloves and cowboy hat, Carrie looked like one of the extra hands they'd hired for this second hay cutting of the season. She wasn't, though, and he'd never been more aware of her femininity. Her green eyes, framed in thick dark lashes, shone. Her skin glowed, and those freckles on the bridge of her nose continued to tempt him.

"Carrie told us about mice and birds and how this field is a whole…" Cam screwed up his eyes. "Eco something."

"Ecosystem." Carrie took a tube of sunscreen from a bag and applied a dollop to Cam's face.

"We looked at bugs too. Carrie's gonna show us some pictures on the computer when she comes back from visiting her mom and dad." Paisley wrapped her arms around Carrie's waist. "Three sleeps. You promise?"

"I promise. I'll be back around breakfast time on Monday." Carrie hugged the children and then turned to Bryce. "I've got my stuff in the truck. I'm leaving as soon as your mom comes by with lunch."

"Yeah, of course." When Carrie had asked to take an extended weekend to go to Kalispell for her mom's birthday, it wasn't a problem. Now, though, and despite the never-ending work to keep him busy, the time without her seemed like a bunch of empty hours Bryce would struggle to fill. "Have fun."

"I feel bad leaving you on your own at such a busy time. I've put meals in the fridge and freezer for you to heat up. If you have to work late out here, I've arranged for the kids to have a sleepover at your mom's." Carrie paused. "Don't forget Paisley's going to a birthday party tomorrow. Melissa's picking her up to drive into town with Skylar. I already wrapped the present. It's in the basket in the family room."

"It's a mermaid-themed party. We're gonna swim with

a real live mermaid. I already packed my swimsuit. Carrie said I need to help you by remembering stuff. While me and Skylar are at the party, Aunt Melissa's taking Cam to the playground."

"And for ice cream." Cam elbowed his way between Carrie and Paisley.

"We'll be fine." Bryce had managed okay before Carrie came into their lives, and she'd only be gone a few days. Why did he now feel like things might fall apart as soon as she left? Like *he* might fall apart. "Mom's pulling up on the other side of the field now. So...bye."

Paisley and Cam hugged Carrie again.

"I'll be back before you know it. Help your dad and don't forget to brush your teeth after meals. Visit Teddy for me too. He'll love those treats we got him from the feedstore. Bye." She straightened and gave Bryce a jerky wave. "Good luck with the baling and everything. The weather looks like it'll hold."

"Yeah." Bryce shifted from one foot to the other.

"You haven't hugged Carrie, Daddy." Cam looked between them. "Whenever anybody leaves or comes back, we always hug."

"Grandma says you can never have too many hugs," Paisley added.

"Sure... I..." Bryce stepped closer to Carrie. "Safe travels." He put his arms around her shoulders.

"Take care." Her warm breath brushed his cheek as Carrie hugged him back, and her hat brim bumped his.

Bryce relaxed into her embrace and deepened it, drawing Carrie closer. He breathed in a faint lemon scent mixed with the hayfield and sunshine. He drew nearer still, and then his mouth grazed the curve of her cheek in a kiss.

"Oops." Carrie jerked back and grabbed for her hat as it tumbled off.

"Daddy's a good hugger, isn't he?" Cam's voice was innocent.

"Uh, he's great." Carrie wedged her hat back on her head.

Paisley giggled behind her hands.

"I better…" Carrie gestured to where she'd left her truck parked on a dirt road behind the trees. "See you Monday." Her face was as red as Bryce imagined his was and not from the sun.

"Yeah." He fumbled with his own hat, which was crooked from hitting Carrie's. "Come on, kids. Let's see what your grandma brought us for lunch."

"Did you kiss Carrie?" Paisley looked from Bryce to the road, where Carrie had already started up her truck.

"No, of course not." His lips had connected with her cheek by accident. It wasn't a real kiss.

"You were holding her really, really close." Paisley tucked her hand into Bryce's.

"I hugged her, that's all. Like your grandma says, the Carters are huggers." But how he'd hugged Carrie was different from how Bryce hugged his family. If the kids hadn't been there, he might have given her a real kiss too.

While Cam ran ahead to check out the field lunch, Paisley squeezed Bryce's hand. "If you want to go on a date with Carrie, it would be okay with me."

Bryce yanked his hat farther down over his eyebrows. "Carrie's your nanny, and besides…" He stopped.

"Besides what?" Paisley skipped at his side.

Bryce's heart flipped. "It doesn't matter. Do you think Grandma brought us a pizza party? Remember she did that last year?"

Distracted as Bryce had intended, Paisley darted after Cam.

If only Bryce could distract himself as easily. His fingers still tingled where he'd held Carrie's shoulders, and his body hummed with awareness of how good it felt to be close to her.

And although Carrie had only just left, without her nearby there was an emptiness inside Bryce neither pizza nor anything else could fill.

"IT'S SO GOOD to have you home safe and sound." In the spacious vestibule of Carrie's childhood home, her mom greeted her with a loving embrace. As Carrie breathed in her mom's familiar floral fragrance, her heart sank. How could she disappoint her mom and dad? She was their only child, and they depended on her.

"How are you doing, Pumpkin?" Her dad gave her a bear hug. "Let's take a look at you." His callused hands lingered on her bare arms. Despite being the president of the family construction company, Frank Rizzo still pitched in on job sites. It was a source of pride he wasn't afraid to get his hands dirty, and he and her mom had instilled in Carrie the value of hard, honest work.

"I'm good." She touched her cheek, still feeling the imprint of Bryce's lips against her skin. All the way to Kalispell, she'd replayed what had happened in the hayfield in her mind. Bryce had only hugged her because Cam had asked him to. That kiss was an accident. It wasn't even a real kiss, only a peck on the cheek. It had also been more than a little awkward because they were both wearing cowboy hats, and the kids were looking on.

"You'll want to change, of course, but you look wonderful." Carrie's mom's heels clicked on the imported-Italian-marble hall floor as they made their way to the family room at the back of the house, which overlooked the patio and pool area. "Ranch life and all that fresh air must agree with you. Your eyes are brighter, and you're glowing."

After leaving Carrie's overnight bag and backpack at the foot of the sweeping staircase, her dad joined them. "Carolina, you are always beautiful, but now there's something extra special. Maybe someone special?" He quirked an eyebrow.

It felt strange hearing her full name, one she'd always disliked, for the first time in months. "Nobody special." It wasn't exactly a lie, but she couldn't tell her parents the truth without sounding like a teenage girl with a crush. "I like High Valley, and the family I work for is nice." She sounded like she was reciting a school lesson. "The kids, Paisley and Cam, are a lot of fun."

"And their father? You've never said much about him." Her mom's eyes, the same shade of green as Carrie's, narrowed. Sophia Rizzo was astute, and despite their differences, Carrie and her mom had always been close.

"Bryce is a good dad and a good employer." That wasn't a lie either, but Carrie's stomach still lurched, and the spot on her cheek where Bryce had kissed her burned so hot she was surprised her parents couldn't see it. "He's the youngest son in a big family, and their ranch is a family operation. Everyone's made me feel really welcome." Although Carrie hadn't realized how much until now, Bryce and the kids, the ranch, High Valley and the Carter family were all changing her.

Her mom still studied her. "You'll be back home in September, won't you?"

"I'm not sure yet." Carrie took a glass of soda from her dad, who'd busied himself with the drinks cabinet.

"But why not?" Her mom twisted her hands together, and her diamond tennis bracelet slid on her slender wrist. "I thought everything had been decided. I'm already—"

"We have plenty of time to talk about Carolina's plans, Sophia." Her dad shot Carrie's mom a warning glance. "Now we have a party to get ready for."

Beyond the floor-to-ceiling windows, staff from the caterer and party planner were hard at work. The backyard was already festooned with pink and white balloons, and a small stage was being set up for dancing near the pool house.

Her mom's demeanor and expression were stiff, and tension radiated from her. "I left several dresses for you to choose from on your bed. I remember small-town life. There's likely no place to shop in High Valley."

Not for couture clothing, but the stores there met Carrie's needs. "I planned to wear the dress I wore for Dad's sixtieth birthday. That was only a year ago." She'd never been a dress person, and even at Paisley's age, she'd been happier in jeans, a T-shirt and her beloved cowboy boots.

"I wanted to treat you." Her mom's smile was anxious. "Besides, most of the people who were at your dad's party will also be at mine. You can't wear the same dress."

Carrie held back a protest. As dresses went, she liked the green one she'd bought for her dad's birthday, and that was why she'd worn it to Cole and Melissa's wedding. And how Bryce had looked at her at the wedding now made the dress special. Part of her wanted to have a memory of him here. "I'm sure whatever you chose for me will be beautiful." Her mom had excellent taste and the money to indulge it. "Where's Aunt Angela and the rest of the family?" The house was quiet, although it was so big there could have been a party in the bedroom wing, and she wouldn't have heard it here.

"Angela's having her hair done, your uncles are golfing and the others haven't arrived yet." Her mom's expression softened. "Although I don't understand why you couldn't have gotten extra time off to travel with Angela two days ago, it's been good for us to have time alone together. I have my sister back, and she…you…" Her mom's mouth trembled. "She loves you."

"I love her too. Why don't you and Dad come visit High Valley later this month?" Carrie hadn't told anyone, not even Bryce, how she'd begun to put her finances in order to see what kind of property she could afford. Or how every night before bed, she checked online to see if any small ranches or farms in a twenty-mile radius of High Valley had come up for sale. She didn't want to divert attention from her mom's birthday weekend, and if her parents came to High Valley, it would be easier to tell them what she wanted to do with her life then. Maybe in the place she intended to call home, they'd understand and support her choices.

Three hours later, dressed in a pale yellow off-the-shoulder cocktail dress paired with white gladiator sandals, Carrie was having more fun than she'd expected. Every aspect of the birthday party had the casual air of elegance her mom had perfected. It was also good to see aunts, uncles and cousins she rarely spent time with because she was on the road so much.

She murmured her thanks to the server, Rob, an acquaintance from the rodeo circuit, who added her empty wine glass to a full tray. Like Carrie, Rob was one of the many cowboys and cowgirls who worked other jobs to earn extra money in between rodeo events. Despite her parents' wealth, as soon as she'd graduated from college, Carrie had been determined to pay her own way rather than depend on her family.

"Want to dance?" Domenic Pasquale, a man around her age she remembered from company holiday parties, held out a hand. When she took it, he swept her into a waltz.

"What are you up to these days?" She made polite conversation. The kind of conversation she'd have to spend her life making if she took that job her folks wanted her to.

"I'm now head of sales." The dance floor was lit with strings of white lights that shone off Dom's dark hair and gleaming white teeth. He wore an open-necked white shirt, sports jacket and dark dress pants along with polished tasseled loafers. "Your dad promoted me last month."

"Congratulations." Dom was attractive, polite and successful. Yet, compared to the men Carrie knew in High Valley, there was something fundamentally lacking about him. Beneath her hand, his forearm was soft, not well muscled like Bryce's, and as he talked about golf and a wine-tasting tour he'd taken on a recent business trip to California, her mind wandered.

As they passed Angela, in a group of Carrie's parents' friends from their neighborhood, her aunt smiled and raised an eyebrow. Angela wore a pale blue dress that set off her silver hair and dark eyes—Carrie's mom had evidently treated her to a new outfit as well.

"I'm sorry, what did you say?" She turned her attention back to Dom.

"Let me know when you finalize your start date. We could have lunch or meet up for a drink after work your first week."

"I haven't signed the paperwork accepting the job yet." Something her parents kept reminding her about.

"From what I hear, the paperwork's only a formality." At Dom's warm smile, more guilt stabbed Carrie's chest. "There's a work trip to New York in September. What do you say about taking in a Broadway show?" His expression was hopeful.

"I guess, but only as colleagues." Carrie stumbled, and Dom eased her closer. He wasn't as good a dancer as

Bryce. "I don't date people I work with." *Or work for.* She worked for Bryce, although not for much longer. But at the end of the summer, she'd be going back to rodeo, so she couldn't date Dom *or* Bryce.

"Of course." Dom's smile slipped. "Have you been to New York before?"

"Once, with my parents. It was fun. Our hotel was near Times Square." Carrie kept her voice light. She liked visiting cities, but she wouldn't want to live in one.

"Your dad says you're going to shake up the marketing department. They're a good, creative team, but they need strong leadership. That's where you come in. Your dad's so proud of you. Your mom is too. Together, they've built a company I'm proud to be part of." As the waltz ended, Dom swung her in a circle like Bryce had done at the wedding. "They'll be glad to have you here at home, where you belong."

Carrie tried to smile as she thanked him for the dance and murmured something about wanting to check in with her folks. "Why don't you dance with my cousin? Sabrina's from Seattle and doesn't know many people here." She gestured to a dark-haired woman who stood alone near the bar, and when Sabrina joined them, Carrie introduced her to Dom.

As Sabrina gave her a grateful smile, Carrie backed away before bending to rub a spot on her heel where the new sandals, which her mom had picked out to go with the dress, had rubbed her skin almost raw. A woman like Sabrina would be perfect for Dom. As well as being smart and attractive, she was an avid golfer, and in the card she'd sent Carrie for her last birthday, she'd mentioned taking a wine-tasting class at night school.

Considering she'd done her good deed for the day, Carrie straightened and glanced around for her parents.

"I almost didn't recognize you without jeans, boots and a hat." Rob appeared with a tray of fancy hors d'oeuvres. "You clean up well."

She laughed at his teasing and took a shrimp appetizer with avocado and cucumber. "So do you." As he asked her about Teddy and their next competition, and they talked about rodeo people they both knew, Carrie felt more at ease than she had the entire evening.

"There she is." Her dad's voice boomed, and her parents came toward her holding hands.

Carrie excused herself from Rob and put on her party face again.

"We're treasuring every moment of having our girl home," her mom added. "We only wish you could stay longer."

"She'll soon be home permanently, won't you, Pumpkin?" Her dad's voice rumbled. "I saw you dancing with Domenic. He looked smitten."

"It was only a dance, Dad." Carrie tried to keep her expression neutral. Her dance with Bryce had changed everything, but one dance with Dom had left her unmoved.

"He's got a good business head on his shoulders, and he's ambitious. Reminds me of myself at that age. The Pasquales are a fine family. Dom's grandfather and yours were friends. You should think about—"

"Now, Frank, leave Carrie to make her own decisions. You want her to come home, don't you?" Her mom shook her head, but her expression as she looked at Carrie's dad was loving. "I've convinced your dad to take time off so we can visit you for a few days later this month. We'll stay with Angela, and the two of you can show us around."

"Great." A weight settled in the pit of Carrie's stomach like the rock on the edge of the hayfield where she'd worked with the kids and Bryce. A rock Bryce said was too big to move, so they went around it instead.

Did her mom truly mean Carrie could make her own decisions, and her parents would accept her choices? She couldn't keep going as she had been, letting them think rodeo and freelance work were temporary, but she didn't want to disappoint them either.

No more avoiding or shirking the truth. This weekend wasn't the right time, but when her folks came to High Valley, she'd tell them what she wanted to do with her life, and they'd either accept it or they wouldn't.

But faced with their loving, proud and expectant expressions, the rock in her stomach got heavier.

Somehow, she knew that when she left Kalispell after this brief visit, it wouldn't feel like she was leaving home. Instead, with each mile that clicked over on her truck's odometer, she'd be going back to her true home. High Valley and the Tall Grass Ranch.

CHAPTER TWELVE

AT THE MONDAY morning breakfast table, Bryce pretended to read the local newspaper, but he was really listening to Carrie and the kids. It had only been a few days, but without Carrie, his house had felt empty. He'd managed fine on his own, but now he didn't want to. Carrie was part of his and the kids' lives, and he didn't know what he'd do when summer ended and she moved on.

"The mermaid had a purple tail. We swam with her, and then we had cake and ice cream and played a game, and I won a prize." Paisley squeezed Carrie's left hand while Cam held her right, and both kids tried to talk over each other, as happy to see her as if she'd been gone a year.

"Slow down, guys, and take turns." Carrie gave them both another hug. "I missed you too."

"Aunt Melissa told Ms. Kristi I could have two scoops of ice cream and three different kinds of sprinkles and strawberries. It was too big for a cone, so I had it in a bowl with chocolate sauce." Cam bounced with excitement. "That was after we went to the playground. I went on the swings and right to the top of the new climbing frame. I was so high I could almost see North Dakota."

"Montana is 'Big Sky Country' all right but not quite that big." Bryce laughed and set the paper aside. Carrie was focused on the kids. That was her job. So why did he feel left out because, apart from a brief greeting, he hadn't had a chance to talk to her. "We missed you. The place isn't the same without you around."

Had he emphasized the "we"? He'd almost said "I missed you" but had caught himself in time. As soon as she'd walked into the house ten minutes earlier, his body had responded to her presence, and, like the kids, he'd wanted to greet her with a hug. More than a hug, to be honest. He'd dreamed of her while she was in Kalispell. They'd been in that hayfield in the moonlight, and he'd held her close and kissed the freckles on her nose.

"My folks say hi. They sent you guys presents." Carrie tickled the kids, and they giggled.

"What kind of presents?" Cam eyed the backpack and small suitcase Carrie had left inside the back door.

"You'll see. After you do your chores." She patted Cam's head. "You must have grown while I was away. I'm sure you're taller." She poured herself a mug of coffee from the pot Bryce had brewed earlier and joined him at the table. "Did everything go okay here?"

"It was fine." He made himself focus on her here in his kitchen, not as she'd been in that unsettling dream. "It was a couple of late nights, but we got the hay in." Dreams aside, he could still get used to sitting with her at the kitchen table while the kids loaded the dishwasher.

"That's great." Carrie leaned back in her chair. "I kept checking the weather and thinking about you. About everyone, I mean." She took a mouthful of coffee and turned to the kitchen window. "The herbs and spider plants look like they've grown. Good job with the watering." The curve of her cheek nearest Bryce had a faint pink tinge.

"We watered exactly like you told us. Cam and I took turns," Paisley said, coming to sit in the chair between Carrie and Bryce.

So much for talking to Carrie on his own. Bryce drained

his mug. He was attracted to her in all the ways a man could be attracted to a woman. But it was more than just physical. It was a kind of soul-deep pull that drew him to Carrie whenever she was near and made him think about her when she wasn't.

"You could be on Daddy's team for the competition." Cam joined them at the table too, and the dishwasher now hummed in the background.

"What competition and where?" Carrie glanced between them.

"At the rodeo. See?" Cam pointed to a picture in Bryce's newspaper. "It's coming to town on the weekend. We'll be there."

"Our family's going on Saturday," Bryce said. "That's Carrie's day off. Your grandma babysits you on Saturdays, so—"

"I'm not a baby who needs 'sitting,' and I bet Carrie wants to come with us." Paisley nestled into Carrie's shoulder.

"Sure, but it's your family day out. I don't want to—"

"Carrie's like family, isn't she, Daddy?" Cam's voice was hopeful. "And you said you needed someone for your team roping competition. You also said Carrie did great herding cows."

"Yes, but…" Bryce's heart pounded. "If you don't have anything else planned, you're welcome to join us at the rodeo." It wouldn't be a date. His whole family would be there. "Like Cam said, I'm looking for a partner in the amateur team roping competition. Heidi, our part-time ranch hand, sprained her wrist so she had to drop out. It's for fun, not truly competitive, and there won't be any professionals. We're a group of local ranchers raising money for charity." His tongue tripped over the words. "If you want to team up with me, you'd be welcome."

"Grandma's on Mr. Gallagher's team." Paisley snuggled even closer to Carrie. "Grandma said they're going to give the young ones a run for their money. That means make it hard for them to win."

"I've done team roping for fun with friends. It was great." Carrie's green eyes sparkled. "Count me in, as long as you have a horse I can ride that's used to roping. Teddy isn't. We'd also need to practice. My skills are rusty, and I don't want to let you down."

Bryce's mouth went dry. It was an expression, nothing more, and it was only a small-town rodeo and amateur event. Even if Carrie threw the rope too soon and they were disqualified, it wouldn't matter. Yet, she meant what she said. "I don't want to let you down either." *On horseback or in life*. His stomach flipped.

"You won't." Her green gaze held his, and it was as if time stopped. He cared about her, and maybe she cared about him too.

"As a former pro, Cole's not eligible to compete, but there's nothing in the rules that says he can't give us pointers and choose the right horse for you. What would you think about Daisy-May? She's an old girl, but she's steady on her feet, and in her day she loved being in the roping ring."

Bryce heard his voice from far away as if it belonged to someone else. As one part of him talked to Carrie about different horses and they made plans to meet in the paddock after lunch, the rest of him was trying to figure out what had just happened between them.

He'd always considered himself to be logical and rational. He made decisions with his head, not his heart. It made sense for Carrie to take Heidi's place. It even made sense for her to go to the rodeo with Bryce and the rest of the Carter family.

What didn't make sense were the feelings churning through him, turning him inside out and upside down to leave his usually ordered world in shambles. Feelings that swept logic and reasoning away.

JOY DREW CINDY to a halt in a shady spot by the slow-moving creek and relaxed her hold on the horse's reins. It was already August, and another summer was slipping by. This summer, though, she'd cut back on her usually busy schedule of family and community activities to focus more on what *she* needed. That was one of the reasons she'd told Bryce she couldn't look after Paisley and Cam all the time, and that choice had also been good for her son and grandchildren. Forced to step up, Bryce had hired Carrie, and both he and the kids were better for it.

"If I haven't already said so, you're looking especially pretty today." Shane stopped his horse, Pinto, a gorgeous American paint, beside her.

Joy turned to him with a smile. "You have, but it's always nice to hear." Joy took his hand as he reached across their saddle horns. "You look very handsome too." With his short, steel gray hair, well-fitting jeans, dark cowboy hat and blue Western shirt, Shane looked as good today as he always did. But it wasn't only that he was handsome; she liked him because he was a good person. Kind, honest and trustworthy like Dennis had been, but Shane was also his own man and had his own place in her heart.

"Thank you, ma'am." Shane's grin was boyish, and he gave her hand a comforting squeeze. "What are you fussing about now?" He considered her with the intent gaze that, at first, had made Joy feel off-balance, but nowadays she knew it meant he understood her, cared and wanted to help.

She could have pretended nothing was bothering her,

but Shane knew her too well to be fooled. "As always, I'm worried about Bryce. When Carrie was in Kalispell visiting her folks, he looked lost, like he didn't know what to do with himself. He kept working—he always does—but the light in his eyes was gone. What's he going to do when she leaves for good?"

"That's up to him and maybe her too." With his free hand, Shane rubbed Pinto's ears. "Our kids have to live their own lives."

"I know, but…" Joy studied Pinto's brown-and-white pattern, and the horse turned to look at her with his vibrant blue eyes. "Also, something's not right with Molly. I talked to her online last night, and although she says she's happy, she's not. A mother can sense these things."

"Molly will be home for her vacation in a few weeks. You'll be able to talk to her then. The computer's great, but a video call isn't the same as in person." Shane's voice was reassuring.

"You're right." Joy pushed her worries aside. She was in a beautiful place with a wonderful man, and she didn't want to spoil it. *Focus on the moment.* She repeated her current mantra to herself.

"I want to talk about us, not our children." Shane dropped her hand and eased Pinto to a walk, and when Joy did the same with Cindy, the two horses meandered side by side along the willow-shaded creek path.

"Us?" Joy's heartbeat sped up. Of course, they were an "us." They'd been dating, if you could call it that at their age, for over a year now, and Shane had become one of the most important people in her life.

"You and me." His breath caught. "You're a fine woman, and I have strong feelings for you. After I lost my Bonnie, I never thought I could care for someone again like I care for you."

"Like me with my Dennis." Joy edged Cindy closer to Pinto to avoid a low-hanging tree branch. Shane's wife, Bonnie, had passed after a long illness, so he and their children had had time to say goodbye. But no matter how you lost your spouse, whether in an accident like with Dennis or not, after a long and happy marriage, you didn't stop grieving. Rather, you learned to live with the grief and moved on because you had to. Joy had found solace in her family, but lately she'd wondered if that was enough.

Shane took her hand again as they came out into an area where the creek widened and was spanned by a covered bridge. The first Carter family had built it when they'd moved to this part of Montana from Vermont way back in the nineteenth century. In New England, such bridges were known as "kissing bridges," and the Carters had always called this bridge that too.

"I won't ever forget Bonnie, and you won't forget Dennis either. That's as it should be." Shane cleared his throat and took off his hat. "We both have our children, their children and our own places, but I bought more land."

"You did?" Joy blinked at the sudden change of subject. For a minute, she'd thought Shane was going to ask her an important question. "Where? In Wyoming?" Her heart sank. Apart from his youngest son, who'd moved to High Valley with him, the rest of Shane's family ranched near Sheridan, Wyoming. It would make sense if he wanted to move back there.

"No." He chuckled, and his eyes held a teasing twinkle. "I bought those acres between Squirrel Tail and the western border of your place."

"That's good grazing pasture. It used to be Carter land, but…" She stopped as emotion threatened.

"But you and Dennis had to sell it to pay some of Paul's medical bills." Shane swung off Pinto and then helped

Joy dismount from Cindy before tethering both horses to nearby trees.

"How did you find out?" Joy never rode out that way because having to sell that land had been hard and something she and Dennis had agonized over. But Paul was more important.

"Zach mentioned it one day when I met him out there checking the fence line. He only told me because I said it was an odd place for a boundary. Your boy didn't tell me anything private, but I knew it must have been tough for you all."

"It was." So tough, Joy tried not to think about it. "Are you planning on renting out the land or going into the cattle business yourself?"

"Neither." Shane wrapped an arm around her shoulders. "I bought that land for you, so what happens to it is your call. When those acres came up for sale, you never said anything, but I knew you were worrying about who'd buy them and what they'd do."

"Yes." Something else Joy had tried not to think about, but it had wormed its way in like one of those pesky bugs that ate her tomato plants. "But buying all that land is too much. You shouldn't have."

Shane cupped her chin in one of his tanned hands. He had strong hands, and she'd seen him rope a cow with them, fix a fence and lift hay bales. But when he held her hands in his or comforted her grandchildren, they were gentle. Like now, touching her face as if she were as fragile as a butterfly. And as she stared into his eyes, his steady gaze never wavered.

"I wanted to. By rights, those acres are yours, and I have the money, so why not? But when I signed the sale paperwork, all I could think of was you and me and a dream I've had for a while now. One day, I hope we can share a

small piece you don't use for grazing or anything else."
His face creased in a brief smile. "If you're willing, we
could build a house there, and it'd be a place to bring our
families together. I love you, Joy, and when you're ready,
if you'll have me, I want to marry you." Lines fanned out
around Shane's mouth, and his eyes held both love and
experience earned from the life he'd lived.

"I love you too." Several tears rolled down Joy's cheeks.
"And yes, I want to marry you. I'm crying because I'm
happy." Happier than she could have ever imagined. She
buried her face in Shane's shoulder, her tears dampening
his crisp cotton shirt. "But I can't…" She raised her head
to look into his eyes again.

"You can't what?" Shane's expression was tender.

"I don't want to make anything official or tell our kids
for a while. At least until September, when Molly's home
and your daughters and their families are here visiting.
And even then, I don't want them to think we've forgotten Bonnie and Dennis."

"I doubt they'd think that, but I can wait a few weeks.
It'll be our secret." He wrapped his arms around her. "I
want to give you a ring, so it'll also allow you time to
choose one."

"For *us* to choose it." Joy hugged him back and then
tilted her face to his. "Yes, we each have our own lives,
but I want us to be a team. With our ranches, our families
and everything. Except for my college classes. I have to
do those on my own." She paused. "I still want to get my
degree. If that's a problem for you—"

"Of course, it isn't." Shane looked at her in astonishment. "I not only want you to get your degree, I'll be the
one cheering loudest when you walk across that stage in
your cap and gown. You're a smart, independent woman,

and I love those things about you. Together, we'll be a strong partnership."

"Together." It wasn't like they were young and just starting out. She and Shane had lots of things to figure out, but they'd take it step by step.

Then he kissed her, and as Joy kissed him back, his strong arms holding her close, she was filled with a sense of both love and rightness.

When she finally opened her eyes and saw the love and loyalty in Shane's gaze, the kissing bridge behind him like a benevolent presence, she also felt blessed.

Life, with all its twists and turns, had brought her here. While Dennis would always be a precious memory, with Shane she had a second chance, and she was excited for what lay ahead.

CHAPTER THIRTEEN

"You've got mustard on your face. Hold still a second." Carrie took a moist towelette from her tote, wiped around Cam's mouth and finished with a gentle boop on his button nose.

The boy giggled and booped her back. "What are we gonna do next?"

Carrie checked the time on her phone. "The team roping event is soon. I need to find your aunt Beth and your sister and then your dad." Beth was looking after all the kids while Carrie and Bryce competed. Since Paisley had wanted to hang out with Ellie and Skylar, and Melissa had a volunteer first aid shift, Beth had kept the girls with her while Carrie had had some one-on-one time with Cam. With Joy and Shane competing too, the whole family would reunite in the stands to support them.

"I want you and Daddy to win." In a small cowboy hat, jeans, plaid shirt and cowboy boots, Cam looked like a miniature version of Bryce. "But I also want Grandma and Mr. Gallagher to win. Is that bad?"

"Nope. You can cheer for all of us." Keeping one hand in Cam's, Carrie scanned the crowd. The visiting rodeo had set up in an open area behind High Valley's riding arena. Along with fairground rides, booths selling food and offering games of chance occupied nearby Meadowlark Park.

"There's Paisley." Cam pointed to his sister, almost hidden behind a towering cone of pink cotton candy. "And Aunt Beth, Ellie and Skylar."

Carrie waved as they approached. At the same time, Zach and several ranch hands from the Tall Grass passed her carrying saddles. Small-town rodeos were the best, as much about family as the competitive events.

"Sorry we're late." Beth sounded out of breath. "There was a long line for the restroom. We bumped into Bryce and he said he'd meet you in the arena. He's getting the horses ready." Zach paused to kiss his wife, and as he continued on with the other men, Beth shielded her growing pregnancy bump with a protective hand.

Now beyond the first trimester, Beth had a perpetual glow, and whenever Carrie saw her and Zach together, her heart got tight. The love the couple shared was sweet, tender and heartwarming. It made Carrie hope it wasn't too late for her, that one day she'd find that kind of relationship for herself.

"Good luck," Paisley and Cam said, hugging her before joining Beth and Ellie.

"I'll need it." Despite her past experience and daily practice this week with Bryce, Cole, Maverick and Daisy-May, Carrie was far from a roping expert. She jogged toward the arena, greeting friends and acquaintances on the way.

"I'm glad I caught you." Kristi stopped her near the arena's rear entrance, where she was manning an information booth. "I heard through the grapevine the old Sutton farm's coming up for sale soon. It's near Diana's ranch but a lot smaller. If you're interested, I can put you in touch with the Realtor."

"That would be great, thanks." Carrie smiled at the café owner. Apart from Bryce, Kristi was the only person she'd told about her dream of having a small ranch of her own.

When Carrie had worked with Kristi on the café's website, they'd discovered a shared interest in sustainable farming. "I have to get ready for the team roping event, but let's talk on Monday. I've got more ideas for branded merchandise. You could sell various sizes of Bluebunch mugs, and I've found more durable, eco-friendly containers for your coffee, tea and muffin-of-the-day club members."

"You're my very own marketing guru." Kristi tipped her white cowboy hat before turning away to answer a question from a visiting competitor.

As Carrie navigated the labyrinth of stalls at the back of the arena, the buzz of conversation melded with the familiar scent of horses, hay and saddle leather. Those sounds and smells gave her the sense of home she'd missed while she'd been away from the competitive circuit.

At the far end of a walkway, Bryce and Cole readied Maverick and Daisy-May.

"Hi, guys." She patted Daisy-May's warm side, and the Appaloosa welcomed her with a soft nicker.

"Hi, Carrie. You saw Beth?" Bryce brushed Maverick, and Cole checked Daisy-May's hooves.

Carrie nodded and made sure the tack she'd packed earlier was in order. "Paisley and Cam are with her. Cam must be going through another growth spurt. He ate two hot dogs, but he was still hungry. I gave him the vegetable snacks I brought with me, and he ate those too."

"You should hear my mom talk about the amount of food she went through with four of us growing boys back in the day. Cam's just getting started," Cole said. Grinning, he turned to Bryce. "Remember not to leave the chute too soon, bro. You're the header, so you have to give the steer enough of a head start." He patted Bryce's shoulder as he left the stall. "And Carrie?"

She lifted her head from adjusting Daisy-May's saddle

pad. "Yeah?" She shouldn't be so nervous. It was a demonstration event, not an official competition, but the top three teams would win a donation to the charity of their choice. Bryce had picked the hospice that had given Ally end-of-life care, and Carrie didn't want to let him—or the charity—down.

"You've been great in practice," Cole assured her. "Just relax, take your time and rope both hind legs. Remember, you won't hurt the steer, so keep your rope nice and tight so his feet don't slip out. Mom says she won't hold it against me that I coached you two. After all, Shane's son helped them, and he still rides on the circuit."

"You're sure it's fair for me to take part? I ride on the rodeo circuit too." Carrie had asked Bryce to double-check with the event officials to be certain. She'd never want to do anything that could damage her own or the Carter family's reputation.

"Double-and triple-checked," Bryce said. "You're a barrel racer, not a roper. They're different sports, so today you're an amateur like the rest of us."

Carrie exhaled. "I sure feel like one. Not even an amateur. A beginner."

"Good luck. May the best Carter team win." Cole laughed as he left to join the rest of the family in the stands, and Bryce and Carrie led their horses toward the warm-up area.

"Are you ready?" Bryce held up one hand.

"You bet." She lifted her hand to meet his in a high five. Even this demonstration event on placid Daisy-May reminded her how much she'd missed competing. With guidance from Bryce and Cole, she'd had fun this week rediscovering roping too. Maybe once she was back on the circuit, she'd ask some of the others to train with her. She stopped near a practice chute and drew in a harsh breath.

"What's up?" Bryce stopped too.

"Nothing." *Everything.*

"Let's go on ahead." Carrie ducked around Daisy-May, but it was too late. Her ex, Jimmy, had already spotted her. Brittany, her one-time friend had too. "What are you guys doing here?" she asked, plastering a smile on her face.

"Britt's cousin's competing in junior bull riding." Jimmy jerked his chin to a boy with a red ribbon being congratulated by a couple who must be his parents. "We're spending the weekend in High Valley."

"I'm sorry," Brittany said. "For everything. What I did. What we… I…we didn't realize you were here." She flicked her long blond hair over her shoulder, and her face flushed as she glanced between Jimmy, Carrie and Bryce.

Carrie shrugged. It was too late for apologies. Since she hadn't talked to either of them after Jimmy admitted he'd cheated on her, there was no reason for them to know where Carrie was or what she was doing. "I'm working on a ranch near High Valley this summer." She introduced Jimmy and Brittany to Bryce.

Carrie patted Daisy-May. "We need to warm up. Enjoy the rest of your weekend. If you haven't already, be sure to stop at the Bluebunch Café for breakfast or lunch. The food's fantastic. Check out Medicine Wheel Craft Center too. They sell gorgeous locally-made souvenirs." She nodded politely and led Daisy-May away to where competitors prepared.

"You said that was 'nothing' before. But it didn't look like nothing just now with those two. To me it looked important and…uncomfortable." Standing beside her, with a patient Maverick, Bryce had an expression of concern.

"It was but it's over." And to her surprise, Carrie wasn't upset. "Jimmy's my ex, and Brittany's a former friend. They got together when I was on the circuit, and he 'forgot' to tell me. I found out when I came home a day early, drove by my favorite Kalispell restaurant and saw Jimmy and Brittany kissing on an outdoor patio. When I calmed down and confronted Jimmy the next day, at first he tried to tell me it meant nothing, but then he admitted he and Britt had been seeing each other for a few months." Carrie shrugged, and Bryce touched her hand in sympathy.

"It's okay," she said. "I'm not even mad any longer. At least I found out what both of them were really like, Jimmy especially. But that's why honesty and trust are more important to me than ever." While having people she'd trusted lie and betray her was never okay, in a way the two of them had done her a favor. She'd have been truly heartbroken if she and Jimmy were engaged or married, and he'd cheated then.

"Still, ouch." Bryce's face was filled with compassion.

"It hurt a lot at the time, but Jimmy and Brittany are in the past." And that experience had helped Carrie learn to trust her instincts. While she hadn't expected to find Jimmy was cheating on her with a friend, she'd sensed something was off with him for weeks. He'd cancelled dates and hadn't texted as often but she'd pushed her doubts aside. She glanced back, and Jimmy was on his phone like always, not paying any attention to Brittany or her cousin. Had he even congratulated the kid for winning a ribbon?

With his dark hair and eyes, athletic build and charming smile, Jimmy was handsome, and he had a good job in finance. He also had an expensive car, designer clothes and liked splashing money around. However, now it was as if Carrie saw him through new eyes. If she were honest with herself, she'd dated him to please her mom and dad because Jimmy's parents were business associates.

And like her folks, Jimmy had always assumed barrel racing was temporary, and never really listened to what *she* wanted. What had she ever seen in him? He was all surface polish and no substance, more focused on himself than anyone else.

As for Brittany, with time and distance, Carrie could even feel sad for her former friend. If a man cheated once, the likelihood was higher he'd cheat again. Besides, everyone deserved a partner who'd put them first, not a guy who spent all his time on his phone and pouted when he didn't get his own way.

She turned back to Bryce and Daisy-May. "I'm fine, really. I only hope the two of them go to the café and Rosa's gallery and spend lots of money. They both like good food, and Jimmy used to go on about the importance of supporting the arts. He should put his money where his mouth is." She chuckled. "Brittany apologized, but it doesn't bother me whether she means it or not. That part of my life is over."

"Good for you." One of Bryce's special smiles spread across his face and made Carrie weak at the knees. "You ready to show everyone what we're made of?"

"Absolutely." Today was about fun, friends and family, and Jimmy and Brittany weren't included. In this new life Carrie was building, instead of trying to please others, she was following her heart and making friends she could trust. Like the women of the Sunflower Sisterhood, Bryce and the rest of the Carter family. And after talking to Kristi, she'd contact that Realtor and ask to visit the old Sutton farm. It was all part of looking to the future, not the past.

She swung herself into Daisy-May's saddle and gave Bryce a thumb's up. "Let's go, partner."

IN MAVERICK'S SADDLE, Bryce made himself relax and eased the horse into the box beside the chute holding the steer. "Just like in practice, buddy." He fingered the rope looped over his saddle horn as the crowd cheered for his mom and Shane. What were the odds of the Carter teams following each other in the charity team roping event?

His mom tossed her cowboy hat into the air and caught it while she beamed at Shane. They'd had a good run, his mom especially, and set a time to beat. But it was even better for Bryce to see his mom happy and having fun.

"Good luck." His mom rode past him on Cindy as she and Shane made their way out of the arena. "And stay safe. No broken bones or other injuries. I went through enough of that worry with Cole."

"I hear you." Bryce laughed, and the tension in his shoulders lessened. He glanced at Carrie atop Daisy-May in a box on the other side of the chute. He was the header, she was the heeler and they were a team. No matter what happened in the arena, they'd handle it together.

As the announcer, a DJ at the local radio station, called their names, Bryce gripped the rope and leaned forward in his saddle. "Here we go." He nodded to the chute attendant and called for the steer.

The chute door swung open, and the steer took off into the arena at a run. Bryce and Maverick followed. Out the corner of one eye, Bryce spotted Carrie and Daisy-May waiting in position. He lassoed the steer's horns and did a quick dally, wrapping the rope around his saddle horn, and pulled the steer off to the left.

The next part was up to Carrie. Bryce held his breath as his gaze found hers for a split second. "You can do it." She couldn't hear him, but somehow he knew she sensed his encouragement.

Then Carrie let her rope fly too and caught the steer under its hind legs.

"Perfect execution." Bryce let out his breath as Carrie dallied up on Daisy-May's saddle horn. "Now for the finish."

He turned Maverick again so they faced Carrie and Daisy-May, and then both horses moved backward. "Gently, that's it." With the steer roped between them, the flag went up, and an official registered their time before releasing the steer, who trotted off.

"Great job." Carrie rode over to Bryce.

"You too." He hadn't compared their time with those of the other teams, but the result didn't matter. They'd shared something more important than a rodeo event. Bryce loosened his grip on his rope and put a hand to his heaving chest. "That was fantastic."

"The way you and Maverick came out of the box and roped those horns. Wow." Carrie's eyes were wide, and her body seemed to vibrate with excitement. "Maybe you missed your calling. Cole's not the only rodeo cowboy in the family."

"I'm happy being a rancher." But her words filled Bryce with quiet pride. Today, he'd stepped out of his comfort zone, and it felt good.

"I'm sorry about skidding on that turn. It was my fault, not Daisy-May's. I held her wrong."

As Carrie talked about their run, Bryce tried to focus. He hadn't noticed a skid, hadn't noticed anything really, except how the two of them had connected. It wasn't through words or even the event itself, but something had bound them together in a way that was soul deep.

"Way to go, guys." As they reached the exit, Cole greeted them. "You're only a second behind Mom and

Shane. Looking at the remaining competitors, I'm guessing you'll get second place."

"If not for me messing up that turn, we might have won." Carrie's shoulders slumped and she frowned as she ducked her head.

"You didn't mess up anything. You were perfect." *And not only on horseback.* The thought hit Bryce and caught him tighter than he'd roped the steer. "It's lucky you'd done some roping before, but we didn't have much time to practice. Don't be so hard on yourself. I wouldn't change anything about you or our run." He stuttered to a stop. Carrie and Cole stared at him, along with Melissa and Skylar, Beth, Paisley, Cam, Ellie and Zach. "I should see to the horses." His face must be tomato red.

"Cole and I'll take care of them." Zach stepped forward. "You watch the final competitors and then the result." A small smile played around his brother's mouth, and he exchanged a look with Cole, who smiled too.

"What?" Bryce dismounted and stood shoulder to shoulder between his older brothers.

"Nothing. We're happy for you." Cole sounded like he was holding back a laugh.

Even though they were adults, there were still times Bryce felt like the "little brother" he'd once been. Too young to join the older boys in their adventures, too old to play with Molly—stuck in the middle of the family. He took a step back and patted Maverick before Cole led the horse away.

"You had a good run," Zach said. "You surprised us, and that's good. If you'd wanted a shot at it when you were younger, you might have made it as a roper on the circuit." After Paul's death, Zach had assumed the role of oldest brother and peacemaker. "It's also great to see you having fun and being part of things again." He turned away to take Daisy-May from Carrie, who was getting excited hugs from Paisley and Cam.

After hugging his kids too, and while Carrie chatted with Beth and Melissa, Bryce leaned against the fence to watch the last few teams compete. He'd surprised himself as well. Unlike Cole, who'd always wanted to be a rodeo star, and Zach, who, because of Paul's illness, had been groomed by their folks to take over the ranch, Bryce's role had never been as well-defined. Molly too had always wanted to be a nurse and work at a city hospital.

Had he fallen into ranch work instead of consciously choosing it? He'd been interested in growing things and science since kindergarten, when they'd done a simple experiment to see how plants breathed. Although he'd considered teaching and, with Ally's encouragement, had earned a teaching qualification, he'd never let himself think seriously about any career except crop science and agriculture. Especially after his dad passed, he'd been needed on the ranch, and along with Ally and their family, work had been his life. He'd never let himself think about anything—or anyone—else.

The others cheered, and Carrie shouted and clapped the loudest.

"We did it." She ran over to him and jumped up and down. "I'd have liked to have placed first, but your mom and Shane did great, and the hospice will still get a nice donation."

Bryce joined in the family celebration, hugging everyone and being hugged in return.

Then he found himself beside Carrie again, and it seemed natural to hug her too—and hold her tighter and longer than necessary as he breathed in her sweet scent and savored her softness in his arms.

It felt right. *She* felt right. And it still would have, even if they hadn't won anything for the hospice. Today, Bryce had made a new memory, a good one, and although he hadn't shared it with Ally, that was okay. Maybe he'd begun to understand what she'd wanted for him. And for the first time, that was okay too.

CHAPTER FOURTEEN

"IN ALL THE EXCITEMENT, I haven't had a chance to say how proud I am of you," Joy told Bryce. She'd finally caught up with him in the family room at the main ranch house during the after-rodeo party she was hosting. "You and Carrie were great competitors." Both in the arena and here, her youngest son looked relaxed, happy and like he was having fun.

"I'm proud of you too, Mom. I hope I'm still going strong like you and Shane when I'm your age." He took a juice box and several pretzels from the tray Joy carried.

"We're not that old, but I'll take it as a compliment." Joy swatted his hand away like she'd done when he was a kid. "If you want more snacks, look in the kitchen. These are for the children."

"Yes, ma'am." His cheeky grin reminded her of that little boy too. Bryce was the most serious and introverted of her children, and she and Dennis had called him their "old soul." Although he usually managed to hide it, Bryce was perhaps the most vulnerable and easily hurt of their family too.

"Stop ma'aming me. That really makes me feel old." She shook her head and handed the tray to Rosa, who was keeping an eye on the kids as they ran through a sprinkler on the lawn. "Shane and I only won by a second, and unlike us, you and Carrie have a lot of years of competition left." Joy winced and rubbed her lower back. "Today was fun, but from now on I think I'll stick to dressage. It's more sedate."

"I always thought Cole's rodeo talent came from Dad, but watching you rope that steer, maybe I was wrong." Bryce's eyes twinkled.

"Maybe your dad and I were wrong about you too." Joy drew him into a quiet corner away from the party. "I was sure wrong about myself. After your dad passed, I never thought I'd smile or have fun again, let alone go on dates. It likely sounds silly, but I thought it would be disloyal." If there was a chance to take away what she suspected might be that same sense of guilt from her son, she wanted to try. "I finally realized your dad would want me to go on with my life as best I could. Not only for you kids but for me too."

Bryce rubbed a hand across his face. "Today was great, but…"

"You feel guilty?"

He gave a quick jerk of his chin.

"There's no need." Joy put a tentative hand on his shoulder. "You'll always love and miss Ally, like I'll always love and miss your dad, but that doesn't mean you can't have fun."

Joy glanced around the room. By the stone fireplace, Carrie chatted with Beth, Melissa, Kate and several other members of the Sunflower Sisterhood. Carrie fit in here as easily as if she'd always lived in High Valley. She'd fit in the Carter family too if Bryce would let himself take a chance. Today, more than ever, she'd seen the strength of the connection between her son and Carrie. She'd watched and waited for the right opportunity, and now she'd found it.

"Here." She dug in the back pocket of her jeans. "Shane won a pair of tickets to that outdoor country music festival on Friday, but we can't go." Joy suppressed a secret smile. They were going to another, larger town to look at engagement rings and planned to make a day of it, ending with dinner and dancing at a place they both liked. "Why don't you go with Carrie?"

"With Carrie?"

"Why not?" Joy willed him to take that next step. "There are some great bands playing, and the Wild Prairie Rodeo Chicks are headlining. I've heard Carrie say she likes their music." Joy did too, but even if she weren't going engagement ring shopping, she'd have given up the tickets to help Bryce.

"That would be great. We'd go as friends, of course."

"Of course, but you won't be going anywhere unless you ask Carrie." Joy put her hands behind her back and crossed her fingers for luck.

"Ask me what?" Carrie appeared at their side. "Paisley and Cam have had a long day. If it's okay with you, I'll take them home and get them settled and ready for bed."

"That's fine. I…" Bryce paused. "I won't be here much longer either, but I want to check on Maverick before I leave. Mom…she offered me…us… Shane won them, free tickets to that country music festival just west of town on Friday. They can't go, so would you…like to go? With me?"

Joy forced herself not to bounce with excitement. Despite sounding like a middle schooler asking a girl he had a crush on to go to the PTA dance, her son had done it. Since he likely hadn't asked anyone out since middle school, and back then it had been Ally, his awkwardness wasn't surprising. Asking someone for a date, and going on one, took practice, no matter how old you were.

"That would be fantastic." Carrie's face lit up with a smile. "I wanted to go, but when I tried to get a ticket the event was sold out. I'm a huge fan of the Wild Prairie Rodeo Chicks."

"It's all set then," Joy said. Was Carrie's excitement only about going to the event or was it also to do with Bryce? If she were a betting woman, Joy would put money on Bryce being a bigger draw than any band.

"Thank you, but…" Carrie's happy expression dimmed. "What about the kids? We can't leave them and—"

"Beth and Zach can look after them on Friday night, can't you?" Joy turned to Beth, who'd joined them.

"Of course. We'd be happy to. Ellie loves Paisley like a little sister, and Zach has fun spending time with Cam." Beth exchanged a sideways glance with Joy as if she sensed something was up and was happy to go along with whatever it might be.

"Excellent." Everything was working out exactly as Joy had hoped. "All you and Carrie need to do is go and have fun." She beamed at her son, who looked bewildered but happy, and then Carrie, who was radiant.

With luck, the weather Friday night would be perfect, and under a big, starlit Montana sky, anything could happen. Bryce, who'd had so much heartache, deserved something good…and someone like Carrie to share that goodness with.

CARRIE SWAYED TO the music, and the warm breeze—seasoned with the scents of barbecue, grassland and evergreens—ruffled her hair. Although she'd been born and raised in a city, those summers at her grandparents' ranch meant she was a country girl at heart.

"Having fun?" Beside her, Bryce moved to the music too, his expression as relaxed as Carrie had ever seen it.

"It's the best. The music and the setting are fantastic." *And the company.* She bit back the words that could have taken the evening in a more intimate direction. Even if Bryce wasn't attracted to her like she was to him, it was getting harder and harder to hide her feelings. Her body tingled whenever his arm brushed against hers, and the musky scent of his aftershave tantalized her senses and made her remember that all-too-brief brush of his lips against her cheek. Something she longed to repeat, without the kids looking on… Would his kiss move to her lips this time?

"Montana's beautiful in all seasons, but summer here is extra special." When the song changed, Bryce took Carrie's hand and led her into a country two-step. "I remember as a kid lying in the field behind the house on nights like this and looking at the stars with my dad. It was magical."

"It sounds like it. You must miss your dad a lot." Carrie followed the step pattern—quick-quick, slow-slow— of the dance her grandparents had taught her as a child.

"I do. Just as I miss my brother Paul, and Ally. Along with my dad, it's a lot."

"I can only imagine." Was that much loss and grief why Bryce seemed so closed and wary of opening up to others?

"Still, like my mom says, life has to go on." There was a bitter note in his voice, gone almost as soon as Carrie registered it.

"It does. But for me, when I think of my grandparents, I hope they'd be happy with how I'm living my life. In a way, trying to live my best life honors their memory." And thanks to that small inheritance her grandma had left her, if the seller was willing to come down a bit on the price, the old Sutton farm might be in her budget. She'd visit the farm once it was officially on the market, but from what the Realtor said, it sounded like the kind of property she wanted.

"This summer, you've shown me how living your best

life is important." Bryce guided her through the steps, and the soft, springy grass brushed their boots almost in time with the music.

"I'm happy to help." As they turned in a circle, Carrie tilted her head back to look at the inky sky spattered with stars. She had a sense of safety and belonging in this rural Montana world—and even more so in Bryce's arms—that she'd never felt anywhere else. "Sorry." Not paying attention to where she was going or the pattern of the dance, she stumbled and caught the toes of his boots with hers.

"Not a problem." His voice was low, and his warm hand settled more firmly on her shoulder and drew her closer. "I'm used to Paisley and Cam stepping on my toes. Your little tap was nothing."

His children. She loved the kids, but they were also why she couldn't let herself get too comfortable with their dad. She was leaving High Valley once school started again. She couldn't risk hurting Paisley and Cam by letting them think she could be a permanent part of their lives. "I bet the kids are having fun tonight." The musicians changed pace again, and Bryce moved them seamlessly into the more difficult cowboy cha-cha. "They love spending time with Zach, Beth and Ellie."

"The kids are lucky to have family who are always there for them. Between my family and your support this summer, I've now got a much better handle on everything."

"That's great." Carrie tried to sound happy and enthusiastic. She should be grateful she'd succeeded in her job instead of wanting more.

"Why am I talking about Paisley and Cam? We have a night off." Bryce guided her through the dance steps, one of his arms around Carrie's shoulders and their hands joined.

"We do." Dancing so close together, the warmth of

Bryce's body washed over Carrie. If she turned ever so slightly, she could—

"Thanks for supporting the Wild Prairie Rodeo Chicks." The lead singer, a woman with long dark hair and rhinestone-studded pink cowboy boots, took the microphone. "We'll be back after the break with one last set. Our good buddies, and a new band joining us this season, will be here. The Lonestar Runners are a sister act from Texas, and I hope you'll love their music as much as we do." Bryce's hands dropped away from Carrie's as they both clapped. "Get some more food, enjoy a hayride or treat yourself to a souvenir T-shirt or CD, but most of all, kick back, relax and enjoy the rest of the night." She waved as the crowd cheered and more country music, this time a recording, blasted from the speakers around the stage.

The night air had turned cooler, and Carrie shrugged into the pink-and-white "Long Live Cowgirls" sweatshirt she'd tied around her waist. "Earlier, when you were getting us drinks and burgers, and I went to the restroom, I stopped at a souvenir stand. I bought a signed CD for your mom and a T-shirt for Shane. I wanted to thank them for giving us the tickets." She patted the small backpack she used as a purse where she'd put the presents and then, keen to return to Bryce, had forgotten about until now. "I hope they'll be pleased. Your mom said they like the Wild Prairie Rodeo Chicks too."

"They'll be thrilled. That's so thoughtful of you." After putting on his own hoodie, a blue one that matched his eyes, Bryce tucked his hand into Carrie's.

Except for when they'd danced together, Bryce had never held her hand. And the way he clasped it now was different—more intentional and personal. All her nerve endings stirred.

"But right now, I don't want to talk about my mom or

anybody else in my family." He gave her a crooked smile. "What do you say we go on one of those hayrides?"

"That sounds great." As Carrie squeezed Bryce's hand, warmth spreading up her arm from his touch, her breath caught at the tenderness in his face.

"I'm having fun." He boosted her up onto one of the hay wagons waiting at the edge of the field and then joined her.

"Me too." Carrie settled into the sweet-smelling hay. The evening had gone too fast, but she wouldn't let herself think about that now. Instead, she'd savor every last moment of being with Bryce, just the two of them. "My grandparents used to take me and my cousins on hayrides. I loved it. Then we'd go back to the ranch house for homemade ice cream."

The driver spoke to the horses, two beautiful Clydesdales, and the wagon moved away along a track that bordered the field.

"That sounds fun." Bryce's leg brushed against Carrie's, sparking the now familiar tingles. "I have an ice-cream maker. If you want to use it, go ahead. I'll be a happy taste tester."

Carrie held on to the edge of the wagon as the horses pulled them down a gentle slope. On the other side of the wagon, their backs to Carrie and Bryce, a family oohed and ahhed at the starlit sky and tried to spot constellations. "I want to try making huckleberry ice cream. I spotted a patch of huckleberries when I was out riding last week. They should be ripe by the end of this month or early September." Around the time her nannying job ended. Carrie's heart squeezed, already anticipating the loss that would bring. Although she'd regain her barrel racing career, she'd lose the kids, Bryce and times like this one.

"I love huckleberry ice cream." The wagon lurched, and Bryce looped an arm around Carrie's shoulders.

"Me too. I'll ask my mom for my grandma's recipe." Bryce wasn't exactly hugging her. He was only holding her because the wagon ride was bumpy, and like a gentleman, he wanted to keep her safe. But even when the track smoothed, Bryce didn't move his arm, and it was natural for Carrie to lean into his body. "My folks are visiting Aunt Angela and me the last weekend in August. I'd like them to meet you and the kids and see the ranch. They're not horse people, not even my mom despite growing up on a ranch, but High Valley will still be fun for them."

And Carrie would finally tell her parents what she wanted to do with her life, and that it didn't include Rizzo Construction. Her dad would have to find someone else to take on the head of marketing job—and, a few years down the line, someone to lead the entire company—because it wouldn't be her. What had been an ever-present sense of guilt was now replaced with relief and excitement about making her own future.

"I'd like to meet them too. For themselves but also because they're your folks." Bryce's voice was low, almost husky. "Carrie, I...you're important to me."

"You're important to me too." Her heart hammered. Was it possible Bryce felt the same way about her as she did about him?

Bryce twirled a loose strand of her hair around his fingers. "Your hair's so pretty. You're so pretty. And I..."

"Yes?" Suddenly it was hard to breathe.

"Aww, Carrie."

She didn't know which of them moved first, but they both wanted the same thing. And as their lips met in a kiss every bit as wonderful as Carrie had imagined, she succumbed to the pleasurable sensations engulfing her. Bryce's lips were warm and seeking, and as she returned the kiss, she touched his jaw and ran her fingers across the roughness of his beard stubble.

It wasn't a quick, accidental kiss like the one in the hayfield with the kids looking on. This kiss was purposeful, real and turned every part of her to mush. Yet, it had a steadiness and sweetness too, along with faithfulness, honesty and care.

As they drew apart and stared into each other's eyes, Carrie tipped over that edge from liking Bryce to loving him with every fiber of her being.

She'd worry about what to do about it later. Right now, what she had here was enough.

CHAPTER FIFTEEN

BRYCE FINISHED MUCKING out Maverick's stall and pulled off his work gloves. Less than twenty-four hours after he'd kissed Carrie, guilt had expanded from his stomach to lodge in his windpipe like something hard and physical. Kissing her had been an impulse. And although he hadn't immediately regretted it, after Bryce had dropped Carrie off at Angela's and gone home, he'd tossed and turned all night, playing what had happened between them over and over in his mind. And when she'd arrived at the ranch house for breakfast with him and the kids this morning, despite it being her day off, he could barely look at her.

Wherever he turned on the ranch and in his house, he was reminded of Ally and now Carrie too. Since a big part of him still felt married to Ally, what was he doing kissing Carrie and enjoying it as much as he had? He also liked Carrie in a way that went far beyond friendship, and without consciously planning to, he'd gotten seriously involved with her. Except, she was leaving at the end of the summer so a future for them was hard to see.

He kicked an empty metal feed bucket aside, and it clattered as it hit the barn wall. Two of the barn cats, Mr. and Mrs. Wiggins, darted out of the way and yowled.

"Sorry." He righted the bucket, hung it in its place from a hook on the barn wall and scratched Mr. Wiggins behind his ears.

"Is everything okay?" Saddle leather creaked as Carrie dismounted. She led Teddy into the barn.

"It's fine." Bryce tossed a ping pong ball for the cats to chase.

"It's such a gorgeous day. Teddy and I rode along the creek and then did some training with barrels I set up in the lesson paddock. I waved at you from the paddock, but I guess you didn't see us."

Bryce muttered something incomprehensible. He'd seen them all right, but if he'd waved back, he'd have also gone over to chat. And before he knew it, he'd have been kissing her again, and who knew where that might lead? Sadness when Carrie left, and he was alone again, for sure.

"Can you grab me a hoof-pick, please?" Her sweet voice caught Bryce's heart and made him ache to hold her. "The one with the purple handle. Teddy picked up lots of dirt and gravel on the trail."

Bryce found the pick and passed it to her, making sure to keep a careful distance between them.

"Thanks." She took the pick and bent toward one of Teddy's front hooves. "It's okay, boy. I'll make you feel better."

Bryce should leave the barn right now. There was nothing to be gained from prolonging the agony of having Carrie so close. And it took a lot of effort to stop himself from wrapping his arms around her and maybe even asking her to spend the rest of her life with him. "If you're all set, I need to get out to the wheat field. Enjoy the rest of your day." That was honest, polite and friendly, so why did he feel like he'd taken a hit to the chest with Cam's soccer ball?

"Hang on a second." Carrie straightened and patted Teddy. "Since your mom's looking after the kids today, I wondered if you'd like to have supper with me and Angela? She's making caprese chicken, and I'm taking care of dessert. It's pizzelles and vanilla ice cream. Aunt Angela has an ice-cream maker too, and I want to practice for huckleberry season." Her warm smile lifted the corners of her mouth and lit up her entire face, including her eyes.

A sharp pain shot through what was left of Bryce's heart. Angela Moretti's caprese chicken was famous in High Valley. And he'd tasted plenty of Carrie's outstanding baking, including the crispy Italian butter cookies she'd brought for the kids. For both the company and food, he'd be a fool to say no, but he had to.

"Sorry, I can't. I'm having dinner with the kids at my mom's." Although he hadn't asked his mom yet, she was always happy for him to join them.

"Oh." Carrie's smile slipped. "Another time then."

"Yeah." Bryce swallowed the taste of regret. It was hard, but it was for the best, not only for him but Paisley and Cam. He couldn't let his kids get hurt, either, when Carrie left. "Since I have an early client call tomorrow morning, I'll be working in my office when you get to the house." Carrie hadn't started out working for him on Sundays, but Bryce had taken on a big freelance project. This weekend, he needed her on what should have been his day off. Who was he kidding? He needed her all the time. Not as the kids' nanny but as a partner, someone special in his life.

"Of course." Carrie returned to picking out Teddy's hooves, and her voice cooled. "I forgot to mention the kids and I are volunteering with your mom at the Sunflower Sisterhood's booth at the town's homecoming event tomorrow afternoon. Is that okay with you?"

"No problem. It'll be fun for them. You as well, I hope. A couple of the hands took vacation time, so I'll be busy here." He turned toward the open door. "Hey, girl." He patted Penny who'd followed a scent into the barn.

"I understand." Carrie hesitated, and although Bryce

didn't raise his head from the dog, he sensed her studying him. "I'll leave a packed lunch for you in the fridge. Paisley needs new swim goggles, and some of Cam's T-shirts are getting small. I could—"

"Buy whatever they need. I'll transfer you money to cover it." Bryce brushed his damp palms against his jeans. Pretending to be oblivious to how Carrie made him feel was harder than he'd expected, but it would get easier in time. It had to.

"Fine." Was that hurt in her voice? "Have a good day."

"You too. It's sure a hot one." Now he'd resorted to talking about the weather. As Bryce left the horse barn, he mentally berated himself. If he hadn't hurt Carrie, he'd offended her, but it was for the best, wasn't it?

"Who or what ruffled your feathers?" Outside the red barn that housed the ranch's business office, Cole interrupted Bryce's reverie.

"Nobody and nothing." He manufactured a smile as he greeted his brother. "Is Zach inside? I want to talk to him about the Herefords. They're arriving at the end of the week." Those pigs would keep him busy too. "I also want to see about getting quotes for a new irrigation system."

Cole let out a low whistle. "Zach's at his desk, but an irrigation system will be expensive. With buying that tractor a year ago, is there enough in the budget? You should get Beth's input too. She's a genius with finding extra cash, but she also runs a tight ship."

"She is, and I already have." Did Cole think Bryce didn't know their sister-in-law oversaw the ranch's finances with the same expertise she'd once wielded as chief financial officer for a major corporation? "Don't you have work to do?"

"Whoa. I haven't seen you so riled since Big Red got into the barley field last harvest. What's up, Little Buckaroo?"

"Don't call me that." Bryce usually took his childhood nickname and his brother's good-natured teasing in the spirit it was intended but not today. "As for that bull, if he ever gets into the barley or any other crop again, he's going straight to auction. I'll drive him there myself." Bryce stepped to one side of the barn doorway, and Cole followed him. "What? You're in my way."

"I'm sorry for winding you up. If something's wrong, I want to help. Melissa will too." Whenever Cole mentioned his new wife, his face got a soft, loving expression Bryce usually considered sweet. Now it only annoyed him more. "I don't need your help. I don't need anyone's help. What I *need* is to talk to Zach and then get back to work." He had to focus on work because…apart from the kids, it was all he had.

"Okay." Cole shrugged, but his expression was still remorseful and concerned. "If you change your mind, I'll be in the yard fixing the tractor belt. As for the Herefords, it'll be fun to try something new. I talked to Carrie, and she's excited about them too. She offered to be there when we unload and—"

"Whatever." Bryce entered the dim coolness of the barn, where Zach's voice echoed from the business office. His other brother must be talking on the phone because the conversation, about a cow, was one-sided and punctuated by intermittent silence.

Carrie. Until he'd met her, Bryce's life had been full, and his kids and work had been enough. Somehow, he had to get back to that place again. It was the only way to keep himself, and his heart, safe.

"Here you go." Carrie handed a woman wearing a High Valley High School, Class of 1992, T-shirt her change along with a reusable shopping bag that held a jar of local honey, two packages of sunflower seeds and a lemon yellow baby blanket crocheted by Aunt Angela. "Thanks for stopping by. Enjoy the rest of your day, and welcome home."

High Valley's weekend homecoming event had started the day before, and the town was busy with visitors. Over the two days, both locals and tourists flocked to the Sunflower Sisterhood's stall on High Valley Avenue in front of the Bluebunch Café.

"Have a seat." Joy indicated one of the folding lawn chairs behind the booth and then took the other one. "You look like you need it. It should be quieter for the next while with everybody heading to the park for the band concert."

Carrie sat and stretched her sneaker-clad feet in front of her. "Thank goodness Beth offered to look after Paisley and Cam for a few hours after lunch. It's been too busy for them to help here, so they'd have been bored. I also couldn't have kept an eye on them and served customers."

"You've been a lifesaver. It would have been hard for me to handle so many people on my own." Joy patted Carrie's arm. "It's good to catch up too. I've hardly seen you these past few days. You'd have been welcome to join Bryce and the kids for supper with me yesterday, but he said you had plans with Angela. I hope everything's okay."

Carrie forced a smile. "Everything's fine. Since Bryce has had to work so much lately, I've almost been living full-time at the ranch. I wanted to spend time with my aunt on my day off." All of that was true, but she'd been disappointed Bryce hadn't accepted her dinner invitation. In fact, since they'd kissed at the music festival—a kiss Carrie still felt on her lips and in her heart—it seemed Bryce was avoiding her.

She feigned an interest in High Valley Avenue. The council had closed the town's main street to vehicle traffic this weekend, and the wide thoroughfare was lined with stalls run by community groups like theirs raising funds for local causes. "If this afternoon's sales are an indication of the weekend total, the Sunflower Sisterhood should be able to make a sizeable donation to the arena's accessibility committee. At least enough to finish putting in more wheelchair-accessible and low-mobility seats."

"Maybe improving accessible parking too." Joy picked up a stack of paper gift bags and began filling them with packages of sunflower seeds, souvenir magnets, pens, notepads and huckleberry-scented tea lights. "I'm glad you and Bryce had fun at that music festival. I love the signed CD you got me, and Shane's wearing his band T-shirt today."

"You two missed a great show." Carrie tightened the lace on one of her sneakers. She'd dropped off the gifts as quickly as possible and declined Joy's invitation to come in for a coffee. Bryce's mom was savvy. Carrie didn't want her to guess Carrie's relationship with her son was strained. There was a new distance between them Carrie didn't know how to fix.

"Bryce is…" Joy paused and tied a green ribbon around the handles of a filled goodie bag, one of their most popular items. "He's complex, and although he looks fine on the outside, underneath he's a wounded soul."

"Of course." Bryce had lost his wife, his dad and a brother. Anybody would be wounded after so much loss.

"No, I don't think you understand." Joy rearranged a tea-light display. "Bryce can sometimes be like a wounded animal. Although they're different in almost every other way, Cole's the same. When either one of them is scared, hurting or overwhelmed by what they're feeling, they run off and hide. Maybe not physically—although Bryce has spent so much time in the fields this weekend, I've been tempted to ask if he wanted to pitch a tent out there—but emotionally. The few times he's reappeared, he's been like a grumpy bear woken from hibernating too early. We've all noticed it."

Carrie gave what she hoped was a casual shrug. "My focus is Paisley and Cam." Letting herself care for their dad, and starting to imagine she might become a real part of Bryce's life and family, was her mistake, not his.

"Cole mentioned Bryce made a fuss about nothing with him outside the barn yesterday, and he also had heated words with Zach about housing those Hereford pigs. I was in the business office at the time, so I heard most of it. I stayed well out of it, but from how Bryce was going on, you'd have thought Zach didn't know anything about livestock." Joy shook her head. "Bryce is usually so easygoing. I don't know what's wrong."

"I expect Bryce will figure it out in his own time." Carrie busied herself filling goodie bags too. What was or wasn't bothering Bryce wasn't any of her business. Although Joy sounded innocent enough, something in her tone put Carrie on alert.

"It's such a pity. Bryce has seemed so much happier and almost like his old self this summer." Was Joy's sigh a bit too dramatic? "With taking part in the team roping competition and going to that family fun day at Squirrel Tail, I really thought he'd turned a corner. I know…" Her blue eyes shone. "Shane had a cancellation this week. There's a family bed-and-breakfast suite free on Wednesday night. You, Bryce and the kids should take it. A little vacation might be what he needs to perk right up. What do you think?"

Carrie swallowed. "Bryce and the kids should go, sure.

Paisley and Cam would love that one-on-one time with their dad." If they were away, Carrie would focus on her freelance work. She'd add the last touches to Kristi's website and design an advertising poster for one of her rodeo clients.

"It would be a nice getaway for you too. Besides, you're like part of the family. Leave it with me." Joy waved at a couple who'd come out of the Medicine Wheel Craft Center. "I'll talk to Shane and fix everything. He likely won't charge you for the suite either. The family who'd booked already paid in full but had to cancel because their children have ear infections. Poor things." Joy stood and waved at the couple again. "Luckily, the family had cancellation insurance, so neither they nor Shane will be out of pocket. With the suite empty, it would be fun for you to use it."

"Fun," Carrie echoed. As Joy talked animatedly with the couple, old friends who used to live in High Valley, Carrie made an excuse about getting a drink from the café.

Spending time in such close quarters with Bryce as part of the family wouldn't be fun at all. Not now when she was so hurt and puzzled by his behavior. He'd even brushed away her offer to help with the Herefords, although raising those pigs had been her idea originally.

She opened the café door, asked the teenage girl behind the counter for a soda and dug in the pocket of her denim shorts for money.

Whatever was going on with Bryce was his problem. If she ended up going to Squirrel Tail Ranch for that so-called "vacation," she'd be there for Paisley and Cam but avoid any activities that involved Bryce. Thanks to her nannying job and free boarding for Teddy, she could afford a ranch of her own sooner than she'd expected. That was what mattered. Yet, as she took the cold can of soda from the girl, her whole body, not only her hand, chilled. Now she wanted more than that ranch. She wanted Bryce too.

CHAPTER SIXTEEN

THAT EVENING, after spending most of the day at the home-coming, Joy put the first aid box in a kitchen cupboard and patted the bandage that covered Cam's scraped knee. "You were very brave, and in a week or so, your knee will be as good as new. Not even a scar."

"You always make hurts better, Grandma." He wrapped his arms around her, and Joy's heart swelled. Small physical hurts were easy to fix and soon forgotten. The bigger emotional ones, like Bryce's, were much harder. "Get an ice-cream treat and go play with your cars on the porch. I need to talk to your dad for a minute."

"Is Daddy in trouble?" Cam paused by the freezer drawer and looked at her quizzically.

"Of course not." Joy made herself laugh. Bryce was "in trouble" all right but not the kind Cam meant. "I'll come and play soon. If you need anything, ask your aunt Melissa." After Carrie had dropped the kids off at the ranch house because Bryce was still working, Joy had asked Melissa and Skylar, who'd popped in while Cole did chores, if they could stay a bit longer. Joy wanted some uninterrupted time with her son.

As the porch door shut behind Cam, Joy glanced around her tidy kitchen. It was the heart of her home—and her family—and many of their most important conversations had taken place around the long harvest table. She'd celebrated at that table, grieved there, and in all seasons of her life, received comfort from loved ones there too. When she and Shane had their own house, that table would come with her.

She fingered the diamond-studded engagement ring she wore on a chain around her neck and pictured Shane's face. In a few weeks, they'd share the news of their engagement with their families, but for now Joy had the time she needed to get used to this lovely but big life change.

"I checked those boards on the back deck," Bryce said, coming into the kitchen. "They need replacing for sure. I'll pick up lumber when I'm next in town. Are the kids ready to head home?"

"In a while. Sit." She gestured to one of the chairs, and her beagle, Gus, and elderly collie, Jess, sat too.

"Okay." Bryce laughed, pulled out the chair and patted the dogs. "What's up?"

"I was about to ask you the same question." Joy grabbed the bowl of peas she'd picked earlier, sat across from him and started shelling the firm green pods. The evening light slanted across the kitchen floor and accented the lines on her son's face. "Has something happened between you and Carrie? When she volunteered with me at the homecoming stall, she was different. Evasive even. I thought you two were friends." More than friends, although it wasn't Joy's place to say so.

"We are, but..." Bryce exhaled and rested his head in his hands. "It's a mess and all my fault."

"If it is, you can fix it." She studied his bent head and the silver strands amongst the brown. Dennis had gone gray early too, but in Joy's eyes, it had only made him more handsome and distinguished.

"I had a great time with Carrie at the concert, and I really care for her. As a lot more than a friend." His voice was almost a whisper.

"Grief and guilt are funny things. They ebb and flow and swirl and slither around until you can feel like you're tied up in knots inside. If you're anything like I was, taking that next step is hard." She set aside the peas and covered Bryce's hands. "The first time Shane kissed me, I felt like I was cheating on your dad. For a few days afterward, the guilt was terrible."

"It was?" Bryce raised his head, and his eyes were troubled.

Joy nodded. "Then I talked to my friends and my grief counsellor, and they made me see guilt is another part of grief. It comes in stages. First there's going out and having fun without your loved one. That's a big hurdle. Then there's letting yourself care for someone else in a special way, and that's even bigger."

"But you did it?" His voice cracked.

"Shane and I both did. He misses his wife like I miss your dad. But although our loved ones were taken too soon, they'd have wanted us to be happy in all ways. I can't live my life as I once did, but that doesn't mean I can't have a new life." The ring tucked beneath Joy's T-shirt testified to that.

"If Carrie makes you and the kids happy, you should see where things go. We both know you can't plan everything in life, so what about instead letting yourself be open to opportunities?" She squeezed Bryce's hands and returned to shelling peas. "Letting yourself care for Carrie doesn't diminish your love for Ally. It doesn't make you a bad person either. Rather, it makes you human and someone who needs comfort and companionship like we all do."

Bryce rubbed a hand across his weary face. "Thanks, Mom. You always know how to make things better. I'll talk to Carrie tomorrow and start by apologizing. I've been weird to her this weekend. To all of you."

Joy chuckled. "We're a family. We can put up with weirdness from time to time. You might want to apologize to your brothers too. Zach and Cole were pretty steamed about what you said to them yesterday."

"It wasn't anything they said or did." Bryce's expression was sheepish. "I took my own stuff out on them."

"They'll understand. I certainly do. It's hard when you're on your own and surrounded by loving couples, but we each have to find our own path."

"I'm happy for Zach and Beth, and Cole and Melissa, but sometimes it hurts, you know?"

"Reminders of any big loss always will, but you learn to live with it. Besides, it's only been a few years, and you've had the kids to worry about. Grief doesn't have a timeline, and you could only grieve in bits and pieces. You couldn't even think about a new relationship because you needed to be strong for your children." Joy came around the table and hugged her son as tight as she'd hugged her grandson. "But you're never too old for a fresh start."

She only hoped her kids would be as happy about her fresh start, and Shane becoming part of their family, as she was.

"YOU TWO ARE doing great with your swimming." Near midday on Monday, behind the wheel of Bryce's pickup truck, Carrie spoke over her shoulder to Paisley and Cam, who were buckled into their booster seats. "Your front crawl is lots better, Cam, and so is your diving, Paisley."

"I'm scared about the test." Cam's voice was small.

"Everybody gets scared before tests. I still get scared each time I go into a rodeo arena to compete," Carrie said. "Take a deep breath and do your best. That's all anyone can ask of you."

That was all Carrie should ask of herself too. She'd

hoped to find a quiet moment to talk to Bryce earlier and try to understand what was wrong. But some cattle had gotten loose, so he'd left the house with Cole as soon as she'd arrived.

"Your teacher said you'll pass no problem," Paisley assured her brother. "I'm scared for my test too. Can we go to the pool again tomorrow afternoon to practice? Aunt Melissa's bringing Skylar then, and we could practice together. Skylar's excellent at swimming. She's younger, but she's way better than me."

"Skylar started swimming lessons earlier. Her grandparents in California have a pool too." Carrie slowed the truck and stared at a ranch on the right-hand side of the highway, where black smoke billowed from one of the barns. "Hang on." She pulled onto the gravel shoulder as an emergency siren squealed, and a fire truck raced past.

"It's a fire. Daddy might be there." Cam bounced in his seat and pointed.

"Or on his way," Paisley added. "Some kids who go to the high school live on that ranch. They rode on our bus last year."

Carrie's body chilled as she spotted flames coming from the barn roof. In the distance, someone led a horse to safety in a nearby pasture. "Sit tight, kids. Here comes another emergency vehicle. The fire department will soon have things under control." She tried to make her voice calm. They had to quell the fire fast before it spread to nearby fields, other barns or the ranch house, but she couldn't leave the children to go and help. She fumbled with her cell phone and scrolled to Bryce's number.

She was driving his pickup because hers was in for a service, and Angela's car didn't have enough space for the two booster seats. If Bryce was here, he'd have taken Joy's car or one of the ranch's trucks.

His phone rang and went to voicemail. Without leaving a message, she tried Joy's number and then Melissa and Beth.

"Hello?"

"Thank goodness." When Beth answered, Carrie exhaled. "I've been trying to reach everyone. A barn's on fire a few miles this side of town and—"

"I just heard. Joy called me. I'm at home with Ellie. If you want to come here with the kids, we're staying put. Bryce responded to the first alarm, so he's already there in his gear. Zach and Cole left around the same time."

"I'll stay here for now. Joy's car's pulling up behind me." The phone slipped in Carrie's sweaty palms, and even the kids were quiet. "Here's your grandma." She got out of the driver's seat and met Joy outside the truck.

"Almost as soon as the emergency call came through, the town sent out an email, and there's a lot on social media too. Everyone wants to support the Irving family." Joy spoke in a low voice to Carrie. "I thought if I drove out this way, I'd meet you coming from swimming. I can take the children back to the ranch if you want to lend a hand moving the horses and other stock."

"Thanks, I do." Before Joy had finished speaking, Carrie was pulling her hair up into a ponytail and taking off her sneakers and replacing them with one of the pairs of barn boots Bryce kept in the back of his truck.

"I have a batch of chocolate chip cookies fresh from the oven." Joy helped the kids unbuckle their seat belts. "How does cookies and milk sound? Your dad will be back before you know it, so we can save some for him."

Paisley, older and more aware than Cam, glanced between Carrie and Joy, and a worried frown creased her face.

"Your dad and the other firefighters will keep everyone safe." Carrie knelt to Paisley's level. "And I'm going to keep the animals safe. I'll be home as soon as I can. Can you save cookies and milk for me?"

"Lots of cookies in Grandma's special tin. The one with the tractor on it." Easily diverted, Cam let Joy lead him to her car.

"You go on," Carrie said to Paisley. "It'll be okay. Your dad needs you to be brave and help Cam and your grandma. Can you do that?"

Paisley nodded and hugged Carrie before she joined Joy and Cam.

Carrie ran down the long driveway toward the barn. Bryce had to be okay. She couldn't lose him. Although she'd tried to fight her feelings, she loved him, and she wanted that love to have a chance to grow. "What can I do?" She met Jon Schuyler, a local veterinarian, by the pasture fence.

"We're loading these guys into a trailer to take to a neighbor's place." He gestured to two beautiful chestnut Morgan horses who stomped and pawed the ground and showed the whites of their eyes. "I could use a hand."

"You've got it." The frightened horses would give Carrie a focus beyond Bryce. Still, her gaze strayed to the barn where firefighters in protective gear trained hoses on the burning structure while several others did the same in the hayloft, where the roof was partly gone. "Easy, boy. You're safe." She soothed the nearest horse and guided it gently toward the waiting trailer.

In a few minutes, Cole appeared with a gray pony, and they worked together to load the precious cargo. "Luckily, most of the cattle are in a far pasture, but Zach and a couple of ranch hands are getting a few calves and some other stock out."

"And Bryce?" Carrie's hands shook, and she fumbled with the first Morgan's trailer tie.

"Last I saw, he was headed into the barn fire." Cole's expression was grim. "He knows what he's doing. He's been trained for it. It's not his first fire either. Try not to worry."

Carrie gulped and went back for the second Morgan, further conversation made impossible by several more emergency vehicles screeching to a stop beside them.

As she focused on horses and then calves, chickens and several pigs, time lost all meaning. Cole made several trips to the neighboring ranch with the loaded horse trailer while Carrie worked on and tried not to look at the inferno that had now spread to the barnyard and an empty chicken coop. *Where are you, Bryce?*

An hour later, Jon, the vet, rubbed a hand across his soot-streaked forehead. "The worst of the fire's out. All the animals have been relocated, and they saved the crops, except an acre or so of the barley field and a vegetable garden. Luckily, the wind didn't change direction, or they might have lost the house too. I was here on a routine visit when the fire broke out. It spread so fast. It's also lucky you turned up when you did. Cole and I couldn't have gotten the horses to safety so quickly without you."

"I was happy to help." Pitching in when neighbors were in need was part of small-town and ranch life. "Did the family have insurance?"

Jon nodded. "If there's anything insurance won't cover, the rest of us will share what we can now, and for animal feed throughout the winter. I heard Joy Carter and Rosa Cardinal are organizing the Sunflower Sisterhood to deliver meals and divide up garden produce."

Carrie would be part of that effort as well, but her priority was to find Bryce. She shaded her eyes with one hand and lifted her damp ponytail from the back of her neck with the other. Most of the firefighters were still clustered by the barn. But at this distance, and with them wearing all that equipment, she couldn't tell them apart. "If you don't need me for anything else, I'll—"

"Carrie. What are you doing here?"

She swung around at Bryce's voice. "Helping. Your mom's looking after the kids." Apart from a yellow safety helmet, he'd removed his outer gear and wore a blue short-sleeved T-shirt with dark pants and boots. "I was so scared for you." She swayed toward him, and her eyes filled with tears.

"Hey, it's okay. The fire looked bad, but I've been called out to worse." Bryce opened his arms, and she almost fell into them.

"I...you're safe... I thought I'd never see or talk to you again." Her voice cracked, and tears slipped down her cheeks. And as she kissed him, and he kissed her back, she was oblivious to any curious onlookers.

She and Bryce had another chance, and that was all that mattered.

CHAPTER SEVENTEEN

AFTER SAYING GOODNIGHT to Paisley and Cam, Bryce sat beside Carrie on the front porch swing. His house faced west, and the sun was a red-gold ball against the far horizon. "When one of my crew said you were at the Irvings' farm today, and then I saw you with Jon and the horses, I was both proud and terrified. Proud because you'd pitched in, and without your help the Irvings might have lost stock, and terrified something could have happened to you."

While Bryce wanted to keep Carrie safe, having her nearby steadied him. She'd been his calm and anchor amidst the chaos of the fire. And now he wanted to tell her at least part of what he was feeling.

"Anybody would have done the same. If your mom hadn't come by, I'd never have left Paisley and Cam. But since she did, I couldn't go on home without doing what I could."

The setting sun picked up matching gold and red glints in Carrie's pretty hair, and in a red-and-white polka-dot sundress he hadn't seen her wear before, she looked feminine and almost delicate. She was strong and tough when she needed to be, though, and Bryce liked that and everything else about her. More than liked. Could he love her? The rush of emotion he'd experienced in the aftermath of the fire, when she'd tumbled into his arms, hadn't subsided. If anything, it had grown stronger.

"What did you say?" He stared at Carrie, mesmerized

by the soft curve of her cheek and the bow of her kiss-able mouth.

"I asked if the kids had settled into bed okay. They were both more worried about you than they let on. They love you so much."

Carrie's expression was puzzled, and Bryce tried to re-arrange his face into a more neutral countenance. "I love them too. I…" He stopped himself. He'd almost said he loved her as well, but for a cautious and logical guy like him, it was too soon, and the feelings were too new. "Cam was asleep as soon as his head hit the pillow. Paisley took longer, but reading a story calmed her."

The swing creaked as it moved back and forth in a gentle motion. The past few summers, Bryce hadn't spent much time on this porch. However, Carrie and the kids had planted petunias in the previously empty containers and brought out this swing from where he'd stored it in the garage. Along with a cheerful, sunflower-patterned wel-come mat, a low table with a candle lantern and strands of white lights twined around the railing, the porch was now as homey as the rest of his house.

"It's a pretty night." Carrie's voice was low. "Peaceful."

No matter what they were doing, or what else was going on, simply being around Carrie gave Bryce a sense of peace. "I meant it when I said I was terrified for you at the fire." As a younger man, he'd never admitted to fear, but life and loss had changed him. "At the music festival, I said you were important to me. What I should have said is I have important feelings for you. When I kissed you on the hayride, it was great, but then I panicked, so I backed away. I'm sorry for being weird."

"It's okay. I think I understand." Her eyes were soft and filled with compassion. "Am I the first woman you've kissed since Ally?"

Bryce nodded. While some women might have been jealous or uncomfortable, Carrie was intuitive enough, and caring enough, to get and accept where he was coming from. Already slow to open his heart and his life to someone else, Bryce also had baggage most other men his age didn't.

"I have important feelings for you too." She slipped her hand into his, and they rocked quietly together for a few moments. "That's a big part of why I don't want to leave High Valley. I've got an appointment with a real estate agent to see the old Sutton farm tomorrow after work. When I'm not competing, I'd like to make my home in this area."

"I'd like that." He took a deep breath. "Shane had a cancellation, and he offered me a free, two-bedroom family suite at Squirrel Tail on Wednesday night. It would mean a lot if you joined the kids and I there."

"Your mom mentioned that as well, and now…yes. I'd love to come with you." Her words came out in a rush, and her green eyes shone.

"It could be the start of seeing where things might go between us." Instead of panic, Bryce felt calm and a fundamental sense of rightness. "I don't want anything to spoil our friendship or upset the kids, but what do you think?"

The only other time he'd gotten serious about a woman, he'd been a teenager, and he and Ally had grown up together. It was different with Carrie. He was different, and this relationship, as it should be, was also different from the one he'd shared with his late wife.

"I think that sounds good." The honesty and trust in Carrie's face touched a part of his heart he'd thought was gone forever. "I know you need time, so I don't want us to say anything to the kids or anyone else right now. Let's take things slowly. I won't be working for you much longer, and after that…" Her face went pink. "Today, at the fire, I was afraid I'd never have a chance to tell you how I feel about you. I want us to have a chance to explore those feelings, Bryce."

"I want that too." He moved closer and read the invitation in her eyes. And then he kissed her, better than any of the kisses they'd shared before because now they were also sharing what was in their hearts.

IN THE TRANQUIL river behind the main guest house at Squirrel Tail Ranch, Carrie dipped her paddle into the water, and the kayak slid forward.

"Are you guys having fun?" From a three-person kayak moving in tandem with hers, Paisley and Cam, who wore orange life jackets, gave Carrie a thumbs-up. Bryce grinned and raised his own paddle in salute. Beneath a yellow life jacket, he wore a white T-shirt with the Tall Grass Ranch logo and black swim shorts. A ball cap had taken the place of his standard cowboy hat, and aviator sunglasses finished the look.

"It's fantastic, isn't it?" She let her kayak drift to watch a pair of ducks paddle into a clump of reeds.

"You got the hang of kayaking real fast." Bryce nodded approvingly. He looked as at-home on the water as he did on horseback or working in the fields.

"You're a good teacher." He was kind, patient and had a way of explaining things that made it easy for Carrie to understand.

"I once thought about teaching high-school science. I did a teaching qualification part-time after I finished college. School in the winter and ranching in the summer would have been a good fit but…life happened." A shadow flitted across his face. "I'm teaching several agricultural workshops next winter. One of my consulting clients asked me for them, and I thought why not?"

"You'll be great." Carrie turned her kayak around to follow Bryce and the kids back toward the rental area. Although life didn't always turn out how you expected, there were all kinds of ways to make dreams come true. You had to take a fresh perspective, that was all.

As they neared shallower water, she rested her paddle across her knees. Before today, she'd only ever been on tourist boats, and they were motorized and much bigger. Kayaking was different. It brought her closer to nature, and the slow pace brought her closer to herself too.

"Here you go." Bryce, already out of his kayak, pulled Carrie's onto the sandy shore and helped her out.

"What did you think?" Carrie gave a hand to Paisley as she scrambled out of the bigger kayak while Bryce did the same with Cam.

"It was awesome." Paisley grinned.

"Look, there's a frog." Cam darted toward the grassy area beyond the small beach, and Paisley followed.

"Your life jackets, you need to—" Carrie stopped.

"They'll be back in a minute, and they'll also be extra safe if they get close to the water, even though we can still see them from here." Bryce laughed and pointed.

Since they'd talked on the porch swing about the feelings they had for each other—feelings both of them had been careful not to name—there was a new easiness between them. And on this brief vacation, Bryce seemed happier and more relaxed than Carrie had ever seen him. He was even more attentive to her too, and with each private glance they shared or brief touch of hands behind the kids' backs, she fell a bit more in love with him.

And this feeling *was* love, she was sure of it. With Jimmy, it had been infatuation, intense but fleeting. Although she hadn't realized it at the time, she hadn't been herself with Jimmy, and over time, she'd downplayed her barrel racing success and freelance client portfolio to be the kind of girlfriend he wanted. Now, more confident in herself, she could be the woman she truly was. Bryce liked the real Carrie, and he was interested in her career too, which Jimmy never had been.

"Are your folks still coming here the weekend after this one?" Bryce pulled both kayaks farther up onto the beach, tucked the paddles beside them and took off his life jacket.

"Yes, Mom said they should be here next Friday night around ten. She'll make sure Dad doesn't work late." As Carrie shrugged out of her life jacket, Bryce helped her, and his hands brushed her arms, making her skin quiver. "They'll likely want to go to bed soon after they get to Aunt Angela's. We can give them a tour of the ranch on the Saturday morning. I'll introduce them to you then too." Afterward, she'd find a private moment to tell her folks she didn't plan on coming back to Kalispell to live or taking that marketing job at Rizzo Construction. She grabbed a towel from her bag and rubbed water droplets off her arms and legs. The water was cold, that was why she was shivering. It had nothing to do with that looming conversation. Still, her parents' visit was more than a week away. She didn't have to think about it now.

"It's too bad your mom and dad can't get here earlier. They could cheer you on at your event at the charity fundraiser. The kids and I will cheer extra loud to make up for their absence." Bryce toweled his muscular legs, and Carrie's stomach somersaulted. He looked good in ranch clothes, but he looked even better in casual sportswear. "How are you feeling about returning to competition?"

"I'm excited." Carrie squeezed river water out of the hem of the oversize T-shirt she'd worn over her swimsuit for kayaking. "Teddy's in great shape, and it'll be a fun event." One she hadn't told her parents about. Preferring she give up rodeo altogether, they weren't likely to cheer her on as Bryce suggested. They'd be upset enough once she finally told them the truth about what she wanted in her life as well as in her career.

At least she wouldn't have the added stress of showing them the Sutton farm. A few hours before her scheduled viewing, the family had gotten and accepted a preemptive offer that, according to town gossip, was far higher than what Carrie could afford. "My folks are looking forward to meeting you and the kids." Except, she also hadn't told them Bryce was more than her boss. That one was easier, though, because she hadn't told anybody and neither had he.

"It'll all work out." As if he'd read her thoughts, Bryce gave her a quick hug and kissed her cheek.

"I hope so." Carrie made herself smile as Paisley and Cam rejoined them. She and Bryce helped with their life jackets and then returned the equipment to the rental place as the kids talked about the frog and getting mud between their toes.

If things didn't work out, what was she going to do? She had an open invitation to stay with Angela as long as she liked, but Carrie wanted her own place to come home to between competitions. And although her parents wouldn't disown her, they'd be disappointed, and she never wanted to do anything to hurt them.

"Like my mom says, don't borrow trouble." As they walked to the main part of the resort to get ice cream, Bryce gave her a supportive smile.

"Why would you borrow trouble?" Paisley giggled. "It's not like a library book."

"You don't really borrow it. It means don't worry about

something before you need to." It was good advice, and for now, Carrie would set her worries aside. "But we don't need to worry about anything because we're on vacation."

"And we're having ice cream and then doing goat yoga and having a barbecue and roasting marshmallows and lots more." Cam took Carrie's hand to lead her to the ice-cream stand.

"We sure are." Carrie laughed with the others at Cam's "schedule" for their day.

As Paisley and Cam went ahead to choose ice-cream flavors, Bryce drew closer to Carrie. "After the two of them are in bed, what would you think about stargazing with me? The patio outside the bedroom the kids and I are sharing would be perfect. It's supposed to be a clear night, and we'd still be close enough to hear them."

"I'd love that."

But most of all, Carrie loved spending time with him and Paisley and Cam. This mini vacation felt like being a couple and a family she wanted to be part of for the rest of her life.

CHAPTER EIGHTEEN

BRYCE LAY ON a blue yoga mat while a curious brown-and-white young goat bleated and nudged his shoulder. "You want to join in, buddy?"

"Mine does, Daddy. See?" On a mat to his right, Paisley lay on her back with a small white goat sprawled on her chest.

As the goat continued to study him, Bryce rolled onto his stomach and glanced at Carrie. She sat cross-legged with a tiny black-and-white goat in her arms while Cam used her phone to take a picture.

"I've never had so much fun doing yoga before. Since these guys are rescues, and Shane puts their welfare first and foremost, they'll still have a good life here when they get too big to cuddle. Maybe goat yoga is something I could offer at my ranch someday. For locals, not tourists." As the special family class, a few beginner yoga moves and lots of animal cuteness, ended, Carrie set the goat aside, got to her feet and stretched in a graceful arc.

Bryce's mouth went dry. Right now, what he wanted most was to kiss her breathless, but he couldn't. Keeping their relationship secret was hard, but it was also the right decision. He wasn't one to rush into anything anyway, and he had the kids to think of. What if he got their hopes up that Carrie would be part of their lives longer-term, and then things didn't work out?

"I'm sorry the Sutton place fell through, but don't be

discouraged. Another property will come up." It likely wouldn't be as close to High Valley and the Tall Grass Ranch as the Sutton farm, though. Given Carrie would often be away with rodeo, when would they be able to spend time together?

"I'm impatient. The Sutton farm seemed perfect, but there must be something else out there that will be even better." Carrie secured Paisley's flyaway ponytail.

Bryce had abundant patience, but unlike Carrie, he wasn't so certain better things lay ahead. However, what if he let himself think that way? It was early days, and he and Carrie would figure things out as they went along. A positive mindset could make all the difference. "What's next, guys?"

"Swimming, visiting the rabbit hutch and Buster, and going on the trampoline." Cam bounced around him.

"Then an arts-and-crafts session for the kids before the barbecue," Carrie added. "I'd also like to visit the horses. Shane has a new mare he's excited about. He thinks she has the makings of a champion barrel racer."

"Mr. Gallagher said he'd let me ride her when I'm bigger," Paisley said as she took Bryce's hand. "Isn't this the best day ever, Daddy?"

"Yeah, it is." And for the next few hours, Bryce focused on each magical moment, especially ones like now when he and Carrie had a few minutes by themselves.

"You missed a spot. Here, let me." He grabbed the bottle of sunscreen from the patio table in their suite's small garden area. "Got it." He checked, and they were still alone, so he dropped several quick kisses on her nose.

"You're very distracting." Still, Carrie kissed him back until they both reluctantly drew apart. "I'll check on the kids. They should be changed for the barbecue by now, but it's way too quiet in there."

As Carrie moved to the screen door, it slid open, and Paisley and Cam came out.

"Don't you two look clean and tidy. Good job." Bryce clapped. "Are you ready for the barbecue and marshmallow roasting?"

"Almost." Paisley had her hands behind her back, and both kids looked as if they were bursting with suppressed excitement. "While you and Carrie went to see the horses, we made something for you in arts and crafts. We hid it in Cam's backpack so you wouldn't see and it would be a surprise."

"For me?" Bryce glanced between his kids.

"For Carrie too. Really, it's for all of us. See?" Paisley took her hands from behind her back to show them a piece of art paper covered with colorful drawings. "It's to remember our vacation."

"There's the frog I saw after we went kayaking." Cam pointed to a picture near the top. "Didn't I choose a good green color?"

"You sure did." Bryce's throat was tight as he and Carrie admired the children's work. "You've got the goats from yoga and your ice cream." He indicated a chocolate cone held by a boy who looked like Cam.

"There's our kayaks and my pink baseball cap." Carrie put a hand to her head and then the drawing. "And Buster and the other rabbits and you kids on the trampoline."

"We drew all of us too. There's me and Cam between you and Carrie." Paisley showed them four stick figures in the center of the paper. "There's Mommy too. She's the angel in the sky watching over us." She pointed to a brown-haired figure perched on a cloud with purple wings on the back of her purple dress.

"I drew the wings, and Paisley did Mommy's dress." Cam leaned into Bryce's side. "Paisley said angels don't have purple wings, but nobody knows for sure, not even the minister."

"Purple was your mom's favorite color. She'd love those wings to match her dress." Bryce hugged both kids as they told him more about the picture. "You did a great job and made a wonderful memory." He blinked away moisture behind his eyes. If Ally could see the kids now, he hoped she'd be proud of them and him too. "I'll get this artwork framed so we can hang it up at home."

"I smell barbecue grilling. Has everyone worked up an appetite?" Carrie glanced at Bryce like she knew he needed a distraction.

"I'm starving. I could eat three hamburgers." Cam rubbed his stomach.

"Let's start with one, okay?" Carrie laughed as they made their way to the main patio, which housed a fire pit and barbecues.

"Today's been great. Thanks for everything." Bryce greeted Shane, who stood behind a buffet table loaded with salads, while Carrie took care of their hot dog and burger orders at a separate food station.

"My pleasure." Shane handed Bryce a tray. "You're welcome at Squirrel Tail anytime. All of Joy's family are." His expression softened before he turned away to serve another guest.

As Bryce filled bowls with mixed salad greens and toppings, he couldn't shake the sense there was something more going on between his mom and Shane than either of them had let on. It was the way the older man had said Joy's name and how his gaze had lingered on Bryce in an almost fatherly way. Still, it was their business, and given his relationship with Carrie, Bryce wasn't one to talk.

After he added a bowl of grated cheese and a glass of

breadsticks to the tray, Bryce returned to the picnic table where the kids waited.

"All set?" Carrie arrived with her tray and began handing out plates of food. "Please don't reach in front of your sister, Cam." She passed Bryce his burger and then set out her own meal.

"But I want cheese, and she's taking it all," Cam said.

"No, he's taking it," Paisley argued.

"Quit it, kids. There's enough cheese for both of you, but if you keep on, neither of you'll have any." Bryce made a mock annoyed face, and Carrie choked like she was trying to hold back a laugh.

As the kids settled and they ate the delicious food and talked about the day, Bryce was at peace in a way he hadn't been in a long time.

And several hours later, as he sat on a patio chair and stared into the glowing coals in the fire pit, that peacefulness, along with comfort and bone-deep contentment, wrapped around him like one of Carrie's hugs. "You're my sleepy boy." Cuddled on Bryce's lap, Cam mumbled something unintelligible.

Without disturbing his son, Bryce gestured to Paisley and Carrie, who'd joined a group to listen to a bedtime story.

"I didn't realize it was so late." Carrie collected their belongings.

"I'm not tired." Paisley's mouth was smeared with chocolate, marshmallow and graham cracker crumbs from the s'mores they'd made earlier.

"You will be when you get to bed." Carrying Cam, Bryce led them back to the suite along a path lit by solar lights.

"Cam left his cow in the truck. Can you find it while I get him into his pajamas and brush his teeth?" Carrie flipped on lights that illuminated the spacious living and dining area as well as the hall leading to the bedrooms.

"Sure." Bryce made sure he had his keys and went back out into the night to the parking lot. Opening a rear door, he found Cam's cow, which his son needed to sleep with, as well as Paisley's bear.

He scooped up the toys, closed the truck door and looked at the starry sky. Maybe Ally was up there watching over him, an angel like in the kids' drawing, but now her memory brought him more solace than pain.

Returning to the suite, voices murmured from the larger bedroom with a queen-size bed and bunk beds he shared with the kids. Carrie was across the hall in her own room.

"Your dad will be back soon with Cow-Cow," Carrie said. "What was your favorite part of today?"

"I had lots of favorites." There was a pause as Cam thought. "But the best part was being with you, Daddy and Paisley."

"That was the best part for me too," Carrie said.

"I love you." Cam's voice was so soft Bryce strained to hear him. "I wish you could be my second mom."

"I love you too." Carrie's voice was muffled. "Right now, I'm your nanny, but even when I don't work for your dad, I hope I'll always be your friend and maybe like an adopted aunt. How does that sound?"

"Daddy?" The bathroom door swung open, and Paisley stepped out ready for bed in horse-patterned pajamas. "Thanks for finding Buttercup. I thought he was in my suitcase."

"What? Oh." Bryce looked at the bear and cow in his arms. "Yeah, here you go." He passed her the teddy.

"Did you get bitten by a mosquito or something? Your face is all red and itchy looking."

"No, it's nothing." *Or maybe everything.*

There was no more uncertainty or doubting his feelings. He loved Carrie too, and like Cam, he wanted her to be a permanent part of their family. Happiness and a sense of rightness surged through him.

As Paisley continued to the bedroom, Bryce glanced at Paisley and Cam's artwork on the coffee table. The pictures they'd drawn were more than a memory. They could also be his future, their future.

A second chance and a new family, together.

A WEEK AFTER her mini vacation with Bryce and the kids, Carrie waited with Teddy in the arena's alleyway and visualized the run one more time. Unlike some of the other horses waiting to race, Teddy stood quietly with no jumping or rearing up.

"You can do it, Teddy Bear. *We* can do it." She rubbed his ears how he liked and shifted in the saddle. Although this rodeo was only a small event—and as a fundraiser for a horse rescue, it wasn't part of the official competition schedule—it still felt good to be back. Having Bryce and the kids here to support her was better still—something she wouldn't have at her first official event since Colorado was too far for them to travel once school started.

The crowd applauded for the previous competitor, and Carrie walked Teddy to the gate, where he again stood quietly. Although Teddy was calm and attentive by nature, a calm rider also made for a calm horse.

"Let's show them what we can do." She spoke softly into Teddy's ear and then straightened in the saddle, focused on the job at hand.

The gate swung open, and they raced into the arena and around the first barrel. "Good job, easy now."

Teddy's hooves thudded in the dirt, and the wind rushed past Carrie's ears as Teddy sailed around the run like he'd gained wings. And Carrie was in what she called "the zone" with him like she used to be before things had gone wrong.

"Go, Carrie. Go, Teddy," Paisley's voice rang out.

"That's it, boy." Teddy finished the cloverleaf pattern, and then they raced to the finish. "Great job." She patted his heaving side. They'd done it. She hadn't hesitated, hadn't doubted herself or Teddy, and they'd had a clean run without touching a barrel. She'd gotten her confidence back, and whether she won a ribbon or not, that combination of mental and physical strength was a personal best in all the ways that counted.

As her name and time were announced over the loudspeaker, she waved to the crowd and three people in particular. Bryce and the kids had come from their seats in the stands to greet her at the gate, all of them talking at once and clapping and cheering.

"Way to go." As soon as Carrie had led Teddy out of the arena and dismounted, Bryce hugged her. "You were fantastic. I don't know much about barrel racing, but even I could see you and Teddy nailed it."

Paisley hugged Carrie too. "I bet you win a blue ribbon for sure."

"There are still some good riders and horses left to compete." Carrie had learned early on to be confident but never overconfident. The latter led to taking unnecessary risks and, possibly, a career-ending accident. "There's Kim Padilla on Mustang Maddie, for instance." She gave a good luck thumbs-up to the two of them. "Besides, the most important thing is how much money we've raised for the horse rescue, right?" And for Carrie, it was proving to herself that she deserved her previous success and was ready to compete professionally again.

From behind the fence, Paisley studied the other waiting riders and horses. "I'm gonna be out there someday. You'll see."

"I don't doubt it." Carrie wrapped an arm around Paisley's shoulders as Bryce and Cam took Teddy into the barn. "But don't forget what's important in life outside the rodeo arena. That's your family and friends. A place to call home. And following your heart and doing what's right for you."

"Why would I forget those things?" Paisley looked bewildered. "Anyway, Cam's gonna be on the circuit with me. We'll have a truck and trailer together. There'll be space for our horses and to live." She turned away to clap for Kim and Mustang Maddie.

"You never know." Carrie spoke under her breath as she clapped too. What you wanted at one point in your life could change. Or you could lose sight of what you wanted and have to rediscover it. Maybe other people wanted different things for you, and you tried to please them instead of being true to yourself. She exhaled and studied the scoreboard.

Since their stay at Squirrel Tail, she and Bryce had spent all their free time together, and for these last few weeks of her nannying job, Carrie had moved into Bryce's guest room to have as much time as possible with him and the kids. They watched movies after Paisley and Cam had gone to bed. Bryce had abandoned his home office to work at the kitchen table, where Carrie did her freelance projects. And on Carrie's day off, she'd gone to the fields with Bryce to check the crops, learning from him for her own ranch. They spent time in companionable silence too, either watching the stars from the porch or over cups of coffee the next morning.

Unlike Jimmy, being with Bryce made Carrie's life better. And since he gave her the acceptance and space to be herself, Bryce made *her* better too.

"Teddy's comfortable." Bryce and Cam rejoined them, drawing Carrie out of her thoughts. "We left him with Heidi to get settled. Heidi says congrats. She watched your run with some of the other hands."

The part-time ranch hand at the Tall Grass loved Teddy, and the horse returned her affection. Since Heidi was a barrel racing fan, she'd come today to help.

"You and Teddy are still in first place." Paisley jumped up and down and pointed to the scoreboard.

"Yes, but there's one more competitor to go," Carrie said. "Digby Dare's a great horse, and his rider's no slouch either."

"Even if you don't win, you and Teddy are still best to me." Cam took one of Carrie's hands and squeezed it.

"Me too," Paisley chimed in.

"Aww. Thanks, guys." Carrie glanced at Bryce.

"Me three." His voice was gruff, and if the look in his eyes wasn't love, she didn't know what it could be.

She held his gaze, and the same look of love must have reflected back at him in her eyes.

"Yay, you did it, Carrie. You won!" Paisley yelled. "Did you see? Digby Dare knocked over a barrel and got a penalty. It's you and Teddy, then Kim Padilla and Mustang Maddie."

Carrie glanced at the scoreboard. She'd missed the race because she'd been caught up in Bryce. That look, that feeling between them and having him and the kids at her side. It made a great day even better. And while it was fantastic to win, it was even better to share her victory with people she loved.

"It's good to have you back." Kim congratulated Carrie.

"Thanks, it's good to be back. You had a great run." As Carrie introduced Kim to Bryce and the children, the other woman gave her a sideways glance and smiling nod of approval.

"What's next?" Paisley wondered after asking Kim for her autograph.

"We'll be presented with our ribbons. There'll be photos too. It's fine with me if you want to head home." As competitors, Carrie and Teddy had traveled to the event before Bryce and the kids, who'd arrived later in his truck. Heidi had also traveled separately because she was spending tomorrow in the area visiting friends who lived nearby.

"Why would we go home early? We want to see you get your ribbon and watch the rest of the events together," Bryce said.

"You saw us get our certificates for passing our swimming tests," Paisley added.

"I did." Paisley and Cam were children and needed adult supervision, but even if they didn't, Carrie would still have stuck around so they could celebrate.

"We'll soon be as good at swimming as Mommy was like we put on our list," Cam said.

"You sure will." Paisley and Cam talked about their mother more often now and those casual references warmed Carrie's heart.

"But right now I'm starving. Lunch was hours ago, and Daddy said we could have supper here," Cam added while rubbing his tummy.

"I did." Bryce laughed. "We'll go home in a convoy together. That's the Carter way." His voice was warm. "Besides, there aren't many houses or towns along that stretch of highway. I don't like to think of you driving it alone at night. I'd worry."

Although Carrie was used to driving long distances alone, knew how to change a tire and do basic maintenance and had a roadside rescue plan for anything more serious, it was nice to have someone who cared and wanted to make sure she reached home safely.

Letting Bryce look out for her and accepting his help didn't mean giving up her independence. It was part of being a team and made her feel closer to him.

She held his steady gaze again, and in it she read trust, commitment and love—everything she'd always wanted but never found. And he came with a family too. She looped arms with Paisley and Cam as they walked toward the prizewinner's area. Children she loved like they were her own.

As Kim chatted with Chelsea, the third-place winner, bits of their conversation reached her. She didn't know Kim well, so she hadn't realized Kim had a husband and kids, and Chelsea, who Carrie hadn't met before, did too. If they made barrel racing and family life work, there was no reason Carrie couldn't. And if she asked, they'd likely be generous with advice and support.

Bryce and the kids wouldn't be alone when Carrie was on the road. They had the whole Carter family.

"It's the Carter way." His words echoed in her head. That "way" was about more than making sure people reached a travel destination safely. It was a way of life and about stepping in when others needed help. If Carrie became part of their family, Joy and the others would do whatever was needed as soon as Carrie asked—maybe even when she didn't. But they'd never be intrusive or take over either.

She joined Kim and Chelsea for the ribbon presentation and smiled for photos.

With some creativity and flexibility, she could have barrel racing *and* Bryce and the children. All she had to do was figure out how.

Starting with talking to her parents.

CHAPTER NINETEEN

BRYCE EXAMINED HIS reflection in the mirror over the utility-room sink at the main ranch house. Should he have gotten his hair cut? Carrie had texted him she and her parents would be here soon, and he wanted to make a good impression.

"You look good." As he came into the kitchen, his mom studied him and then straightened his shirt collar like she'd done when he was a kid.

Wearing the apron Bryce had given her, Paisley stood behind his mom's baking island, stirring a wooden spoon in a big mixing bowl. "After you and Carrie show Mr. and Mrs. Rizzo the ranch, we're having a tea party for them with cookies and lemonade on the porch."

"I'm decorating the cookies and drawing them a special picture." At the kitchen table strewn with colored markers, Cam was intent on a drawing pad.

"That's great." Bryce glanced at the kids.

"Be yourself, and it'll be fine." His mom gave Bryce an encouraging smile.

"It's strange, you know?" The last time Bryce had met a girl's folks, he was twelve. Now he was in his midthirties. Carrie wasn't a girl, and he wasn't an awkward middle-school boy either.

"It was strange for me when you kids met Shane for the first time too." His mom patted his back.

"It's not the same." Who was Bryce kidding? Carrie was important to him like Shane was important to his mom.

Her expression teased him. "If it isn't, you have nothing to be worried about, do you?"

As Bryce went out the back door, a white SUV pulled up and parked in the driveway by the house.

Carrie clambered from the rear seat, and her parents got out the front. Her dad, a barrel-like man with thinning steel gray hair, paused by the driver's door and spoke into his phone. Her mom pointed to the pasture and spoke to Carrie.

Bryce walked toward them with a welcoming smile. Maybe he should have brought the kids with him, but at the time it had seemed easier to meet Carrie's parents on his own. At least Paisley and Cam would've been a distraction and taken attention off him. "Mr. and Mrs. Rizzo. Welcome to the Tall Grass Ranch. I'm Bryce Carter." He extended his hand, and Mr. Rizzo took it in a beefy grip.

"We're so pleased to meet you." Carrie's mom, an older version of her daughter with brown hair threaded with silver, greeted him too. "But please, call us Sophia and Frank." She clasped his hand in turn. "We feel we know you. Carolina's told us so much about you and your sweet children."

Carolina? Bryce glanced at Carrie, who made an embarrassed face.

"We named our Carolina after my mother." Frank grunted and put his phone away. In a white open-necked shirt, dark dress trousers and shiny loafers, he looked like he should be at a wine-tasting evening at Squirrel Tail rather than on a working cattle ranch. "My parents, Carolina and Antonio, came to America with nothing, but with hard work they—"

"Dad." Carrie interjected. "You and Mom are here for a

tour, and Bryce is taking time out from a busy day. Would you like to start with the horse barn?"

"I'd love to see the horses," Sophia said. "I had a pony when I was small. She was called Mabel." Her smile had the same warmth and sincerity as Carrie's.

"You never mentioned anything about a pony." Carrie stared at her mom in astonishment.

Sophia's laugh was light. "It was a long time ago. Another life."

Bryce cleared his throat. "Let's head over to the pasture. The horse barn's beyond it."

Despite Sophia's smile, Carrie's mom and dad were a lot different than he expected, and it wasn't because they lived in a city. They had an air of wealth and sophistication that would set them apart anywhere, not only here. Carrie had said her dad worked in construction, but Frank looked like he'd be more at home in a boardroom than on a building site.

As for Sophia, her "office job" must also be pretty high-powered. An expensive-looking watch and several bracelets sparkled on her arms, while diamonds twinkled in her ears, at her throat and on her wedding finger. In crisp jeans, a pale pink T-shirt with a floral-patterned scarf looped around her neck and immaculate white sneakers, she too looked like she'd been headed for Squirrel Tail and ended up at the Tall Grass Ranch by mistake.

"Carrie says you've got a big spread." Frank fell into step beside Bryce. "Ever think of expanding into corporate ranching? I hear there's good money in it."

"The Tall Grass Ranch has always been a family operation. We want to keep it that way." Bryce kept his voice even. "Watch your step." He gestured to a mud puddle. Frank, to his credit, moved around it unfazed.

"Family operations can grow into multinational corporations. I'd be happy to—"

"That's Bryce's horse, Maverick, with Teddy," Carrie broke in. "The other ones are Scout and Bandit. They belong to Bryce's older brothers. Bandit's retired now, but he was a rodeo horse. Bryce's brother, Cole, was a cowboy. He rode professionally on the circuit." Carrie's words came out in a rush, unlike her usual more measured way of speaking.

"Teddy looks wonderful." Sophia stood by the pasture fence and held her hand out, palm up.

"He's a fantastic horse," Bryce said as Teddy came to greet them. "You should have seen Carrie and him competing in a charity event a few days ago. How the two of them raced around those barrels set the standard for sure. My kids and I almost cheered ourselves hoarse when Carrie and Teddy came first. We're so proud of them."

"You raced in a charity event?" As she patted Teddy, Sophia raised a groomed eyebrow, and her expression was puzzled.

"It was only a small thing. To raise money for a local horse rescue." Carrie's cheeks were pink.

"Don't be so modest." Maverick, Bandit and Scout sidled up to the fence to check out the visitors too, and Bryce dug in his pocket for treats. "It was small, but it attracted talent. The kids and I are excited to see Carrie compete in official events this fall. My daughter's keen on barrel racing. It's wonderful for her to have Carrie as a role model. Carrie gives Paisley lessons too, between pitching in with chores, rounding up cattle and working in the fields. We couldn't have managed without her at haying time."

"I…" Carrie stuttered, and she glanced between Bryce and her parents. Instead of the humble pleasure he'd expected, her expression was more one of horror.

"Haven't you been working as a nanny?" Frank stepped away from Scout's nose while keeping his gaze on his daughter.

"Of course, I have, but the whole Carter family is involved in ranch work. Paisley and Cam have daily chores, so I'm in the barns with them. Besides, I'm boarding Teddy here, and I—"

"There must be staff to look after Teddy." Frank shook his head, and he, like Sophia, looked puzzled. "What about your freelance business? Have you given your clients notice you won't be available after Labor Day?"

"I…not yet." Carrie seemed to shrink into herself.

"Where are your priorities, Carolina?" Frank tutted. "And what's this about rodeo competitions in the fall? You'll be back in Kalispell."

"Which reminds me," Sophia said. "You still haven't told maintenance the color of paint and carpet you want in your office. And Human Resources is waiting for you to sign the paperwork they emailed. My assistant needs to book your trip to New York City with Dom and arrange theater tickets. The client's a fan of Broadway shows. If you fly out a few days after Labor Day, you can rent a car and check on that hotel project upstate too. It's running behind, and the civil engineer says—"

"Mom. Dad." Carrie sounded anguished. "Let's talk about this later, okay?"

Dom. New York. Office. Human Resources. Theater tickets. Hotel project. Bryce tried to make sense of the words. "What's…you're going to New York and not that rodeo in Colorado after Labor Day? With Teddy? Who's Dom?"

"Not with Teddy. At least, not to New York City. Dom… works for my parents. It's complicated. I need to talk to my folks. I planned to do that later today. Nothing's been decided yet. Not officially." Carrie's lower lip wobbled.

What was going on? Carrie wouldn't have lied to him, not after her ex and former friend had hurt her with their dishonesty. There was a big misunderstanding somewhere.

"It's not complicated at all." Frank's tone was decisive. "You're returning to Kalispell as soon as this nannying job ends to start your role as head of marketing at Rizzo Construction. We've been more than patient with you to get barrel racing and freelancing out of your system, but now your duty is to your family and our business. We'll work together these next few years so you can take over the whole shebang when I retire. That's always been the plan, and as far as I know, nothing's changed."

"Frank, honey, Carrie's right. We should talk later." Sophia looked almost as distressed as her daughter.

"Carrie?" Bryce took her hand and then dropped it. Her folks thought he was their daughter's boss. As long as she looked after Paisley and Cam until the time they'd agreed on, it shouldn't matter to him whether she went to Kalispell, New York City or anywhere else. It did, though, more than anything.

She stared at him, and although her mouth worked, nothing came out.

And as he waited for her to speak, he read the truth in her eyes. If Carrie hadn't outright lied to him, she hadn't told him certain things about herself and her family. Important and life-changing things.

Her dad didn't only work in construction, her family owned a construction company. A successful one that had made them wealthy. Her dad and mom expected her to work for that company and live a life a world away from rural Montana. They likely wanted her to marry a man from that world too, maybe even that Dom guy.

Bryce swallowed and rubbed Maverick's ears. "I should get going. Like Carrie said, I have a busy day. It was good to meet you both." He touched his cowboy hat to Sophia and Frank. "Carrie can finish showing you around. After your tour, Paisley, Cam and my mom, Joy, will have a tea party set up on the porch. The kids are making and decorating cookies for you."

"Bryce, I'm sorry. I can explain. I meant to tell you about my family and their plans for me, but I…it was never the right time." Carrie sounded choked, like she was fighting back tears.

"I don't understand." Her dad looked between them. "Was Bryce expecting you to keep on being a nanny for his kids? Didn't you only take this job for the summer?"

"I did, but… I didn't mean to mislead any of you." Carrie gave Bryce a pleading look.

"It's fine." It wasn't, but Bryce wouldn't get into that now. "Enjoy the rest of the weekend." He made himself look at and speak to Carrie as if she were any other employee. "I'll see you Monday morning. Can you be at the house around seven thirty? I have a meeting in town at eight." It was cold, businesslike and as effective as putting a bandage meant for a minor cut on a mortal wound.

"Of course." Carrie took a step toward him and then stopped.

Bryce turned on his heel. He didn't know where he was headed, only that he had to get as far away from her as possible. And everything that reminded him of what he'd thought they'd shared.

"I WANTED TO talk to you before. I should have, but I thought you wouldn't understand." From her perch on the sofa in her aunt Angela's tidy living room, Carrie reached for another tissue from the box on the coffee table. She rarely cried, but now she couldn't seem to stop.

Her parents sat in matching green-upholstered armchairs on the other side of the table. When they'd returned to Angela's after an awkward tea party with Paisley, Cam and Joy, Carrie's aunt had evidently realized something was wrong and excused herself to work in her garden.

"We still don't understand." Her mom dabbed her eyes with a tissue as well. "From everything you said, we thought competing in barrel racing was temporary. Like your freelance work was temporary."

"I let you think so because…" Carrie couldn't think about Bryce and the betrayal and hurt in his eyes and on his face. She'd meant to tell *him* the truth too, but she hadn't wanted to spoil the magic of their quiet moments together. Because she couldn't face the reality, she usually avoided hard conversations and wanted to please instead. The real reason hit her in the solar plexus. And now, because she hadn't stood up for herself and been honest about who she was and what she wanted, she'd messed everything up. In some ways, she'd been as dishonest as Jimmy and Brittany. "I didn't want to disappoint you." But she'd disappointed herself, Bryce and her folks anyway.

"So instead, you as much as lied to us? I thought we raised you to tell the truth." Her dad's face was red, and her mom put a soothing hand on his forearm.

"You did, but…" Carrie took a deep breath. She was an adult, not a child, and it was more than time she took a stand. "I'm sorry."

Her father harumphed. "Don't fuss, Sophia. Carolina knows where her responsibilities lie."

"I do." But from now on, she wouldn't let herself be pushed around either. "I'll always love, respect, care for and support you as a daughter should. However, I can't work for Rizzo Construction as head of marketing or any-where else in the company. Not now and not ever. I'd hate working in an office all day, and I wouldn't be good at it either. Being CEO would be even worse. You need some-one who can grow the business like both of you have done." As a vice president and head of business development, her mom was as much a part of the company's success as her dad. "That person isn't me." There, she'd said it, and de-spite everything, it was as if a weight had lifted off her shoulders.

"But, but…what will you do? How will you live?" her dad sputtered.

"I want to compete in barrel racing as long as I can, continue with my freelance work, and with money I've saved and what Nonna left me, I want to buy a small farm or ranch of my own." Now that she'd started, the words weren't as hard to speak as she'd expected, and more weight lifted.

"Your dad and I are worried for your future." Her mom's tone was conciliatory. "A ranch is fun for a summer va-cation but not to build a life, at least not for you. It's hard, rough and exhausting work."

"Don't you understand, Mom? I'm not you. You couldn't wait to leave the ranch, and you love the life you and Dad made together." She glanced between them. Her folks were a team, and it was understandable they wanted the best for her. However, it was up to Carrie to decide what that "best" was.

"I know you're not me, and I don't want you to be. I love you for who you are." Her mom sniffed and patted her eyes again. "Your dad and I both do, but what about a pen-sion plan and benefits? Healthcare and everything else?"

"Your mother's right." Her dad's expression was more sad than angry, and Carrie's heart pinched. "You have to be sensible. The Carter family's ranch is scenic, and from the sounds of it, they're doing okay now, but what happens if there's a drought or something else beyond their control? Like barrel racing and freelance work, agriculture's risky. If you don't want to join us in Rizzo Construction, surely you can see you need a permanent and secure job? When you come back to Kalispell, I'll talk to my friends, and we'll get you fixed up with something else. You can still ride Teddy as a hobby."

"Dad." Carrie exhaled. "I know you care and want to help, but it's my life and I need to live it my own way."

"Looking back, I was the same, Frank." Her mom's voice sounded both resigned and concerned. "My parents wanted me to stay on the ranch, but I wouldn't hear of it. If I'd done what they wanted, I'd never have met and married you. Carrie needs to make the right choices for her."

"But when we're gone, who will look after you, Carolina? You're over thirty and still on your own. Since you didn't hit it off with Dom, I can introduce you to someone I met at the golf club. Gino's a good man from a fine family. He'd love to meet you. He has a secure, well-paying job as an attorney with the county and a pension too. Say the word, and I'll—"

"Pappa." The Italian name from Carrie's childhood came out unprompted as frustration mixed with love. "I don't need a man or you and Mom to look after me. I can look after myself." She didn't want any man but Bryce, not that she could tell her parents. And even then, she'd imagined they'd be equal partners looking out for each other, and she'd still have her own agricultural business.

"You're our only child, our daughter. Part of me will always see you as my little girl, no matter how old you are." Her dad let out a heavy breath. "And your mother and I aren't getting any younger."

"What your dad's trying to say, badly, is we miss you."
Her mom's mouth trembled. "If you lived nearby, we'd see
more of you."

"And I miss you, but I can't do what you want."

Her dad stood and muttered something about going out
to see Angela in the garden.

"Frank…" Her mom raised her hands in a helpless gesture and came to join Carrie on the sofa.

"I'm sorry I've upset you," Carrie said. "But if I come
back to Kalispell, I won't be happy." She rubbed her face
as her dad's footsteps echoed on the tiled floor of the hall
and then the front door shut with a sharp click. "I don't
want to live a life like yours."

Her mom gave Carrie a crooked smile. "Each generation thinks they're different, when, in reality, we're much
the same— even your pappa."

"I didn't mean to judge you." A knot hardened in Carrie's stomach. "You're happy with your life, and that's
great, but it's not for me." Had her mother ever had regrets? If so, she'd never voiced them in Carrie's hearing.

"Your grandfather Rizzo didn't want me to work in the
business. He was very traditional and thought a woman's
place was in the home. Your dad overruled him. Just now,
you sounded as your father did with his father." Her mom
sighed. "We each need to make our own choices, as well
as mistakes. I have regrets, yes, but they're likely not the
ones you think." As if she'd read Carrie's mind, her mom
stared at Angela's collection of angel ornaments displayed
in a glass-fronted cabinet. "I love your dad and you, and I
love being a wife and mother. I love my job too and how
I've worked with your dad to build the business into what
it is today."

"But?" Although Carrie and her mom were close, they'd
never talked this honestly.

She took Carrie's hand. "Your dad works too hard, and he won't listen when I tell him he needs to slow down and ease into retirement."

"So that's why you've been pushing me to join the company?" Carrie leaned into her mom's shoulder like she'd done as a child.

"In part. There's the family legacy, of course, but I thought if you came on board, your dad would be able to relax. I want us to have a lot more years together and time to have fun and enjoy life. When your dad went with Zach to see the ranch's office setup, and you took Paisley and Cam to wash their hands, I talked to Joy. She and her husband had all sorts of plans for their retirement, but then she lost him. Along with you getting hurt barrel racing or on the road, losing your dad is my biggest fear."

"Oh, Mom." Carrie hugged her. Why hadn't she realized her parents were vulnerable? And why hadn't she also realized how similar she and her dad were, both of them determined to do things themselves and their own way? "I can't imagine Dad not working, but I have an idea. Instead of me, why don't you ask Sabrina to join the business? At your birthday party, she asked lots of questions about the company, and she just finished her MBA."

"Your cousin Sabrina?" Interest and maybe even relief sparked in her mom's eyes. "Your uncle Marco and aunt Lynn never wanted her to have anything to do with Rizzo Construction. Marco has always been set on Sabrina moving to Washington and working in politics. You're too young to remember, but Marco once had political ambitions himself." She stopped and laughed. "You really think Sabrina would be interested? She lives in Seattle."

"I don't think there's much to tie her there." Between the job and how she'd looked at Dom, Sabrina would probably book a moving company before the contract paperwork was even final. "If you ask Sabrina, and she says no, then we'll have to come up with another plan." Carrie grinned. "I doubt it, though. I bet she and Dom would be perfect for each other, or if not, Dad could introduce *her* to that Gino guy."

"Your dad shouldn't have interfered. I told him it was a bad idea to try to set up you and Dom and now Gino. Your dad isn't as traditional as his parents were. Even though I come from an Italian family too, my ancestors are from the north of Italy, whereas the Rizzos are from the south. It sounds silly now, but when we got engaged, there was upset because your dad's parents wanted him to marry the daughter of a friend whose family came from the same village back in Italy."

"Really?" Carrie shook her head. "It sounds like something that would have happened hundreds of years ago, not in the twentieth century."

"Oh yes." Her mom's smile was bittersweet. "It worked out eventually, but at the time it was hard. Your dad only wants to see you happy and settled, but he's always been a fixer and problem solver. Even though he goes about it the wrong way sometimes and doesn't listen, he has what he thinks are your best interests at heart. Like the company. Like Domenic." Awareness dawned on her mom's face. "It's Bryce Carter, isn't it?"

Carrie nodded. "I love him, Mom. I love Paisley and Cam as well. But I made a big mistake in not telling him the truth about you and the job and everything. And I don't know how to fix it." *If* she could fix it. Some of her dad's problem-solving ability would come in handy right now, but she'd created this mess, so it was up to her to deal with it.

"All you can do is try. Like you did with your dad and me today." Her mom's voice was comforting.

"What if Bryce doesn't forgive me?"

"That's up to him, but if he doesn't, forgive yourself and focus on the future. *Your* future and that ranch you want to have. Life's a journey, remember? There are lots of mistakes along the way, but hopefully we learn from them. I didn't realize it then, but growing up on the ranch was idyllic. As I grow older, I miss it. Not the work, mind you, but if that's your dream, I won't stand in your way."

Carrie hugged her mom tight, too choked up to speak.

"Now, let's go find your dad, and you can tell us about your plans for this ranch." Her mom's voice was thick with tears. "Send me your competition schedule. I'd like to come and see you ride at as many events as I can. I'm planning to go part-time with work in a few months, and when I do, maybe your dad will see sense and join me." She gave Carrie a watery smile. "I'll talk to him about Sabrina and everything else. It'll take time but he'll come around. Despite that nonsense about wanting to look after you, he knows you're a strong and independent woman, and deep down, he wouldn't want you to be any other way. My only true regret is being so busy with work that I missed out on things in your life. If you'd be open to it, I'd like us to spend more time together."

"I'd like that." Enveloped in her mom's embrace, Carrie felt the warmth, security and love she'd always found there. But now, she also found new strength and confidence. As far as work went, she'd gotten the life she wanted.

Now she had to figure out the rest—the love and family that would make a happy life even better. And as soon as her parents left, she'd do whatever it took to earn back Bryce's trust.

CHAPTER TWENTY

LATE ON SUNDAY AFTERNOON, Bryce spread fresh straw in Maverick's stall and cleaned the automatic waterer. Carrie's parents would be on their way back to Kalispell by now, and since Teddy wasn't in his stall or the pasture, she must be out with him. Bryce had spent most of the weekend working, and in between tasks, he'd stayed home with the kids to be sure he wouldn't bump into Carrie or her folks in town.

So far, he'd avoided her at the ranch, but he still had no idea what he'd say when he saw her. And having left it that she'd turn up as usual for work tomorrow morning, he had to figure out a strategy soon.

How could he have been so wrong about the woman he'd planned to propose marriage to? He'd thought he'd known her, but he hadn't, not at all. He patted Maverick, left his stall and latched the door.

Outside the barn, the air was cool and fresh, and although it was still summer, the seasons had begun to turn. A horse's hooves clattered, voices rang out and Bryce swiveled in the direction of the creek path. One of those voices was Carrie's, and that distinctive whinny belonged to Teddy. Even though she hadn't seen him yet, it was too late to duck back into the barn or continue on to the ranch house to pick up the kids.

"Thanks, but I'm heading in." Carrie waved to Melissa, who rode Daisy-May, and Cole, on Bandit, before saying something else Bryce couldn't catch. Then she turned and spotted him in the barnyard.

He made his expression neutral. He had nothing to be embarrassed or ashamed about. He wasn't the one who'd hidden big parts of who he was.

"Hi." She stopped Teddy beside Bryce and dismounted.

"I'm on my way to the house. If you need anything, Heidi's in the barn." He rubbed Teddy's ears to avoid looking at his owner.

"I do need something. I need to explain." Carrie's face flushed red. "I wanted to come and talk to you as soon as my parents left, but you weren't at your place, and I didn't want to text."

"I've been working today. Harvest's coming." Bryce put his hands in the front pockets of his jeans so she wouldn't see them shake.

"Of course. The wheat's looking great." She hesitated. "I wanted to apologize and say sorry again." She fiddled with Teddy's saddle. "But I also wanted to say I never meant to lie to you. My parents kept pushing me to join the family construction company, and for this summer, I wanted to avoid thinking about it and what they expected of me."

"Head of marketing's a big leap up from nannying." Bryce swallowed and tasted betrayal.

"Not for me." Carrie moved toward him, and Bryce made himself step back. "I'd hate that job or any other kind of office work. I wouldn't be good at it either, but I was too afraid of disappointing my parents to tell them the truth. That's why I let them think barrel racing and my freelance work were temporary. I'm working on it, but I've always been a people pleaser. My only true act of 'rebellion' was wanting to be a professional barrel racer. I even went to college to please my mom and my dad."

"I get they must worry about you, but…" Bryce stopped. If he kept talking, he'd be drawn to her again. She hadn't been honest with him once, what might she not be honest with him about again? He couldn't take that risk. Not for himself and not for Paisley and Cam either. "Apology accepted so let's consider the matter closed." It sounded formal, cold and unfriendly, but it was what he had to do.

"You don't understand. I'm not going back to Kalispell or taking that job with my folks or any other one. I told them the truth. When I'm not competing in rodeo, I'm staying here in High Valley. At first, I'll live with Aunt Angela, but I'm still looking for a farm of my own nearby."

No matter how much it hurt, Bryce had to tell her what he'd decided. "It was a mistake for us to develop a personal relationship. You're the kids' nanny, and I should have respected that. I put you in an awkward position." Paisley and Cam had gotten way too attached to her, but a clean break would be best for all of them. He tipped his hat. "If you'll excuse me, I'll—"

"You didn't put me in an awkward position. I'm a temporary nanny, and we didn't tell Paisley, Cam or anyone else in your family we were more than friends." Carrie's breath came out in short jerks.

Only Bryce knew he'd been a fool. That should have been comforting, but it wasn't. At least he didn't have to give uncomfortable explanations. Being with Carrie right now was hard enough. Being around her for another week—in his house and at meals—would break his shaky resolve. His mind raced, and he glanced across the barnyard to the ranch house. The T-shirt Cam had gotten ice cream on at lunch flapped on the clothesline. As Bryce watched, his mom came out of the house carrying a laundry basket.

"I'll still see you tomorrow morning, then? Around

seven thirty like you asked?" Carrie's voice was hesitant. "I planned to take the kids to get new shoes and backpacks for school and then to the café afterward as a treat."

"Actually..." As the screen door shut behind Bryce's mom, something shut in his heart. His mom wouldn't mind. It would only be for a few days, and she looked after the kids all the time. "Since school starts so soon, my mom can babysit. I'll pay you for this last week, but you'll have more time to get ready for your first competition. Look at any farm and ranch properties too." His heart constricted at the thought of Carrie being so close but also far away. Still, it would be easy to avoid her, and when their paths did cross, he'd be friendly like with any other acquaintance.

"Your mom? But I haven't said goodbye to Paisley and Cam. I can't disappear on them. I also meet my commitments." Carrie's voice was tight, and her eyes shone with unshed tears.

"You can still drop by any day this week. Just let my mom know beforehand." And Bryce would make sure he was in the outlying fields, where there was no cell phone service, so he wouldn't give in to the temptation to call Carrie. "Don't worry about not meeting a commitment. I'm releasing you from it." So why did he feel like a jerk? "You could even take a vacation. Leave Teddy here as long as you need." He wanted to be generous, but even to his own ears, he sounded pompous.

"I'll pick up the things I left at your place when I say goodbye to the kids." Carrie sniffed and smoothed Teddy's mane. "I'll also find somewhere to board Teddy as soon as I can. Maybe at Diana's. She has a few empty stalls in her barn."

"Good." The backs of Bryce's eyes burned. He'd never broken up with a woman before, and it hurt. "Take care."

"You as well." She led Teddy into the barn, and the horse's hooves made a dull clopping sound on the hard-packed dirt.

And as Bryce went to the ranch house, he tried to convince himself he'd done the right thing. He'd miss Carrie for a while. The kids would too. But any relationship, especially a marriage, had to be based on honesty and trust. He couldn't risk his heart, or his family, on any other kind.

CARRIE KEPT HERSELF together while she stabled Teddy and chatted to Heidi as if nothing was wrong. She also kept herself together while she drove back to town. But as soon as she turned into Angela's driveway and parked her pickup in the space beside her aunt's car, the tears came.

She rested her head on the steering wheel and gave in to emotion. Bryce didn't want her. She'd betrayed his trust, and he'd never forgive her. Gulping back sobs, she grabbed a handful of tissues from the box on the console.

She'd never forgive herself either. If only she'd stood up to her parents long ago. If only she'd been honest with Bryce from the start. However, it was pointless to ruminate on what might have been. Somehow, she had to come to terms with what was.

After blowing her nose, she stared out the truck window at Angela's backyard. A vegetable garden occupied one side of the property, while a profusion of flowers and herbs bordered a patio with a lawn swing and glass-topped table surrounded by chairs. Shade trees edged the fence to give the yard privacy, and the two-story, white-painted house with green trim drowsed in the late-afternoon sunshine, blinds closed against the heat. It was peaceful and, in a more rural setting instead of in town, the kind of house Carrie wanted for herself one day.

She unclipped her seat belt, got out of the truck on wobbly legs and aimed for the swing near a patch of purple alpine asters.

"Carrie?" The back door of the house opened, and then Angela was beside her and wrapped Carrie in a hug. "What's wrong? I heard your truck and then when you didn't come inside, I... Oh, honey."

Her aunt's kindness made Carrie dissolve into tears again. "Everything's wrong, and I don't know how to make it better."

Ginger, the small white mixed-breed dog Angela had adopted from the local shelter, hopped onto the swing and nosed Carrie's arm.

"Does this trouble have anything to do with Bryce Carter?" Angela's expression was wry.

"Did my mom—"

"She didn't say a word. I guessed." Angela rubbed Carrie's back in a soothing motion.

"I didn't tell Bryce something I should have, and I said I was sorry, but it's no good. He's paying me for my last week of nannying, but his mom's looking after the kids. If I stay here, I'll see him, and—"

"That's his problem, not yours." With a final pat, Angela released Carrie. "As for Joy looking after Paisley and Cam, I talked to her not more than an hour ago, and she didn't mention anything." Her eyes narrowed. "Don't let Bryce run you out of town. I hope you aren't thinking that way."

Before this summer, that was exactly what Carrie would have thought. She'd have packed her bags and hit the road, leaving her troubles behind as easily as she moved between rodeos on the competition circuit. But she was different now, and despite Bryce, those changes were good.

"It crossed my mind but no. I love High Valley. I have friends here. Family. You." She gave her aunt a tentative smile. "I want to make my home here." In addition, Paisley and Cam had already lost their mom and grandfather, and she didn't want them to lose her too.

"Then let's go."

"Go where?" Carrie raised her tearstained face to stare at her aunt.

"We have some farms to look at."

Angela collected her purse from the patio table and scooped up Ginger. "The old Sutton place is coming back on the market. Something to do with the previous buyer's financing falling through. Billy and Marie Hogue's farm will be up for sale soon as well. For the right buyer, they'd likely take less than the asking price."

Carrie gulped and took more tissues from Angela. She'd heard how fast news traveled in High Valley, but this was the first time she'd experienced the efficiency of the local grapevine herself. "Don't we have to make an appointment with a Realtor and wait until both places are actually *on* the market?"

Angela laughed. "For the Sutton farm, yes, so we'll have to look at it from the road. However, I talked to Marie Hogue after church, and she said we'd be welcome to drop by—informally, of course—any time. My mamma would be so happy the money she left you will go to realize your dream. If you'd told me what you wanted earlier, I could have contributed from the start, but it's not too late."

"That's really nice, but I can't accept your financial help."

"You can, and you will. Come along." Angela gestured to her vehicle, and Carrie followed her. "My husband and I weren't blessed with children, and this summer, well…" She stopped and buckled Ginger into the pet restraint in the rear seat. "You've become like a daughter to me. If you need a bit extra for a down payment, I want to give you money now I'd have left you after I'm gone."

"But…" Carrie settled into the passenger seat as her aunt got behind the wheel.

"No *buts*." Angela gave her an impish grin. "We're family. Although I lost sight of it for a while, family comes first. Understand?"

"Yes, ma'am." Carrie grinned back. Although she could be crusty on the outside, underneath Angela was kind and loving. Carrie would find the means to pay her back, but right now she'd accept her aunt's generosity in the spirit it was given.

"I can see the wheels turning in that smart and pretty head of yours." Angela accelerated out of the driveway and headed for the highway. "I don't want to hear any talk of repayment. I'm not rich, but your uncle's estate is finally settled, and I have enough. I worried for more than a year about how I'd manage, but now? I have more money than I ever expected, and that's the truth. Having you nearby for keeps will be a blessing, and I'm a fortunate woman."

"I'm fortunate too." More tears threatened, but they were happy ones this time. "Thank you."

"I should be thanking you." Angela tooted the horn at Kristi outside the Bluebunch Café. "After your uncle passed, I was angry. I didn't like myself, and I suspect a lot of folks didn't like me either. Nina stuck with me, though, and made me see I wasn't helping myself or anyone else by being cross, bitter and judgmental. Then Melissa and her sweet Skylar came into my life, along with the Sunflower Sisterhood. Thanks to their friendship and after reconciling with your mother and having you to stay, I'm truly living again."

Guilt slithered through Carrie, and she looked out the passenger window at a garden edged with pink and white hollyhocks. "Apart from when I first came to High Valley, we've hardly spent any time together."

"You're young, and you have your own life. Knowing you were around made all the difference." She gave Carrie a fond smile. "Bryce Carter will come to his senses, you'll see, but no matter what, you have to go on and live your own life."

Carrie did have to go on, and looking at properties was only the start. "Which place are we seeing first?"

"The Hogue's farm. It's closer to town, and I also hear there's a problem with the septic system at the Sutton place."

"How did you—"

Angela shook her head and slid her thumb and index finger from one side of her mouth to the other.

Yet more information via High Valley's unofficial news source. Carrie focused on the landscape, its vastness healing and filling some of the empty, hurting places in her soul.

Ten minutes later, Angela turned onto a gravel road that dipped into a small valley before coming out again onto flatter land. In the distance, a white mailbox sat at the end of a long tree-shaded lane.

"Did you hear anything about the Hogue place?"

"From all accounts, it's in good order." Angela turned into the lane with the mailbox. "Billy and Marie have done well, and they both come from successful farming and ranching families. Now that I think of it, Marie's related to the Carters on her mother's side."

Carrie hugged herself. She'd have to get used to casual references to Bryce's family. They hurt now, but it would get easier in time. It had to. She looked at the fields on either side of the lane. One was pastureland where two bay quarter horses grazed. The other side lay fallow, and while it looked like an untended pile of dirt, Carrie knew better.

There was a lot going on underneath, and this time of rest would lead to higher crop yields in the future.

As they came to the end of the lane and pulled up in front of the farmhouse, she drew in a soft breath. A white frame house, with three upstairs gable windows trimmed in blue, nestled against a low hill sheltered by trees. A wide porch wrapped around the house on three sides, and a white barn, also trimmed in blue, snuggled amidst more trees.

"Pretty, isn't it? A bit like my place in terms of architecture and layout. The house could use a coat of fresh paint, but that's minor. Billy's not as spry as he once was, and he's never been one to hire anyone for jobs he'd rather do himself. They'll miss this place, but Marie wants to move into town to make things easier for Billy." Angela got out of the car and unbuckled Ginger. The dog dashed out to greet a golden retriever, who said hello with several happy barks and a wagging tail.

"It's beautiful." A vegetable patch sat to one side of the house, and in a field beyond, ripe wheat waved against a sailor-blue sky dotted with high white clouds.

"In terms of acres, it's smaller than the Sutton place, but Billy and Marie have made the most of what they have." Angela tucked her car keys into her purse and waved to a couple in their late seventies or early eighties who'd come out of the house and onto the porch.

"It's perfect." And just like that, thoughts of the Sutton farm fled, and Carrie fell in love. She hadn't walked the fields, seen inside the house or checked out the barn, but she felt the rightness of this place down to her bones. Her name wasn't on the title, but the Hogue place was already hers in her heart. She could picture Teddy in that pasture and her own crops growing in this earth. She could also see herself on that porch with friends, family and, one day, when she didn't travel as much, a dog. Maybe she'd raise goats too, along with offering horse boarding.

Unlike men, horses were easy to understand, and a horse had never hurt her like Jimmy and Bryce had. She turned in a slow circle as contentment washed over and through her. She wouldn't run away or give up the life she wanted because Bryce had let her down. And while she'd let Bryce down too, if he were truly the man she wanted to spend her life with, he'd have listened to her, understood her and genuinely forgiven her, instead of pushing her away.

"What do you want to see first? The house or the barn and fields?" A small smile played around Angela's mouth.

"The barn and fields." Although where Carrie would live was important, the barn and surrounding fields would be at the heart of her new life. A life that would be good, rich and full in things that mattered and fulfilled her—even without Bryce.

CHAPTER TWENTY-ONE

"WHEN WERE YOU going to mention you expected me to babysit Paisley and Cam this week?" On Sunday evening, Joy waylaid Bryce as he came out of the barn after late chores. "Who's watching the kids now?"

"Ellie. I hired her to babysit tonight and tomorrow morning until noon. After that, I can watch them while I work from home. I was going to talk to you soon. Like now." He looked everywhere but at Joy. "How did you find out?"

"Angela Moretti called me with a question about the next Sunflower Sisterhood meeting. She mentioned it was good of me to fill in on short notice since Carrie wasn't working for you this week." In the light coming from above the barn door, Joy studied her son. Unshaven, his eyes dark-shadowed, hair unkempt and shirt buttoned the wrong way, he looked almost as bad as he had after Ally passed.

"Did Angela say anything else?" Bryce's voice sounded anguished.

"No, should she have?" Joy resisted the urge to smooth the lock of hair that tumbled across her son's forehead. Even if he was behaving like a child, he was a grown man.

"No, of course not. So, can you look after Paisley and Cam? I let Carrie leave early. She has stuff to do with getting ready for her first official competition."

"You 'let' her leave? I suspect you 'told' her to go because something happened between the two of you."

"It's…over." Bryce shrugged, but the casual gesture didn't mask his hurt.

"I'll look after the children, but I'm doing it for their sake, not yours."

"Thanks, Mom. We can always count on you."

That was one of the problems. "No, you can't. I'm not your on-call free babysitter." Joy had to take a firm stand with her son for his own good and hers. Although Bryce didn't know it, her life was about to change. Once she and Shane were married, Bryce and the rest of the family would have to get used to Joy not always being as available to them as she was now.

"What do you mean?" Bryce finally met Joy's gaze.

"I love Paisley, Cam and you, but one of the reasons I said I couldn't provide full-time childcare this summer was because you were relying on me too much."

"But I—"

"It's the truth, and it's partly my fault. I didn't say no before, but by forcing you to find someone else, I made you take a step forward—a step you needed to start rebuilding your life." She touched Bryce's stiff shoulder. "Carrie made the kids happy, and she seemed to make you happy too. She was a good influence on all three of you, and I was glad."

"I let myself get personally involved with her, and that was wrong." Bryce examined his boots.

"How so? Ally wanted you to find happiness again." And although Ally had also asked Joy to encourage Bryce to be open to a new relationship, until this summer he hadn't been ready.

"She told you too?" Her son's voice cracked.

"Ally and I had lots of talks in the last few weeks of her life. She was taken too soon, but she made the most

of the time she had. You could learn from her example."
Joy needed to get through to Bryce, but how?

"Carrie's great, but she's not Ally."

"Of course not, and you wouldn't want her to be." Joy
exhaled with frustration but also understanding. She'd
been where Bryce was, but unlike him, she hadn't stayed
stuck there.

"I don't, but it's not the right time. Maybe when the
kids are grown, I'll meet someone. Besides, Carrie's not
ready to settle down. She's going back to barrel racing."

"Maybe you're thinking about 'settling' the wrong way.
Some barrel racers have husbands and children. If they
make it work, there's no reason you and Carrie couldn't
do the same." Bryce had always been stubborn, and when
he made a decision, he stuck to it. While that was a good
quality in many ways and made for a devoted and committed husband, it could also be infuriating. Now, he was
making excuses for why he and Carrie weren't right for
each other.

"I appreciate you want to help, but it's my business not
yours."

"It's partly my business because you're my son, and it
concerns your happiness as well as my grandchildren's."
Joy glanced at the horse trough filled with cold, fresh
water and briefly considered dunking her son's head in it
to shock some sense into him. "Breaking off whatever relationship you had with Carrie and not allowing yourself
to see where it might go is a big mistake. For you as well
as Paisley and Cam."

"Drop it, Mom. I know what I'm doing." Bryce closed
and locked the barn door with a clatter.

"I hope so, but if you find you're wrong, it's okay to
change your mind." She patted his arm, but he shrugged off
her touch. "Remember hockey? You were so determined

to play because Zach and Cole did, but it took you most of two seasons, and the coach talking to me and your dad, to get you to admit you really wanted to try curling instead."

"It's not the same. Besides, I was good at hockey. Not like Zach, but at least as good as Cole." Bryce started across the barnyard, and Joy followed him.

"But you excelled at curling, and you loved it. You still do." Joy and Dennis had tried to make sure their kids knew they were valued as individuals and had discouraged them from competing with each other. Even if they'd missed the mark with Bryce, it wasn't too late. "Whether it's in sports or life, as much as you can, you should do what gives *you* joy. There are always chores like shoveling manure." She tried to joke. "But there are wonderful things too, and I thought you'd found something special with Carrie."

"Can I drop the kids off with you at seven thirty on Tuesday morning? I'll make sure they eat beforehand."

"Forget about breakfast. They can eat with your brothers and the ranch hands." Joy bit back everything else she wanted to say. Like that old proverb her nana used to quote, "You can lead a horse to water, but you can't make it drink."

"Thanks, Mom. You're the best." As they reached the gate in the fence dividing the barnyard from the lane leading to the ranch house, he gave her a one-armed hug.

"You're the best too." She returned the hug. "I only hope you realize it."

She'd done what she could to help Bryce, but now he had to help himself. Changing himself, and changing his life, had to come from him because *he* wanted it, not because of Joy or anyone else.

BEHIND ONE OF the long tables set up in the elementary school's playground, Carrie stacked paper plates and napkins alongside platters of precut vegetables, bananas, cookies and other kid-friendly snacks. "I'm glad you asked me to join you." She smiled at Melissa, who set water bottles and juice cartons on an adjacent table. "It's fun to share the back-to-school excitement." Volunteering at the school's welcome back barbecue, a tradition in High Valley on the Friday afternoon before school officially started, also made Carrie feel part of the community.

"Since I'm the newest member of the PTA and don't know many others yet, I'm glad you're here to keep me company." Melissa greeted a kindergarten student who clutched her big brother's hand, a boy Carrie recognized from the field trip in June. It had only been a few months, but since then, everything had changed, especially Carrie herself.

Across from the tables, on what was usually the basketball court, Zach, Cole and Bryce manned barbecues along with Ellie and several other teens. "Here you go." Carrie spooned carrot strips and cherry tomatoes onto a paper plate for Skylar. "Have a great year at school." Carrie needed to focus on the kids, not Bryce.

When Skylar grinned and showed Carrie the new sneakers Melissa had taken her to buy, Carrie's heart hurt a bit more. She'd missed back-to-school shoe shopping with Paisley and Cam, and she also missed them almost as much as she missed their dad. Except for a brief goodbye at Bryce's house, when the kids and Joy had been as teary as Carrie, she hadn't seen them in almost a week.

"Carrie." A pair of arms went around her waist as Cam hugged her.

"Where have you been?" She hugged him back and then embraced Paisley. "I looked for both of you as soon as I got here."

"I helped my new teacher put up posters and organize the art cupboard," Cam said with quiet pride.

"I helped too," Paisley chimed in. "Mrs. Benson used to be my teacher." She clung to Carrie's hand. "I miss you. Grandma's fun, but she's not you."

"I miss you." Carrie swallowed a ball of emotion. "But I was only ever going to be your nanny for the summer."

Paisley fiddled with a piece of hair. "Daddy's been really grumpy since you left."

"It's harvest season. He's likely tired from getting the crops in and the cattle moved." Despite that immediate twinge of concern, Bryce's mood wasn't Carrie's business. "Did you hear I bought a farm? I'm staying in High Valley, so that's good news, isn't it?" She made her voice cheerful. It *was* good news. The best. And she was determined to focus on what she had, not what she didn't.

Carrie had made an offer on the Hogue farm as soon as it was officially on the market. Billy and Marie had accepted it, and she'd take possession in mid-October. Between rodeo and everything she needed to get organized before the sale closed, she'd be too busy to think about Bryce.

"Ms. Kristi told us about your farm. It sounds nice." Paisley didn't even smile when Carrie added an extra cookie to her plate.

"If it's okay with your dad, you can both visit me. I bet there are dinosaur fossils there, Cam."

The unhappy expression Cam had had when he was being bullied was back, and he shook his head when Carrie offered him cucumber sticks with his favorite dip.

"How's everything at the ranch?" She missed it too, but to avoid bumping into Bryce, Carrie made her visits to Teddy brief.

"Okay, I guess." Cam shrugged. "I talk to Teddy when I do chores with Uncle Cole."

"Teddy appreciates you checking in on him. I do as well." She'd given notice at the Carters' barn and would move Teddy to Diana's ranch the following weekend. Cam would soon miss Teddy too. "Have a great year at school." She made herself repeat what she'd already said to all the other kids.

"Oh, Carrie." Cam hugged her again and pressed his face into her shirt. "Can't you come back to look after us?"

"Please?" Paisley's voice was pleading. "It's not the same without you. Grandma doesn't play like you, and riding lessons aren't the same with Uncle Cole. He knows about barrel racing, but he doesn't do it himself. And when I asked Daddy if we could go to one of your competitions, he said he'd see. That usually means no."

"Your dad knows what's best for you." Carrie's voice cracked, and she focused on the school's vibrant Welcome Back banner so she wouldn't look at the kids and cry. "You'd better go get a hot dog or hamburger."

"I'm not hungry." Cam still clung to her.

"I'm not either." Paisley set her plate back on the table.

"Come on, kids. Carrie's busy, and you're holding up the line." Bryce joined his children. "I took a break to help you get food."

"Carrie did that already." Paisley made a sulky face.

"Can we go home?" Cam gave Carrie another hug before she gently extricated herself from his grasp.

"We can't go home until my volunteer shift finishes." Above the children's heads, Bryce's gaze met Carrie's. "Congratulations on buying the Hogue farm."

"Thanks. I'm excited about having my own place." And Billy and Marie were thrilled Carrie would take care of the property as they had.

"The soil quality's excellent near that ridge." Bryce took Paisley's and Cam's plates and moved the kids along. "Good luck with whatever you plant. Winter wheat should do well there."

"I'll keep that in mind." Carrie made herself nod and smile as if Bryce were any other parent.

Then he and the kids were gone, and Carrie was once again left with a hole in her heart—and her life—bigger than the big Montana sky.

"Are you okay?" Melissa's face was filled with compassion. "I can look after both tables if you need a break. As long as she sits down, Beth can help too." Melissa indicated Zach's wife, who was unpacking more water bottles from a box the grocery store had donated.

"I'm fine." If Carrie took a break, she'd fall apart, and she didn't want Melissa or anyone else to know how much she was hurting.

"You're not really, but I understand." Melissa's voice was gentle. "If you need to talk, I'm here."

"Me too." Beth joined them. "The Carter guys are great, but…" She hesitated.

"Sometimes they're also maddening and frustrating." Melissa rolled her eyes. "Bryce has to realize how fantastic you are for him and the kids."

"Of course, he will," Beth added. "He's stubborn, but we saw how he acted around you."

Carrie tried to smile. Melissa and Beth meant well, but they didn't know Bryce like Carrie did. They also didn't know how she'd betrayed his trust. While part of her would always love him, she had to move on.

Letting herself hope for a miracle would only lead to more heartache.

CHAPTER TWENTY-TWO

"SORRY WE'RE LATE, MOM." On Saturday afternoon, at the end of the first week of school, Bryce greeted Joy in the ranch house kitchen. "Hey, Molly. Great to see you." He hugged his sister, who'd flown in from Atlanta the night before, and Paisley and Cam welcomed their aunt with excited cries.

Before this week, Bryce had been certain he'd done the right thing by sending Carrie away. However, everything was a mess, himself most of all, and things weren't getting any better. He was lonely, and even when everyone was home, the house still felt empty, as if its heart and soul had been ripped out. And seeing the affection between Carrie, Paisley and Cam at the school barbecue was a poignant reminder of what, and who, they were all missing.

"We've been waiting for you." His mom's face was pink, and her blue eyes sparkled. "Come through to the family room. Everyone's here, as well as Shane and his kids and grandchildren. The buffet table's ready, but we wanted to tell you something first."

"We?" Bryce glanced at Molly, but she looked puzzled too.

"Shane and I." His mom was almost girlish as she led them to join the others. Bryce's folks had loved hosting informal parties, and after his dad passed, his mom had continued the tradition on her own. This get-together was to celebrate Molly's return home for a short vacation, so why was Shane's extended family here? And why was his usually casually dressed mom wearing a filmy blue-and-gray floral-patterned dress and heels?

"Shane." Bryce shook hands with the older man. Instead of his usual jeans and T-shirt, Shane wore beige dress pants, a white shirt open at the collar and a navy jacket.

"Thanks for joining us." Shane looked around the family room, where everyone talked in small groups. "If I could have your attention for a moment, please?" He took Bryce's mom's hand. "Joy and I want to share some news with you."

Conversation ceased, and expectant faces turned toward them. Bryce joined Zach and Cole by one of the big windows that overlooked the horse pasture.

Standing beside Shane in front of the fireplace, his mom's smile mixed happiness with apprehension.

"Last month, I asked Joy to marry me, and she said yes." Shane beamed. "I'm a lucky man, and I'll be honored to call her my wife."

Muted clapping broke out, but Joy held up a hand to ask for silence.

"Neither of us expected to find love again, but we did, and I'm grateful." Joy looked at each of her children in turn, and her gaze lingered on Bryce. "I'll always love my first husband, Dennis, like Shane will always love and remember your mom, Bonnie." She smiled at Shane's kids. "But there's room in our hearts for each other, and we hope you'll be happy for us."

"Of course, we are." Zach stepped forward to offer congratulations, and then, led by Cole, the room erupted in applause, whistles and cheers.

As everyone surrounded the happy couple and admired Joy's engagement ring, Bryce hung back. He liked Shane, and Shane and his mom were a good match, so why did

he feel so empty and miserable? He made himself con-
gratulate his mom and Shane too, join in the toast Zach
and Shane's oldest daughter proposed and then, although
he wasn't hungry, fill a plate with food from the buffet.

"You're happy for us, truly?" His mom stopped him by
the punch bowl.

"Yeah, I am." He made himself smile. "Shane's a good
man. Dad would have liked him."

His mom's expression softened. "Me marrying Shane
will change things, of course, but I'll still be nearby to
help you when I can. As an engagement present, Shane
gave me that land your dad and I had to sell to pay some
of Paul's medical bills. We want to build a house there."

"That's great." Bryce filled a glass with fruit punch.
"It's also fantastic to have the land back in the family. I
bet it won't be long before Cole asks to use some of it for
his stock contracting venture."

"He already has." His mom laughed. "Your brother
never holds back in asking for what he wants."

Bryce laughed too, but it was hollow. His mom and
Shane having a new home together made sense, but it also
meant his mom was moving on, and their family, the heart
of which was this ranch house, wouldn't be the same. "Be
happy, Mom. That's all any of us want for you. It's what
Dad would have wanted too."

She hugged him before going to talk with Shane's
daughters and their husbands.

As Bryce filled glasses with fruit punch for the kids,
his thoughts drifted to Ally. Why could he tell his mom to
be happy and not put that advice into practice for himself?

He no longer felt guilty or that he was betraying Ally by
letting himself care for Carrie. However, Carrie not telling
him about her folks expecting her to return to Kalispell
and work for the family business stung. It was more than

that, though. Faced with her obvious remorse, anyone else would likely have been able to forgive her and go back to the way they'd been with each other, but he hadn't. That was about him, not Carrie.

He set his drink and untouched plate of food aside and returned to the window as the party went on around him. Daisy-May, Maverick and most of the other horses grazed peacefully in the sunlit pasture. Bryce had taught Ally to ride with Daisy-May, and she'd loved the gentle horse. The scene blurred as memories tumbled through Bryce's mind. Ally as a teenager riding alongside him. Their college graduations and then Ally on their wedding day. A few years later, Ally giving birth to their babies. And then Ally getting sick and how Bryce had been so sure the doctors would make her better.

He grabbed the window frame to steady himself as realization shot through him. He'd lost his wife, the person he'd loved most in the world. But until now, he hadn't understood why and how that loss meant he hadn't been able to truly move on.

With Carrie, letting himself love her had gotten mixed up with those awful memories of loving and losing Ally and made him afraid to love and lose again. He'd used Carrie not being fully honest with him as an excuse. Instead, Bryce hadn't been honest with himself—or her.

He finally knew what he wanted and what he had to do to get it, but he had to do something else, something just as important, first.

Whirling away from the window, he asked Melissa and Beth to keep an eye on Paisley and Cam and give his apologies to his mom and Shane. Then Bryce left the ranch house at a run and got into his truck.

Fifteen minutes later, he parked by the fence outside High Valley's cemetery. It occupied several acres of rolling land alongside a small stream tucked behind the town's first church.

He walked past older gravestones to the newer part of the cemetery and found Ally's marker with her name and birth and death dates. *Beloved daughter, sister, wife and mother.* The backs of his eyes smarted as he knelt on the grass by the stone.

"I've been an idiot." He glanced around, but there was nobody nearby except a white-haired man by a grave a few rows over. Now retired, Mr. Kuntz used to manage the feedstore. He'd lost his wife young and had never re-married or, as far as Bryce knew, even dated. Now, with his kids grown and scattered across several states, he was on his own.

In the light breeze that rustled the trees, Bryce could almost hear Ally's laughter. "What have you done this time?" He could almost hear her voice too and picture her teasing expression.

He rubbed a hand across his forehead. How to explain what he'd only just understood himself? "Even though you aren't here, you're still in my heart. You always will be. You're part of Paisley and Cam too. You'd be so proud of them. But now..." He took a deep breath. "I've met a wonderful woman, and there's room in my heart for both of you. I love her. Carrie's good for me and the kids, but I ruined everything."

"You can make it better." Ally's voice was so clear it was like she was beside him. "You make everything bet-ter."

She'd always had faith in him, but after she died, Bryce had lost faith in himself and, apart from the kids, every-one else. "The whole time you were sick, and then when you passed, I wanted to be there for you like always..." He gulped. "I did my best but I've been so scared. I was scared of losing you, and since then, I've been scared of losing the kids. I've also been scared of letting myself care for anyone else. I know you wanted me to be happy, but I couldn't. I bet you understood all that, even though I didn't."

More laughter, but this time it was loving, and the wind brushed his face like a tender kiss.

Anyone overhearing him would think he'd lost his mind but instead, Bryce had found it again and found himself too.

"I have to go, but I'll be back soon and with Paisley and Cam. I stayed away because I couldn't face coming here, so I kept the kids away. That was wrong. But now, we'll bring you your favorite flowers, and I bet Cam will want to draw you a picture of Daisy-May. Paisley can tell you about girl stuff she doesn't want to share with me." He looked at Mr. Kuntz, who held a framed photo and, with his head bent, seemed to be talking to it like Bryce was talking to Ally. "I love you, Ally, but I love Carrie too, and I need to go tell her."

If he didn't, and if he let the fear of loving and losing stop him, he'd end up like Mr. Kuntz, alone and talking to someone who could never answer back.

When instead, Bryce could have a life rich in love, family and everything else that, with Carrie by his side, would make the rest of his years better.

While he hoped it wasn't too late for Mr. Kuntz, either, what if, in the end, *he* was too late? *No.* Bryce ran back to the truck and jumped into it to head to Angela's house. He'd fight for Carrie's love as long and as hard as it took. And rather than living his life in fear, from now on he'd live it with hope—in himself, in her and in their family.

CARRIE LED TEDDY out of the barn and into the horse trailer. "I know, buddy. You've been happy at the Tall Grass

Ranch, but you'll be happy at Diana's too. Besides, it's only a few days until we're on the road again." She loaded Teddy into the compartment, closed the door and tied him down but left the outside window open so he could look around while she returned to the barn to retrieve a few last things.

From Teddy's peg in the tack room, she picked up his saddle blanket and a set of reins, and then, for the last time, walked along the barn's central aisle.

The horses usually stabled in this part of the barn were out in the pasture, so it was quiet apart from the soft coo of pigeons and the rustle of barn cats playing in the straw.

"Bye, boy." Mr. Wiggins wrapped himself around Carrie's ankles, and she bent to scratch his ears. "Look after Bryce and the kids for me, okay?"

In the barnyard once again, she stopped to silently say a final goodbye.

Cars and trucks were still parked near the ranch house for Molly's welcome home party, and while Carrie had been inside the barn, people had spilled out of the house onto the porch. Although Joy had invited her to the party, Carrie had thanked her but declined. It had been hard enough to be around Bryce and the kids at the school's barbecue. A family gathering would be much harder, and Carrie wasn't ready to face that yet, if ever.

She turned back to the trailer to close Teddy's window, but as she patted him, a pickup truck sped along the gravel driveway and squealed to a stop by the fence.

It was Bryce's truck, but he never drove that fast. Yet, it *was* him. Carrie shaded her eyes against the bright sunlight as his familiar figure, topped by a white cowboy hat, opened the barnyard gate and ran toward her.

"Thank goodness you're here." Bryce skidded to a halt, put a hand to his side and gasped for breath. "I went to Angela's first. She said you'd come out to the ranch to load Teddy an hour or so ago, so you might be at Diana's by now. I'd have gone there next."

Carrie should have been at Diana's, but she'd lingered here because it was hard to say goodbye to a place that meant so much to her. "I'm on my way." She gestured to her truck as Teddy looked at them out of the still open trailer window.

"Please wait. I have to explain. And say I'm sorry. So, so sorry." Bryce's face was red, and his expression was both desperate and despairing. "Please, will you give me a few minutes and listen?"

"Okay." Carrie's heart pounded.

"When your folks were here, and I found out they expected you to go back to Kalispell and take that big, important job, I was hurt and angry you hadn't told me."

"I should have, and I'm sorry too, but—"

"Forget it." Bryce gulped. "Yes, you should have been honest, but what you did or didn't do isn't why I pushed you away. It's because of something else." He came closer, and from the horse trailer, Teddy neighed. "It's about me, not you."

"I don't understand." Carrie stared at his dear, familiar face with the serious, now anguished blue-gray eyes that saw into her soul.

"I only just figured it out myself. As soon as I did, I had to find you." He took off his hat and held it in front of him. "I ended things between us because I was scared. I was so afraid of losing you that I couldn't let myself love you in case I lost you like I lost Ally."

"But I'm not sick, at least, not that I know of." Carrie's voice shook, and she clutched the saddle blanket and reins.

"No, but I've been letting fear rule my life in all kinds of ways. I don't want to live like that anymore." He took a deep breath and got down on one knee. "I love you, Carrie. Please give me another chance. I'd like us to be a family. You, me and Paisley and Cam. You're going away, and I... I want to fix things between us before it's too late. Will you marry me?"

"Marry you?" Love, happiness and excitement fizzed inside Carrie. When she'd let herself imagine a proposal, it had never been in a barnyard, but this was real, right and perfect. She didn't need flowers, candlelight or a fancy meal. She only needed Bryce.

"Yes, please marry me because I need you by my side and want us to build a life together. I'll support you in rodeo, on your farm and in everything else. I'll be there for you no matter what, to care for you and love you forever. And maybe, if you're willing and the timing's right, we'll have a child or two of our own one day." Bryce's face held all the kindness, loyalty and trust Carrie could ever want.

Teddy neighed again, louder this time, and Carrie glanced back at him. He nodded as if he understood and was giving his approval. Having Teddy nearby made this moment even more perfect.

"Yes, I'll marry you." She dropped the saddle blanket and reins and took Bryce's hands to pull him to his feet. His cowboy hat went flying, but he ignored it, his gaze focused only on her. "I love you, but I need you to promise me something."

"Anything." He moved to draw her into his arms, but Carrie stayed where she was.

"From now on, we have to trust each other with the hard things along with the good and sharing our fears. Can you do that with me?"

"Yes." His voice caught. "It's hard, but I know I'll be able to do it with you by my side."

"Just like I know *I'll* always be able to truly be myself with you by my side. You 'get me.'"

Bryce gave her a teasing grin. "Now can I kiss you?"

"I can't think of anything I'd like more."

As their lips met in a kiss to seal their future, Teddy snorted, and then Daisy-May, Maverick and several other horses joined in from the pasture while a cheer went up over by the house.

"Come here, kids." As Carrie and Bryce drew apart, she gestured to Paisley and Cam, who along with Joy, Molly, Bryce's brothers and their wives now hovered in an excited group by the barnyard fence.

"We've got something important to tell you." Bryce kept one arm around Carrie and hugged the kids with the other after they ran to join them.

"Are we gonna be a family for real?" Paisley stared wide-eyed between them.

"For absolutely real," Bryce said.

"For always? You promise?" Cam wrapped his arms around Carrie's waist as if he feared she'd disappear, and he was determined to hold her in place."

"I promise. Forever and always." And as Carrie looked at Bryce over the children's heads, her vow was as important as the one she'd make in front of a preacher. "I do."

EPILOGUE

JUST OVER A month later, Bryce rode Maverick across harvested fields and along the lane to what was once the Hogue farm but now belonged to Carrie. On this Saturday afternoon, the October sun lay in mellow ribbons across the fields, and the farmhouse gleamed with fresh white paint with blue trim and a matching blue front door.

As Bryce rounded a curve, Carrie came toward him on Teddy. They met under one of the big trees that lined the lane, its leaves now russet, orange and gold. "I missed you when I was in Texas." she said, leaning across Teddy's saddle to greet him with a kiss.

"I missed you too." He took her left hand, on which she wore the simple solitaire diamond he'd given her to mark their engagement.

"The outside of the house looks great. You and your family did a fantastic job finishing what I started. Thank you. I wish I could have been here for the painting party weekend." Carrie and Teddy rode beside Bryce and Maverick as they made their way along a field where Carrie had seeded winter wheat.

"I wish you could have been here too, but that's rodeo life. It's hard being apart when you're competing, but it also makes our time together even more special." He took her hand again. "It's not official yet, but you're a Carter in all but name."

She smiled and squeezed his hand. "I've been thinking

about our wedding. I'm keeping the name Carrie Rizzo for barrel racing, but everywhere else I'll be Carrie Carter." She drew Teddy to a stop under a towering American red maple, the tree now the brilliant autumn red of its moniker.

"And?" Bryce stopped Maverick. He wanted to marry Carrie as soon as possible, but she had a busy competition schedule, and he didn't want to push her. They'd get married when the time was right and they were both ready. They also needed to figure out where they'd live and all the other details that went into making a life together.

"What would you think about having a double wedding with your mom and Shane at Thanksgiving?" She squeezed his hand once more. "Before you say anything, hear me out."

"Okay." Bryce nodded and tried to contain his excitement.

"My mom and dad are finally okay with me not joining Rizzo Construction, and my cousin's doing great at the job that was supposed to be mine. She and Dom have hit it off too, so everybody's happy. But…" She hesitated and gave Bryce a half smile. "Now my folks, my dad especially, want our wedding to be this huge extravaganza with hundreds of guests, a multicourse sit-down dinner and me in an enormous dress and veil flanked by an entourage of bridesmaids, flower girls and all the rest."

"If that's what you want, it's okay. Truly." Although the thought of such an elaborate wedding made Bryce cringe, marriage was about give and take, and compromise started long before they exchanged vows.

"It's not." Carrie gave a mock shudder. "I told my parents that, but they've asked me to take more time to think about it. I don't want a big wedding, and I'm not going to change my mind, but it's still uncomfortable and awkward."

"You're getting good at standing up for yourself."

Bryce teased her gently. "You're getting good at winning first-place ribbons too. Between us, the kids, your folks, rodeo, this farm and freelance projects, I'm so proud of how you're handling everything." He was in awe, but together they were learning how to make their careers and family work. He leaned in for another kiss.

Carrie kissed him back and then laughed. "Although my parents will be disappointed that I don't want the wedding they're dreaming of giving me, they'll come around in the end. Look at how my mom and I convinced Dad to semi-retire and spend summers here." She hesitated again. "If we get married at the same time as your mom and Shane, I could have the simple, no-fuss wedding I want. We could also start our married life sooner. And Molly and your other out-of-state family members wouldn't have to make two trips here."

"You'd like that?" Happiness rolled over Bryce, along with love—the kind that would last a lifetime.

"I would." She nodded and patted Teddy. "I'd like to include some of my family's Italian traditions, though."

"I'd like that a lot." Bryce swallowed as emotion threatened to overwhelm him. "As long as my mom's okay with it, that kind of wedding would be perfect."

"Your mom thinks it's a great idea. In fact, she suggested it." Carrie's cheeks went pink. "I talked to her earlier when I was driving home. I called her about that exhibition of Paul's art we're putting together, and then we got talking about the wedding. She asked if I had any ideas about a dress yet, and somehow…she was so kind… I opened up to her."

"My mom has that way about her." Bryce was glad she did because without his mom's gentle nudging, he might still be mired in grief and loneliness.

"She does." Carrie grinned. "She might have had an ulterior motive, though, because she also asked if I'd be interested in renting my house to her and Shane while their new place is being built. Before the baby comes, Zach, Beth and Ellie are moving into the main ranch house. They'd like more space, and it's closer to town so more convenient for Ellie's school. And Cole, Melissa and Skylar are moving from the house Melissa's been renting in town into what was Zach's house until they build their own place."

"It's like musical houses instead of chairs." Bryce blinked as he tried to follow his family's housing plans. "Does that mean you want to live at my place? I thought… Ally and I lived there, and I don't want you to be uncomfortable."

"I won't. Your house is the only home Paisley and Cam have ever known. I don't want to disrupt the kids' lives, and I'll be happy on the main ranch property with the family nearby. Besides, I'll be working here at this farm most days when I'm in High Valley. If you're open to having another painting party, we could do some redecorating and make your house more ours."

"That sounds good to me." Bryce's voice cracked. "It was my lucky day when that goat got loose."

"The goat?" Carrie stared at him, puzzled. "Oh, you mean Sammy."

"Without him, I might never have met you." Bryce linked one hand with Carrie's as they walked Teddy and Maverick along a path leading uphill between more maple trees.

"It was my lucky day as well. I love you, Bryce. Now and forever."

"I love you too." And he'd spend the rest of his life showing her how much.

* * * * *

WESTERN

Rugged men looking for love...

Available Next Month

Redeeming The Maverick Christine Rimmer
The Right Cowboy Cheryl Harper

....

Fortune's Secret Marriage Jo McNally
Home To Her Cowboy Sasha Summers

....

 LOVE INSPIRED

His Unexpected Grandchild Myra Johnson
His Neighbour's Secret Lillian Warner